"Set in the aftermath of war, this follow-up to *Havemercy* is rife with intrigue, betrayal and magic. Like its predecessor, this story is told by alternating narrators, and the multiple viewpoints bring four new characters to life. Cultural differences are skillfully depicted and create a setting rich in history and tradition that draws readers into the exotic landscape."

—*Romantic Times,* 4 out of 5 stars

Praise for HAVEMERCY

"I was captured by the book's pace and the voices of the narrators. Jones and Bennett have written a really pleasurable book, and I look forward to reading a second one from them."

—CHARLAINE HARRIS, *New York Times* bestselling author

"Delicious! The characters are unique, entrancing and believable: dinner-party guests you never want to see go home. I will gladly walk again in this city, now that I know my way around."

—ELLEN KUSHNER, author of *The Privilege of the Sword*

"A dazzling cast of memorable characters! *Havemercy* is a wonderful debut from two talented new authors."

—LYNN FLEWELLING, author of *Shadows Return*

"Warning: the dragons in this remarkable first novel are wickedly innovative creations. Once they take flight in your imagination, they may supplant your childhood memories of their fairy-tale cousins. I, for one, will never think of dragons again without hearing the roar of these metallic monsters."

—DREW BOWLING, author of *The Tower of Shadows*

"Debut coauthors Jones and Bennett have created a freshly imagined fantasy universe with magically powered metal dragons, a hard-living, tough-talking crew of dragon riders, and tales of hidden identities, long-kept secrets, and loves that prove stronger than magic."

—*Library Journal*

"Jones and Bennett vividly convey the testosterone-saturated world of fantasy fighter pilots in this fast-paced debut."
—*Publishers Weekly*

"These ladies write like a house on fire, delivering fantasy's most pleasant surprise since Temeraire himself took wing in 2006. Jones and Bennett have reinvented dragons yet again, this time in a steampunk context. But the bulk of their story is driven by some of the most sensitive and authentic attention to character you're likely to see this side of Westeros. . . . *Havemercy* works beautifully as a rich and rewarding stand-alone adventure. It's an impressive debut for its 20-year-old creators and one of the few truly notable titles of 2008."

—SFReviews.net

"Each protagonist has a distinctive voice, from Royston's catty sarcasm to Rook's unrestrained anger, and each undergoes sensitive and realistic changes because of their relationships. The few flaws are minor compared to the strengths of this fantasy that satisfyingly concludes within the same volume in which it started."
—*Booklist*

"Dragons, like elves, are so common in fantasy literature that the palate can get tired of them. They can be used in new, interesting ways . . . but often they aren't. *Havemercy* is one of the interesting ones. . . . The world they've created is one I want to know more about and their characters are interesting."
—SFSite.com

BY JAIDA JONES AND DANIELLE BENNETT

Steelhands
Dragon Soul
Shadow Magic
Havemercy

STEELHANDS

JAIDA JONES AND DANIELLE BENNETT

BALLANTINE BOOKS • NEW YORK

2012 Spectra Mass Market Edition

Copyright © 2011 by Jaida Jones and Danielle Bennett
All rights reserved.

Published in the United States by Spectra, an imprint of the Random House Publishing Group, a division of Random House, Inc., New York.

SPECTRA and the portrayal of a boxed "s" are trademarks of Random House, Inc.

Originally published in hardcover in the United States by Spectra, an imprint of the Random House Publishing Group, a division of Random House, Inc., New York.

Map by Neil Gower

Cover illustration: Paul Youll

ISBN: 978-0-553-59305-1
eBook ISBN: 978-0-345-52637-3

www.ballantinebooks.com

9 8 7 6 5 4 3 2 1

Spectra mass market edition: July 2012

To Aunt Roberta and Uncle Michael,
for showing me the world outside Victoria
—*Dani*

For the one and only curator
of the Secret Museum of the Air
—*Jaida*

ACKNOWLEDGMENTS

As always, we have to thank our fabulous and tireless editor at Spectra, Anne Groell, who has always given us more care than any one person (with a new baby!) should have time to give, and our agent, Tamar Rydzinski—same deal! We're also incredibly grateful to our assistant editor, David Pomerico, and copy editor, Sara Schwager, without whom this book would be little more than a very heavy manuscript with *so* many errors. Once again, we have to thank ruthless Mom— who remains ruthless, and possibly even gets more ruthless with age; Uncle David, for ferrying us around in that glorious clown car; Grandma Fay and Grandpa Terry, who offer songs and jokes and stories; Nick, who makes the best pad thai ever; Bob, for occasionally using his indoor voice; Toni, for making sure we look fashionable whenever we have to leave the house; Taid, for not complaining too much about the typo; Marjorie, for the delicious fruit bread; Matthew, for always being on our side; Jonah, for the sound track to our lives; Andrew, for pretending we're cool enough to hang out with him; and, of course, everyone at Thremedon, whose enthusiasm and creativity far surpass our own and remind us of why we love to write in the first place. Here's looking at you, kids.

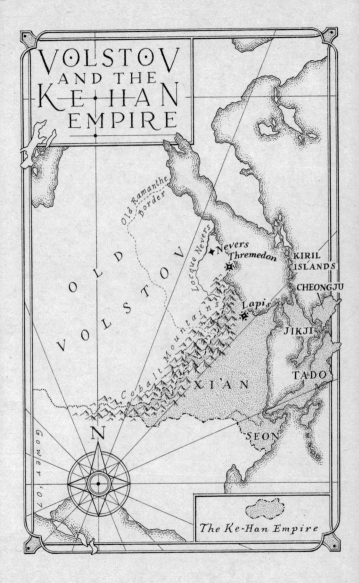

VOLSTOV
AND THE
KE·HAN
EMPIRE

Old Ramanthe Border

OLD

VOLSTOV

Locque Nevers

Nevers
Thremedon

KIRIL
ISLANDS

CHEONGJU

Lapis

JIKJI

Cobalt Mountains

XI'AN

TA·DO

SEON

Gowler '07

N

The Ke·Han Empire

STEELHANDS

CHAPTER ONE

ADAMO

The way I saw it—and probably would 'til the day I died—
was that both times the rug was pulled out from underneath
my boots, it was somehow because of that whelp. Not even
the whoreson who usually gave me all my trouble. It was
the *brother* of the whoreson who usually gave me all my
trouble.

I'd never asked to be anybody's pen pal, since I'd never been
much for writing letters in the first place and all the people
I'd ever cared to know lived in the same city as I did. The
end of the war had fractured some things though, sent little
pieces skittering all over, and one of those pieces just happened to have a brother with a real sick sense of humor, at
least by my understanding.

Dear Adamo, the letter began—no Chief Sergeant or nothing, which was technically correct, but seemed oddly personal
to me.

> *It is my sincerest wish that this letter finds you well, that
> its contents are not despoiled before you've had a chance
> to read them, and most of all that this information doesn't
> bring you trouble.*
> *I will jump straight to the sticking point and hope that
> you can forgive me: While in the desert, Rook and I very
> nearly saw the resurrection of a dragon. Havemercy, spe-
> cifically. A pair of magicians from Xi'an had pieced her
> together from old, found parts and somehow managed to
> get a hold on her soul as well. Please don't mistake me for
> a philosopher; the soul is a device both magical and me-*

chanical, with the essence of a powerful magician inside to give the creation life. These men had planned on using a woman to house the dragon's soul—a decidedly unmechanical vessel, but one that perhaps seemed easier to control. I tell you all this because Rook and I were not alone when we made this discovery. There was an agent of the Esar present, and what she learned she has no doubt already passed on to her master.

I know that the Esar is a secretive man, one who guards his possessions jealously. In light of that, I considered the possibility that he might never share this story with you and thus felt duty-bound to impart it myself. The dragons belonged to more than just one man, however powerful that man might be.

I have no counsel for what you might do with this information, my own strengths lying largely in the theoretical and analytical fields. I merely felt that it was the right thing to pass it along and hope that you do not find yourself too at odds with my assumption.

That was it—the vital parts anyway. I'd squeezed out a lot of the hand-wringing that came afterward and there were three more long paragraphs all about how Rook had taken to the desert like a camel and nearly became prince of the nomads, but that wasn't the shit that was going to get me arrested.

He'd wrapped up the whole thing with *Best wishes.* After crafting a letter that read like Thom was putting *every ounce* of that enormous brain into getting me arrested, he ended it with "best wishes."

I'd met some cracked little teacups in my time, but he had to be the absolute worst.

"So the thrust of the matter," I concluded, myself, "is he says you need a living, breathing human being to bind their soul to, and he thinks the *ethical implications* of something like that would be devastating. Not just for Volstov, but for everywhere else." I reached for the letter to get the *proper* phrase, the one he'd used that'd made me laugh out my breakfast, although it wasn't for pure humor. "Oh yeah.

'*Just* devastating.' He feels compelled, because of our time together, y'see, and because of his brother being 'one of us,' to make sure I'm aware of a situation that, as far as I'm concerned, could probably take my head off my body a damned sight easier than flying."

And that, as anybody knew, was dangerous enough. Commanding the members of the Dragon Corps from Proudmouth's back wasn't exactly the job a sane soldier volunteered for, was it? Even if the truth was I'd never really volunteered for it in the first place—I was just a whole lot better than most people at holding back all the shit I wanted to say when somebody more important was doling out the steaming heaps.

Bitter, my good friend Royston might've called it, but it wasn't really that. It was just practical thinking. My theory was, the less you got involved, the less chance there was of someone important taking exception to your head and the way it sat on your shoulders.

Which was why I didn't appreciate getting this crazy letter from a man I already knew thought more of the ethical implications of something than he did of the personal ones. In other words, me holding this letter, getting it over breakfast and breaking the seal and reading it with my buttered rolls, would've had more implications in th'Esar's eyes than just ethical ones.

Sometimes, a man just didn't want to know.

And that was kind of the tactic I was taking right now. Because in that letter, the words that loudmouthed, proud-arsed, crazy-eyed ex-airman Rook's damn *strange* little brother had used—such as "resurrection" and "soul"—sounded a lot to me like playing at things I wasn't meant to play at. More often than not, I gave my hand away at cards.

"So, I burn it," I said, with only a hint of uncertainty. I didn't want to be the man who went to his friends asking for advice with his mind already made up. No man was ever more of a burr in the arse than that one, and I wasn't going to be him. Not even in my old age.

Across from me, Royston took a neat little sip of his coffee. Then he reached up to smooth the two, maybe three, gray hairs growing at his left temple—the ones no one would notice if he wasn't so damn self-conscious about them. After all, he was considerably less advanced into his forties than myself. In fact, I thought it was downright rude of him to remind me.

"Well, it is a conundrum," he said finally.

He was doing it to needle me, I told myself, but years of getting used to the behavior never quite meant you became master at dealing with it. I snorted, just giving him the rise he wanted, not to mention buying him extra time to think up a more clever response, then handed it over.

"Well," I said, filling up the air. I hated to watch people *read* things, and Roy knew it.

"Reading," Roy replied quietly, with that distant air he only got when he was putting his mind to something complicated or talking about his boy.

Now that was a mess of worms, I told myself—a can of them that'd already been opened—and to avoid hurting certain feelings I had to throw myself into the task of teasing Roy every chance I got, just so he'd know how I felt about the matter. But it'd probably take a few years before I'd be comfortable sitting in the same room with the two of them. Pointing out that a man was still a baby was no fun when that man was in the room, if only because teasing babies just wasn't right no matter who you were doing it for.

Those thoughts seemed to occupy enough time that Roy finally cleared his throat, tossing the letter down between our coffee cups. I eyed it unhappily, this simple-enough-*looking* thing that I knew wasn't going to prove simple for me— at least not now that I knew about it.

I wasn't the sort of man who could just sit on information. I'd been bred to *act,* and all this sitting around and hemming and hawing was starting to chafe at my very last nerve. Wouldn't've expected it to be the quiet that got me in the end either, but the world was a strange place.

"I'll look into it," Roy said.

"Somehow, I knew that'd be your answer." I sighed. "But with a nose that large, I suppose you can't help poking it into things."

"Dark-mooded as you are, it isn't anything *yet,*" Roy continued, too distracted by his thoughts to let the teasing get to him. This *wasn't* a normal coffee we were having, and for whatever reasons, that made me even more clench-jawed. There was no way I wasn't going to tear into some poor, hopeful tactician in my afternoon lecture that day and be hearing about it from the wealthy parents a few days afterward. Couldn't I please be easier on their precious offspring? The lecture room wasn't part of the Airman, as far as *they* could tell.

And, the worst one: *This isn't wartime anymore, you know.*

Not that I was against the war being over—not even when it was all I'd ever known, which meant I knew a whole lot more about it than the sap-eyed creatures who shuffled into the room and daydreamed about their ponies back in the country while I tried to impress upon them the importance of strategy, or coax some milk of inspiration out of them in return for all the milk they'd sucked from the world, probably right up until the moment they were sent away to 'Versity. Maybe they missed it now. Maybe if I bottled some and gave them all nap times and dollies, they'd be more inclined to think about what the differences would be between an airstrike and a land strike.

And Brothers and Sisters of Regina help them if one of them ever questioned the *real* importance of discussing airstrikes again, since wasn't that a moot point these days anyway?

Nothing in war or the possibility of war—and definitely not during the preparation for war—was a moot point. I'd drum it into their skulls yet, and if not me, then some future generation of real war drums. Not exactly comforting, but it was a salary and I hadn't been fired yet—no matter how much some parents objected to the shouting.

"Oh, it's something," I muttered. "You mind hanging on to it?"

"You're acting uncharacteristically suspicious," Roy told me, which was true.

"Boy who wrote that's the opposite of any good-luck charm I've ever had," I explained, backward country as it sounded. "Some men carry around a rabbit's foot or a lock of their true love's hair or what have yous. Well, the way I figure it is, I'm *not* carrying around anything he touched."

"You know what this means?" Roy said.

I shrugged.

"It means if I'm caught with this information on me before I—before *we*—decide what to do with it, the Esar will be very, very displeased." This was just one more reason that sending all these words in a *letter* was more than just bad luck; it was suicidal stupidity. "He already doesn't like me, though I'm sure his feelings about you are much more complicated. I might even be exiled again. Once is painful enough; twice just seems excessive, don't you agree?"

"Well, look on the bright side, anyway," I replied. "Maybe you'll find yourself another . . ."

"One of these days, Owen," Roy told me, in a tone I really didn't like, "you're going to find yourself falling in love. And I can only hope it will be the most outlandish—the most wildly inappropriate—coupling that Thremedon has ever seen."

"Considering that rumor with Margrave Holt and his greyhounds—" I began.

"I think you need a good walk to clear your head," Royston suggested. "And, for that matter, so do I."

I wasn't inclined to take Roy's advice any more often than I had to. Listening to a man like him when he told you what was best for you would only give him the hot air he required to fill his own head. And as much as I teased him about his nose—great honking detail that it was—the size of his head as it was remained quite tolerable. For the time being, in any case.

But he *was* right about the walk, as he was right about so many other things that he had no business knowing, let alone sharing.

That was the problem with old friends—and magicians, to boot. Putting both attributes in the same man was like committing yourself to a life sentence, though I'd never actually give him the satisfaction of acknowledging that.

The point was, I did need a good walk to clear my head.

And I intended to take it, but I needed some time on my own—if Roy would allow it. Which he usually didn't.

"Along the 'Versity Stretch perhaps?" Royston suggested, already out of his chair and straightening his waistcoat—some gold and black brocade fashion that looked like it cost about as much as the entire coffee shop. I'd seen everyone wearing the sort recently; leave it to Royston to lead the trend. "You might become inspired for your next lecture."

"Head's not gonna get much clearer if you come along," I pointed out, dropping a few coins on the table for politeness's sake. "When you talk, I can't hear myself think."

"Who said I expected you to be able to?" Royston asked.

"Oh, I don't know," I said, putting on my coat. "Little someone by the name of Mistress Common Courtesy?"

"I can assure you that *were* I ever to take a mistress, it would *not* be her," Royston said, tying his scarf in a fussy kind of knot before heading for the door.

Wind hit us both square in the face, cold as frozen steel and just about as sharp when we stepped out into the street. Just like always, my muscles tensed all over—though not from the cold, because who would I be if I couldn't handle a little of that? No, it was more like the memory of what wind on my face had meant once and how hard it was to teach your brain something once the rest of you'd gone and figured it out already. All I had was my two boots firmly on the ground, and they weren't going anywhere but down the road. Maybe toward the Rue around where they'd erected those fool statues of me and the boys.

Small miracle no one'd knocked a piece off or written anything vulgar on 'em yet, but that'd come with time. Hell, if some of the boys had been boys still and not just statues, they'd probably have done it themselves—or at least the ones that *could* write, with messages to each other about the night before, what kinds of women they'd been with and fancied themselves to have pleasured, sharing it so all Thremedon could know *just* the sort of men they were looking up to.

But I had to steer clear of those would've-beens, else it'd be another lane I was walking down.

"If I'm not wrong, we're bound to see a bit of snow to-night," Royston commented, slipping his hands into his pockets alongside my letter. He shivered theatrically—for my benefit, I guessed, since there wasn't anyone else around who was looking. And also, so anybody watching—if there was even anybody who cared—wouldn't notice that piece of paper sliding into his coat. Thremedon could be a paranoid place. And, without the war, the gossips had little else to talk about.

The winter chill had come to Thremedon about three weeks prior, though my old bones still hadn't got properly used to the cold in the air. Roy insisted it was the source of my being "out of sorts," as he put it, like we both didn't know that meant real mean and even a downright whoreson some-times on top of that. Roy'd said something about how I should consider retiring down south, not taking into account that talk of retiring was the one thing that made me madder than all this cold. I wasn't an old man *yet,* thanks, despite how my bones felt, and I wasn't about to lie down and roll belly-up just to make anyone's life easier. Least of all my own.

"Guess Hal's in for some shoveling," I said, because I really couldn't help myself when it came right down to it. Be-sides that, what kind of man shied away from a good joke when he had such material to work with?

"Mm," Royston agreed, so that I wasn't even sure he'd heard me. *He* was probably thinking about the contents of that letter, which was what I was meant to be doing instead of twitting Roy like usual. Maybe I thought if I just stuck to my routine, the solution to all my problems would come floating down from the sky like the golden spirit of Regina herself.

The real problem was, I didn't want to know any of this.

I'd made an all right Chief Sergeant when there'd been a time for one, fair assessment being we'd done our jobs in the end, and that was more than you could say for most. Defi-nitely more than you could say for whatever Ke-Han bastard had my job on the other side of the Cobalts. So I guess you could say I was fairly comfortable with a position of authority. I'd kept those boys in line, after all—a fact that seemed *about* equal to hog-tying an Arlemagne chevalier and getting him to see reason—and come out the other side relatively unscathed. Mental scarring aside, of course.

Which was all a very fancy way of saying that I'd kept worse than dragons at bay. *Certainly*—and that was a quote from the letter, too—*certainly* a man of my caliber would be better suited to judging the information in the letter than anyone else the writer could think of.

I was already regretting being as kind to Thom as I'd been. I should've thrown him to the wolves on the first day and let nature take its course; that was the way things worked in the wild.

Except, of course, we were supposed to be better than animals in the wild—civilized people—and acting that way was what'd gotten us the bad-luck charm in the first place.

If I had any kind of luck at all, or if whatever still remained from the war was holding firm, Roy would think of something. He was better suited to the ins and outs of court dealings, ironic as that was, seeing as how he'd been exiled once and I hadn't.

The street stones were coated in a thin, near-invisible sheet of frost that melted in the shape of our boot prints as Royston and I made our way along the Stretch and toward the fountain, both of us lost in our own private imaginings—though I got the sense that mine were a lot darker than his, at the minute. Probably thinking of Hal shoveling the snow, Regina help us all.

"Whatever you—*we*—end up deciding," Royston said, breath puffing up little clouds of steam in the cold air, "I feel like you ought to know that things . . . aren't exactly copacetic in the Basquiat at present."

"I'd be real interested to hear what that has to do with me," I admitted. The streets were less crowded than usual—probably because of the cold—and I could already see the distant, misty gray outlines of a few statue heads and shoulders rising above the buildings. Mine being the biggest one, despite us all knowing that Compagnon'd been proud owner of the largest skull in all the Dragon Corps.

"Well . . ." Royston began, like now that I'd actually agreed he didn't have any idea of where to begin. "My sources inform me that relations with the Esar are not exactly what they *used* to be, and you of all people know what they *used* to be was hardly that sturdy to begin with. Anyway, it's as bad as it's ever been, and that might not put him in the most forgiving of moods at present. A war always does make the enemy seem clear. But once that clear enemy is gone, and one is so used to having one . . ."

"Thanks for the theorizing," I said, because if you let Roy talk too much, you'd never come to the point of anything, "but if you do have a plan of action, do you think you might let me in on it? It's damned cold out."

"I intend to talk to my sources," Roy repeated, blinking once. "Do keep up, old friend."

"So by your sources, you mean a certain lady of the tower," I said, just for confirmation. Funny thing about running in the same circles as Roy, you met all sorts of people you'd never have cause to know about otherwise. Lady Antoinette definitely seemed like the type who'd prefer you not to know about her. At least, not until it was too late.

"She's as acceptable a source as any when it comes to his moods," Royston said. "And this letter has the sort of information she should know."

"It doesn't seem anyone should know about it, to me," I said. Damn me if I was going to have to talk to th'Esar about anything, least of all what rights I had when it came to the girls. I'd been taken off my post, considering it didn't exist anymore. I wasn't anyone except Professor Adamo, teaching two classes to 'Versity brats just because there was a statue of me in the middle of the Rue, and that made people assume I knew things. Made people whisper about me, too, and maybe pity me a little. "So I guess that just means I'm waiting."

"I'm afraid it's the only thing you *can* do, at the moment," Roy murmured, voice far off. His mind had moved on to whispers and secrets, concerns of the Basquiat that apparently—thanks to Rook's fucking brother—had somehow become my fucking problem. "This is hardly like planning an assault on the other side of the Cobalts, is it?"

"Nothing really is, anymore," I said. Not like I missed it.

"You don't have to look so dark," Royston assured me. "At least, not yet. I'll let you know when you do. You *know* how the Esar gets into these moods of his; I'm sure it'll all pass over like so many storm clouds in the end. I just thought it best to forewarn you, lest you make an uninformed decision and run off to the Esar without me."

"Sounds to me like I'd do better without you if he's not feeling too warmly about the Basquiat," I said.

"I suppose that will be for you to decide," Royston said with a shrug. We rounded the corner that led to the mouth of the Rue d'St. Difference, filled with all sorts of fancy hat shops—Luvander's included—which just went to show how a woman was judging her fashions these days. To our right was the open courtyard that held our statues, mine in the middle and the boys lined up on either side of me, in proper formation like we'd never quite managed with the living examples. They sure brought the customers in for Luvander. "Bastion," Royston added, "what on earth is *that . . .* ?"

There was a shabby little crowd gathered around them, which wasn't so unusual except that the group had suitcases with them, and their clothes were—as Roy might've said— decidedly countrified. Even for someone like me who didn't much care one way or the other, it was easy to pick 'em out. Despite how it was only a carriage ride away, there was never too much mixing between the outer country folk and those who were born and bred in Thremedon. For good reason, according to people like Roy—which I couldn't help but feel made him a snob, since without the proper shepherding, the former were liable to be swallowed up in the shuffle. Not to mention having to keep up with the changing fashions. Some of us city folk couldn't even manage that.

"Looks like hayseeds to me," I said, eyeing them. Young people mostly, at least a dozen or more. They seemed cold— just as dramatically cold as Royston had been himself a few moments ago. They probably couldn't take the difference between Thremedon and the countryside—always warmer out there, or so I was told—and one of them had taken the liberty of sitting on his suitcase, which made him look both unimpressed and damn tired, too. "Why? Are you interested? I know you've a fondness for country folk."

"You know," Royston said, "the more often you say a thing, the less funny it becomes."

TOVERRE

Thremedon was even more beautiful than I had ever imagined. As grand as she was always described, mere words could not capture her vital essence. Even in my wildest dreams I could not have envisioned such splendor, not to mention the fashions—the delicate brocades and elaborate waistcoats—worn by all the passersby, and not a one of them looking out of place. And the statues of the airmen were taller than the barn back home! We'd arrived in the milliners' district, and in the windows I could see hats with pearl-droplet veils and—my heart could not be still to see it— real peacock feathers!

What glory, I thought, and tried to keep my mouth from hanging open as though I were a dying fish. No matter how I felt like one.

I was deeply enthralled—and even more deeply grateful that Father had not come with us to the city proper to say his good-byes. His presence would have ruined it, and his disapproval of my gawking would have dampened my spirits. Father belonged in the countryside, with his precious mud and chattel. Here *I* was, ready for the 'Versity's winter quarter. The weather was frigid, my nose running more freely than a gossip's chatter, my fingers beginning to grow numb, but I would never wear the woolen gloves that had been packed for me. They were simply too humble for a place so grand, and I intended—for the first time in my life—to belong somewhere.

Not to mention, at long last, that I was finally free.

Where would I go first? I wondered. What delightful hole in the wall would be my choice of public alehouses to frequent? When would I meet my first poet; when would I find my first love? It was far more likely in a place like this, and I knew already about all the scandals. I might create one of those myself, depending on the lover I chose to take; the thought itself felt like lightning. Father would hear of the news and clutch a hand to his chest, suddenly quite unable to breathe, but there would be nothing he could do about my actions. He would never leave the manor in order to acknowledge my transgressions.

"Watch yourself," a voice beside me said, just before the carriage driver threw my bag at me.

It almost knocked me down. A suitcase full of woolen gloves and books was bound to be heavy. Worse, it was flecked with mud from the journey over. I attempted to catch my breath though the sudden impact had certainly winded me.

"You've got a little bit of something on your chin," Laurence said. "I think it's drool from all that staring. Do you want my handkerchief to wipe it off?"

I turned to face her, only somewhat indignant. The cold air made her cheeks so pretty, whereas I knew that I would be covered in strange pink blotches all over my skin. She was wearing the dress I'd suggested, the nicest garment she owned—I'd given her my advice in the hopes that we would *both* fit into city life as more than pitiable country bumpkins— green to complement her eyes; without it, they'd just look gray. And the particular color was so flattering on a redhead.

Chances were, she would have much better luck finding *her* first love in Thremedon than I would. Nonetheless, I would encourage her *and* counsel her on what to wear, for I intended to be a solid friend despite all my jealousies. As her fiancé, I would always be there for her.

"Well, here we are," she said. "I bet *you're* loving this, anyway."

"Aren't you?" I asked.

Laure shook her head and made a face. "Too cold," she said. "I told you I should've worn something a little warmer."

"You look exquisite," I told her, as the carriage driver handed off her bags. At least he was more delicate with hers than with mine; the benefits, I supposed, of being in a lady's presence. "All you need now is a hat. I had no idea they'd be this popular."

"A warm hat, I hope," Laure said. "One that will cover my ears. And a scarf, maybe?"

I took her hand, tugging her over to one of the shop windows. Inside was an array that could only be described as luscious; I wished that the men's fashions were as extravagant as the women's. There was one with a wide brim and a little white veil that would have suited her very nicely, and it was even the same green as the rest of her dress.

"Well, bastion," Laure said. "Would you look at *that* monster?"

To my horror, she pointed at the hat in question by tapping her finger on the window, leaving behind a faint smudge. I fought the urge to clean it—an establishment as fine as this would have help of their own to do that—and had to admit the hat she was talking about, an immense red velvet affair, was a little too much even for my tastes. I couldn't imagine the sort of woman who would wear it in earnest although I did wish I could see her dress.

"Red doesn't suit you, anyway," I told her.

She grinned. "So you've said."

If only I'd had more of an allowance, I thought sadly. I wouldn't spend it all, of course, but neither would I hoard it. I would make one insane and wicked purchase, then keep it forever in my private little 'Versity room, to remind myself of how glorious life could be—would be, one day.

Father, of course, would not have approved. I sniffed—and it wasn't because of the cold.

"Fine day for a little window-browsing, ain't it?"

I'd *begged* Laure before we came not to use such language—to clean herself up in mind as well as in body, so to speak—but the voice was not hers, and not one I recognized. Curious, I peered over my shoulder and was met with an assault to the eyes as well as to my nose. There was a man standing before us, about three days of beard growth covering the lower half of his face and a fine layer of dirt and grime covering everything else. He wore gloves, though his thumb was poking out of a sizable hole on the left, and when he smiled I could see that he'd replaced one of his teeth with what looked like a low-grade precious stone, the sort my governess had always worn, though those were bound to be paste more often than not.

I fought the urge to hold my nose, but the effort it took not to leap back by at least a block was incredibly trying. This man was dirtier than Father's pigs, and he was standing so near to us. My skin crawled, and Laure stepped closer.

"New here, ain't you?" the man asked, apparently not bothered by the fact that neither I nor my robust fiancée had engaged him in conversation. "I can tell by the bags and all. *Real* sharp, Old Drake is. Thought I might ask as to your final destination, me with a hansom cab and all to spare, and the weather turning sour the way she's bound to do past midday."

"We'll manage, I think," Laure said, with a sniff of her own that probably *did* have more to do with the cold than anything else. Her sensibilities had never been delicate. I, however, was gagging. "Thank you for the offer."

"Well, now, no need to answer right away," Old Drake said, licking his false tooth thoughtfully. He reached for the nearest bag—one of Laure's, borrowed from her mother for the trip—and hefted it up as though to test its weight. "Just that this seems like an awfully heavy load for a pretty young lady such as yourself to be carrying *any* distance, no matter where you're going."

"I do have some help," Laure said, "not that you'd *know* it," she added in a quieter tone, for my own benefit. This was followed by a *look*—one of her finest—which clearly stated this was one of many situations wherein she would welcome the aid of a knight in shining armor. A *real* fiancé, so to speak—perhaps one of those large, statuesque men we'd seen upon arriving, the heroes of the war, with broad shoulders and square chins.

Unfortunately, all she had was me, and I wasn't about to get any closer to that man than I was already standing at present. I reached up to adjust my scarf, pulling it over my mouth and nose to keep out the smell.

"Skinny little weed like that won't be much help at all," Old Drake tsked. He still hadn't put down Laure's bag, and I was beginning to wish I'd learned how to recognize a Provost man when I saw one in the street. Did they wear uniforms, I wondered, or were they merely meant to appear in a time of need, like children's guardian magicians? If one were to rescue us now, it would be very noble indeed. "No, *my lady,* I'm afraid I *am* going to have to insist you come along with me. 'Twouldn't be chivalized otherwise."

"I *think* you mean chivalrous," I said, so that at least Laure wouldn't be able to say I'd done nothing when we were making our claim to the Provost.

I supposed one couldn't expect *every* city adventure to be a pleasant one.

"Excuse me," said another stranger, and my heart positively leapt into my throat. If this was one of Old Drake's counterparts or cronies, we were absolutely sunk. I was of no use at all in a fistfight, and Laure could only handle one grown man at best, *perhaps* two, but the latter was only if she had a weapon of some sort. There was nothing available save for me and a few hats, and all the beautiful passersby I had been admiring were ignoring us as though we were invisible. It was possible this kind of shakedown occurred all the time.

In short, we were royally fucked—a delicious and outrageous phrase I'd heard upon our arrival in the city though not one I could see myself *uttering* anytime soon.

I squinted into the sharp wind, prepared for the very worst. But what I saw was not at *all* what I'd been expecting. When I described it later in my journal—and I surely would, with a colorful flourish here and there to make sure I never forgot *exactly* how it all happened—I would have to express how *remarkably* it seemed to be one of the statues from the square come to life. The terror of the Cobalts, a real-live member of Thremedon's Dragon Corps, arriving on the scene to rescue us from being taken for a ride like your average pair of country bumpkins.

Then the wind forced me to blink and I realized it wasn't a statue, but rather a man of flesh and blood. He was young and blond and rather large, which explained my earlier mistake. And, it seemed, he was staring at me with an expression of quiet puzzlement.

"I'm sorry," he said, turning to Laure, "I didn't mean to interrupt anything. I only saw the pair of you standing here and I thought I'd come over."

"No harm done," said Old Drake, setting Laure's bag back down at her feet. However tempting a catch we might've been before—a deceptively peaceful young woman and myself, posing no real physical threat—this newcomer was clearly a discouragement to whatever Old Drake had planned for us. "Welcome to the three ladies, and here's hoping your visit's a prosperous one."

He offered a funny little bow and a tip of his hat—the threads at the top had come undone and it flapped like an ugly, open mouth—and melted back into the crowd. At last, I felt the ice in my chest begin to thaw, even if the rest of me was still *quite* chilled.

"Are you heading toward the 'Versity?" asked our savior, pushing his hair from his eyes. He was wearing thick woolen gloves of an unassuming gray that matched his eyes, and his winter coat had clearly seen better days, but he was also divinely handsome. *He* could have comfortably worn anything in the milliner's shop and still carried it off marvelously.

Some people simply had such complexions.

"We are," Laure said, shooting a look toward me that suggested she knew exactly what I was thinking. If only she had not always been quite so discerning! "Thank you. Your timing is . . . particularly apt."

"Oh, that," said the young man, ducking his head. "Well, I didn't want to say anything in front of him, but it seemed like you might need some help if that's not too presumptuous. I'm Gaeth, by the way. Heading to the 'Versity meself."

"Laurence," said Laure, holding out her hand instead of dropping a curtsy the way I'd expressly shown her. "And this is Toverre. We thought we'd do some looking around the city, but I think perhaps we should take that as a sign to move on."

"Pleased to meet you," Gaeth said, shaking her hand. "And your friend. Is . . . is everything all right with him?"

I realized I'd been caught staring and promptly changed

strategies, busying myself with my own suitcases to make sure everything was in order, and also since it was evident that Gaeth would want to help Laure with hers. It was a clumsy tactic, at best, but the tips of my fingers and toes were beginning to go numb from the cold and I wasn't operating at my best. Here I'd thought we might have a *few* days of being equally alone and unappreciated in the city. That showed how little I knew.

"Here, I can take that," Gaeth said, appearing before me to tug the leather case from my hands.

"That's not necessary," I said quickly, voice snapping. It wasn't at *all* the handsome rejoinder I'd had planned. Perhaps I was smarting slightly from the implication that I was Laure's "simple" companion—though I supposed that was what I got for not responding in the first place. "Surely you have your own bags to tend to."

"Got them sent ahead to my room," Gaeth said, hefting my bag over one shoulder as though it were filled with nothing more substantial than straw. "'Course, I haven't been to my room yet, so I've got to hope they're there at all."

"That was smart of you," Laure piped up, handing over one of her own bags gladly before she picked up the other. "I wish I'd thought of that."

"My mam arranged it all," Gaeth said, starting off down the street with Laure and leaving me to struggle after them. At least he'd taken the heavier of my bags. In the city, one could be grateful for saviors and small miracles.

Thick clouds had begun to form in the sky above us. Despite Old Drake's more nefarious intentions, perhaps he hadn't been lying about the weather. I was looking forward to spending the winter months in something warmer and finer than an old barn converted to extra housing. No matter how Father insisted it had been properly insulated—and that a real man should have no trouble with it even if it were not—there were terrible drafts from all corners, and the bathroom always smelled stubbornly of horse no matter how many hours I spent cleaning it.

Here in Thremedon, I would have my own space, and I could give it a smell of my choosing. Exotic incense from a

merchant bartering in Ke-Han goods would be *quite* daring,
I thought. It might even make me the talk of the dormitories,
though I hadn't yet decided what sort of reputation I wished
to cultivate among my peers. Something remarkable, of
course, and one that had nothing to do with dragging my
suitcases along the cobblestones after my fiancée and someone who looked like an artist's dream. Were he chiseled from
marble, surely, the craftsman would throw down his tools
and cease to work ever again. He represented the absolute
pinnacle of someone's ideal, and I was not about to allow
Laurence to scare him away as she did all the others, with her
peculiar cleverness or with her fists, depending on the sort of
mood she was in that day.

"It *is* a boy's name," she was saying, as I drew nearer. "If
you think that's bad, you should've seen me before my father
let me dress myself. Nothing but cotton shirts and trousers
my entire life. This is the longest my hair's ever been, too.
Just lucky the notice came when it did, or else I'd've looked
a fine fool among all these *fancy* ladies."

"I'm sure that isn't the case," Gaeth said. He seemed just
slightly uncomfortable. It was inevitable, of course. Laure
brought people together, regardless of class or age, in that
they were all to some degree put off by her candid nature.

"Toverre told me so," she confirmed most traitorously.

"Well," Gaeth said, stopping in front of a simple doorway.
"Here we are."

The bottommost step was crumbling, and all the paint
worn off the knob. The window lowest to the ground was
dirty inside, and all cluttered with plants and books. For a
moment I had no idea what our newfound savior could possibly be talking about.

"Here we are where?" I asked, feeling my nose twitch.
A marvel, considering how very *cold* it was.

"'Versity housing for first-years," Gaeth replied. He
fished an envelope from his coat pocket and from it procured
a simple key. How magical it all seemed, yet also, how very
mundane. "I assume you'll have to get sorted with your
schedules and your rooms, but I can help you with your bags,
if you need me."

"Seeing as how we almost lost them, that'd be nice," Laure said. No doubt he would find it charming that she had not thanked him.

I could have done so myself, except that I was too busy staring in abject horror at the state of the carpet inside the dormitory building, just past the doorway, where Gaeth was still standing. Boot marks and stains everywhere, and even something that looked like a mess made by a house cat.

Surely there had to have been some mistake.

"Are you *certain* this is the place?" I asked, grateful for the thin, more fashionable gloves I was wearing; they would shield me from whatever lingered on the banister and the doorknob even if they didn't do their job in the cold.

"Seems it must be," Gaeth replied. "You've . . . never been to Thremedon before, have you?"

"I think it's more than all right," Laure said, giving my arm a gentle squeeze. "We'll just have to get used to it, that's all."

Used to it, I thought in terror, but I could not allow my comrades to see me balk at the idea. It would take all my courage and a day of scrubbing—if my room was in any similar state—but I would be able to manage it. Perhaps there was a common room of some sort that would be in better repair, regularly cleaned if I was lucky. And a little adversity would harden me into the man I intended to become.

"Used to it," I repeated, gathering my wits and my breath and my scarf around me before I stepped inside my home for the next full tutoring year.

BALFOUR

I was beginning to hate the Arlemagne people more than I'd ever hated the Ke-Han. Yet dirty, strange, and traitorous thought that it was, I continued to harbor it. I was just lucky there was no one around to read it on my face.

At least my first week in the Airman had taught me how to hide my emotions more than adequately for a collection of mere diplomats—although someone would have easily been able to tell what I was thinking had I been sitting with my fellow airmen in the common room. They'd have sensed it even playing darts or exchanging stories of conquest, and suddenly I would have heard my name, *Balfour!* from Rook or Compagnon or Ace, most likely. Then it would have been *Hang his trousers from the window!* or perhaps *Let's see what will happen if we set fire to his socks!* and all the giggling that usually followed such delightful experiments. Not to mention my need to write home for another pair of socks *and* trousers. It was always so difficult to explain to Mother.

I missed it like hell and burning, and I supposed I likely would forever. I was always reminded of them somehow, just as I was of the little scars at my wrist where my skin ended and metal began.

One of the magicians who'd fitted me for my prosthetics had told me I was suffering from phantom limb—and he was right, though I was also suffering from phantom airmen alongside it.

Only at present I was suffering from all-too-tangible Arlemagne diplomats more than anything else, and not even rubbing at my wrists under the table could distract me from the gaping despair I suddenly felt. It was hopeless. After all we'd done to Arlemagne, they would never really forgive us.

At that, I thought of what Rook would have done in my situation—found someone to call a Cindy, insulted a wife or two, and insinuated he had slept with them all and could ride their horses better, too, making everything far worse but at least far more entertaining—and then I smiled from the fond memories it brought because quite obviously I was going insane.

"Well," Diplomat Chanteur, a large man with a red nose who had once spat on me by accident while speaking of the troubles involving one of our Margraves and their own Crown Prince, "I am famished from all this talking. Despite what little your people have to offer by means of food, perhaps it is time for us all to lunch?"

"What a wonderful idea," I said. "I commend you for your sharp thinking."

Privately, I thought to myself that such sharp thinking would have been better appreciated almost two hours ago—

about the point at which my stomach finally gave up growling.

In the Airman, one could have meals at any time one wished to, provided one was also prepared to share one's meal at least three ways, depending on who was awake at the time. Then there were the boys complaining that there wasn't enough, that it tasted like pig's shit, that they'd chipped a tooth and how did I intend to pay for it? Despite all the talk, the bastion could also be silent on occasion; not so with the Airman. So it was not that I preferred providing breakfast and lunch and dinner for men just as picky about their food as the Arlemagne were—and the Arlemagne loathed Volstovic fare, especially Volstovic attempts to serve traditional Arlemagne dishes. Nostalgia hadn't taken hold of me quite so badly, at least not yet.

"Don't commend me," Chanteur suggested. He stood in his chair; it creaked almost as loudly as his back. "Commend some better chefs, that's what I say."

"My lord," I told Chanteur, bowing stiffly as he brushed past me on his way out. "It has been a pleasure, as always."

What an excellent liar I was.

The diplomats all filed out after their leader. They were dressed fashionably, a few of them absolutely reeking of perfume. Those who didn't smelled distressingly of other things—a sharp body odor that reminded me of myself after a particularly grueling flight, only with less oil and more human sweat. I cleared my throat, keeping my head down and my thoughts to myself. When they'd arrived in Thremedon, they'd been expecting a cold winter. What they hadn't been expecting was a hot room in a bastion tower, and I didn't envy them their brocade coats and stiff ruffles.

How I ever managed to be given this position, I had no idea. It was because I wasn't as slippery as Luvander, who'd managed to wriggle free of all obligations, or as intimidating as Ghislain, who'd said he planned on heading out to sea, and no one, it seemed, felt like arguing with him. Adamo and I had unfortunately been caught up in some bizarre, terrible system of being rewarded as living heroes.

And as for Rook . . . I had been informed of his progress

here and there by Thom, who seemed to be weathering those troubles with his usual distress and stubbornness.

"Lost in thought, I see?" a familiar voice said beside me. "Or is it simply that your stomach has digested itself? I'd personally eat a bale of oats right now, fine cooking aside."

Now that Thom was gone for parts unknown, fighting his way through the desert and dealing with the discomfort of sand in his trousers, there were few people left in Thremedon I could consider my friends. The man standing in front of me was one of them, I supposed, partly because we'd known each other in school when we were younger, and partly because he'd managed to adopt me diplomatically on my first day of talks. In class, we'd always conducted a particular rivalry for top marks, but in the practice of diplomacy I was at last willing to concede my defeat; his years of experience in the field were more suited for this than my own.

Even if I sometimes *wished* I might have conducted the talks from atop Anastasia—then I surely would have had an advantage. At the very least, it might have hurried the pace along.

Still, in the absence of my dragon, I was glad to have a childhood companion at my side. We'd fallen out of touch when I'd moved to Thremedon and into the Airman and he'd remained in the country, but the years between us didn't seem to have made things too abruptly awkward. He'd even asked me how I was with only the barest of glances at my hands and never shied away from shaking when we met.

It was comforting, in its own way.

"Troius," I said, smiling this time not because I was thinking of—or like—my old comrades in arms, but rather because of some more present emotion.

"You still remember my name," Troius said. "That's an *excellent* sign. Quick! To the kitchens, before we lose our minds to starvation."

"Were I truly experiencing starvation, I don't think my first concern would be my mind," I confessed, falling into step with him despite my better judgment.

The men from Arlemagne didn't like to see too many of us conferring together at once. It made them feel plotted against, or so Troius had informed me on our third day of talks when I'd asked him why he didn't see fit to take his meals with the rest of us. Personally, while I understood the need for diplomacy now more than ever—the war effort was over for the present, but one never knew what the future might hold—I didn't particularly enjoy all the conceding to Arlemagne comfort.

But then, I supposed, that was why I had been given this task and not Adamo. I was better bred for it, and my nature was such that—outwardly, at least—I seemed more eager to please.

I could think of thirteen other men who would never have bothered, though of course it was because of one of them that we had to be so bastion-blasted cautious with the Arlemagne all the time.

That, and the business with the Arlemagne prince. As far as our foreign friends were concerned—and I use "friends" in the loosest sense of the word—Volstov was the equivalent of a pretty whore and Thremedon what lay beneath her layered skirts. They were humoring us with the talks, perhaps, but they showed no signs of truly respecting us.

Nor would they send us their royalty again, but that was a different matter. On that front I supposed I didn't blame them.

I had learned to live without respect before, and certainly my life would continue without it in the future. Of all the airmen, I was the only one who could count himself a member of the *second* generation. My brother had died in an air raid against the Ke-Han, brought down somewhere in the skies over Lapis, and it had been all the others could do just to get his dragon back in one piece. That was how they'd explained it to my parents, and again in a letter from the Esar himself—with a painful lack of detail. No body had ever been recovered. It simply wasn't worth the risk to the other dragons and their riders to try to find him.

Indeed, Chanteur's rudeness paled in comparison to the arsenal of hazing leveled against me once before by the other airmen—vicious, personal reminders that I was not my brother and never would be, as though I hadn't enough of those on my own. It had been in some ways easier to deal with than the simple grief I'd seen on my parents' faces, quiet and resigned every time that they remembered I *was* Balfour, and not someone else entirely.

By comparison, a blue handprint on the face didn't seem all that bad. But I *wouldn't* miss all the piss in my boots. A man had to have some standards.

"You look like the dog's breakfast," Troius said, steering me through the seemingly endless halls. "Don't worry, things are bound to look up sooner or later. They can call us a corrupting influence all they like, but their men visit the 'Fans often enough, don't they? Nothing says hospitality like satin sheets and low lighting. We'll welcome them into our beds and eventually find places in their hearts."

"If that's the case, then I imagine they'll want to do some redecorating at the bastion," I said, trying and failing not to picture it. I had to suppress a curious giggle that did not sound quite like me.

Diplomatic venues were largely the same in every country, I imagined; all around us were soothing neutral colors and no decorations that could be considered offensive to anyone, no matter what their heritage might be. I'd considered it a privilege when the talks had first started—no one I knew could lay claim to ever having entered the bastion for anything other than criminal charges—and I'd even written a letter to Thom proclaiming as much.

He was very interested in the procedures, if distracted somewhat by his own diplomatic proceedings with Rook.

Now all I could really think was that it was *much* different from a building decorated with naughty portraitures that looked as though they'd been drawn by someone with either very little understanding of anatomy or a generous overestimation of the weight a woman's back could support. Not to mention, there was no Madeline here. The Airman's own personal mascot had started out as a papier-mâché bust of someone's ideal woman but had gradually grown to a full-size mannequin. When the boys had run out of materials, they'd started using Raphael's books, which I'd always felt lent her a dignified air. There was ancient poetry on her breasts, and a line of translation from the Old Ramanthe over her upper lip that Ghislain always said looked just like a healthy mustache.

The closest thing to any kind of mascot in the bastion was a marble carving of a lion, whose creator had had no flair for humor or personality. The stone beast practically scowled.

Troius laughed as we rounded the next corner and a symphony of smells assaulted me. All at once, I felt my mouth begin to water. No matter what Chanteur said about our food, I found the chefs at the bastion dining hall to be quite satisfactory. I was even managing to put on a little weight, which my physician said would serve me well after all that I had been through.

"Diplomats *are* whores, in a sense," Troius said, taking a tray from the clean stack in the corner. "We make concessions and do our best to wheedle and flatter our way into a better position. Plus, we negotiate the price before we'll get into bed with anyone. It's just common sense, really—but don't tell anyone I ever said something like that."

"I'm beginning to regret my career in politics," I said, eyeing the bean stew and a basket of freshly made crusty white rolls.

"It's not *so* bad," Troius reasoned, serving himself some of the sliced ham from another tray. "Look on the bright side: You could've been sent out with that envoy to the Ke-Han. That didn't turn out so well for them, did it? Though I suppose making it back all in one piece says something. Although I *did* hear Margrave Josette came back with a little souvenir of her own."

"Don't gossip," I said, spooning up my much-belated lunch even as I cast an eye about for empty tables. "She could be here."

"It's only the truth," Troius reasoned. "Though her souvenir could likely snap my neck like a toothpick, so you're probably right. Discretion it is. Lunch is on me, by the way."

"Thank you," I said, too surprised to do anything but take him up on the offer.

Privately, I couldn't help but disagree with his statement, even if I knew exactly how foolish it sounded, even in my own head. The danger in Ke-Han had been quite real, and to desire *that* was the mark of a certified lunatic, with papers to attest to his condition. Still, the idea of facing down a mad emperor in a foreign land that was struggling to rebuild itself sounded slightly more interesting than staring across the table at Chanteur's red face day in and day out, while he feigned forgiveness for all our political transgressions like a country lord dangling a carrot in front of his mount's depressed nose.

I'd been raised—or at least I'd been made a man—on a steady regimen of simply not knowing when my life would be forfeit. At any moment, any one of us airmen could have died. In the end many of us had, and I hadn't yet gotten the opportunity to ask those yet living how they coped without a steady diet of adrenaline on a daily basis.

We never saw each other all that much—I suspected it was because it was a little too painful for us.

I was in some ways a recovering addict—an analogy I disliked immensely but one I seemed resigned to making all the same. I *would* consult the others one day, and perhaps thereby learn the key to living a normal life.

Chief Sergeant—now just Adamo—would certainly have the answers if no one else did.

The eatery was crowded, though not so crowded as it would've been hours ago at a proper time for lunch. There were long tables set out for groups, if they wished to continue chewing at their problems at the same time as their lunch, and the smaller tables for what I viewed as much saner folk—those who wished to take their meals alone or with a friend, forgetting all about politics in the meantime.

Perhaps that meant my limitations were showing, but I didn't know how else to get through the day. Truly, if I didn't have meals to break up the monotony of diplomacy, I would surely lose my mind.

That was how I'd word my next letter to Thom, I decided. It sounded suitably dramatic, and I hoped it would make him laugh as his letters did for me, describing in great detail his trials and his own peace talks with a single man instead of a nation.

I couldn't imagine brokering any kind of personal treaties with Rook, but then, Thom had blood on his side. If anyone was stubborn enough to accomplish it, he was.

"I have a question for you," Troius announced after we'd seated ourselves, and once I'd struggled somewhat setting out my napkin on my lap. Unfortunately, it was at the precise moment when I'd taken too large a bite of my stew. I managed not to choke, however, and instead chewed carefully before I swallowed, eyes watering from how hot it was.

"Ask away," I said, thinking the better of reaching for some water. It was possible I would knock the glass over; my fingers worked poorly when my mind was otherwise engaged.

"Well, let me preface it by saying I don't want to make you uncomfortable," Troius said, instantly rendering me uncomfortable already. "You know that. And certainly don't feel as if you have to answer or anything, I'm just curious, and what with the cold snap hitting and all . . . How *are* your hands feeling?"

I clenched them involuntarily, though the gesture was a natural one and not an accident, the way it had been when I'd first gotten them. They responded in the same way my old hands had, but they didn't *feel* the same. I'd set up several mental blocks about them straightaway. There had been magicians to help me out of that bad habit, of course, but Troius was right. The cold *did* make a difference. They ached at the scars some nights, and if I accidentally touched my face after walking through the streets at night I got a frightful shock, even *with* the gloves, but it wasn't so bad as to be intolerable.

There were many who'd fared worse. I considered my hands a gift more than anything. And at least the gloves themselves kept too many people from staring, unless they knew what they were looking for.

"I've offended you," Troius said, leaning back in his chair with a regretful air, like a hound being scolded by his master. He even looked a little like one, dark eyes and darker hair that framed his face in much the same way as a bloodhound's ears. "I truly didn't mean to."

"It's all right," I said quickly, before I could decide for myself whether or not that was true. "Really, it's no trouble at all. I just forget about them sometimes, which is actually meant to be a good thing, I'm told."

Another lie, but another diplomatic one. I didn't mind applying my talents for good every now and again, and lying for Troius's benefit made me feel much better than lying to flatter Chanteur's ego.

"Probably means you're getting used to them," Troius agreed cautiously. He pushed his fork around on his plate before halfheartedly spearing a piece of meat. "They're serving you well, then?"

"No complaints," I said, which *was* partly true. I couldn't have asked for a better substitute, and I'd grown accustomed to the occasional moment of clumsiness they caused me. The fact that I didn't want a substitute at all was my own difficulty to overcome and nothing a magician could do for me.

"You know, I've always wondered," Troius said, then stopped, shaking his head. "No, never mind. It *would* make you uncomfortable."

I smiled. "Trust me when I say that I have known men who made it their favorite pastime to ensure my discomfort," I assured him. "Just knowing those aren't your intentions is enough for me. Go ahead; ask away."

Troius chewed his ham, casting around with the same hesitation that everyone used when they asked me how I was feeling. They were curious, a little repulsed; some managed the courage or the insensitivity to ask anyway *because* of their curiosity. And so few actually wished to touch me.

"I've just always wondered how you control them," Troius said at last. "Bit of magic in it, isn't there?"

"So I'm told," I confirmed. I rubbed the back of one glove, metal finger pressed against the fabric, and felt absolutely nothing. "I . . . know they're there, but of course, I can't *feel* any part of them."

"One might even say they work like one of the dragons did," Troius added. There was a familiar light in his eye—the sort any man displayed when bringing up that topic.

I hid my wince as well as I could, pretending it was the spices that made my eyes unfocus rather than some distant loneliness. Anastasia had been my last tangible tie to my brother. What was more, she had been my *only* tie to a group of men with whom I'd practically lived my entire adult life. I could hardly call them friends, so in the absence of our shared employment, I had nothing *to* call them. "Yes, of course, one could say that," I confirmed. "Although these hands aren't a separate part of me at all, nor do they have a personality of their own. It was never really something I understood, mind you. Just something I trusted."

"Must be strange," Troius said, attempting to sound comprehending. I appreciated the effort despite how impossible the thing would be. "But you never have trouble with them at all?"

"They can be a little clumsy," I admitted. I wished the conversation could have ended a few questions earlier, but it was good practice for my diplomacy. "But with time and practice, I'm told I'll master it. Like real hands."

"Like a natural part of you," Troius said, shaking his head. "The things these magicians can do these days, you know? Incredible."

"Almost like magic," I agreed, with a touch of humor that was as much to comfort me as it was to make my companion laugh.

"Almost like magic, indeed," Troius said. He wiped at the corner of his mouth with his napkin, tossing it down neatly onto his plate. "Well, back to diplomacy, then, eh, Balfour?"

I folded my own napkin, tucking it gently under my plate. I'd lost my appetite some time ago, in any case. "Quite," I agreed, and followed him out.

LAURE

There was a draft in Toverre's room, so for the time being he was lingering in mine—which itself was smoky, some problem with the fireplace no one was coming to fix for us, so I was fixing it myself. In thanks, Toverre had started to unpack for me.

It wasn't so bad, I thought. At least not as bad as Toverre was making it out to be.

"There's something caught in the flue," I said, even though I knew he wasn't listening. It was more like explaining it out loud for my own sake. "Don't know if this is a good idea or not, but I'm going to try for it anyway. Is there anything in here like a poker? Would you mind looking under the bed for me?"

I heard Toverre draw in a sharp breath. When I turned around he was toeing the bottom of my coverlet anxiously, but he sure as rain wasn't on his hands and knees like I was.

"Never mind," I said. "I'll look for it. You just keep unpacking."

"That *was* my plan," Toverre replied, stepping away from the bed gratefully and tugging a handkerchief out of his front pocket to wipe his hands, "but I'm afraid I've found something very disturbing in your traveling bags."

There was dust under the bed—enough to make me sneeze pretty loudly—but at least that gusted it all away. There was the poker, I realized, reaching out for it and brushing past something disturbingly sticky on my way. A ball of tape, I realized as I pulled it out, holding it up for Toverre to see.

Toverre made a face of real horror. "Don't try to distract me from my point," he said. It was obviously pretty hard for him to breathe, but he'd always been too easy a mark for any *real* teasing. "Please, Laurence, *do* put that somewhere . . . away."

There was a wastebasket in the corner of the room, which already had a few balls of dust and other strange remnants of the room's previous dirty, scummy student. I tossed it in there, grimy with dust and dirt and some unknown black substance, then moved to the fireplace with my newfound poker. Flimsy piece of work, probably made light so none of the fools living here was ever tempted to clobber themselves—or a student rival—with it in the dead of night. But there was something warped and metallic stuck in the chimney shaft, and I was getting it out. If not just to make the room more hospitable, then certainly to see what it was. Aside from all the scorch marks on it, it was shiny.

"You *know* it's not polite to look through a woman's personal effects," I told Toverre. "So what'd you find, anyway? There's nothing embarrassing in there."

"You brought trousers with you," Toverre murmured, sniffing unhappily. "And a man's riding boots and shirt."

I stabbed at the bit of metal a tad too viciously and it clanged, but the distraction bought me a little bit of time. Being born a man—peculiar as he was—Toverre would never be able to understand what it meant to be a woman in Volstov, no matter how many times I'd *tried* to explain it to him. And as much as Toverre's father wanted him to be someone else, mine was wishing right along with him. He might even have accepted Toverre, though he couldn't ride half as well as I could and was terrified of barnyard animals, besides. The only weapon he'd ever managed to wield successfully was a butter knife—although he knew pretty well which piece of silverware came first and second and so on during a fancy dinner service—but, bastion help him, he did have the necessary parts to make a son, which I didn't.

It was pretty simple, really. Da just wanted a boy. Why else would he name his sweet little daughter after his favorite uncle?

"Don't worry," I told Toverre. "Breathe normal. It's not like I'm planning on wearing them all over the place and all of the time. I thought I could wear the trousers underneath my skirts when it got really cold, and the shirt to bed at night. Besides, it's not like I have *so many* dresses."

"You thought you'd wear these trousers under your skirts," Toverre repeated. Like *I* was the one most likely to go mad.

"No one's going to know," I said. Another clang, and a little shifting of embers and stone, and I knew I was close to shaking the thing free. Now I just had to hope it was something put in there by some troublemaker, and not an actual part of the fireplace that was necessary for making it work.

"My dear Laure," Toverre said, "this simply will not do. Here we are, in Thremedon at last. It is time to remake ourselves."

"Oh yeah?" I asked. "Into what?"

He might've answered, except I managed to shake the

metal free at last. It fell down into the still-hot embers of the fire I'd lit—before I knew the room had been booby-trapped, that is—and I poked it quickly out onto the carpet, while Toverre watched me, covering his mouth with his kerchief. So as not to breathe in any unseemly fireplace poison, I assumed.

"Well," I said, a little disappointed. "It's just a plate. Wonder how that got up in there. Don't you?"

"It's *ghastly,*" Toverre said, his voice slightly muffled because of the cloth. "What if it has the remains of someone's meal on it? You ought to put it back immediately."

"It's made for eating off, not for being stuck in the flue," I told him. I bent down so as to be able to wrap my skirts around it before picking it up. It *had* been in the fire, and nothing held heat like metal did.

I'd often wondered how the men in the corps didn't burn their breeches off, riding the dragons the way they did and them being *all* fire and metal, but when I'd asked my da he'd just said I had too practical a mind for my own good, and to go feed the chickens already. The question shouldn't bother me, anyway; it wasn't like *I* was going to ride them, especially not now they were all gone.

"You're not planning on . . . *eating* from it," Toverre said, not even as a question because he couldn't possibly imagine the answer would be yes.

It really was too easy to get a rise out of him. Maybe I should've gone a little softer on him, like I would've had we been sparring for real, but if he didn't toughen up now—in the middle of all his planned personal renovations, bastion help us—then there really was no hope for him.

"You never know when it might come in handy, having a spare plate in the room," I told him. "What if I'm entertaining company? Or if I want a midnight snack for when I'm studying?"

Toverre finally deigned to seat his bony behind on the very end of my bed, folding one leg up to his chest and resting his chin against his knee. He looked like a finely dressed bundle of twigs—perhaps a scarecrow dressed in a noble's clothing or a portrait from a book about the first magicians, none of whom had ever looked quite human to me. Hard to convey what a man with no heart looked like on the outside, probably, even for the best artists. The girls in the country had all found him handsome enough, I expected, in that beautiful, ghostly way of his. Everyone did, right up until he opened his mouth and all the crazy came pouring out.

All the long eyelashes and dark curls in the world couldn't make up for someone who'd only take the road to the nearest marketplace on *even* days, not odd. And if he so much as breathed in trail dust, he'd be coughing for a week. People didn't like being told they had dirt under their fingernails, and his behavior only got worse when he was talking to somebody he actually *liked*.

He could be a pain in the ass, but he didn't try to grab my breasts or look up my skirts, and he didn't make any stupid comments about how *grown-up* I looked in my mother's dresses, either. We'd known each other since both of us were learning to walk, and I liked him all right.

Someone had to, after all.

"I can't even begin to tell you how wrong it would be to try and entertain guests in this room," Toverre said, lowering his kerchief at last. I was surprised he hadn't spread it out over the bed like a protective doily or something, but then, maybe the thought just hadn't occurred to him.

Or, miracle of miracles, he was actually loosening up a hair. *That,* however, seemed less likely than me securing an invitation to dinner with th'Esar himself. Even if our reasons for coming to the city had been directly thanks to His Highness, I didn't cherish any illusions about him wanting to meet us or anything like that.

Apparently, after the war and once all the dust had settled, th'Esar had realized that there were all sorts of people in Volstov—outside of Thremedon—with good heads on their shoulders and no means of expanding their minds. I guess it had something to do with the fact that the man who'd figured out how to stop the magicians' plague had hailed from somewhere around Nevers originally. All the best minds in Thremedon hadn't been able to accomplish what he did, and th'Esar probably didn't want to get caught with his trousers down like that again.

Of course, that *wasn't* how it'd been put in the letter Da got, but it *was* the general thrust of things. It was a postwar scholarship program, and Toverre and I'd been lucky enough to qualify because of our location. Besides which, Toverre was the only young man of age to be found for miles in either direction.

We'd accepted because you didn't say no to th'Esar. Though, to be honest, Toverre's father was happy enough to be rid of him, and *my* da would do all right so long as the stableboy didn't leave his employment seeking other work. Toverre was delighted, but I was reserving judgment—at least until I saw what Thremedon was *really* like.

The letter came in early fall, just after the war ended. Winter term started up, like you'd guess, at the beginning of winter. That didn't give us much time for getting ready, and everything had happened in a flurry of packing, Toverre's bags more than triple the size and quantity of my own, before he'd forced me to go deep into my old things and bring along several of the dresses I'd discarded as too fancy or too light for the winter.

Seasons change, he'd insisted, and even though it seemed like an awful lot of trouble to go to—not to mention an awful lot of crinoline and lace taking up space in my bags—I'd agreed to go along with his suggestions.

Dealing with Toverre was remarkably like dealing with a herd of cows when only one of them had reason to be spooked but all the rest panicked anyway. If you just stood to one side and allowed them to do whatever they wanted, both parties would come up smelling like posies. Or at least, no one the worse for wear.

I picked up my new plate and set it on the windowsill, figuring I'd decide what to do with it later. Now, at least, I could probably light a fire in my room without feeling like I'd been transported to a blacksmith's.

"Are you even listening to me?" Toverre demanded, arms crossed over his chest.

"You said you couldn't begin to tell me what was wrong with it," I reasoned, going back to stoke the coals with my poker. "So I just naturally assumed you wouldn't. Tell me, that is."

"You're making fun of me," Toverre said, wrinkling his nose with a disapproving sniff. I wanted to ask him if he needed to blow his nose, but the mere idea would've caused spasms of horror or something worse, probably. And me standing there without any of the cleaning solvents that usually soothed his more serious fits of dirt panic.

Fortunately for both of us, someone knocked at the door.

"Looks like someone already heard I was entertaining," I told Toverre before I could help myself, and went to answer the door. I even wiped the knob first with my skirts, just so Toverre wouldn't faint dead away then and there. A thin layer of dust and grime came off on the fabric.

Maybe he'd think that was worse.

Standing in the hallway was the same young man who'd helped us with our bags, hand still raised from knocking like he hadn't quite expected me to get to the door that fast.

"Hello," he said, glancing over my shoulder toward the fire, and where Toverre was knotted up on the end of the bed like a piece of burned twisty-bread. "I hope I'm not interrupting anything. I just wanted to see how the two of you were settling in."

"Well enough now," I said, racking my brain to remember his name. "I'm sorry, I'm shit with names. It *is* Gaeth, isn't it?"

I knew that Toverre would berate me later for using indelicate language, but there were certain points of etiquette that didn't make any sense to me. And wasn't it more polite to ask than to pretend all afternoon that you knew someone when you didn't? But that was probably just my practical mind getting the better of me once again.

Could've done without saying "shit," though. Probably.

"It is," Gaeth said, looking marginally relieved.

"Would you like to come in?" Toverre asked pointedly, because I hadn't yet. I could've told him that there were better ways to try and upstage me as a hostess, and sounding like an old magician who lured children into her lair to suck their bones clean *wasn't* one of them.

It was all in the tone of voice, really.

For whatever reason, instead of giving Toverre a funny look and suddenly remembering he had a pressing engagement elsewhere, Gaeth stepped inside, leaving me to close the door behind him.

Da would never have stood for a closed door at home with two boys in my room, but as far as I was concerned, he didn't have anything to worry about. Toverre was no danger to a woman's virtue, and I could tell by the way he was behaving that Gaeth was about to be the millionth lucky customer— the next great love of Toverre's life.

It wasn't so unattainable a title as all that. In fact, it rotated at least once a week, changing heads more often than the Arlemagne crown. He was a hopeless romantic—emphasis on the hopeless part—and anyway, no one ever found him out since his way of showing affection was pissing all over a man verbally.

They ran for the hills, and this one would, too. I glanced out of the window and wondered, for a moment, what would serve for hills here in Thremedon. Only the spindly tops of buildings winding their way up the cobblestone street broke up the gray skyline. I couldn't see much from this angle, but Toverre'd already discovered you could see the Basquiat if you opened the window and leaned out.

Though why anyone would open a window in this weather was beyond me.

From his perch, Toverre made a strangled sound and leapt suddenly in the direction of one of my half-unpacked bags. He looked like a cricket, all long legs and bent-up elbows.

Of course, both Gaeth and I looked after him immediately, to find him shoving my undergarments deep into the suitcase.

"I came at a bad time," Gaeth said. "Didn't I?"

"We were just unpacking," I told him, grateful at least that *he* hadn't blushed. Toverre's cheeks were pink as he did up the snaps, my private items locked safely within. If only he'd shown a little less delicacy, my honor mightn't have been compromised so quickly. "It's not a bother, anyway."

"You could have given us *some* warning, actually," Toverre said pointedly.

Gaeth cleared his throat, shrugging lopsidedly. It was *definitely* love in Toverre's eyes, and I didn't quite blame him. Gaeth was clearly of good stock, and if he'd've been a horse, Da and I wouldn't've argued for a second before buying him. Nice skin, good teeth, dark eyes. He was healthy, too, with strong coloring. If he made a pass at my skirts, I was going to clobber him.

"Just . . . wanted to make sure you settled in fine, like I said," Gaeth said at last, probably because nobody else was talking. "Is that . . . soot on your face?"

I brought my hand up to my cheek, and some cinders came floating out of my hair as I did so. Toverre winced dramatically, in the middle of polishing one of the brass buckles on my biggest suitcase.

"There was a problem with the fireplace," I explained, pointing to the plate on the windowsill. "Had a plate in it."

"There was a boot in mine, actually," Gaeth said.

Toverre made a little clucking noise. "I haven't even checked mine yet," he said mournfully. "Do you think . . . No, I can't *bear* it. I'd never crawl up into such a dirty, *dirty* place."

"Could always give it a once-over for you," Gaeth offered. Little did he know what he was getting himself into, doing something like that. "I've got a meeting with a finances advisor before supper, but after that I'm free."

"As long as you don't touch anything," Toverre said. "And I mean *anything*. Leave everything the way you've found it, and . . ." His eyes darted to me, looking for all the world like a drowning man, and I tried to send him some form of encouragement through sheer will alone. ". . . thank you," he concluded at last, though he sounded like there was a stone he was trying to pass when he said it. At least the actual words came out, which was a step in the right direction for poor Toverre.

"I'll help, too," I offered. "But I'm going to touch everything; you know I can't help myself."

Gaeth laughed, relaxed and steady, and Toverre even managed to join in, despite looking incensed. And just like that, we'd made our first friend in the city.

It only figured that he wasn't actual city folk.

CHAPTER TWO

TOVERRE

Our first day of classes began in the bitter cold, the air so sharp that by the time we'd made it to the classrooms a delicate snow had begun to fall, dusting the rooftops of Thremedon like sugar powder upon a fancy cake. The whole city looked like a piece of wedding confectionary—at least, it did to *me,* but Laure had put her boot in a little yellow puddle only a few steps past our dormitory building, so she refused to agree with me about how lovely it was.

I had to walk down 'Versity Stretch on her other side the rest of the way.

Being a school with no separate campus for its students meant that the 'Versity was crammed right up against the city itself, so that even while making their way to classes, students might observe the most fascinating aspects of city life. I'd discovered that if I followed the Stretch long enough I would wind up at the mouth of the shopping district Laure and I had wandered into on our very first day in Thremedon. It was labeled *Rue d'St. Difference* on my map, and I'd practiced saying it so that I might sound as casual as possible when I finally did suggest it as a meeting place to a lover or newfound companion.

It had been difficult to get my desired amount of private time in my room for such practicing—Laure's company was one thing, but Gaeth, too, had come to unstick my chimney just as he'd promised. There'd been a small metal pan normally used for cooking jammed in the flue, and I'd made him promise to take the thing with him, now that I knew it was there. Laure had suggested we might collect an entire dinner service at this rate, but not one whose practical use could be *condoned*.

Later that night, I'd been forced to lie with my stomach on the ground in order to properly inspect the floors for any soot or dust that might have come loose in the proceedings. I'd found none, but it had eaten into my time *considerably*.

There were shops along the 'Versity Stretch, too, but smaller ones, no doubt wishing to cater more to poor students and the size of their wallets. No remarkable hats to be found *here*, though I did espy several bookshops, a few cafés, and even a very small market—but I could see easily enough from the state of its shriveled fruits and unimpressive vegetables that I would not be giving such a place *my* business. There was a little apothecary hidden away down a narrow corner that sold poultices and remedies for those unfortunate enough to take ill in the winter months. I made a note of its location, quite sure that I would be availing myself of its services sometime in the future.

Despite my chimney being stopped up in the same manner as Laure's had been, my room had remained persistently chilly and drafty from the first.

Still, it was difficult to remain in a dreary mood when one's surroundings were no longer dreary in the slightest. Various men and women—dressed so smartly that it was impossible to imagine they weren't headed somewhere terribly important—used the Stretch as a thoroughfare to get from one place to the next despite *clearly* not being students or professors of the 'Versity proper, and the street was terribly crowded, even though I hadn't yet seen very many other students. I personally felt like a very small fish in a very large, overcrowded ocean—and one with very dull scales indeed. And I had no affection for the way men and women walked past you as though you didn't exist, jostling you this way and that without so much as a by-your-leave. They never covered their mouths with kerchiefs when they sneezed, either, and I knew without a doubt I would be sick before the week was out.

"Why're you making that face?" Laure asked me, nudging me in the side with her elbow.

"I can smell whatever it is you've gotten on your boot," I replied. This was very true. "I told you, you should have changed it right away."

"I've had worse on my boots," Laure said. "*Way* worse, too."

This was very true, as well, but I couldn't bear to think about it.

The Stretch was wide, but branched off into a great many side streets along the way. One of these was my dear Rue d'St. Difference, which made up a border of sorts, as I understood it, with the neighboring Charlotte district. I was absolutely *itching* to see the lower town, but I hadn't mentioned this to Laure for fear she'd try to knock the idea right out of my head.

If we were to keep going and make a sharp right, I realized, we would land ourselves smack where we'd been dropped off in the carriages—back at the statues of the Dragon Corps, though that was one landmark I'd seen quite enough of for the time being. One of them smelled like Laure's boot did, and besides, it seemed rather morbid—to me, in any case—to erect statues of men who were both living *and* dead, and group them together like that. It was like inviting bad luck—though perhaps such superstitious notions were regarded as entirely outdated in the city.

Luckily we were only meant to follow the main road for a bare few twists before we came to the central class buildings—which looked, I realized, just the same as the regular housing, with no discernible difference whatsoever. I had been hoping for something a little more grand, or perhaps a longer walk through the city so that I might drink in more sights and sounds, but no such luck. Seeing as how it was very cold indeed, I supposed I could accept this—at least for the time being.

But as soon as classes were out for the day—and we had only two introductory lectures to begin with, the latter of which concluded around lunchtime—I intended to go exploring. Bold and intrepid as such actions were, I would have my stalwart companion, Laure, with me. Perhaps we would start by drifting in the wake of the more-elaborately-dressed people around us to see where they ended up. Or perhaps we might even make our way to the Basquiat, though we had no real business there. This time, there would be no bags that could be lost, and we would also be wandering with the aid of a local map.

"I think this is it," Laure said, holding up a crumpled piece of paper, which had a smudge of grease on the right-hand corner. She'd been eating while looking at her syllabus again, it seemed. "*Cathery* 103."

By the side of the door was a silver plate announcing that the building we were standing in front of was, indeed, Cathery. Someone shoved past us without any word of apology and took the steps two at a time. I sighed heavily. It would be so unpleasant if this was to be standard procedure. Had all real Volstovic chivalry been lost?

"Don't worry," Laure said. "I'll school that idiot later." With her woolly-gloved fingers, she grabbed my hand and tugged me inside, where it was distressingly empty but at least very clean. The wood paneling and banisters even gleamed.

I supposed the lecture buildings were what the 'Versity institution showed off in order to give a good impression of their dealings. They certainly could not use the first-year dormitories.

It had taken a great many hours scrubbing on my hands and knees to get my room into a state that could be deemed serviceable, so much so that the cold seemed like a minor discomfort by comparison. I hadn't been left very much time for unpacking, but then I rather appreciated the neatness of everything in my various cases and saw no need to court disaster by using the ramshackle dresser the 'Versity had provided. The lining in the drawers was stained and dirty, and there had also been a piece of brown candy melted and stuck to the underside of one of the handles.

I had no intentions of ever touching that, handkerchief protecting my fingers or no.

How I'd managed to hold on to my breakfast after that ordeal was anyone's guess. I was being far braver than anyone would ever give me credit for. Certainly more than Mother and Father had ever been given reason to expect, and certainly more than was indicated by the look Laure leveled at me when she saw the state of my room earlier that morning.

To my immense relief, we were not the first to arrive to our class. In fact, despite the relative quiet in the halls, about half the seats had already been taken. Perhaps there was simply no lingering about between lectures—a small note of etiquette that I filed away both for myself and Laure, who I knew would try to linger the first chance she got, now that we'd seen it was unacceptable. She had such a knack for contrariness.

I hesitated in choosing a seat, as I always did. The room appeared to have filled from the very back first, then forward, as there were a great many seats available in the front rows, a moderate number in the middle, while very few remained at the back, which had the highest elevation. Of course, it didn't matter *overly* much to me, as my suspicions were that those students who chose to sit very far in the back did so in order to sleep, and that was not a crowd I wished to become a part of. However, I also did not wish to seem too eager by sitting in the front row, either. There was a seat that might've been perfect—to the left and nearby a window—but to my great misfortune there was already someone sitting in it.

"Just *choose* already," Laure said, nudging me in the back with her books. "My legs are going to start cramping from standing around."

"All right, if you're going to be *impatient*," I said, casting desperately about for a halfway-decent compromise. Perhaps somewhere in the middle would do, and next day we'd come earlier so that I might be completely satisfied with my choice: a seat that I could stick to for the rest of the term. "Though I have to say, I would expect you to have more strength in your calves."

"We're sitting here," Laure said, stalking past me and plopping herself down in a seat near the middle of the class.

I supposed it could've been a worse selection.

More students filed in after us, alone or in groups of twos and threes, filling up the empty seats and setting out their books, ink bottles, and pens. I did the same for myself as well as Laure, to keep her from getting ink on her fingers and touching her face as she had proved prone to doing in our formative schooling years. Even worse would be spilling ink down the front of her dress. Seeing as how we were not studying to become artists, such a detail would be unforgivable.

I tugged my pocket watch from its hiding place, checking the time. It was only a few minutes until half past the hour; I did hope our professor wouldn't be late. Then I arranged my pens in order from smallest to largest on the desk in front of me before deciding it would probably be better to group them by color.

At half past, the professor entered the room. He was on the tall side, with a ferocious red mustache that looked like the brush Gaeth had used to unstop my chimney. I could feel Laure staring at him, and under any other circumstance I might have done the same, were it not for the younger man he'd approached to confer with beside his lecturer's podium—someone who'd been sitting there all this time, I realized, and I'd been too caught up in trying to choose a proper seat to notice him right away.

He had dark hair that fell into his eyes, and *freckles* all over his cheeks and nose—something I had always been disappointed that Laure had never exhibited, not even in the height of summer. (Laure did not freckle; instead, she burned.) The young man in question was clearly older than the rest of the first-years, though not so old as to be a professor, and when he turned his head to pick up a sheaf of notes I could see a darling thumbprint of ink against his pale neck.

Somehow, it was more endearing to me on him than it ever was on Laure. I could imagine him resting his hand there dreamily, and I tugged at the collar around my own neck at the very thought.

"Well, I see that most of you are here already, so why don't we get started?" the professor with the red mustache said, wringing his large, meaty hands together and leaning back against his podium instead of taking his place behind it. "This here's theory and history of the magicians, so if you're in the wrong place, feel free to leave now. No harm done; I won't take it personally. Nor will I even remember your faces as you file out, I'm sure. I'm Professor Ducante, and this is my lecturer's assistant, Hal, and the answer to the question that's burning in your fresh little minds is *yes,* I *will* be requiring you to take notes. I don't care how good your mind is; memory's no match for a pen and paper. I'd best hear you all scratching away mightily for the next hour and a half, and if your hand's not cramping by the end of each session, you're just not doing it right. I hope that's clear."

Hal, I repeated privately to myself, the name thoroughly unremarkable and somehow perfect all the same. He'd given a shy little wave upon being introduced, and I'd felt my pulse speed up in reply. It was a reaction he'd never know he'd inspired, of course, but it was there all the same, unmistakable to *me.* I drew in a deep breath, no longer prepared or even listening remotely to what the professor was saying, outlining the basics of the course we were to be taking, no doubt.

And I usually so enjoyed outlines.

I was in the middle of observing the way Hal drew his thumb nervously up and down a crease in one of his papers when Laure elbowed me sharply in the ribs.

I turned to her, distraught and also a little indignant. She couldn't have known *already* what I was thinking. It was just too unfair.

"That's *Hal,*" she whispered, eyes wide as though she thought that meant something to me. A little of what I was thinking must've shown on my face, too, since she rolled her eyes and looked as though she wished to elbow me much harder. "*The* Hal. Are you even listening? The one who came here and saved the city, not to mention all the magicians?"

The gears in my brain began to click and whir once more—clogged as they'd been by Hal's freckles and the gentle manner in which he stood to one side observing the rest of us, even making his own notes from time to time. *This* simple soul was the man who'd saved Thremedon? That made him a hero, on top of being everything else, which added up to a great deal in my eyes.

It was almost too much to bear, really.

"I just want to say that I'm looking forward to getting to know you, and that if you ever have any problems, I'm . . . that's what I'm here for," Hal was in the midst of saying, obviously picking up on a cue from the professor that I'd missed simply because I hadn't been paying attention to him. His voice was gentle. If Laure had made me miss some of his speech with her gossip, I would—well, I wouldn't be able to do anything to her in revenge, but oh, how I would sulk! "Other than that, I hope that you enjoy the class and—if you don't mind my saying so—welcome to Thremedon."

Something loosened in my chest, like a whole host of doves being set free at a king's coronation, when Hal finally smiled at the class. He was a far cry from the statues outside, a thin coating of snow now frosting their austere features— hard men carved from hard stone and ranged together like the Cobalt Mountains themselves to ward against any invading danger. Hal was small, his nature warm and inviting. His wrists were delicate, and he was the first person to welcome us to Thremedon *without* also trying to relieve us of our valuables. Besides which, it was thanks to him we were even here in the first place.

Now that my gratitude had become more personal in nature, it was stronger than ever before. All the awfulness of my cramped little room, the dust in every corner, the taffy on the dresser handle, the pot in the chimney, and the foul man who had attempted to steal my things seemed insignificant in the face of this new life I was starting.

Something dropped against my desk and I looked over at it to find a crumpled ball of paper. Its inelegance told me at once it was a present of some sort from Laure, and I nervously unfolded it, spreading it out beside the rest of my notepaper, attempting to smooth the wrinkles.

CUT IT OUT!!! it read in Laure's unmistakable hand. To emphasize her point, she had even underscored "out" three times, and employed a matching three exclamation marks.

"You up there," the professor said, pausing midlecture, with a voice so sharp it commanded all our attention. I swallowed miserably, stomach swooping in terror. Was it possible he had noticed Laure's indiscretion, and we were in trouble on our very first day, not even halfway into our very first hour?

I waited for the blade to fall, but somehow, it did not.

"I'd like to see your pens *moving*," Ducante continued. "That goes for all of you. Since this is *history* of the magicians, I daresay the *history* I'm giving you might just be the most important part."

My fingers twitched and began moving of their own accord, neatly marking down the date in the top right corner of my paper before I began to copy down, word for word, everything our professor was saying. At that moment, somehow, Hal looked up into the audience of the lecture hall and met my eyes—as though he had sensed my fear and sought to ease it somehow.

Only a bare moment later he looked away, but I was content in knowing he had seen my face even if he would not remember it.

That evening, when I pulled out my notes to look them over just before tucking the sheets around myself in bed, I would not remember a single word written there, in my spindly writing, as it had been said. My mind—and my heart—were far too full of other things for that, I was afraid.

And so began my first love in Thremedon.

ADAMO

I wasn't in a good mood at all that morning. Part of it was because it was the start of a new term, and, even though I hated leaving a job unfinished, I hadn't managed to teach my class from the previous term anything worth a damn. I guessed that was weighing on my conscience just a little bit, not to mention how much the idea of doing it for another two months was sticking in my throat like a fish bone.

Another part of it was the dream I'd had in that weird part of dawn when dreaming gets a little too keen and a little too detailed for a man's liking—about the day we'd received word from whatever lackey was in charge that day that the dragons, *our* dragons, were being disassembled, and no, we wouldn't be seeing what remained of them again.

But never let it be said Owen Adamo spent his time lingering over *dreams*. He just took his crankiness out on the poor cannon fodder first-years in his lecture room, instead.

My lecturer's assistant was a Margrave's son who'd gotten out of joining up for the war effort because of some loophole about the importance of his studies meaning he was needed more at home than out there on the field. It'd worked out well for him to exploit it because it was doubtful he'd have been able to find the balls to actually kill a man in real combat. He was obsessed with strategy nonetheless and considered himself something of an expert on the matter, which meant he didn't like my style of teaching one bit. His name was Radomir—not Radimor, as I'd called him for the first two-thirds of our first term together because I didn't have room in my head for the names of people I didn't like *or* trust—and I found that ignoring him worked best.

I cleared my throat. It was one minute before the lecture was supposed to start, and the last of the lost, lonely little stragglers were filing in and taking their seats. I could feel a few of them staring at me, no doubt taking this class so they could gossip about the man teaching it rather than discuss the fine art of war or anything. Anyway, it was obvious that near to none of them had the head for any decent thinking. There was one in the back who was already asleep, and I didn't know if I was more or less disposed to liking him than I was to the few who'd crowded around the front row, leaning forward like so many carrion birds, ready to eat up what I said and never once question any of it.

But it wasn't too fair-minded of me to judge them before they proved they were the idiots I suspected, now was it? There were a few keen faces among the rabble—a girl with red hair and sharp green eyes and some ink on her nose being one of them, as well as a towhead who might've served himself none too bad in the war itself if he hadn't clearly missed the age of conscription by a year. Maybe these ones could prove me wrong, and I welcomed the challenge. *If* you could call it that.

"Right," I said. "Get all those papers and pens and ink-wells and the like *off* the desks; there won't be any note-taking in this class. Not today, and not for the next two months."

I enjoyed the moment of shock they *all* displayed at that, then waited for the chaos of paper being shuffled and ink-wells being bottled up to calm down, so I could have the rest of their full attention, or whatever half attention passed for it.

"I'm no professor," I said. "If you learn only one thing this term, which you just might, I'm certain it'll be that. I'm going to be calling on the lot of you at random, and the way you pass is through contribution. Thinking, then saying something. Extra points for anyone who says something not necessarily smart, but *interesting*. So I'm expecting you all to listen. You lot in the back, tell me to speak up if you can't hear anything."

Out of nowhere, a hand lifted. It was the first willingly raised hand of the term, and I quietly said a prayer that it wasn't some know-it-all looking to impress the rest of the class while fluffing up his own ego. I took the owner of the hand in.

It was the girl I'd had hopes for.

"Well," I said. "You there. Speak."

"If you want us to think before we say something, wouldn't it be better to call on those of us who've volunteered, instead of picking us out at random?" she asked. "Thinking on our feet, is . . . difficult, for some people, and it might be kinder to help them get the knack of it first."

"Guess that all depends on how much of the class you want to take with you," I said, not chewing on her question too long before firing back a proper response. If you gave some of these whelps an inch, they'd take the whole 'Versity Stretch. "A lot of strategy—good strategy—means knowing when to scrap your plan in the field and come up with some-thing new. Something better. That kind of recalibration takes tactical thinking, and it's *not* something you can learn by gnawing on your books and writing neatly in the margins."

"So it's a part of the class, then," the girl said. "As much as anything else?"

I thought about that one for a minute myself, allowing a

quick look around the room to see if the others were paying attention. It was about the ratio I'd expected, some listening in and others taking advantage of the distraction in order to do whatever they damn well pleased. That didn't bother me, so long as they kept it to themselves and didn't distract the rest of the class with it.

My expectations weren't very high, and my hopes were even lower than that.

Time with the airmen had taught me that you had to pick your battles. And sometimes, having the attention of, say, no more than one-third of the class was better than trying to wrangle all of them at once. Divide and conquer. That was tactical thinking in practice.

"I guess that's about right," I conceded. "Maybe the most important part, even. Curriculum says you've got to take at least two exams to make up a proper grade, but the rest is up to me, and I've had enough classes now that this shook down as being the best way for going about it. Any better ideas?"

"It just seems a little different from everything else we've done," said the girl. I was beginning to get tired of thinking of her as *the girl,* too, but I wasn't the sort of professor who passed around a seating chart and made all the good little boys and girls write their names in their places so that I'd know who was who and who was showing up. That seemed like the mark of a doddering old fool who'd been teaching so long that his blood had turned to chalk and ink.

"There's times when different's bad, I'll give you, but this isn't one of 'em," I reasoned back, settling into the discussion now. "I hate to keep harping on this one point, since it means you'll figure out that's my *only* point sooner rather than later, but in the heat of battle, adapting quickly to the differences that crop up—and bastion knows, *they will*—can mean you staying alive one more day ahead of everyone else."

"What if you come up with a really good plan in the very beginning, though?" the girl asked. There was a skinny little scarecrow sitting next to her, I'd just noticed, and he'd begun to tug on her sleeve. Probably trying to get her to shut up, for all the good it'd do him. He looked like one swift right hook'd take care of him then and there, and something told me the redhead had at least one swift right hook in her. "Isn't *that* the point of strategy? Planning ahead so that you'll have the upper hand when it comes to dealing with your enemies?"

Somehow, against all odds, I found myself smiling as I leaned back against my desk, arms crossed like I was addressing a much smaller room of much larger personalities.

It'd been a long while since anyone had engaged me in anything *close* to what might be called a good debate—given me a reason not only to tell 'em I was right but to explain the reasoning behind it so that *they* believed it, too.

That was the only kind of teaching I'd ever wrapped my head around, and I'd managed it with loads more stubborn folk than this one. From somewhere behind me, I could hear Radomir give a slight, dry cough. He was always complaining about his constitution in winter, so I didn't pay him any mind.

"Things always go to shit after takeoff," I explained, and there was a collective creak of the desks as students either leaned forward or back in their chairs, depending on how they felt about colorful language. Some of the ones sleeping in the back had actually woken up from their dreams of being swaddled babes in arms, and they looked kind of regretful they hadn't chosen a seat closer to the center of action. "The reinforcements you're depending on don't arrive in time, for any number of reasons that don't matter because what counts is you're fucked now. Or some idiot overslept and forgot to give your girl—your dragon—a good once-over before you left at night, leaving her harness loose. Little mistakes, the small things you don't even think about—say the weather changes and all of a sudden the battlefield's a mud pit, or you're flying sideways through sheets of rain. You can't always avoid 'em, but what you *can* do is train your mind to be ready. Keep calm in the face of everybody else feeling fucked sideways. That make sense?"

The girl sat back in her chair, silent, but I could see the cogs turning in her head, unlike some of the others who just looked dumbfounded, or a little too pleased by the naughty words I was using. She really was thinking it over.

Radomir cleared his throat again. I invoked the professor's right of ignoring his lecturing assistant and kept my eyes on the girl instead.

"That does make sense," she said finally. "Only . . . This doesn't mean you'll be moving the class unexpectedly to another room or—I don't know—making it rain just to see what we do in a crisis, right?" She almost sounded disappointed, too.

I was surprised into laughing. She wasn't making fun of me—at least I didn't think she was, mostly because of the look of pure suspicion on her face, like she wanted me to know I wasn't going to get the jump on her and she'd show up to class in a coat and tall rubber boots every day for the next two months if she had to.

The boy sitting next to her hid his face in his hands.

Little did he know he had a real firecracker to contend with. Or maybe he *did* know, and that was why he looked so close to crying.

"No," I said, once I'd finished laughing. "They're pretty understanding here at the 'Versity that I don't have the same training as the other professors, but I think they'd be mad as hogs before feeding time if I pulled a stunt like that. Not because of how much they care about *you* lot, of course, but out of respect to your parents, most of whom're paying your way through this and don't want to buy you any new clothes on top of every other expense."

The truth was, since these kids were from the country and not the brats of the upper class, I probably *could've* gotten away with it, but I hadn't taken leave of my senses enough for it to seem like a good idea just yet. I was going to be *that professor* sooner or later—the one no one wanted to be assigned to, more like a commander of troops than a teacher—which was exactly what I was anyway, so where was the harm in that? I'd like to see those in charge complain to me about that one. They wanted me lecturing here at the 'Versity for status's sake. Now they had me, for all the good it'd do them.

Anyway, I'd keep it in the back of my mind for whenever I wanted to take an early retirement.

"Pardon *me,*" Radomir said. I wanted to commend him for finally finding his voice after all that throat clearing, but I wasn't supposed to twit my assistant in front of the class, or so Roy'd told me. Something about fostering a united front, but I had a feeling it was because his boy had been made a lecturer's assistant a few months back and he'd developed sensitive feelings toward everyone in that position as a result.

"Yeah?" I asked.

"Well," Radomir said, holding up the syllabus like a white flag, "I simply wanted to suggest that if you were *finished,* it might be time to continue outlining the requirements. Unless you had something else planned for the rest of the class that I simply haven't been informed of. We *did* go over this together if I recall correctly."

I could've thumped him on the head for that one, but he had the right of it, and anyway, the last thing I needed was for this girl—or worse, her parents—to decide I'd singled her out somehow even though she didn't exactly seem like the type to take offense.

She even looked a little disappointed when Radomir checked us, like she'd been enjoying our little match as much as I had. That was more what I'd imagined teaching might've been like in the first place, which was the only reason I'd agreed to it, before I'd learned enough to know my mistake. That and not wanting to retire just yet, but nobody had to know it.

"Right," I said. "There's a whole list of books on here but there's only one required reading, and that's one with a whole mess of pretty little diagrams. Helpful, too. Pictures are good for visualization and, like I said, I'll be calling on you lot at random. Best do your reading the night before. I know the look somebody gets when he doesn't know what he's talking about, either, so tread careful. Everybody's got that?"

It took me by surprise as much as anyone to find how little time was actually left in the class after that. It was a shortened day, of course, so as not to load too much into their soft, fragile minds at once, I imagined, but normally the first days dragged on *forever.* I wasn't the kind of professor who had a lot of things to go over, and after my introductory speech we mostly spent the rest of the time staring dumbly at each other, and me using all the skills I planned to teach in order to avoid questions about what it'd been like to lead the airmen.

Somehow "a royal pain in the ass" never seemed to be the answer anyone was looking for.

Anyway, ready for it or not, the bell for class's end rang while I was still explaining to some weed-brain why full frontal assault was never a good plan. Punctual as you'd like, my students started to shift in their chairs, all eyes turned uncannily in my direction.

"You can go when you hear the bell," I told them, and refrained from adding, *My boys always did.*

The girl with the red hair had already packed her books and pens up, so it didn't take her long to sling her bag over her shoulder and brush out her skirts. I saw her exchange brief words with her companion before making a beeline through the crowd toward me. The scarecrow followed her but hung back. I didn't blame him; even *I* was a little intimidated, though I knew better than to show it.

"Ah, the beginning of another term," Radomir said, tapping his stack of papers against my desk so they all fell in line. "You know, if you planned your lectures in a more linear fashion beforehand, you might—"

Quickly, I made the decision between having a conversation I'd had at *least* three times before and meeting this girl head-on to see just how offended she was, on a scale of one to screaming mad. I held my hand up to Radomir, then left him in the dust.

To be fair, he'd be just as happy having that conversation all by himself.

"My name's Laurence," the redhead said, holding out her hand. Up close, she looked like one of those portraits in a locket that Raphael had collected, all fiery red hair and a stern gaze. The countryside, Raphael used to say, *did* breed them like that.

But none of Raphael's girls, I was fairly certain, had ever sported a man's name before.

"I have a brother named Laurence," Radomir said from over my shoulder, suddenly showing interest. I knew that tone all too well, and I wasn't going to let him get away with it.

"Go file your notes," I told him in no uncertain terms.

Radomir made a sharp, pained noise, but at least he had the sense to do as he was told.

"Anyway, the reason I'm here is, I wanted to ask you about something," Laurence said, as Radomir shuffled off, probably feeling extremely sorry for himself in the process. If it'd really been important to him, he would've stayed and fought for it. Civilians took orders too easily or not at all.

"Go right ahead," I told her. "But I was serious about the rules here, which means you don't need to bring your parasol to class or anything."

"Parasol," Laurence said, and snorted. "More like an umbrella and a tarp, with all that mud you were talking about."

I should've known she wasn't a parasol type. I felt pretty close to ashamed and shrugged my apology. "That'd be more useful," I admitted. "Now. About that question."

She shifted the weight of her books from one arm to the other and tapped her boot against the floor. I noted a strange smell suddenly—it reminded me of the Rue after a holiday night, when everyone had been up late drinking and leaving sour little presents all along the cobbles for those who were up early the next morning—but I didn't know where it was coming from, and making a face while talking to a young lady was never considered good manners. "So you were Chief Sergeant of the Dragon Corps, right?" Laurence asked finally. "That's what you said at the beginning of the class."

"Either that, or having some trouble with my memory," I replied. I hated that question, but I was man enough to weather it. If not now, then when would I get my sorry self over it?

"Rode a dragon and all?" she asked, eyes getting keen.

"Only when the bell rang," I said.

"Heard you rode Proudmouth," Laurence continued. "And she was a crusher, if I know 'em, right?"

"She was," I confirmed.

Laurence nodded, not looking pleased with herself, just

thinking hard. "But crusher or not, they all breathed their share of fire, right?"

"Most compact form of long-distance firepower we had," I explained. "The fire was offensive primarily, but defensive as well. If any of our girls hadn't been able to breathe fire, or if something'd jammed up the works—lost a man that way once, and I'm not proud of it—then she'd be dead in the air, and her rider along with her."

"I'm sorry to hear that," Laurence said. "But if you were riding on top of these big metal girls like they were horses only larger and more dangerous, and they were breathing fire all over and everywhere in the heat of battle, I've always wondered . . . How was it your clothes never caught on fire? Pants, specifically. I'd imagine with them up against all that hot metal it couldn't've felt too nice, now could it?"

"*Enough,* Laure," her companion said suddenly. In truth, I'd forgotten all about him. But there he was, reaching out and grabbing her arm and trying to pull her bodily toward the door. "We're so sorry to have bothered you with our technical questions, Chief Sergeant—Professor—but we'll leave you to your business now. Thank you very much. Good day."

"To*verre,*" Laurence said. "Stop that at once; he was *going* to answer! How did your pants not catch on fire, Sergeant Adamo?"

"Simple enough," I said. "It's because I wasn't a liar."

Both Laurence and her friend stared at me for a long moment. Then, out of nowhere, Laurence burst into laughter while her friend continued his efforts to tear her away with renewed vigor.

"That's a good one," Laurence said. "I guess it's His Highness's royal secret, then, and you're not allowed to tell me?"

Somehow, something about leaving her with that impression rubbed me the wrong way.

"Had a saddle," I said, folding my arms over my chest. "Wasn't made out of metal, and it fit up against Proudmouth's spines. That way, nothing important of mine down there was impaled on any of the scales, either. Kept us fixed in one place. Kept us from falling off, too. There was a harness for holding on, and the harness helped control the flames, although most of that she did herself—*she* was a real tactician. As for the pants, the suits we wore when we were out on a raid were made special to keep us insulated. Doesn't mean some of us didn't come back singed all over, and one of my boys lost a pant leg in a close call. But there were provisions for keeping us from getting charred as a campfire, and everything else we left up to skill and luck. You got burned, it was your own damn fault. Do you see what I'm saying?"

"Thanks," Laurence said. "Bet *you* never got burned."

"Only once," I said, but that was once she was out of earshot. I followed her red head out the door, the last of the students to leave.

"What a remarkable conversation you just had," a fresh voice said from the front row. I turned around, and there was Roy, lounging happy as you please in one of the seats, playing with a pen one of the first-years probably left behind. "Did that young woman just ask you how you avoided flaming pants?"

"Hope you weren't here for that *entire* lecture," I said. "Don't you have anything better to do with your time?"

"Of course not," Roy said, setting the pen down and unfolding himself from behind the desk. "I enjoyed it very much. I do believe she likes you."

"At least that makes one of 'em," I said gruffly. "So get to the point."

"I was here to pick up Hal, actually," Roy explained, casting one of his long-nosed looks at Radomir as he guided me out of the classroom. "Also, I did want to talk to you about other things. Dinner at my place tonight?"

"Will the teacher's assistant be there?" I asked. These were the kinds of things you had to make sure of before you agreed to anything.

"Of course he will," Roy replied. "Before you make the joke, I'll do it myself: He's a growing boy, and he needs to eat." He clapped me on my back before heading down one of the long hallways, sharp new boots clacking on the wood. "Shall I see you at eight?"

"You eat too late," I grumbled, but he'd already known my answer. What point was there in even saying yes?

BALFOUR

One of these days, I *was* going to make it down that last little block of the Rue, all the way to the statues, where Luvander had set up his hat shop.

It wasn't that I was worried anyone would recognize me in the flesh from my stonier counterpart. That was never an issue since he was far more proud-looking than I, not to mention so tall it would have been impossible to compare the details of our faces. If I kept my hands shoved into my pockets and my collar turned up, I would look like any other citizen, and no one idling near the memorial and reading the plaques would ever be the wiser that an ex-member of the Dragon Corps was walking among them. The better for them. It really wouldn't live up to what they must have thought.

That was what had taken Ghislain out of the city, I expected, since a larger man would have had trouble hiding in plain sight the way I did, and he was nearly the size of his own statue—a sight people were much more likely to recognize. It made me wonder if he'd seen the shop, or indeed if he'd anchored in Thremedon at all since leaving.

I wasn't at all certain that I would, given the opportunity to leave in the first place.

In any case, I *had* promised Luvander I'd visit the establishment, and I didn't intend to go back on my word. It was just that—what with one thing and another, and also my own private reticence—I never quite seemed to make it there.

Some days, I was too busy with my own work even to contemplate the trip. But on others, I really had no excuse. I took long walks to clear my mind yet managed to bring myself around in circles rather than stop at the designated place.

It was for the best, surely; this was what I told myself. There was little sense in showing up at such a place before I was ready, with no idea what I would say or what to expect. It would be doing a disservice to Luvander, not to mention if

I happened to come at a particularly busy time of day I'd be interrupting his business with my staring. He might feel obligated to entertain me, and it was possible he'd tell his customers who I was—that would be the worst of all, especially with all the handshakes.

If Luvander had only chosen some more private line of business, perhaps it would have been easier. But it was none of my business what anyone chose to do with his life. Rather, it was more that I'd never pegged any of my fellow airmen as aspiring milliners.

Then again, there was a lot we hadn't known about one another. With so many things the others hadn't ever learned about *me,* I supposed it would have been foolish indeed to assume I'd learned everything about *them.*

But all that was conjecture. Time to focus instead on the business at hand—literally the business at *hands.*

Before me was a far smaller task than marching through the city until I came to the Rue. It was almost so mundane as to be entirely insignificant, though it troubled me more than I was willing to admit to anyone but myself—and even then sometimes I had difficulty with it. I'd somewhat lost track of the days because of my current routine of lively debates with the representatives from Arlemagne; but one that was marked upon my calendar, in no uncertain terms, was my monthly checkup and overhaul. I could have called it my day for polishing if I'd had anyone to joke with about it. Nonetheless, if I wished to have hands that didn't work in the *slightest* as opposed to making do with what I had now in order to keep up the pretense of being somehow more normal, by all means, I could avoid the appointment.

But I would not—especially because I feared the retribution from the magician in charge of my prosthetics.

Magicians—at least the ones I'd met—seemed to enjoy being rude almost more than the airmen had, though a magician's rudeness was more about being sly and less about dangling you by the ankles out a window.

Admittedly, my hands were a less startling sight than they'd been to me in the beginning, but there were still nights when I woke from dreams of flesh and bone only to wonder with a violent start what beastly metal nightmares had attached themselves to my wrists. There were those who might have found them beautiful—I had no doubts about this, since they represented a rather pleasing triumph of machinery and craftsmanship—but to their owner, they only signified a replacement that fell considerably short of the original.

Also, painfully enough, they reminded me of Anastasia. They were even made of the same metal.

My fingers were silver in color, though the rest was not, since I supposed all the tarnishing would have made that impractical. When I'd asked, I'd been told that the materials were closer to steel—something my body was less likely to reject—and sensibly sturdy as well. They wouldn't rust, so long as I made sure to dry them carefully should they ever get wet, and they shone brightly in the light—alien and eerily beautiful—even if I felt no particular affection for them one way or another. The palms of both hands were smooth and cold to the touch, as well as the fingertips, and there were even little grooves where each piece fit together that a fortune-teller might still read my fate by.

It was the backs of my hands—the part I was supposed to know better than anything else, or so the saying went—that everyone seemed to find the most interesting. There was no steel plate to be found there, but a series of minute, interlocking gears and pulleys that turned as I moved and made the softest of clicking sounds whenever I did something as simple as drumming my fingers against the table. Somewhere inside that, past what looked like the workings of the most intricate clock I'd ever seen, there was a vial of concentrated magic that was worth more than my weight in gold. Worth more than my statue's weight in gold, in fact. And I hadn't the faintest idea how it worked.

It was the same way Anastasia had worked, after all, and I hadn't needed to understand what was inside her in order to know how well she flew.

I'd had to commission gloves of a sturdier fabric once it became apparent that the gears were going to tear right through all my best pairs, and it simply wouldn't be possible to go without. The diplomats from Arlemagne would stare, not to mention everyone else, and I would be worn down from answering the same questions day in and day out. My hands looked strange; I would be the first to admit it. And I had memory enough of what I'd once been—what parts of me I was missing—without everyone else knowing about it, too, the instant they laid eyes on me.

The construct itself was a less exact science than the dragons had been, chiefly because the dragons were created as their own separate entities whereas these hands had had to be made specifically to tailor to the rest of my body—a part of me that was at once integral yet utterly unnatural.

One day, I'd been told, or at least "ideally," they would be able to fit a panel onto the back and cover things up once and for all, leaving me with smooth metal skin and, I supposed, the freedom to wear more delicate gloves again. But that final piece of the puzzle couldn't be put into place until after years of fine-tuning, and the magician couldn't make adjustments without turning me loose in the world to see what problems I ran up against. "Trial and error," I believe was the term, and I was growing rather weary of it. Especially when my right hand stopped working completely during my very first postwar bath—at least, the first I was allowed to take on my own, without nurses and healers watching over me.

Still, I had no right to feel ungrateful. I'd lost my hands, but I'd kept my life, and that was more than so many of my fellows could say. Without any further delay, I tugged my gloves on—extra thick to keep the chill from getting into the metal, which in turn made my wrists ache—did up the buttons of my coat, and left.

After the end of the war, once the Esar's plans for me had become apparent, I'd thought it prudent to rent my own quarters in the city rather than returning to my parents' estates. It made for a much shorter commute between home and the bastion every day, and I had a very lovely view of the Basquiat from my window. In fact, I lived close enough that I could take the Whitstone Road to cut across the Rue and be in upper Charlotte—and therefore, the Crescents—before the sun set.

The days were growing so short in winter and the early dark played havoc with my moods.

It would have been more convenient for me if the magician tending to my follow-up appointments had been operating out of the Basquiat instead of her own home, but the Esar had his own way of doing things, keeping magicians and politicians separate. If the rumors I'd heard were true—as much as I hated listening to idle gossip, more often than not there was truth to be found in it—then he didn't trust the magicians at the Basquiat as much as he once had.

That was a tense area that could've used a little diplomatic intervention, I thought, and it made me wonder why we were bothering so with the Arlemagne when there were matters within Volstov that needed tending to, but I was no ruler. It wasn't my place to suggest these things. The problem would be resolved in its own time, and certainly without any help from someone like me.

There had always been a struggle between members of the bastion, the Esar's handpicked favorites, and the Basquiat, whom magic herself had picked. And the Esar, I suspected, did not like being reminded of forces more powerful than he. Since he was no magician, it was all something of a sore spot.

The air was bitter and still as I made my way down the road, thankful for the absence of the sharp winds that had attempted to flay the skin from my bones earlier. If I kept to this path I would eventually come to the 'Versity Stretch—as I already had, more than once—where Adamo had long since finished giving his lectures for the day. I had no idea at all where he was currently staying—whether he had a place in the city, too, or if he was taking advantage of the professors' quarters, now that he was one. It didn't seem like information I should want to know, and yet I'd spent a good portion of my life knowing every small detail about men I now seemed to go out of my way to avoid. Even though we hadn't liked each other, we *had* lived with each other. I knew when each of them liked to take their showers, when they slept— when they did *not* sleep—and what kind of woman each one preferred. At the time, I'd been desperate to escape and live on my own, exactly as I was now.

Yet my private quarters were too private. If the upstairs neighbors weren't at home, all was too quiet, save for the wind howling outside the window on the colder nights, or the sound of the dog above shuffling around his favorite bone.

It didn't make sense. Perhaps if Thom had been there, he might've explained it to me, but he wasn't, and he had troubles enough of his own. I wasn't about to write to him with mine.

I always knew when I was getting close to the Crescents, because abruptly the city planning and even the buildings themselves ceased to make any kind of logical sense. They rose up around me like abstract paintings—a chimney here, a steeple there, and now and then a large round room supported by a twisted scaffolding structure that didn't look as though it could possibly bear the weight. It was difficult not to feel like you were about to become part of an architectural accident in the Crescents, the way the houses all leaned toward the streets like they couldn't wait to be the first one to topple over and crush you.

The houses never did fall of course, but I couldn't help being glad the wind had died down, all the same.

The sun was just beginning to set, bruising the sky a lovely gray-purple, when I made my way to Crescent Number 27—a tall, crooked affair made of polished white stone, with a set of silver chimes hanging in the entranceway to ward off evil spirits. There was a light on in the tower but none at ground level, which wasn't so unusual. The tower was her workspace, and she'd probably gone up there to prepare her instruments beforehand, or something of that nature.

For someone so intimately involved in the proceedings, I had very little understanding of how they worked. I tended to look away when the gears were out. I supposed they disturbed me more than I was ready to admit to myself.

I knocked—rather loudly, just to be sure she'd hear it from upstairs—the sound rattling the gears in my knuckles. It was an uncomfortable sensation, like grinding your teeth in the night. I rocked between my heels and the balls of my feet, glancing up and down the street out of idle curiosity. It wasn't as crowded as it had been up near the Basquiat, but then I *had* come around dinnertime. Most people were either inside with hot meals on the stove or still hard at work, I imagined, with little crossover between the two. I hesitated, then knocked at the door again.

The problem with magicians—aside from getting around their quirks, which often translated to sheer rudeness—was that if they were working on something, it was nearly impossible to get their attention. I'd let myself in once before—after knocking and waiting in the streets in the heat of summer for nearly half an hour—only for her to demand why I'd come so late.

I wasn't about to make that mistake again, and the light *was* on in her workroom. Yet even though I'd taken up with ruffians, breaking and entering wasn't something I wished to add to my list of "unexpected things I'd done because of the strange crowd I spent my time with." Sighing, I tried the door before I could talk myself out of the idea and found it unlocked.

Perhaps we'd both learned something from that little incident, then.

There was a gray cat in the entranceway, as well as several pairs of women's shoes on the floor and matching coats hung up along the wall, but the house was otherwise silent. The cat wound around blue satin boots, rubbing its face against the toe, then yowled enigmatically at me.

Almost on instinct, I reached down to let it sniff my fingers. It did so just as one of my metal knuckles let out a hiss and a creak, and the cat's ears folded backward, the fur over his spine prickling up in mistrust.

"I'm sorry," I whispered, glad no one was around to see me offend, then attempt to *rationalize* with, a simple house cat. "It startles me, too, you know."

The cat sniffed and turned its back on me, bolting deeper into the house.

I should have expected something like that, I thought, and shut the door behind me so as not to let in too much cold air.

"Hello?" I called, just so I wouldn't seem *too* much like a burglar in the night. Or a madman who spoke only to cats. "It's Balfour, you remember . . . I don't think I'm late this time, unless I got the date wrong, in which case I'm terribly sorry."

There was no reply. Whatever she was working on must have been incredibly engrossing, and it wasn't something I wanted to interrupt, either. I knew that from experience, even if the rest of what I knew about her was very perfunctory indeed, though we'd been acquainted for many months.

Her name was Ginette, and I'd heard her refer to the cat once or twice as Kerchief, though I wasn't sure if that was his full name or just a pet name she had for him. She kept her house neater than I'd been led to believe most Margraves did—they were usually too busy with their spells or their books for cleaning. Or maybe she kept a maid.

I peered past one door—the kitchen, it seemed from the shadowy shapes of pots and pans hanging from the wall— but no lamp was lit. It would be strange indeed for anyone, even magicians, to conduct experiments in the kitchen in the dark, rather than in their studies or their workrooms, and so I passed the silent kitchen by.

The hallway twisted away from the foyer and circled past the kitchen in a clockwise direction. I almost tripped on a few small steps before I found myself passing her private rooms. I cleared my throat outside each doorway, and even knocked on one, but there was still no answer.

I felt more and more like an intruder with each step, but I made it to her workroom without the Provost and his men suddenly appearing to arrest me.

This was eerie, to be sure, but I'd been an airman of the famed Dragon Corps. Presumably, I didn't spook easily— although I was beginning to wish I'd gone to see Luvander's hat shop instead and ignored my appointment. There were so many times being that kind of man served you better than doing things *right* ever did, or so I'd learned from living with my fellow airmen: those good old days when I was punished routinely for bringing up what we ought to have done, and they had a jolly time ignoring just that for a night of rowdy fun.

The door to Ginette's workroom was half-open, and a light was on in the room, though I knew instinctively there was no one inside. No sounds at all came from within, not the usual tinkering clatter of metal on metal or the creak of the floorboards as she moved from spot to spot at her long wooden tables. I hesitated, wondering if *I* should be the one to call the Provost and his men, then gently nudged the door open.

The light in the window, I saw now, was coming from a lamp on one of her worktables, which had all but completely burned through its oil. It was giving off its last dramatic, guttering sparks now; if I'd come a little later, I would have assumed she wasn't home at all.

By the dying light, I could see the signs of unfinished work on one of her tables—a small black bowl full of little cogs next to a glass jar filled with some clear liquid, containing an assortment of long, lean metal tools. One large cog and an empty vial were placed between those items; all her other tools were in their proper places, or at least what I could assume were their proper places from my cursory assessment. I'd spent a great deal of time staring at her tool wall—a collection of hammers and tweezers, pincers and wrenches, ranging from very large to so small they looked like toys for a doll—while she operated on me. I knew what went where practically by heart.

It looked to me as though she'd been suddenly called away in the middle of an experiment. Judging by how much oil a lamp such as the one she'd been using usually held and how much had burned down, it must have been some time before the hour of my appointment. It was possible she'd thought she'd be back in time.

I did hope everything was all right. She'd never mentioned family, but then, neither had I. Our conversations were limited to discussing how my hands felt that day, and why there were bread crumbs caught in the gears—that sort of thing. But I had to assume she had someone, and I wondered if said someone had suddenly fallen ill. It wasn't like her to miss an appointment. That much I *did* know about her.

The cat—Kerchief—appeared at my feet again, winding around my ankles. I didn't reach down to pet him, and managed not to trip over him, though he followed me all the way from the empty workroom and down the winding halls, yowling at me when I let myself out.

CHAPTER THREE

LAURE

"We *are* going out tonight," Toverre said, "and I *need* you with me. I can't do this alone, Laure. That's final."

If he'd just said *Please, Laurence,* that would have done it for me. An *I need you* got me every time, but *That's final* always sounded too much like orders for my liking. I wanted to help him, I really did, but I knew the moment I agreed to it he was going to tell me I couldn't go in what I was wearing, and whether he knew it or not, that was always something of a slight. I knew how to dress myself the same as anyone else, but we couldn't all have an eye for what color went with what fabric like *some* people. Truth be told, it didn't seem like all that useful a skill to me anyway. More like it made a person crazy, trying to match things all the time.

Just look at what it had done to Toverre.

Not to mention, it was bitter damn cold—another reason why I was opting for warmth over coordination—and we had reading to do. Knowing Toverre, though, he'd probably done all his reading three weeks in advance, underlined the good parts, and reread them twice already. He did stuff like that.

I wasn't so lucky. I liked to savor what I was reading, except for the boring books, which I didn't like to read at all. The assignments we had for the strategy of war class weren't bad, and I didn't mind doing them first, but some of the history books could put a girl to sleep as soon as she cracked open the cover.

That was why I'd been putting *those* off as long as possible, standing in front of the mirror instead to try to see whether arranging my skirts just so would hide the fact that I was wearing trousers beneath them and woolen socks beneath that. It wasn't that I believed Toverre about making the women and possibly some of the men faint in the streets at the sight of me—the Thremedon women kept their legs covered, too, I wagered, though probably with something fancier than a pair of heavy riding pants—but I thought maybe if Toverre didn't have to look at it, he wouldn't have that much cause for complaint.

It was a long shot, but my da had always said that a fool's hope was better than no hope at all.

Yet no matter what I did, the skirts weren't quite long enough to hide the rumple of fabric where I'd tucked my trouser legs into the tops of my boots. A small detail, maybe, but one I could be sure Toverre would notice right away. And he wouldn't stop complaining until I did something about it.

A knock at the door and me rushing to answer it messed up all my arranging anyway. Being left out in the hall too long gave Toverre the urge to clean it—something I knew from the last time I'd opened the door only to find him staring fanatically at dust on the wall sconce.

Only it wasn't Toverre at my door, but a large package, wrapped in brown paper and tied around the middle with a length of twine. I stared at it for a moment, not understanding what was going on, until Toverre gave a huff from behind it and shifted his weight impatiently.

"Aren't you going to let me in? There's a *stain* on this rug that wasn't here the night before, and that means it's *fresh*. I do sometimes wonder whether we're living with humans or animals. Father's prize pigs were cleaner than this."

"*Do* come in," I told him, stepping back so that he could make it past me with his heavy burden. "What's that?"

I knew he wouldn't tell me—one of the few things Toverre enjoyed more than cleanliness was a good surprise—but that never stopped me from hoping he might slip up one of these days.

"It's for you," Toverre said, which wasn't an answer at all. He deposited the package on my bed with a lot of fuss and crinkling of the paper, then crossed his arms over his chest. "Well, go on. Only *do* close the door, so whatever that stain smells of doesn't waft in."

I couldn't smell anything from where I was standing, but I kept that to myself, shutting the door and giving it a firm nudge on top of that, since the wood of the frame was a little warped. I could've shaved it down with my da's plane in no time, but I hadn't brought that with me.

Then I turned my attention to . . . well, I supposed I'd have to think of it as a present even though it wasn't my birthday and it certainly wasn't Toverre's. If this was some city holiday he'd learned about and hadn't given me fair warning of in advance, I was going to clout him a good one.

"Hurry up," Toverre said crossly, which was his way of being shy and nervous. "It's not going to snap at your fingers, *and* it's getting late."

I supposed I was being silly. Da never savored the moment just before opening a present, and neither did Connor, who worked with the horses.

Without any further ado, I plucked the all-purpose knife from my boot and cut through the knot in the twine. I saw Toverre wince out of the corner of my eye at the idea of a lady carrying a knife in her footwear like a common highwayman, but what else was I supposed to do? He was the one who wanted to roam the city late at night to take in the pretty lights and enjoy the *ambiance,* and after what'd nearly happened to us on our first day, I wasn't going to let myself be caught off guard again. I had my virtue to protect, not to mention Toverre's.

I tore through the stiff paper without bothering to try to save it—though I would be able to use it to get the fire started in my room again later, after we got back and we were both freezing cold. Sitting in the center of the package, neatly arranged, *of course,* was a pair of black boots with shiny silver buttons all up the sides. They looked sturdy as well as fashionable, and when I picked them up I felt something soft folded beneath them.

"The boots are from my mother," Toverre explained, spitting the words out quickly. "Well, from me, but I sent home to get them *from* Mother. After what happened to your last pair, I remembered you were the same size. And *also,* these will go much better with your clothes than those old brown ones. It's a pity the buttons aren't gold, since they'd match your hair better, but mother has different coloring and I didn't want to seem too demanding. I'm sure there's a button shop somewhere. We'll find it, and, no worries, *I'll* put them on."

"And what's this?" I asked, indicating the fabric swaddled up beneath. There were three different colors in all—black, white, and green—and they looked *suspiciously* like women's undergarments.

After all this time, was Toverre finally taking an interest in what was underneath my clothing?

Not likely, I told myself, fingering the soft cotton, feeling fond despite myself.

"Ah, well," Toverre said, clearing his throat. "Those are . . . *not* my mother's. I didn't think you'd approve of that; it's hardly proper. But I simply couldn't have you tramping around Thremedon with trousers under your skirts, Laure; it's beastly. I gather these are what the women use here—woolen stockings and extra petticoats and the like. They'll be serviceable *and* they won't make your legs look like tree trunks, which is a great disservice to your legs, considering what a fine shape they are." On that last note, he almost sounded jealous, I thought. I shook out the green pair of stockings, their empty feet dangling with a knot of thread at each toe.

"Nice save," I told him, not really annoyed. I knew already I'd be heading into the city with him even in spite of the way he'd asked me. It was hard to be angry with someone who'd just given you a nice, thoughtful gift, and maybe he'd planned it that way, but that didn't really seem like Toverre. The present itself was Toverre all over, though, finding a way to insult me just before he made me realize he'd been thinking this whole time about my problem and what might make me more comfortable.

He was as sweet as a hand-raised dove when he wanted to be, though at first I'd thought of him more like a hawk, wild and strange and ready to turn on you and claw your eyes out at any moment. There was also his nose, hooked like all those of the other members of his father's family, but I'd never thought of that as a flaw, really. It *did* somehow make him look handsome.

"You'll have to leave so I can get changed," I told him, clasping the green set to my chest. I knew he'd approve of the choice, since he was always going on and on about how the right greens made my eyes look like something more than the gray we both knew they really were. It didn't seem all that important to me, since they were going on *under* my skirts, but I knew it was the kind of thing that'd put him at ease.

"I'll turn around," Toverre said, facing the fireplace. "But if you think I'm going back out into that hall to wait, you've taken leave of your senses."

"I didn't actually think that," I admitted.

"I know," Toverre replied. "You're always very clever."

"Thank you," I said as sincerely as I knew how. "It's a wonderful present."

Toverre's shoulders stiffened and I imagined him scowling fiercely, though since he'd turned to stare into the fire, I couldn't actually see his face.

"You're welcome," he said after a moment's silence. "Just hurry up and put them on. I need to know right away if something doesn't fit."

He didn't have to tell me twice. Lingering would've only meant spending more time half-naked in my room, which was feeling colder and colder day by day, what with the absence of the plate in the chimney. I was going to have to do something about that, maybe try to keep the fire lit *all* the time, but that didn't seem too practical. And I could always put the plate back—now that it was clear to me why someone had put it up the chimney in the first place.

I was probably the only girl in Thremedon tonight getting undressed with her fiancé in the room and thinking about fireplaces.

It hadn't always been like this between Toverre and me. I'd liked him fine while we were growing up, of course, and

when I'd heard about the arrangement our families had made
I'd counted myself pretty lucky, given my other options.
Sure, Toverre was as mad as a badger in winter and not as
slow-moving, but he was kind and we got along and he didn't
have a nose like a fat red tomato like Ermengilde's fiancé
had. *And* he'd never once tried to look down my blouse. I
hadn't known the reasons for that then, of course, but he
seemed pretty ideal to me at the time.

On top of that, it was funny to get mud on him and watch
him run home crying.

One night, during one of Da's dinner parties when all the
young ones were left to their own devices, I'd even gotten
undressed for Toverre on my own inspiration, *with* him
watching. I'd stolen some of the wine from the cellar and
dressed myself in one of my mam's old corsets because I already knew it made me look particularly grown-up—which
really meant that it pushed my breasts together and up in a
way that men seemed to find near impossible to resist. We
were going to be married, I'd reasoned, and Toverre had said
he was all right with it—even implied he was looking forward to the ceremony, that rotten liar—but the look on his
face after I'd unlaced my top told me everything I ever
needed to know.

We did spend the night together after that, though I'm sure
it wasn't what either of us had been expecting. Toverre lay
with his head on my chest instead, and told me all about the
boy his mother had hired to work in the stables.

I'd liked him, too, because he knew how to handle the
horses and didn't boast about it.

In the morning, I'd realized I wasn't heartbroken, just *extremely* embarrassed, and Toverre and I had finally decided
that in order for our friendship to continue as it was, we'd
never speak about that night again. Also, I wouldn't throw
mud at him anymore. I'd agreed to the latter only because we
were too old for it by that point. All in all, making that big
mistake of mine *had* made us closer, if not in the specific
way that I'd intended, and when I heard that stableboy laughing with the blacksmith about Toverre's obsessive cleaning

two weeks later, I stopped liking him *and* gave him a bloody nose for it.

Even if Toverre didn't love me the way I'd wanted him to—the way a husband should love his wife—Toverre and I were in this together. If anyone ever *did* come along—if they managed to run the gauntlet of Toverre's complete insanity and come out unscathed—then they were going to have to go through me, too. And if anyone in this city so much as looked at my crazy fiancé cross-eyed, then they were going to find themselves with my fist in their face.

It was an indelicate thought, so I kept it to myself. I didn't want to be sending Toverre into fits of fainting on top of everything else. Poor thing probably thought he knew how to take care of himself, but he definitely didn't.

Speaking of which, he was fidgeting by the fireplace like an impatient child, checking his pocket watch, tapping it exactly three times on the right side, then sliding it carefully back into his pocket. I did up the final laces in the front of my dress, tugged at the skirts, and turned around. The woolen underclothes *were* much more comfortable than wearing pants underneath my dress had been, and I could already see that they made everything look sleeker. They weren't even as itchy as I'd expected, either.

"Huh," I said out loud, looking down at myself.

"What is it?" Toverre asked, not turning around. "You've put them on backward, haven't you? I just know it."

"I *was* going to say they look wonderful, but now you've ruined it," I told him, smoothing out my skirts. "The boots fit, too."

"I thought they would," he said, glancing over his shoulder—like he was afraid I might be wearing nothing *but* the boots and undergarments, and I guess he had his reasons to watch out for something like that—before turning to face me at last. "You and Mother are the same size in most respects. Not up *there*, of course, but your shoes."

"Watch it," I told him, tugging on my coat to discourage any more talk of my bosom. This coat was the one piece of clothing I knew would always pass muster, because Toverre had bought it for me as a gift last winter. Big buttons, high collar, a deep bottle green, and all of it very flattering. No doubt he'd tell me it was going out of style soon enough, but until then I was planning on wearing the hell out of it.

"Guess I'm ready," I said, holding out my arm to him.

Toverre tugged on his sleek gray gloves, reaching out to touch the doorknob the way most people picked a rat out of a trap.

With the help of a map he'd procured somewhere, we made our way to the Amazement, Thremedon's theater and entertainment district. It was close to the 'Versity Stretch, but not *too* close; students probably didn't need any extra distracting, I was coming to realize, with a stack of books up to my waist to get through in the next two months.

Toverre wasn't planning for us to take in any shows, of course, but wanted instead to "drink in the sight of the people who *were*." The sun hadn't yet set fully, but the skies were growing dark, and the streetlights had all begun to glow faintly in the dusk. It was pretty as new snow in the country, and that was *before* we came to the row of theaters proper, with their establishments lit up in all different arrangements of color, each proclaiming why its show was the only one you should think of seeing.

Men in sharp, dark coats with their collars turned up walked side by side with women in neat little fur hats, heeled boots stepping carefully around the patches of ice littering the streets. And Toverre had been right; they were all matching, down to their gloves and their muffs. Some of them even matched the men they were walking with. There were some men walking together, of course, and even women alone with no chaperones—unheard-of business in the countryside, but something that made me wonder just as much as I was sure the lean young men leaning on one another made Toverre wonder. Or perhaps "wonder" wasn't the right word for it, but it was exhilarating.

Even though it was marked clearly on the map as a part of Thremedon, I felt like I'd stepped into another world entirely.

Close by, a group of children were gathered around a poster with a beautiful young woman painted on it. The title read *CINDERFOLD* in garish, snowcapped letters, and, in smaller print, *starring Angerona Greylace,* but underneath that someone had written a word that made me laugh and Toverre gasp with how dirty it was. So that was what all the young ones were staring at, I realized. Before I knew it, one of them even reached up to pull the poster down, rolling it up and tucking it under his arm as he ran away, followed by the rest of the gawkers.

"Well," Toverre said.

"Think of it as romantic," I suggested. "Have *you* ever heard of Angerona Greylace?"

"Not at all," Toverre admitted. "But trust me, by tomorrow, I will have. She must be very famous."

"For one thing or another," I replied, a little bit too practical to keep up the pretense of romance any longer.

Another group of women moved past us then, and they were the sort to give a simple country girl pause, no matter how much she tried not to think about things like how her hair looked or whether her nose was turning red in the cold. They wore little drop earrings and had white powder all over their faces, and I could see how fine their dresses were underneath their light coats. They must have been very cold, and they were practically running as they laughed among themselves—out of one small set of back-alley doors, across the cobblestones, and into another, larger door that opened onto the main street. A sign above the door said it was *The Cobble.* It appeared to be some kind of eatery, judging by the smells that drifted out of it.

"My educated guess is that they are actresses," Toverre said simply, with a sniff. "Too much perfume, and one of them was very plain. They can't possibly play more than supporting roles." Then, with a mischievous tone I'd never heard him use before, he added, "Let's follow them."

I was all for it, and about to tell him so, but before I could do so, something caught my eye.

"Hang on," I said. "Isn't that Gaeth?"

I knew it was before Toverre answered—we'd taken enough meals with him, even sat next to him in a few classes, for me to recognize the easy slope of his shoulders, the relaxation of every movement. He was definitely a country boy through and through, but the sort who came from the other side of Nevers, men and women renowned for their comfort in the sunlight and their lazy demeanors. Besides which, I recognized his threadbare gray coat because it was missing part of the collar, like some stubborn horse had bitten a piece out of it.

Maybe it had, but I couldn't imagine any animal taking offense at *him*.

"Hey there!" I called out, startling a few of the people around me. "Gaeth!" As much as Toverre would be horrified by my clumsy tactics, saying hello to the one person you actually knew in a city as big as this one was only polite.

Everyone but Gaeth seemed to hear me at first. Then, very slowly, he turned around, like he was waking up from some deep dream.

"Oh," he said, as we drew up to him. "Laure. And Toverre. What are you doing all the way out here on a school night?"

"Couldn't we ask the very same thing of you?" Toverre demanded, the talons coming out. Apparently having latched onto Hal wasn't making him any less sharp with Gaeth. I'd never known him to have it out for two people at the same time; I didn't know whether that made Gaeth lucky or just a real poor son of a bitch. Maybe Toverre was just flustered.

"Suppose you could," Gaeth agreed.

I sought out Toverre's foot with my own and stepped on it lightly. He winced with his entire body, but for some reason, Gaeth didn't seem to notice. It had to be that lackadaisical, old-country demeanor, I supposed, but then he'd never seemed as far off as this. Long day, maybe, I thought, and felt a little sorry for him.

"I was just on my way back from the Crescents," Gaeth continued without further prompting, like he'd suddenly re-membered an important fact. "It's dormitory protocol, to make sure no fevers make their rounds this early on. Guess, what with people living so close together, that kind of thing's all too easy."

"*Is* there something going around?" Toverre asked, face suddenly even whiter than before.

"It's a *precaution,*" I told him. Honestly, did he not know how to listen? "I'm sure it'll be all right."

"You'll be called in soon, like as not," Gaeth said. "Just a simple blood testing, and nothing else too awful, I'd suspect."

"Oh, *needles,*" Toverre murmured.

"Barely felt it," Gaeth said.

"Some of us have very small veins," Toverre shot back.

In an attempt to make sure nothing too awkward happened between them—Gaeth was easygoing enough, but Toverre had a way of provoking even the gentlest of folk—I decided to step in, and in my brand-new boots, no less. "We were just going to get something to eat," I said, having decided that once my stomach'd started growling only a few moments ago. "You hungry, Gaeth?"

"She means to ask if you would like to join us," Toverre corrected. At least he was picking at me now, but I was used to it. I could take it.

"Maybe another time, hey?" Gaeth suggested. "They said I should head straight back to my rooms after the visit. And I don't want to argue with those in charge, at least not right away."

"Who said?" I asked, but Gaeth had already turned and started off down the road, and not in the direction of the 'Versity Stretch, either. "Weird," I said, turning to Toverre.

"Not very," Toverre replied. "Because you would *expect* someone like that to have a coat that smells of horses."

ADAMO

I arrived at Roy's place in the Crescents about ten minutes too early. Leave it to a man of war to be early to meetings—never early on the battlefield, though, where being early was just as bad as being late. This tendency of mine was especially bad with Roy, who always liked to be fashionably late. And the last thing I wanted was to have the door answered with a scuffle of noise and laughter after the long pause it took when the people you were calling on were trying to get dressed and make it look like they hadn't just been going at it like rabbits. No one ever did a good enough job of tucking in their shirts or combing out their hair to put one past me.

No, I'd already had my life's share of catching Roy *in flagrante,* and I wasn't going to tempt fate any more than I already was, just by paying a social visit.

So there I stood, down on the street in the Crescents, ignored for the most part by anyone who did pass by, waiting for the city bells to ring out the hour. I was damn near certain that Roy—or his boy, if he even cared halfway what happened over the top edge of his current roman—knew I was already out there. I could assume I was being made fun of upstairs, in the top room of Roy's Crescent tower. But I'd weathered worse insults than those. Dealt out worse ones, too. They'd roll off me.

At least the building wasn't one of the crazier structures I always passed walking from my new place in the middle of Charlotte up to the Crescents, seeing for myself easy enough why th'Esar had trouble with magicians. They fancied form over function now and then—though I didn't think they were so stupid as to live in buildings that would actually screw them over, or whatever they were working on. No, it was more a display of what they could do—how they could defy nature and still come out on top—that must've made the fire in th'Esar's mustache stand out a little more against the gray, whenever he caught sight of it. It *was* a bit of a nose-tweak, if you asked me, and the kind of thing people with Roy's disposition for tweaking noses really went in for.

It was a sight different from the simple buildings in Miranda, where all th'Esar's people lived. There, the houses and the offices were just straight up and down, made of solid brick or white stone or marble, no rooms on stilts or hanging towers.

I didn't prefer either since, by my taste, both were too fancy.

The first bell of the hour was struck up by the bastion, ringing down over the rest of the city, clear as day. Good, I thought, because I was starting to get just a little cold, what with the sun setting hours ago and me just standing there growing moss.

I rapped on the door without hesitating—I wasn't one to question if I should wait until after the bell couldn't be heard anymore, so as not to sound desperate or whatever these little details meant. After that, I could hear some noise from within the house, and a quicker footfall on the stairs that told me all I needed to know.

The boy was answering the door for him.

If that meant Roy was trying his hand at cooking again, I thought, shifting my shoulders and grinding my teeth, then there was probably going to be a fire in Charlotte tonight. Tragedy for the ages, though wouldn't it please th'Esar to have what remained of his little magician problem taken care of by one of their number?

The latch clicked and the door swung inward.

"Welcome, Adamo," Hal said, leaning against the door for a moment and looking nervous. Well, he had *some* thoughts for self-preservation in his head, at least, while I was beginning to believe Roy had none at all. "I hope I didn't keep you waiting too long. Please, come in."

Didn't have to ask me twice. The wind picked up just as I stepped inside, stomped the frost off my boots on the mat, then sniffed the air suspiciously for any signs of something burning on the stove.

Hal cleared his throat. "Royston's changing his vest," he explained, almost too softly for me to hear him. How did he hope to get anywhere in life being so quiet like that? Whether he was a delicate flower by nature or not, it was up to the gardener to make sure his prized bloom didn't get knocked over by somebody's fart.

And that was enough flower-metaphoring for me for the rest of my days.

It wasn't that I didn't like Hal in particular. He seemed all right enough, and you had to have more than *just* dumb luck to help save an entire city. And it wasn't that I was against Roy's particular tastes, either, because if *that*'d been the problem, we wouldn't've been friends for so damn long. I was just fine with whatever made a friend happy, provided of course that it *did* make him happy. But Roy had a type, and that type was always too damned young to see who he was and know him for a good thing. They always ended up leaving, which was why there was no point in me getting attached to them.

No point in Roy getting attached to them, either, but that was another story for another day, and I sure as shit wasn't planning on meddling.

I sniffed the air again, shrugging out of my coat before Hal could offer to take it or something, which would've embarrassed both of us, and Roy probably would've come down right in the middle of us struggling over it, demanding to know why Hal was trying to steal my coat in the inner hall.

Wouldn't've been the *first* time Roy took up with someone who turned out to love stealing more than he loved Roy, and right up until that business with the Arlemagne prince, I'd've said he was the worst of the lot by a mile. You'd think that kind of thing would put a man *off* looking for partners half his age, but Roy was nothing if not stubborn as a mule, despite how he hated mules and all their country ilk. I guess the rat'd been charming, in his own slippery way, but he'd helped himself to several pieces of the good silver *and* sold one of Roy's prized first editions before anyone was the wiser.

Never saw him again. Lucky for him, anyway.

How we'd gotten that book *back* was a story in itself, but the simpler version involved a lot of cracking heads together while Roy made things explode, then refused to speak to me, because I'd been right about that crook all along and he needed somebody to punish.

Before he'd taken up with the thief, he'd been with the actor, up-and-coming in the Amazement, who'd *quite* enjoyed the boost in status Roy'd brought him. Of course, he'd cut loose once he'd decided he'd met all the right people, and Roy wouldn't go to the theaters at all that season for fear of running into him, which seemed like a damned waste of season tickets if anyone asked me. Which, of course, they never did.

The most recent—before the country boy—had been the infamous Crown Prince of Arlemagne, whom I'd only met the once, completely by accident, when I'd left the Airman to stretch my legs and ended up at Roy's place in the Crescents as friends sometimes do. The prince'd looked like one of those dolls they sold to little girls along the Rue, blond pony-tail and blue eyes and roses in his cheeks. They'd been having *tea,* of all things, and I couldn't understand a damn word of Arlemagne myself, but Roy'd been kind enough to take pity on me, explaining that tea was not *all* they were having and would I very kindly escort my dragon-stinking ass else-where, since all my scowling was putting a damper on the mood.

There was no way that one could've ended well. Even if the Arlemagne *didn't* get their knickers in a bunch about men kissing other men—and they did, as I understood it, al-most as much as they didn't like being slapped on the ass in public—you couldn't just up and have an affair with the heir to the throne and expect everything to run smoothly after that.

Honestly, I didn't know who was stupider about that one.

For a man I knew could be impossibly clever—*when* he had the mind to be—Roy had about the same amount of good sense as a common house cat, but with less grace to stick the landing. He'd gone and got himself exiled for that one, and that was where he'd met Hal—the latest in a long line of young men who didn't look back when they slammed the door. He'd lasted longer than the others, though. That was one good thing I could say for him.

It was with no small amount of trepidation that I was com-ing to accept him in my own way though I still felt like I was waiting for the other boot to come down, so to speak.

But it didn't mean that I couldn't be polite as I knew how in the meantime. Some people around here had manners, like greeting your friends when they paid a visit.

"You said he was changing, right?" I asked Hal, partly to make sure he wasn't *really* cooking and partly because all the silence between us left me feeling distinctly uncomfort-able. It wasn't that he was unfriendly—quite the contrary, actually—but more like if you let him, he'd drift off to an-other place altogether. That usually left me holding the thread of the conversation and feeling like an idiot once I'd realized what'd happened. I was used to dealing with simple folk whose everyday thoughts didn't work the same as dreaming. When Roy said *Hal's different,* I believed him all right. "Hasn't taken it into his head to try making dinner or anything like that, has he?"

"Bastion, no," Hal said, shaking his head with a little laugh that didn't seem unkind. There wasn't any mocking in it, anyway. "I don't think he'd eat at all if we didn't go out."

"True enough," I agreed. "He burns bread just by looking at it. I've seen it happen."

Hal laughed again, touching the knob of a coat hanger on the wall beside him. "I tried to bring him a cheese sandwich once. He told me to add lettuce, tomato, salt *and* pepper, then to take out the cheese and bring it back to him when I was done."

"And you actually did it?" I asked, since not only would I have told Roy *exactly* what he could do with a good cheese sandwich, I'd probably have threatened to give him a demonstration just so I'd know he'd received the message.

Hal shrugged lopsidedly, one shoulder higher than the other. "I don't mind. If I'm home, then I usually have the time to spare anyway, and I'd rather he eats than doesn't."

"Now, there's a sensible statement if ever I heard one," I said, and I even meant it, too. "If he ever gets it into his head to start dieting again or something like that . . ."

"You can count on me," Hal said, with a little burst of firmness. So there *was* some steel under all those wispy clouds of his. Guess I shouldn't have been all that surprised. It took a lot to be able to deal with someone like Roy on a daily basis. I knew it firsthand from my years in the 'Versity, back when there'd been so many students you couldn't just choose to have no roommate at all, which would've been my preference. It would've been Roy's, too, considering how poorly he got along with both friends *and* enemies when it came to living together day in and day out in such cramped quarters.

Around the end of the winter semester, I'd decided I was either gonna wring his neck with my bare hands or we were gonna end up friends for life. He was too smart for his own good—too much of a smart mouth for his own good, I mean—and I'd taken to sitting in back of class with him just because he made me laugh with his comments. No one else seemed to appreciate that about him, so I guess I ended up unconsciously resigning myself to sticking around for the long haul. Just 'cause he needed someone with the patience to put up with him for that long, and it sure as shit wasn't gonna be the other fly-by-nights he associated with.

Some days, I still wasn't sure I'd made the right decision. Especially when, in senior year, the bastard locked me out of our room all night so he could make time with our linguistics professor.

I was willing to bet there'd been some lingual action going on, but if it had anything to do with tutoring, I'd have eaten my boots. He was my best friend, but I wouldn't live with him again for all the gold in th'Esar's vaults *and* a night with th'Esarina, beautiful as she was. There were limits to a man's patience, after all, and living with Roy was *my* limit.

"Sorry to keep you waiting," Roy said, appearing at the top of the stairs. Finicky bastard always did like to make an entrance, especially if there was an audience, though it didn't seem to matter much either way because we were both used to him. "We're ordering in. I hope you don't mind."

"My stomach's had enough of your good old-fashioned home cooking to last a lifetime," I told him. Having food brought in was like reprieve from battle at the last moment, as far as I was concerned, and I wouldn't be paying for it in the trenches afterward, either.

"You told me you *never* cooked," Hal said, with a smile like he already had some idea where this was going. He hadn't taken his eyes off of Royston since he'd appeared on the stairs, which was sweet in its own way, if also a little nauseating by my own personal standards. No carriage could run on three wheels.

"There is a very good reason for that," Royston said, shooting me a dark look. "Though one wouldn't expect a man of war to be so squeamish. *I* ate it, anyway."

"Man can be more than one thing at the same time," I said, which was true enough.

The caterer arrived before we'd even made it into the dining room. Despite the Crescents' completely off-the-rocker design and how easy it was to get lost just trying to pass through it, somehow the deliveries always made it there, probably because it gave them most of their business. Roy intimated that it had to do with some magic spell or other, but I had a feeling it was more to do with the fact that most magicians didn't have time for making dinner, and coin was the real magic at work.

The dining room itself was a cozy enough place, or at least I'd always liked it: dark mahogany furniture and a small chandelier set over the table to give off light. I didn't know my ass from my top end when it came to decorating a room, but I had to hand it to Roy. He had a knack for putting things together so that they just *felt* right. It wasn't a skill I could've used in any way—put down a chair and a table and a bed and you had yourself a house you could live in just fine—so I didn't envy him so much as I enjoyed reaping the benefits from time to time. There was a stack of books in the corner, no doubt related to whatever rubbish Roy was working on at the minute and couldn't bear to be parted from, and I saw something on the china cabinet shelf that looked distinctly like an essay or some lecture notes. That made me shudder, bringing to mind my own lecture notes, which were currently just a list of pupils I didn't like, as well as the ones I knew I wouldn't like by the time the week was out.

I supposed I wasn't the sort of guest you'd bother to clean up for in the first place, and bastion knew Roy wasn't the sort of person to go around dusting. He refused to hire a maid, too, because, in his words, they "moved things around" to his dissatisfaction.

He *had* once employed, as far as I knew, a young man to come in and sort through the ruins of the upper floors once a week, but it'd ended badly—to the enormous shock and surprise of all involved parties, one of whom was me.

Despite not having a taste for what the rest of the world called real food, Roy did know how to order when it came to dinner. My own favorite part of the meal was definitely some kind of roast bird coated in brandy and lit on fire to get its skin all burned and crackling. Roy'd done the honors, of course, showing off pretty obviously for Hal, but it was equally obvious to me that Hal enjoyed it, so who was I to be the sour apple in the bin?

Except apparently that was my newfound purpose in life, and I was just gonna have to embrace it with open arms.

Halfway through the duck—and more than halfway into some kind of noodle dish with mushrooms—I got sick of watching Roy push vegetables around on his plate like that would trick anyone into thinking he was eating them. Besides, I'd come so we could have a real discussion, and even if I didn't feel entirely comfortable talking in front of Hal about something that could get the both of us arrested—and get Hal arrested just for watching us talking about it—he did have that whole saving-the-city thing under his belt. Maybe he'd even be of some help.

I just had to hope, *if* anything were to happen, he'd come down on Roy's side more strongly than he came down on th'Esar's.

"Oh dear," Royston said. "You have that look on your face."

"I don't have a *look*," I told him. "I was just thinking."

"Yes, that's the one," Roy said, spearing a bright orange piece of carrot and finally lifting it to his mouth. I guess mocking me brought his appetite roaring to the forefront. As much of an appetite as he ever got, anyway. "Have you made any decisions since the last time we spoke?"

"Been thinking about it," I said, which sounded lame even to me. If Proudmouth'd still been in one piece, she'd have definitely let me have it. "In between classes and all. During classes sometimes, too. But I'm feeling that the right thing to do is let the boys know, even if that means setting the light to the fuse myself. It might make things a little messier than if I was the only one of us with the information—then I could say something like, I was gonna make an executive decision on account of being ex–Chief Sergeant and all—but if Rook knows, then it isn't fair to keep it from the rest, you know? And I'm *not* Chief Sergeant anymore, just a civilian, so it's not really up to me who gets to know what."

"You're hardly 'just a civilian,'" Roy said.

"I'll get you some water," Hal said, getting up from the table and clearing his plate while he was at it. Had to hand it to the boy, he had excellent timing. And maybe he *could* read a room as well as he could read a book.

"I suppose this is the part where you lay all your wisdom before me and tell me I'm acting like a eunuch in the 'Fans, all frustration and no equipment," I said, leaning closer and taking care not to land my elbow in the duck.

"No," Roy said, fingers steepled together in thought. "I won't pretend that I am any better equipped to judge this situation—and I'm *certainly* not one to be rational when it comes to dealing with privileged information. It just seems to me that if this were news the Esar wanted known, he'd have announced it by now."

"When does th'Esar ever want matters known?" I asked. But it wasn't really a question that needed answering.

"Exactly my point," Roy agreed. "One can only imagine he's using this information to his own benefit as we speak, or thinking up a way how. If that's even possible, since the creation of the Dragon Corps was only afforded to him by wartime provisions. We are not, as you may have noticed, currently at war. Such extreme measures are illegal, even *for* the Esar. I can't imagine most members of the *bastion* condoning it, much less the Basquiat. But . . . there's another matter that's come to my attention."

"Oh, *great,*" I said, meaning it with every fiber of my being. "Why's it that as soon as it starts raining, the rain turns to piss? I must've been a real son of a bitch in some past life, I'm telling you."

"Don't overreact," Royston said, chiding me softly. "It might not be anything. It's only that Margrave Ginette's been absent from the Basquiat for several days. No one's seen her, or had a word of communication for that matter, and she's not the type just to drop all her responsibilities without warning. She had a fair few—work that a great many of us were interested in. I'd been meaning to talk to her myself, only I've been busy."

I snorted, knowing full well the kinds of things he'd been

busy with. "Why's it that *I* know that name from somewhere, then?" I asked.

"Who knows?" Royston replied, leaning back in his chair. "An indiscretion in your wilder youth, perhaps? She was a very beautiful young woman. I'd say she was just your type, but then, I've no idea what your type even is."

"Not your type," I said. "You can bank on that."

Roy assumed that funny, wry smile of his. "Of course not," he said.

It was bothering me, though, a familiar name I couldn't place. What business had I ever had with magicians? It'd be a real laugh if she was one of the ones who'd worked on my girl, but then, those names'd never been released and I was pretty sure all those who'd worked on the dragons were no longer in the city—either removed to make sure they kept their secrets or because they didn't want to stick around and reap whatever "reward" th'Esar had coming for them.

I wasn't one for treason, though my thoughts could've easily been called treasonous. I just knew on which side to butter my bread, what separated night from morning, and how little you could trust th'Esar when he promised you something. I tried to remember if it was nostalgia getting the better of me or if he hadn't always been like that, chasing down shadows at every turn. But I guessed the war could make even the strongest mind jump at noises that weren't there. I sure as shit wouldn't've wanted to be in his position; I was just lucky I hadn't been born underneath a heavy crown.

No, I'd just been born to be a part of something—somebody, which was the way I'd always looked at Proudmouth—a damn sight bigger than I was. Then, just as quick as you like, it was over and gone.

At least I still had my hands, I thought, staring down at them and feeling sorry for myself, whether I liked it or not.

"Any luck?" Roy prompted me.

"Yeah, actually," I said, the whole thing dawning now. "Balfour mentioned her once, back at the beginning. Margrave Ginette was working on his—you know. His hands. Looked into her to make sure th'Esar was giving him proper care, but those I asked said she knew a fair bit about that kind of thing, so there you have it."

"Of course, you *would* do something like that," Roy said, almost fondly. I didn't like his tone.

"Care to explain what that one means, or should I play questions?"

"It's just that you're such a mother hen," Roy said. "Don't get mad, you *know* it's true. I bet it's killing you to spend all your time with new recruits when you want to be looking after your old ones."

"Anyway," I said loudly, because Hal'd just come back into the room, and whether or not I was slowly taking a shine to him, this wasn't a conversation he needed to hear. Wasn't a conversation *I* needed to hear, either. It'd give me indigestion. "What's that have to do with the mole on Lady Greylace's left tit?"

"How colorful," Roy said. "I'll have to remember that one."

"And you," I told Hal, "should probably cover your ears."

"Oh, no," Hal replied. "I've already heard that one."

I cleared my throat and Roy took his water from Hal at last, covering up a laugh and sputtering just a little on it. "I'm not sure yet," Roy said finally, dabbing at the corner of his mouth with his napkin. "Margrave Ginette was working on mechanics on a much smaller scale than your dragons ever were. Little things—like your friend Balfour's poor hands. The letter you showed me suggests a more . . . massive resurrection, as it were? How terrifying to think such a thing was discovered on that side of the Cobalts. No wonder there's been no public statement."

"Grinds my guts," I said.

"I just can't imagine there being any connection," Royston said, sounding disappointed. I'd've admitted it: I was, too. "I had hoped . . . Well, never mind. At least you've decided to tell the other airmen about the possibility. If you're *sure* that won't make matters worse. Haven't you even wondered about it?"

"Not for a second," I said. "It'd be the same as dragging my mother out of the grave, slapping a new arm on her, a new leg maybe, then having her walk and talk and make breakfast for me again, just like when I was a schoolboy."

"What a horrendous picture that is," Royston said, "but I do think I see your point. Well, I'm sorry, in any case, for intimating I had some piece of the puzzle when it seems I really did not."

More information to clog up the necessary stuff I was trying to keep in order, I told myself. And wasn't that just Royston's style? "Well, thanks," I told him. "It's always so refreshing, talking to you."

"The same for you," Roy agreed. "Now, what about dessert?"

CHAPTER FOUR

TOVERRE

I was being most outrageous, but I had followed him out of the classroom all the way down the 'Versity Stretch, and now we were sitting in the same café. Together, but not together, for he had not yet noticed me.

Laure had told me when I suggested it, in no uncertain terms, that she wasn't going to be a part of this, not even for a second. Following people to gape and gawk at them and indulge in dirty thoughts was wrong, and that was where she drew the line, apparently. She had no idea that my thoughts really were as pure as the driven snow.

I simply wanted him to notice me.

And notice me he would, even if it took me weeks more of following him just this way, mapping out the places he stopped, noting what windows his gaze lingered upon. I would know everything that he liked, would have myself familiar with every shop and bookstore that he preferred. I would make note of and subsequently read the books he carried under his arms, and—at long last—I would gather up the courage and determination to speak with him, armed with the necessary tools to impress him.

That was really all I desired. Laure would understand eventually that there was absolutely nothing dirty about that.

There was, however, something very dirty about the table in front of me. I looked around for the waitress, to inform her she had done a very poor job of cleaning the table after its prior inhabitants, but she was nowhere to be seen. I inched my chair very carefully around the table and away from the coffee stain, then allowed myself another—very daring— look at the object of my affections.

He was waiting for someone, that much was clear. I'd spent enough time watching people that I knew the signs not of impatience but of private longing. Every time the door opened, for example, he cast a casual glance around the café, not anxious—his company was not late, then—but hopeful. He had that air about him, like someone on his birthday, alive and bright with anticipation. I had never seen him like this before though I hadn't yet had that many opportunities to observe him outside the classroom we shared. Then, he seemed somewhat intimidated by the large crowd, reminded of us only when he had cause to look up from his notes.

It was on one of these moments, the door opening and a gust of cold wind blowing in and his eyes lifting from his book, that I hoped he would catch sight of me—as unlikely a possibility as it might have seemed to anyone else. Being of an amiable nature, he would no doubt strike up a conversation, and perhaps even invite me to sit at his table, whereupon I would do my best to impress him with how well—not to mention how quickly—I was adapting to Thremedon's crowded streets. That was my ideal, the scenario I'd dreamed up while observing the object of my affections, and I was more fond of it than any master craftsman of his wares.

Still, one had to be prepared for all eventualities, and loath though I was to consider the larger picture, I was forced to contemplate the odds given to me by our location. There were several men and women sequestered at tables, sipping at their hot drinks and twining their fingers together and generally behaving in a way that made me ill and jealous at the very same time.

How uncanny.

I began to steel myself against the possibility that he was meeting a young woman. She might well have been someone like Laure, with a pretty face and an upturned nose and exceptionally large attributes filling out the top of her dress. Laure herself referred to these last as a pain in the behind more than anything else, and told me I should try having them for a day to see how lovely they really were. But she didn't know—or didn't care—the effect they could have on a man.

If I *had* been gifted for a day with a chest like Laure's, not to mention the body to go along with it, I'd most certainly not have been wasting my time crouched in the corner of a café that 'Versity students seemed to favor. I would have been out enjoying myself and trying on fine clothes.

The bell above the door jingled merrily once more, and this time when Hal looked up I saw the most attractive expression pass over his face. It was like the smile I'd seen him share with the class at least a half-dozen times over a scintillating part in the lecture, and yet *different* somehow, much more personal. Dare I say more intimate? I sought to memorize that look as surely as I had memorized the others, to sketch a living picture so I might always remember it, even on days less fine than this one.

It was nearly impossible to keep from craning my head around at once to see if I could get a better look at whoever had kept Hal waiting. My patience paid off, however, as a very well-dressed gentleman passed into my peripheral vision just moments later. I particularly admired the cut of his black coat and the embroidered vest beneath, and even allowed myself a second—quite scandalous—to note his handsomeness, despite the fact that he was evidently closer to my father in age than he was to me. He had dark hair and a well-trimmed goatee.

Hal rose to meet him, taking both gloved hands in his own.

Perhaps he was a professor, I thought. He did have that air about him, though without the chalk dust on his gloves. They could have been there to discuss research or a project or an essay.

But all my hopes of its being a 'Versity-related meeting were dashed when Hal leaned in to kiss this man full on the mouth.

I had to look away after that—not for the same reasons of propriety that anyone in the country would have turned away, but for how quickly my heart was beating and how hot my face felt. I wasn't given to a pretty blushing—that was more Laure's domain, though she blushed so rarely—but my face *did* see fit to turn mottled shades of tomato red whenever I was feeling any one emotion too strongly. Or perhaps when I was feeling everything at once and couldn't make heads or tails of it.

When I dared to glance back at their table, the man had removed his coat and gloves, but Hal remained latched onto one of his hands as though it were an anchor. No one around them was commenting on it, and no one was even staring at them, save for me.

I'd heard stories of what it would be like in Thremedon, told in hushed whispers of disapproval over breakfast and before bedtime until the day I'd finally left for the city. I hadn't taken them in the spirit they were intended—they seemed less a warning to me and more a promise—but neither had I let on to my family that all their cautionary tales were falling on deaf ears. They might have stopped telling them then, and I'd have had nothing to look forward to at all.

In Thremedon proper, a man could embrace another man as he might embrace a woman. He could even *kiss* another man right in public and no one would give it a second thought or catch him out back behind the barn to pummel the air—and the deviance—out of him. It was an alternative to marrying a woman, however much I did care for Laure, and being forced to produce dozens of filthy babies for the approval of my relatives and to the benefit of my father's name and pride.

What was more, though I hadn't known it before, I'd found myself attracted to someone whose preferences were the same as my own. This was the first time such a thing had happened to me. I had to press my hands against the table's surface to keep them from trembling. It was too much freedom to contemplate all at once.

I'd wash them—and my gloves—later.

Now, however, there was the problem of making my exit since the law of averages dictated that, for however many times I'd looked over at Hal and longed for him to look back at me, my getting up in the hopes of leaving anonymously would be the one thing that managed to draw his attention. No matter how quietly I moved, making an effort not to scrape my chair or—bastion forbid—bump into anyone else, I was rather effectively trapped.

As much as I was happy for Hal, I didn't actually wish to stay and observe his tryst as it progressed. That *would* fall into the category of an invasion of privacy, or what Laure termed "creepy," and never once had such a thing been part of my intentions.

A shadow fell across my table, and just as I was about to assure the waitress that I didn't want anything currently, thank her for her time, and inform her of the coffee stain, I realized it was someone I knew, not the waitress at all.

"Toverre?" Gaeth asked, as though he didn't already know. It was a curious kind of politeness that didn't quite make its way back around to being coy, I'd decided, and it didn't *exactly* bother me.

Mostly because it seemed he wasn't even aware of it himself, which made it endearing instead of completely awful.

"Hello," I said, instantly more panicked than concerned with impressing him. No one *really* ever spoke to me without Laure present, too. Or, at least, no one *came over* to speak to me, given the choice between that and the chance to avoid talking to me entirely. Gaeth obviously hadn't learned that lesson yet, but he would in time.

At the present, I supposed I had only to be grateful for the very large shield he made, which hid me quite effectively from Hal's table.

"Are you meeting someone?" Gaeth asked, casting a glance to the empty chair at my table. "I'm probably interrupting."

"I was just leaving, actually," I told him, making a decision then and there. It would look less suspicious if I were to leave now, and I could hide behind Gaeth until we made it out of the café and onto the street.

Our professor—the former Chief Sergeant of the Dragon Corps—would have been *so* proud of my sudden burst of strategy. Thinking on the spot when all your plans went to piss, as Laure would have said.

"Have you tried the coffee in this place?" Gaeth asked, as I pulled on my coat. He was still wearing that beastly gray monstrosity of his—I supposed he didn't have anything else—but one couldn't be picky when it came to one's instruments of escape. I was less inclined to be forgiving of his shabbiness than I once had been, now that I'd had some time to absorb how important fashion was to Thremedon. "I think it's bad, but then I've never been much of a fan of coffee in the first place."

"It's cheap," I sniffed, arranging myself on his right side before we set out together. "I suppose that's why the students like it."

"That's what I heard, too," Gaeth admitted, holding the door open for me. If he was under the impression that a show of good manners was going to cheer me in the slightest, then he clearly had no understanding of the depth of emotion a person like me was capable of.

A shame, really. Considering how handsome he was, he had absolutely no finer breeding.

In the light of day he seemed a little flushed but less absent than he'd been when I'd run into him with Laure in the Amazement. His eyes were clear, the whites very white and not at all bloodshot, and his nose dry. He didn't *appear* to be suffering from a fever, but one could never be too careful with those *healthy* country boys and their ilk. They'd be fine one second, then dead of the plague the next, and at no point in between did they show any signs of it.

"Uh," Gaeth said, a look of concern creasing his brow. "Did I say something wrong? Or do I have something on my face?"

"Neither," I said, deciding it'd probably go beyond the bounds of our precarious friendship if I tried to feel his forehead. That was for the best; I really didn't want to touch him, anyway. Laure often remarked that I "got meaner than a horse at a shoeing" when I'd been embarrassed by something, and I supposed she wasn't far off. The expression, while inelegant, had a certain grim flourish that left little to the imagination. Even if Gaeth himself hadn't been the origin of my discomfort, I still couldn't shake the awful knowledge that he had been witness to my public heartbreak. "It's nothing. Never mind."

I'd intended to set Gaeth free down whatever street he chose in order to let him get away, but when I turned in the direction of the path I'd followed to get here, for whatever madcap reason, he chose to come along with me. I was cross with him for invading my privacy, since I'd been planning on losing myself in my jumbled thoughts, but it soon became apparent that he wasn't like Laure. He certainly wasn't willing—nay, waiting—to jabber my ear off at a moment's notice. In fact, I was so grateful for his silence that I didn't even particularly mind having to slow my pace considerably in order not to get too far ahead of him in the crowd.

Perhaps he had thoughts of his own to consider, thoughts that were slowing him down.

It was colder than it'd been when I'd left the 'Versity Stretch that afternoon to follow Hal, and I blew on my hands, rubbing them together to try to coax some warmth into them. I'd been cursed with poor circulation as a child, and as a result I tended to feel the cold more than most. The chilblains were the worst, swelling my fingers and toes and cracking before they finally healed, sometime just before summer.

"Do you want my mittens?" Gaeth asked all of a sudden.

I cast a look at his coat and tried not to imagine *too* vividly what any mittens he might've owned would look like. Wearing them over my gloves would be impossible, in any case. I'd have looked quite the fool.

"I think I'll manage," I said carefully, modulating my tone so that Laure wouldn't be able to ask me why I'd scared our new friend away when he was only trying to be polite.

"Nah," Gaeth said, digging around in his pockets for something. "You'll end up with chilblains for sure, and then won't you be miserable. Here, I bought these for my mam, but I don't think anyone'd be the wiser if you wore them back to the dorms. They're new, so . . . you know, you don't have to worry. About them not being clean, that is."

I stared at them, completely bereft of any words that might have helped me to extricate myself from this situation with the proper finesse. A witty retort about women's gloves, perhaps, or even something about chilblains, which as I knew only too well were horrid when experienced firsthand. Had he merely guessed or had Laure told him I was susceptible? The only part my mind could process—*completely* unhelpfully—was that the mittens were a rough, brown leather and looked as though they were lined with some kind of fur.

"Take 'em," Gaeth said. "They probably don't have fleas. I mean, they definitely don't have 'em. I checked."

"Hardly a convincing endorsement," I muttered, but I took them nonetheless, tugging them on. The fur made them warm, though they were bulky enough to make my hands feel very clumsy.

"You should get warmer gloves yourself," he added. "The ones you're wearing are nice and all, but they don't look like they help much with the cold. What you really need is something woolly, like the ones Laure's always wearing."

"Ah, yes," I sniffed. *"Those."*

"Something wrong with 'em?" Gaeth asked.

I checked to see if he wasn't making fun of me, the way Laure would have, or really anyone else in his position. It didn't seem that he was possessed of enough guile to do so, but I wasn't about to lower my defenses just yet.

"If you must know," I told him, "they're ugly. And they itch. They get dirty easily and they don't look at all like what anyone else here is wearing."

"Oh," Gaeth said, nodding and shoving his hands into his pockets, though not before he tugged his cap down farther over his head. "Everyone here must have right cold hands, then."

"I suppose it doesn't bother them," I told him. Was he really so thick-skulled, or had he not noticed he was dressed differently from everyone else on the busy streets of Thremedon?

"I don't know *much* about city folk," Gaeth admitted. "Not yet, anyway. But I can't see as how cold hands wouldn't bother someone."

"They must be used to it," I said, employing a tone of finality that I hoped would end this strange, circular discussion. I cast about for another topic of conversation. I didn't want to ask him about his hometown because I could already picture it—a vast stretch of muddy country, a barn full of cows, and

Gaeth himself in the middle of it, contentedly looking after his repulsive chickens and pigs. It was agonizing—not the least because I'd known dozens of boys exactly like Gaeth back home, and most of them turned out as hardheaded and unimaginative as the cattle they raised. Moreover, the idea that I would carry any sort of fondness for someone so *obviously* lost when it came to the sophistication of Thremedon was downright mortifying. How could I? I was a different man now!

If only Laure had come along, she would have been able to save me though she would have made me pay for it later on, when it was just the two of us again.

"Well," Gaeth said, putting a hand on my arm. "Here we are."

And so we were, back at the dormitories already. I didn't flinch at his touch, yet he withdrew his hand almost immediately with a little nod of apology. "Sorry," he added, looking sheepish. "Forgot you didn't like that."

"Are you going inside as well?" I asked, hoping I didn't sound too desperate for him to answer in the negative. Any more of his company and I would probably expire. Once I was alone, I could begin castigating myself for allowing him to touch me without even a rebuke. Was I no better than a horse myself, to be wooed by something so simple as a gentle hand and a calm demeanor?

If that was how it was going to be, I'd have no choice but to end it all.

"Nah," Gaeth said. "I was feeling a bit warm, so I thought I'd walk around some more for a bit. Winter air's bracing."

Here was the sort of boy my father would have preferred to have as a son, I thought, with some slim bit of jealousy. But mostly, I felt relief. Laure's father would have been happy with him, too, and it was a wonder she didn't hate him for it. No; she rather liked him, and I could hardly pretend I didn't understand the reasons why; simple as he was, he had an awful kind of charm about him. Yet it was something *I* would have preferred to forget.

"It's been . . ." I began, just a pleasantry, but found myself unable to think of anything to say. Instead, I began to tug the mittens off, but Gaeth held up his hands.

"You keep them for now," he said. "I'll come back to pick them up later. Gets cold in your room, doesn't it?"

"It does," I replied, surprised he remembered. He waved at me as he turned away from the bottom step, moving off through the straggling students making their way across the cobblestones, in and out of buildings, laughing or gossiping with their friends. Soon enough, he'd disappeared from view.

I watched him for a few moments longer than was necessary but mostly out of confusion, feeling my brow wrinkle unpleasantly. In the wake of my failure with Hal, I'd quite forgotten about Gaeth, and I'd imagined he'd be only too relieved to find himself free of my attentions. Either that was the case, or he really *was* feebleminded and thought us perfectly capable of being friends without the addition of Laure to keep everyone sane. For what could he and I possibly have in common?

Then I began to feel the cold too keenly, while everything I'd seen earlier in the afternoon came flooding back to me and I forgot about Gaeth completely. I had so much to tell Laure, and even though she'd complain at first about how wrong it was to watch people when they didn't know you from a hole in the wall, I knew it was a good enough story that she'd listen.

She *would* stop scolding me. Eventually.

BALFOUR

I hadn't heard any further news from Ginette, and there was a strange aching in my wrists that was beginning to grow worse with each passing day. It troubled me, and not just for the obvious reasons of my own personal discomfort.

I'd never thought Ginette would be the sort to leave a job unfinished. Return visits to her home in the Crescents proved fruitless; speaking to her neighbors offered no clues as to her whereabouts. And, when I asked a few of my companions in the bastion if they'd heard anything about Margrave Ginette,

I was met mostly with disinterest or vague rumors. Troius said he'd heard from a friend of his that she'd gone missing, and he was certain there'd be a replacement found soon enough to look after my hands if she didn't show up.

That, however, wasn't exactly what I was concerned about.

"You worry too much, Balfour," Troius told me, clapping me on the back. "I know you've seen hard times, but they're over now. Go out, get some fresh air, maybe see a healer for the way those wrists hurt? And things will be fine in no time. I'm sure it's all meant to work out."

I could agree with him about one thing, and that was the matter of getting some fresh air. Which was exactly what I was doing, sitting outside on the steps of the bastion, watching the passersby and making sure I didn't stare too long at any *one* person, thus causing some personal offense.

The Arlemagne diplomats had put a momentary hold on our proceedings, and I'd learned—through Troius and other idle gossip—that it was because there was a royal marriage being arranged. Considering the preferences of their crown prince, which had become apparent to more people than he might've liked during his tenure in Volstov, I felt bad for both the bride *and* the groom in the arrangement. But it was hardly my place to worry about matters of state in a country that wasn't even my own, one that I had never seen and probably would never have reason to visit.

The worries of others, though, proved a distraction from one's own. Since I no longer had a ready-made diversion in the form of thirteen other men being as loud and as violent as possible with one another, I'd resorted to this: observing strangers and doing my best *not* to come up with little stories about who they were and where they were going in life.

There was clearing one's mind, and there was abandoning sense entirely for a flight of fancy, and I could still tell the difference well enough.

I was currently following the movements of a young man in a gray coat and cap, walking distractedly back and forth in front of the Basquiat. His demeanor was a familiar one; I could have recognized it from anywhere since it was the same countrified awe I'd exhibited on *my* very first visit to Thremedon.

That, however, had been a very long time ago, and I soon lost sight of him. The area was a busy one, filled with magicians and diplomats and other nobility alike. This made it ideal for losing oneself in the passersby, all of whom looked more important than you, and busier, too. I knew I was playing right into the Arlemagne opinion of Volstovic diplomats, sitting outside instead of performing any duties within the bastion, but they *had* been the ones to call a halt to the talks. Diplomacy wasn't like any other job, where if one project fell through you simply attempted to find another one with which to occupy yourself. I supposed I could have marched down the hall to where Margrave Josette and Lord Temur were conducting relations between the new Ke-Han emperor and the Esar's representatives, but I hadn't been briefed on the particulars, and if they had need of me, I'd soon know.

I'd heard from Troius—not information I'd requested, but which I'd received nonetheless—that it wasn't the *only* place that they were conducting relations, either. Apparently it was all very scandalous, but I'd never been an idle gossip, and there was no one I knew now who would appreciate the news.

A small crowd was gathering around the Basquiat, a collection that looked like it might've been a tour group, and the magicians on the premises were doing their best to avoid it— one even came so far as to see the group, stop in her tracks, then turn smartly on her heel to take the back entrance in. Fortunately for her, the square was so crowded that it was difficult to notice these things unless one had set oneself apart for such a purpose.

Now and then, a carriage would make its way down from the palace grounds, and everyone drew out of the way to guess at who was within it. That was the only time the crowds parted a little, making it easier to see what was going on.

It was easy to tell when a carriage was coming by the clatter of horse hooves on cobblestone. I strained for a moment, thinking I heard the familiar rhythm, and a moment later I was sure of it. *Someone* important was coming down from the palace.

There was something to be said for training your senses to become an airman, after all. I was feeling very keen these days, though not keen enough, apparently, to solve the mystery of where Margrave Ginette had gone.

The carriage slowed as it came to the bastion, and I quickly lifted myself from the steps so as not to be in the way of anyone coming or going.

"Balfour Vallet?" A man stepped out of the carriage, dressed in the white and gold uniform of the Esar. I had a momentary twinge—it had always been *Airman Balfour* in the city, with no need for a last name—before the reality of the situation came crashing in around me and I felt a familiar surge of adrenaline. Social nerves, one might call them. I'd suffered from them ever since I'd been a boy.

"Yes," I said, somehow resisting the urge to hide my gloved hands behind my back.

"His Grace requests an audience with you," said the man, giving me some idea of what "requests" truly meant. It meant show up if you wanted to keep your head, Balfour, and there's a good lad.

I missed Thom suddenly, if only because he could talk his way in circles around everyone he'd ever met—he'd tamed *Rook,* for bastion's sake—and that was exactly the kind of man you wanted at your side during a meeting with the Esar. I had my own diplomatic training, of course, but that wouldn't be nearly enough to protect me.

Even when he was trying to help you, he was a very intimidating man.

"Of course," I told the Esar's man. "I'll come at once; thank you."

With no further hesitation, I climbed into the carriage. The driver shut the door behind me, and I felt the body of it shake as he climbed up into his own seat.

Ever since the end of the war, the Esar had taken a special interest in me—perhaps because he had been friends with my mother when they were much younger. Hence the position, I supposed, and the expert care. Perhaps he merely wanted to apologize about Margrave Ginette's untimely disappearance and make sure that I had a fitting replacement to continue with the upkeep of my hands.

And maybe, right after that, Anastasia would fly over the city with my dead brother on her back.

The ride was quick, if uneven. The upkeep on roads had gotten very bad during wartime, when most official funds had gone to the conflict, and the driver seemed to be going out of his way to hit *every* bump in the road, veering to avoid pedestrians and taking sharp turns a little too quickly. All the jostling wasn't doing much for my peace of mind *or* my wrists, but I knew as well as the driver that the Esar never liked to be kept waiting.

No doubt that was the reason for our breakneck pace.

I knew that I had no rational reason to fear a meeting with the Esar since I most certainly hadn't done anything wrong, but one's guilt did not always coincide with another man's preconceived notions, and the Dragon Corps's final meeting with the Esar was still quite vivid in my mind.

It was one thing to be brave when thousands of lives were at stake and you were part of the only damned crew that could put an end to the war, but I had little delusions about my own ability to re-create that same atmosphere of victory on my own.

If I was in for something as simple as a discussion, then I didn't have anything to worry about. But it was never something simple when it came to royalty. I'd seen the strange twists and turns the Esar's family line had taken in the past, and I knew the history behind every untimely royal death, as well.

It was because of this, perhaps, that I wasn't able to convince myself of anything.

The carriage bounced to a halt and the Esar's man sprang out ahead of me to lift the catch on the steps. I emerged from the carriage somewhat disoriented, but the beauty of Palace Walk made me catch my breath just as it always did. Even in winter, when the trees were bare and no lanterns lined the path, it was quite lovely in its minimalism.

"I assume you already know the way," the Esar's man said,

bundling the stairs up under the carriage again. They fell into place with an ominous *click*. "If you don't deviate from the path, it'll take you right inside. Should be someone waiting to escort you to His Highness from there."

"I see," I said, tugging my gloves on a little straighter. My fingers were stiff from the cold. "Well, thank you very much for your assistance."

"And for yours," the driver agreed.

The one unfortunate thing about Palace Walk was that it was largely empty: Servants used other entrances for their comings and goings, and unless there was a party—a favored family visiting from their country estates, or perhaps a ball—most of the people with business in the palace were already within. I couldn't get lost in a crowd, and I couldn't distract my mind by observing others. I had only myself to think about, and the large, white stone building looming before me was causing me to feel very small indeed.

There were guards bundled up in coats to open the doors for me, and they did so, nodding as though they knew me, which made me slightly uncomfortable—if only because I most certainly did not know them in return.

Someone *was* waiting for me in the inner chamber, but it wasn't another servant, or even a guard as I'd half expected. She was sitting on a low, ornate couch beside one of the few, long windows that was still gathering the winter light, her voluminous skirts shimmering just slightly like an oyster pearl in shades of white and pale gold, with an overlay of blue. There were little pearl drops hanging from her ears, though her throat was bare, and she wore long gloves that extended nearly up to her shoulders against the cold. Her hair was the same gold as her dress, drawn back from her face and swept up off her neck—held there by what I could only assume was some little magic charm but was in all likelihood a hidden talent with pins that I'd never understand.

I had only ever seen the Esarina in passing and from a distance, but it was unmistakably she seated before me.

"I . . ." I managed, as my brain refused to follow where my mouth had already ventured forth. What was the proper depth of bowing for a woman of her station? I knew it, and yet the sight of her caused me to forget it almost immediately. "I am sorry . . . and humbled, Your Majesty. I must have gotten turned around somewhere. I didn't mean to interrupt you."

"Not at all," the Esarina said, standing with a hushed swish of her skirts. "You are Balfour Vallet, Adelaide Vallet's son, are you not? I am acquainted with your mother. She speaks very highly of you."

"You're too kind," I said, still not quite managing to convince myself that I hadn't tripped and hit my head somewhere along the walk. This felt like an ambush, though too subtle to be planned by the Esar. If he wanted to hit you on the back of the head, he did so, and was done with it. "Or perhaps she is."

The Esarina laughed, covering her face with a fan that had suddenly appeared in her hand, and I slowly let out a breath, keeping my head bowed. Perhaps I'd been lucky enough to receive a stay of execution.

"You are here to visit my husband," she said, composed once more. "I will take you to him."

"*You* will?" I blurted out, before I could help myself. Evidently I was doing my best to see any pride my mother had once shown in me dashed against the rocks. Since they were acquaintances, my mother would hear about my behavior in a letter, and *I* would hear about it soon after, in a letter of my own.

"It is not among my usual duties," she admitted, turning her face to the side for a moment, so that I caught a glimpse of the loose pearls threaded through her hair. "But servants talk, and guards *certainly* talk, since they've nothing but standing all day to occupy their time, and I've been led to believe that this is a delicate issue, one that my husband would like to keep among as few people as possible. Since he finds it difficult to keep things from *me,* I offered to perform this service for him."

The way she said it made me think that the Esarina had a hand in making it difficult for the Esar to hide things from her. I thought of what Compagnon would say—he'd be jealous, and I couldn't help but feel I was doing this for his sake—and I steeled myself in order to make the best of an utterly mystifying situation.

"I am honored to have such an escort," I said, finally recovering what little remained of my manners.

Surely the Esar wouldn't have coerced his wife into escorting me to my own execution. That was the thought I used to calm myself as I held out my arm, not to mention a litany of other reasons why my panic was unfounded.

The Esarina laid a gloved hand delicately against my own, and we made our way through the twisting labyrinth of corridors that somehow always managed to make me feel like a lost mouse in a 'Versity student's experiment, despite my being lucky enough to have a guide who very clearly knew where she was heading. The piece of cheese at the end of this particular maze, however, was the Esar himself, seated on a dais and looking much the same as he had the last time I'd seen him, if a little more gray about the beard and hair. There was barely any orange left in his mustache.

I supposed the war had taken its toll on all of us, one way or another.

At that moment, I realized that the Esarina must have had an intimate feel of the stiff, metal joints beneath my gloves against her arm, and I glanced over at her in horror, only to find her watching her husband instead of me.

"I'll leave the two of you to your business," the Esarina said, letting her hand fall from my arm. She gathered up her skirts and curtsied low, bowing her head deeply. "My lord."

"Our thanks, as always, my lady," the Esar said, waving his hand in dismissal.

I folded my hands behind my back and straightened my spine, doing my best to ignore the tickle in my throat that'd come on me unexpectedly.

"No doubt you are wondering why we called you here," the Esar said, once the door had closed behind the Esarina and we were alone in the private audience chamber.

No witnesses, my mind pointed out, and I stamped the thought out ruthlessly. I couldn't afford to be irrational.

"I am curious, Your Highness," I admitted, not seeing the harm in that. "Although, as I'm sure you already know, our talks with Arlemagne have been put on hold for the time being, so I . . . That is to say I wasn't doing anything of importance, when the summons came. It is my honor to serve you," I concluded. A little official flattery never hurt.

"You've no idea at all why you have been summoned?" the Esar repeated back to me, just to verify. He shifted in his chair, and I felt suddenly as though I was being watched. Perhaps my initial impression of our being alone in the room together, with no witnesses, had been too hasty. "By your knowledge, there's no reason at all we might have to invite you here to speak with us?"

"Not anything I can think of," I said slowly, racking my brains. I did hope this wasn't a test. "Unless it's about my hands."

"Curious," the Esar said, leaning forward suddenly in his charge, so that I almost felt he was about to lunge at me from the dais. "Why would it be to do with your hands?"

"It *is* the topic most people are interested in, once they learn about it," I replied. "That, and my time as an airman of your Dragon Corps—though the latter they have more difficulty believing. With the former . . . I am simply able to show them the evidence."

"And how much evidence have you given?" the Esar asked, rubbing at the side of his jaw, where his beard was freshly trimmed. "How many people have you shown?"

"I wear gloves, as you can see," I replied, "since the sight often . . . troubles people. As a diplomat of Volstov, and a servant to Your Highness, I thought that distracting those diplomats with whom relationships are already so tenuous would be unwise. And . . . a little vanity, too, no doubt plays some factor in it."

"How very prudent of you," the Esar said. "Do you have trouble with them?"

"The hands?" I asked. He nodded, and waved for me to continue without waiting for him to speak. I swallowed, throat feeling dry, but carried on. "It took some time to master them. In the first month, I found myself able to operate only a few of the fingers. Now even more complicated tasks—

replacing the oil in a lamp, managing a fork and a knife at the same time—pose less and less trouble."

"So they are a part of you now, and do as you command?" the Esar asked.

The Esar would think of it that way, I realized, but I nodded once. "Indeed, Your Highness," I replied. "Though they do not feel natural."

"That doesn't matter," the Esar said. "It is of no consequence to us. I am told that you have had difficulty with the magician who treats you."

"I cannot seem to find her," I explained, forgoing any jokes about losing a Margrave. I didn't think he would appreciate them. "No one knows of her whereabouts. She lived alone, and left no information, it seems."

"No one can find her?" the Esar asked. "You are sure about that?"

"Your request for my presence came at a fortuitous time," I said. "Since missing my most recent appointment, I've been . . . concerned about the state of the prosthetics."

"Of course," the Esar said, leaning back in his chair. There was something on his mind, but it was far beyond my capacity to know what. "We'll find someone else and send them to you before anything more discomfiting should happen to you. The way out is the same as the way in."

I bowed very deeply, wishing more than ever that the Esar was a more approachable man. Or at least deigned to answer as many questions as he raised during any simple conversation. I wanted to know, of course, about Margrave Ginette, but to push my luck—even for her sake—would have been about as suicidal as my final mission with Anastasia.

It was so much easier to be a hero in wartime, I thought, ashamed of myself. But I left the room without furthering my case or hers.

If the Esar had an agenda, he didn't want me to know it. And I, being his subject and therefore his servant, had to abide by that. It was law.

I saw no further sight of the Esarina on my way out, and the halls of the palace were eerily quiet, like a summer estate in wintertime. The carriage that had brought me was waiting outside, the driver and the horses alike stamping their feet with the cold and impatience, and they were even so kind as to deposit me not in front of the bastion but at my own home. I tipped the driver somewhat clumsily, my hands so stiff I could hardly move them.

He eyed me strangely, tugging at his cap. With a clatter, he and his equipage were gone.

It was quiet along the streets after that, and I fumbled with my key as I made it up the apartment steps into the long hall. No one was waiting for me when I opened the door, and I was able—after so much excitement—to convince myself that I preferred it that way.

LAURE

Of all the things I hated—exams, mending clothing, being told I had to ride sidesaddle, talking to people I didn't like— it was possible I hated appointments with a physician most of all. Especially when they were someone I didn't know, like an old man with wrinkly, cold hands, attempting to be kind while I mostly wanted to grab my clothes and hightail it out of there, fast, before anyone could see me.

Back at home, the local doctor was just like that, and when he came I usually hid in the pantry, then in the barn when my pantry deal was found out. I never got sick anyway. I didn't have any need for him.

With this damn 'Versity appointment, I didn't even know what to expect, or whom. Even worse, Toverre had his in a few days, so we couldn't even go together for support. For Toverre's sake, I'd have to pretend like sitting in the foyer of some stranger's house while an apprentice took my measurements wasn't one of the least comfortable things I'd ever done in my life. Considering how many times I'd fallen off a wild horse, put my foot in my mouth at the dinner table, and gotten stuck on the shelves while trying to get myself out of the pantry, that was saying something.

Toverre was going to *hate* it.

If only Gaeth'd been around, I would've pressed him more

for details on what it was like—whether they leeched any blood or *kept* any blood, that kind of thing. I had no idea how it worked in the big city, just heard rumors from the stable-boys about what crazy shit they did to you in Thremedon. But I hadn't seen Gaeth in a few days, even though I'd been keeping an eye peeled for him. For a lad that big, he didn't have much trouble disappearing on you.

The apprentice checking up on me was a weedy little man, but up close I could see he was even younger than I was, with freckles and thin orange hair. He'd be bald by the time he was twenty.

I had to think mean thoughts about him because he was writing all kinds of things down about *me*—my height, my age, my weight despite me being a lady, and the day and year I was born—checking my tongue with a flat wooden stick, peering into my ears with some device that was sharp at the tip, which *really* made my skin crawl.

All this seemed much more complicated than it'd ever been at home and, in my opinion, couldn't've been too necessary.

He just needed to get to the bloodletting and be done with it, I thought, because too much longer steeling myself and I was going to talk myself right back into wanting to run away again.

Not like I couldn't take care of myself when it came to these little things, of course, and it wasn't like I was *scared* or anything. I didn't like being made to wait, while in the next room I could hear all kinds of things being prepared. It wasn't going to hurt and even if it did, I didn't mind. I just hated all the anticipation.

"Can we get on with this?" I said, sharp and exasperated. It made the apprentice jump, and he fiddled with his spectacles nervously.

"I'm sure she'll be with you in a moment," he replied, the nostrils of his otherwise thin nose flaring wide. "There's a lot to prepare in advance."

"Oh yeah?" I asked. "Like what?"

That, of course, he didn't answer. Maybe he didn't know.

Maybe he was as uncomfortable as me and was pretending not to hear so that he could escape as quickly as possible.

Stood to reason *one* of us got to escape, anyway, and he was probably in a better position for it than I was. I bet Chief Sergeant Adamo—Professor Adamo now; it must've been awkward for him, what with people slipping up all the time and calling him the wrong thing—would've come up with some brilliant getaway strategy, pants on fire or no.

Then again, if I'd had a dragon to command and call my own, there wouldn't be *anyone* making me wait more than five minutes for anything, and definitely not in a cold little physician's room, either.

A girl had her dreams, and I had mine. I'd heard all about how it was the dragons that did the choosing, and not th'Esar or any magicians from the Basquiat, either. So what if one of the dragons had gone and chosen a woman, just because she liked one better? Probably the only reason that none of 'em ever had was because no woman had been presented to the dragons in the first place, but sometimes when I'd closed my eyes at night back home, I'd imagined what it might be like to slip through all the nets just to get my chance to stand in front of one of those beauties and have her pick *me* out of the lot of 'em.

After all, if the dragons were girls, why couldn't the riders be?

"Thank you for your time," the assistant said, bobbing his head and scuttling out of the room.

I managed to keep from sticking my tongue out at him while his back was turned, but only by imagining what Toverre would say if I told him I'd done it. Sometimes, I thought, he should've been the lady and not me. He'd still have been ten kinds of crazy squeezed into one person, but at least he'd've had all the right airs, not to mention all the right clothes. And if I got to be the boy of the two of us, Da'd be happier, and I would be, too, because of it.

I swung my feet back and forth, trying not to feel too antsy. I was almost grateful when the door opened again—and I never thought I'd end up in a position where I'd be looking forward to a little bloodletting, but that was what Thremedon had done to me.

My physician was a stout woman—something I wasn't expecting at all, to be honest—with black hair and sturdy, square-shaped hands that would've been aces at soothing horses if she'd been born on a farm. I guessed she was aces at soothing patients, because the sight of her even relaxed *me* a little. That put my good sense at about the same level as a horse's, apparently.

"Sorry to make you wait so long," she said, looking over the chart her assistant had left behind before she glanced up at me. "I'm Germaine, and I'll be your attending physician for the next half hour or so. We got a lot of you country folk in today, as you can probably imagine. Preliminary check says you're fit as a fiddle, so that's good news. We're just going to draw a vial of blood for some more advanced testing, then we'll get you out of here, Miss . . . Laurence, isn't it?"

"It's Laure, actually," I told her, hoping I wouldn't have to get into the whole explanation.

"I see," Germaine said, checking something off on the chart, though she probably wasn't striking through the *nce* at the end of my name. Didn't strike me as professional. "That's good to know. I didn't want to be looking at the wrong chart after I've gone and given you a clean bill of health."

"That *would* be awkward," I agreed. Anything to get this over with more quickly.

"Is there anything you want to ask me about?" Germaine asked, folding the chart against her chest and giving me what amounted to a kindly look. Or at least, the closest thing to it that it seemed she could manage. "I know that it can be difficult, being away from home, and Thremedon's certainly an acquired taste. At your age, you probably have most of the basics figured out, but if you have any questions about your body and what's good for it, then now's your time to ask."

"Nothing that comes to mind," I answered—too quickly, I realized, since I could see the disappointment in her face. She probably thought I was lying, or maybe too dirt-stupid to ask the important questions, but I knew most of the things she wanted to talk to me about already. All the natural things, at least, that I could see happening with the horses just by being with them all day. Lying with a man led to having babies; I'd been getting my monthlies for years and they were the same pain in my ass as ever. And unless there was a potion they'd invented in Thremedon to shrink the size of my chest down to something more sensible, then I was sure there was nothing this woman could do to help me. Even if she really wanted to.

"You seem certain enough," Germaine said; there was some questioning in that, too.

"I'm betrothed," I told her, putting an end to the discussion. She didn't need to know that my fiancé was Toverre, and that he was about as inclined to do things to my naked body as I was to his, these days.

"I see," Germaine said, ticking something else off on the chart. It was maddening to know that there were strangers writing down all these things about me to keep as long as they liked—worse still that I wasn't allowed to read what any of it said—but at least she'd gone for my bluff. "Well, if you ever change your mind, I'm here from noon to eight on weekdays. It might take time to schedule an appointment in the next few weeks, but after the start of term rush is over, it should get easier."

"Thank you," I said, not wanting to seem like *too* much of an ungrateful boor right off the bat. The poor woman was just trying to do her job, and I wasn't making it any easier by acting like a particularly sullen cow. "I'll be sure and remember that. *If* I need anything."

"Well," said Germaine, with a little sigh, "I suppose you're anxious to get out of here."

"Yes, ma'am," I said, before realizing it'd probably been one of those rhetorical questions.

Lucky for me, she didn't seem to mind that I'd gone and answered anyway though she did gesture for me to scoot back up in my seat. I leaned back, staring up at the whorls on the wooden ceiling, and noticed a place where there must've been a leak, because the plank was warped and stained. A little bit of tar would solve that problem, easy. Didn't these city folk know *anything*?

"Roll up your sleeve," Germaine said, setting my chart down. "I'll be right back."

I did as she'd told me, biting down on my tongue. She didn't leave the way she'd come in but instead went through a door I hadn't noticed at the back of the examining room— probably because it was painted white, the same as the walls. She'd put the chart facedown on the counter, so I couldn't even try to sneak a glance while she was gone, and I didn't know if she'd be out of the way long enough for me to hop down off the table and scamper across the room to check it out. It'd be just like me to get caught with my hand in the cookie jar, and seeing as how I didn't know what the punishment for peeking at your files would be in Thremedon, I decided to be a good little girl and wait for my bloodletting like everyone else. Even though I shouldn't have to be cautious when it came to my own files, but all Toverre's obsessive behavior was starting to rub off on me.

Curiosity was liable to kill me if I kept focusing on it, so I turned my sights to something else instead.

Germaine had left the door slightly ajar when she'd gone through it, I realized, because it left a long sliver of dark against all that boring, white wall. That was probably where they kept the really mean-looking instruments they didn't want anyone seeing until they stuck you with them. We did the same with the horses at the stables, and even though Da never bothered to brand our cows, Toverre's parents had a separate room for that kind of stuff that smelled of burning hide, so they had to keep the doors locked at all times. If I leaned back, I could even see all sorts of weird, silvery equipment that I didn't recognize, and the tools I *did* recognize were ones I'd never seen in a physician's office before. Shears and pliers and all sorts of cogs, big and small, littered the slice of desk, illumined by bright lamplight. It looked more like a clockmaker's desk than anything. I didn't like the idea of *that* one bit, because if she was a clockmaker, then *I* felt like the clock, but I was probably getting ahead of myself. Maybe it was a hobby she kept on the side. You never could tell with these Thremedon folk.

Also, I was getting a crick in my neck from leaning so far back on the table.

The door creaked and I heard footsteps, so I straightened up, tugging at a piece of my hair and trying not to look like I'd been sneaking a look at something that didn't concern me. This Germaine woman seemed pretty passive as far as physicians went, and I was a head taller than she was besides, but they were all pretty big on the rules here. I didn't want her to decide she didn't like me right before she was about to stick me with a needle, either, which was just plain common sense.

"I'm sorry to keep you waiting again," Germaine said. She sounded a little out of breath, like she'd been climbing stairs or something. It made me wonder how big the space behind the examining room really was, or why they kept the bloodletting equipment so far away from everything else they needed, but it was probably top secret physician stuff, and none of my civilian business. I clenched my jaw and refused to look at the needle she was holding. That was the only way to do it so you didn't spook yourself.

"It's fine," I said, because what else was there to say really? My arm was getting cold, and my heart was racing.

She rubbed the soft crook of my elbow with something that made it colder, then snapped her fingers to one side to get my attention.

I *always* fell for that stupid trick, even if it was for babies.

The actual needle never hurt as much as all the waiting leading up to it, and this time was no exception. It was like a pinprick, and I'd had worse than that during my forays into mending clothes, despite how many times I'd tried to explain that I just *wasn't* made for it. Hurt more to take the needles out of my fingers, too, or when I forgot a pin somewhere and stepped on it.

This wasn't so bad. I'd been acting like a big baby, imagining all kinds of things that weren't there, and all over a simple blood testing.

It was my head that needed testing, I thought, but that

wasn't the kind of thing you could joke about with a physician.

Germaine offered me a tight smile and checked her watch—a pretty little thing made of gold, or at least colored to look like it was. On the face were all these foreign symbols—things I'd never seen on a watch before, not even in the history books I'd *finally* cracked open late the night before, which talked all about how magicians of Volstov had once told time by the sun and the moon. It had two hands like a watch did, though, and a third little one that went ticking in a circle though not in any kind of recognizable rhythm.

I'd ask Toverre about it later. Maybe it was the newest fashion in Thremedon to wear a watch that didn't actually tell time.

"All done," Germaine said at last, which was my cue to look away so she could pull the needle out again. Blood didn't bother me, not my own or anyone else's, but it hurt more when I looked at it, and I was brave, not *stupid*. I'd forget all about it if I just put it out of my mind. "Very good. No squirming or anything; a few of the boys before you fainted when they stood up."

"Got all the squirming out of the way in advance," I told her. "And I've never fainted in my life."

"You're a very sensible girl," Germaine said, tying a clean bandage tight around my arm and sliding her funny watch back into her pocket. The vial of my blood was sitting on a little tray between us, clearly labeled with my name and date of birth. It was much darker than it ever looked when I bloodied my nose or scraped my knee, and there was something creepy about it. Fascinating, too.

Then, just as I was about to ask what came next, Germaine plucked the vial up and whisked it out of my sight. Maybe she didn't want it to become homesick, so far away from the rest of me.

"We'll let you know the results in about a week," she told me, offering me another one of those tight smiles of hers. "Keep the bandage on for at least an hour, don't wash tonight, and check to make sure there's no infection. But there shouldn't be."

"Good to know," I said, remembering one of Da's stable-boys who'd died because of a needle that wasn't clean. That sort of thing made me shudder, though I wasn't about to let it happen to me.

"Thank you *so* much for your time," Germaine said, lingering at her secret doorway. She wasn't going to step inside, not while I was still hanging around. It piqued my interest, sure, but the whole thing left a bad, metallic taste in my mouth, like sucking on a ha'penny. I wasn't too keen on sticking around.

I rolled down my sleeve over the bandage, stretching my arm out and making sure all the blood didn't rush to my head when I stood up.

It didn't.

Only an idiot would faint after something like this, I thought. *An idiot who didn't know not to look at the needle while it was going into 'em.*

"You, too," I said, even though we both knew we were just doing our jobs.

CHAPTER FIVE

ADAMO

Luvander had always said, to anyone who'd listen to him and even to those who weren't listening at all, that when he made it out of this war he was going to open up a hat shop on the Rue d' St. Difference, and no amount of the boys' jeering was ever going to stop him.

With the money he'd received as a stipend for being a Volstovic hero, he proved he wasn't a liar, although in my opinion it was easier for him with most of the boys not being around to make good on *their* promises of jeering.

If there'd been any of them left—besides me and Balfour, who was too quiet for it, and Ghislain and Rook, who were smart enough to get their clever asses out of Thremedon because she held too many memories for them—they would've been lined up in front of the store howling and hooting and jeering at all hours of the day *and* night. They'd've been proud of him, too, of course, but they'd've scared so many customers away he wouldn't't've lasted too long. And the last thing I needed to see in this lifetime was Compagnon putting on one of those big velvet hats and parading around to impress all the others, and whatever poor lady shoppers were caught up in the chaos along with them.

Those were my boys, all right.

As it was, the location of the shop was pretty much ideal for those who wanted to say they'd bought their hats from *the* milliner airman. Him deciding to call it Yesfir after his girl was another stroke of genius, and, I guessed, also a tribute in its own way. Most importantly, Luvander liked to shoot the shit, which was part of the reason, in my personal opinion, he'd wanted to be a shopkeeper in the first place. He loved all that gossip—not the sort that was passed along by the lower maidens about guttings and knife fights, but the high-end crap, like which Margrave was having an affair with which member of the Arlemagne court, and who'd been found having a little ménage à trois with the Wildgrave Gaspardienne?

It was exactly the kind of ambiance I wasn't suited for, which was why I didn't spend too much time scaring away his customers and looking out of place, like a sword-and-leatherware mannequin that'd been delivered to the wrong store.

I had been there once, back when it opened, a small place selling outrageously priced hats and some gloves, too. *In honor of Balfour,* Luvander added to me, privately. But also, apparently, because gloves were all the rage these days.

They probably weren't anymore, knowing how quick Thremedon fashions could change. One day, all the men *and* women were dressing like the airmen, and the kids were charging around in the streets pretending they were flying. The next, you saw the ladies wearing silks from the Ke-Han, and everybody was gossiping about what'd happened on the other side of the mountains.

I wasn't too insulted by it. They were fickle and it was nice not to be the center of attention for a change. Now, if they started building statues in the middle of the Rue of Ke-Han emperors and warlords and shit, then I'd've felt slighted, but I didn't think th'Esar'd be stooping to that level anytime soon. And as for the rest of it, people could wear what they liked.

In the end, I wasn't too surprised to see that all the hats in Yesfir's window were shades of blue and green now rather than the patriotic red and gold of a few months before. With all the feathers, it looked like a slaughtering house for peacocks.

A little bell jingled over my head when I opened the door.

"I am *so* sorry to tell you we don't serve men here," Luvander said from behind the counter, just wrapping something up in a box with pretty white paper. The boys would've loved to see this, and maybe he knew it. Maybe that was *why* he was doing it, carrying on the joke for them that couldn't laugh about it anymore. "Unless you're buying something for a sweetheart—but I doubt it; what mad wench would settle for you? Or you fell off Proudmouth one time too many in your day—in which case I feel it's my duty to tell you none of these styles suit you, *except* maybe the purple one with the white veil."

"Just browsing," I told him, glancing around and shuddering. I'd been a bachelor for a long time—long enough that maybe I was coming around to accepting I'd never have children, much less grandchildren, but no matter how desperate I ever got, I wouldn't take up with a woman who'd wear hats like these. No offense to Luvander and his perfectly serviceable wares, of course. They just weren't my style.

"I suppose I can allow that," Luvander said. He finished up his packaging with a ribbon and a bow—even Yesfir would've crowded into the shop to make fun of him for that detail, I thought, but then again, Proudmouth wouldn't have been too keen with the way I was handling, or failing to handle, my students. What our girls didn't know was for the best these days, all things considered. "But please, don't touch anything. You're not delicate enough. You'll *tear* something."

I rolled my eyes. "Good to see you, too, Luvander," I said.

"You'll have to forgive me," he said, grinning. "I've just always wanted to order you around. You can't blame me for taking my chances now, can you?"

"Guess I can't," I agreed.

It seemed funny to me that women would flock to have such delicate accessories sold to them by a man with a big purple scar on his throat—wasn't it the kind of thing that made the daintier sex faint clean away?—but he'd covered it up for the most part with a white scarf, tucked into the front of his vest. He looked good, healthy, like he was living well and taking care of himself. I didn't have anything to scold him about.

"But don't you think this would look sweet on Balfour?"

Luvander asked, plucking up a little blue number with a peacock feather sewn right onto it.

It actually, somehow, reminded me of him.

I opened my mouth, then closed it again right quick. I wasn't about to wade into *that* hill of fire ants for any reason. Besides, I knew when a man was having a laugh at my expense, along with someone else's.

"I'm so sorry; it appears I'm still teasing you," Luvander said, setting both the box and the fancy little hat aside with a loud crinkling of wrapping papers. "I suppose it's my own small way of letting my nerves get the better of me. Not to mention paying you back for all the times you woke me up by shouting in the night. Soiled my pants more than a few times because of you, so I might as well make you squirm now, right?"

"Too much," I told him. "Don't need to know *what's* in your pants, Luvander."

"Hah!" Luvander said, coming out from behind his counter. "I suppose you're right, at least about that." He paused for a moment, pushing aside one fancy curtain and peering out onto the street. "*He's* never been here yet, you know. Balfour, I mean. Said he'd come and he never did, that charming little snake. It's because all those diplomats got hold of him, and he perfected a no that sounds just like a yes."

"He was probably just worried you were going to rig a bucket of glue to pour down onto his head the minute he crossed the threshold," I told him, eyeing the door. The layout of the shop was perfect for that kind of setup. Ghislain and Jeannot would've had it up there in no time, teamwork never being a problem when you shared the common goal of making another man miserable. "And then you might've put that fancy little peacock number on top of the glue, and he'd be wearing it for weeks, at least until the glue flaked off."

"I would never!" Luvander said, putting a hand to his throat like a woman grasping for her pearls. He took that opportunity to tug the scarf up to cover the mean hook of his scar, where it'd started peeking over the top. "Wasting an expensive hat like that—you have *no* idea. And the glue'd be *murder* to get off the floors. I haven't broken even yet, much less made enough to hire a shopgirl for that kind of thing."

"Bet you a shopgirl'd work here for free," I said. "You could hire some fresh-faced 'Versity student who's all ideals and no brains; she'd be falling all over herself to work for one of the famous airmen. Just a little something to write home about; she'd be the talk of the town."

"Speaking of which, how *is* your professoring coming?" Luvander asked, leaning his head on one hand. Some of what I was feeling must've shown on my face because he glanced over my shoulder toward the door, then shook his head. "That fantastic, is it? Seeing as how we're still waiting for the silver-tongued—and silver-handed, I suppose—diplomat to arrive, you might as well go ahead and tell me. Unburden yourself. No one I know will care, even if I *do* use your misery for idle gossip."

I snorted, rubbing at the back of my neck. "Same as always, it'd seem. 'Versity's started some new program that takes kids off the farms and crams 'em into our schools, so that's been going about as well as you'd imagine." I remembered the girl who'd asked if our pants caught on fire midflight, but she was just about the lone bright spot in a dark sky of children who'd been taught how to count cows and what to do when the crops came back poorly and not much else.

They were useful things to know, for certain, but it didn't mean the students were going to have an easy time of it picking up the basics of strategy.

"Oh dear," Luvander said, taking in the look on my face. "Perhaps I shouldn't have asked. Should I put on some tea? Or—I can't even remember—are you more of a coffee man?"

"Tea's fine," I said. Too much coffee set all my nerves to sounding like the Airman's bell, and I'd had enough of that at the Airman, not to mention the 'Versity.

I couldn't even count on the fingers of both hands the number of times I'd jerked to attention when the signal for class starting or ending rang out through the lecture room. It was a good thing my pupils were so blissfully unaware of everything or else they'd've seen me start for the door every time.

"Excellent," Luvander said, scampering away like an overgrown grasshopper dressed in Miranda's finest. "Tea's all I have, anyway." He disappeared into the back of his shop, hollering out to me like we were back in the air. "I hope you're all right with black tea, of course. The latest fad is all this green powder and leaves they've been bringing over the Cobalts as a gesture of goodwill, but you know—it's the funniest thing. I can't bring myself to drink it. What do you think?"

I didn't think that was so funny, myself, but that was probably me being old-fashioned again. Not willing to move on with the times and see my world changing.

"It smells like gunpowder," Luvander added, popping his head back around the corner. "Isn't that strange? Why anyone would want to drink something that looks like algae scraped off the docks and smells like the sky in wartime is beyond me. I suppose that's why I have such trouble with it. *Welcome,*" he trilled, as the bell over the door jingled merrily behind me. "It breaks my heart to tell you this, but I simply must inform you that we are actually *closed* for the evening. Please come back another time, remind me of my inhospitality, and I'll see if I can't manage a discount for you."

"Oh," said a soft little voice that hadn't hardened itself up any since I'd last heard it. "I . . . Did I get the time wrong? Or were we supposed to meet somewhere else?"

"Hey, Balfour," I said, just so he wouldn't take Luvander too seriously and let himself be chased away. "Took you long enough, but the time's still *almost* right."

"No," Luvander said, stalking out from the back and around his shop counter. "Not *Balfour.*" He came right up to the man and stared at him, eyes bulging like a dead fish's did on the chopping block. "No, you look very much like him, but I'm sorry to inform you that my friend Balfour is no longer with us. If he *was,* you see, he would have no excuse—none whatsoever—for having taken so long to come and visit my shop. And me. What a cruel prank to play on a man, especially a veteran hero of war. Entirely without taste."

"Hello, Luvander," Balfour said. He was wringing his hands a little, and I could see that he'd taken to wearing gloves again. Probably because he didn't like people staring at what currently passed for his hands—an ironic touch that didn't slip my notice. He definitely wasn't used to them yet, though I had to wonder how long it was supposed to take for a man to grow accustomed to such a strange thing. "It's a lovely shop. Really, just marvelous. The colors in the window are—"

"All right, all right, I guess you *are* Balfour after all," Luvander said, waving his hand. "Stop now before you embarrass yourself and our former Chief Sergeant. You didn't salute him, but I think he'll forgive you."

"I'm sorry," Balfour said, shooting me a pained look. "For being late, I mean. And I suppose for not . . . Did you *want* me to salute you?"

"Bastion, no," I said, shuddering at the thought. "That's all we need: for th'Esar to think we're brewing some kind of revolution in here. But just in case, you'd better lock the door, Luvander, seeing as that's all of us."

"Yes, sir," Luvander said, saluting me *just* to be a burr in my trousers. He turned the lock, and flipped the hand-painted sign in the window from *Open* to *Closed*.

I felt relieved once he'd done it, though I couldn't've said why. I wasn't the sort of man who jumped at shadows, but Royston's missing Margrave had me on edge. I'd have to ask Balfour if he knew anything about her once we'd gotten all these pleasantries out of the way, and judging by the way he'd been so quick to agree to this little tête-à-tête, it seemed like he might have some stuff to get off his chest, too.

"Is someone boiling water?" Balfour asked, interrupting my train of thought.

"The tea!" Luvander said, scampering off again into the back, and leaving the pair of us to follow in his wake.

Balfour seemed too pale by my standards, but he'd gained some weight since I'd last seen him, so he wasn't all rail and

bone and long shadows under his eyes like he'd given up living along with his hands, and I guessed that was a start. The
gloves were probably a good sign, too, since he'd always
seemed to like fussing with them before, and I definitely
caught him sneaking a peek at the lavish displays Luvander'd
set up in the corner of his shop, gloves in blue and green and
purple.

His own were navy, made of stiffer, heavier fabric, and
matched his coat.

Of all my boys, it was always Balfour who concerned me
the most. He had all the manners and donkey shit it took to
get along in the world, and he knew how to talk to people
without insulting their dicks or their wives, but he couldn't
take care of *himself* worth a damn and he'd never figured out
how or when to tell someone to take a walk off the far end of
the Mollydocks. This whole diplomacy thing was just about
the worst thing for him, as far as I could tell, since it suited
his strengths way too much and didn't challenge him to
speak his real thoughts. He'd've been better off hitching up
with Rook and Thom, or even setting sail with Ghislain.
Sure, it might've ended up with the sharks getting a special
meal of fresh Balfour meat, but somehow I didn't think so.
Ghislain would've kept his head above water if he needed the
help.

But Balfour was always surprising you. He'd even done
better than his brother, in the end. Just needed a chance to
prove that to himself.

Not that I was in the habit of comparing my riders, mind.
Every man had his own style, and so long as he could do his
job right, then the rest was none of my business. Hadn't been
any of my business when they'd brought Balfour to us in the
first place, a nice little piece of nepotism to fill the void left
by Amery. No one ever got around to asking Anastasia what
she saw in him—maybe just the family resemblance—but
the way they took to each other was more than enough to
shut the mouths of any whoreson who said she'd been forced
into accepting him. Balfour was a natural, and damned if
some days I didn't think Anastasia had picked Amery just

because she'd smelled Balfour on him, and not the other way around.

They were both good in their own ways, but Amery never would've lasted in the situation Balfour had thrust on him. He'd've cracked some heads together and ended up on trial for murder after the first day of finding piss in his boots.

Good man, Amery, but he'd had no better temperament than the dragons when you pushed him.

The back room of Luvander's shop was crammed full of fancy white boxes, rolls of ribbon, and all sorts of other packing and shipping supplies that I didn't know anything about, and that didn't interest me besides. There was a round wooden table with some chairs scattered around it, a little oven in the corner, and some kind of countertop with mugs and tins of tea littered across it. The kettle on the stove was shooting out steam.

"Do you live down here?" Balfour asked, peering around. I was just waiting until he caught sight of what I had: some kind of wooden mask about the size of half a man, carved in the image of some poor bastard's worst nightmare, with its features all twisted and its mouth wry and snarling. It was hanging on the wall above the table, so he was bound to see it eventually. It looked to me like the damn thing wanted to eat us. Why Luvander'd chosen to put it on display over his sweet little dining set was beyond me.

One of the weirdest of the whole bunch, I always said.

"I live upstairs, actually," Luvander said, busying himself with pouring the tea. "This is just where I take my meals so I can stay in the shop at lunchtime."

"Very efficient," Balfour said, before he startled suddenly and grabbed at my arm. "*Bastion!* What on earth is that?"

"Oh, Martine?" Luvander asked, shooting a glance toward the mask. "Ghislain found her on one of his expeditions and decided to bring her back for me. Well, for the shop, really. Like a housewarming gift. Or should that be shopwarming? He said she's supposed to be good luck, but I think she'd scare the customers if I left her out front. So I leave her back here, and I haven't left anything burning on the stove yet. I think she's working."

"It's . . . She's . . . *Hideous,*" Balfour said, not bothering to try for good manners on that one.

"Ghislain not around much these days?" I asked, making it sound casual.

"You know how he is," Luvander said, setting the teapot down on the table and gesturing for us to come over. "Once he sets his mind to doing something, he won't hear a word against it. He's got balls of pure dragonsteel. Of course, he won't tell me *what* he's set his mind to, but one does recognize the behavior all the same."

"You're still in touch with Ghislain?" Balfour asked, reaching out to his cup and not warming his fingers over it, the way I'd done. I guessed he didn't have to, but it was a sobering detail to take in all the same.

"We write now and then," Luvander explained, "and he drops off letters. Sometimes by pigeon. He's training them on his boat, you see."

"His boat?" I asked, at about the same time Balfour asked the same.

"Of course," Luvander replied, blinking owlishly. "He used *his* stipend to buy one, as you both know."

"Thought that was for . . ." I began, then shrugged. "Well, I can't say *what* I thought that was for, actually."

"I think he thought it was the closest thing he'd get to flying again," Luvander said, blowing on his tea to cool it. "Wind in his hair, surrounded by a great expanse of open blue all around, you know. Or maybe he always wanted to be a sailor when he was little; I didn't think to ask. Although I'd wager a lot of what he's doing—if Martine is any evidence to go by—is less like sailoring and more like pirating. Where do you even suppose they have faces like that?"

"Not where anyone's named Martine," I said.

Luvander laughed, and Balfour even smiled; I watched the latter as he touched the side of his teacup and lifted it to his mouth, the motions only a little awkward. Not to sound soft, but it made my heart ache to see him like that, and if he wasn't getting the best care th'Esar had, I'd be speaking to the man myself, crown or no.

"So, that's it, unfortunately," Luvander concluded. He gestured to a map pinned up above his sink, where a few pins had been stuck in haphazardly. "He's somewhere down by Ekklesias, by my calculations. Then again, I know absolutely *nothing* about how to calculate these things. It's very possible I'm wrong."

"How helpful of you," I said.

"Lucky that Yesfir didn't travel by sea," Balfour added.

"That's brave of you," Luvander said, looking scandalized. "Where'd you get *that* edge? Is it Arlemagne? You're going to have to tell me all about them at some point; the best gossip is *always* Arlemagne."

"I'm not really sure . . ." Balfour began, back to his old self.

The banter just served to remind me of how few of us there were; only three where there'd once been fourteen. When I thought of a meeting like this, not too chaotic, everybody present getting his turn to shove a word in edgewise, it felt like somebody walking over my future grave. Sure, there were two more out there—one of them terrifying foreign countries and one of them terrifying foreign seas—but the one terrifying foreign countries, and what he'd found while terrifying 'em, was the reason I'd called this haphazard little meeting together in the first place. Like as not, it was time to bring this meeting of Volstov's ex-airmen to order.

I cleared my throat.

"Something go down the wrong way?" Luvander asked, looking up at me slyly. "Do you need a pat on the back? I'd feel awful if you choked because of *my* tea."

"That's enough outta you, Luvander," I said. It sounded just like old times, and boy, did it feel good. Luvander bowed his head and cleared his throat and listened to me, and I stood up from the chair that was too small for me anyway, just so I could be sure I had their full attention front and center. "Got a letter from Rook and Thom a week ago," I continued. No use beating around the bush and letting them get unfocused again. I almost waited for Compagnon to giggle, then corrected myself, moving on after that a sight more quickly. "Would've come to you both sooner, except I needed

to look into things myself—exercising my rights as *ex*–Chief
Sergeant. Hope there's no complaints, or subsequent mutinies."

"Neither of us is made for leadership," Balfour assured
me. He sounded almost devious when he added, "No offense
meant, Luvander."

"And none taken, Balfour," Luvander replied blithely.

"Enough chatting," I said, and set my teacup down. "What
I learned from Thom was that, somewhere out in the desert
to the south of here, a Ke-Han magician found some way to
make Havemercy fly again." I let that sink in—Balfour in
particular looked like he was going to be sick all over the
table—then pushed on gamely. "They had enough of the
right parts to build her up like a puzzle, and they pulled some
trick to get her up and running. But she wasn't the same as
she once was, because whatever magic horseshit they did to
her fucked her up. So in answer to your question of whether
or not, right now, there's a dragon flying—there isn't. Now,
the rest doesn't make much sense to *me,* since it's not my
area of specialty. All I know is, according to this letter, an
agent for th'Esar was involved, which means we have to assume th'Esar knows about all this. He just . . . doesn't know
I know about it. *We* know about it. But what we *don't* know
is more important—what he intends to do about all this.
Could be nothing; could be something. My thoughts on the
matter are, seeing as *who* we are, we deserve to know, one
way or another. We should be in on his current proceedings."

"I wish I'd made a more soothing tea," Luvander said at
last over a very difficult silence. Balfour's fingers were precise enough that he could pinch and twist at the fabric of his
gloves, which he was doing, and Luvander, who was usually
in constant motion, was sitting as still as the statue of him
just outside. "I wish Ghislain *was* here. And Rook."

"And all the others," Balfour added pointedly, "but they
aren't. And maybe it's for the best. But, Adamo . . . May I
speak?"

I grunted. "No one's stopping you. Believe me, if I just
wanted to hear myself talk, I'd get a mirror instead of bothering you both."

Balfour looked away, gripping his cup very tightly. With hands like that, I wondered how he didn't break it. "There isn't any way for him to rebuild the corps," he explained slowly. "The magicians wouldn't allow it. It was a special allowance for Volstov during wartime, but we aren't at war anymore. And despite how . . . awkward things are with the Arlemagne, they aren't looking to be anything more than allies with us. There are currently no external threats to Volstov."

"That wouldn't stop th'Esar from making provisions," I said, "and you know it."

"I *have* felt it," Luvander said softly, then laughed. "'It'— listen to me—I really don't know what I'm saying. But I've felt *something*. I thought it was just missing people, you know, the usual this and that. Missing my darling most of all. But what if it wasn't as simple, or there's more to this than I thought?"

"No need for that kind of conjecture," I told him, putting a hand on his shoulder. "Though I know what you mean. It's a tempting thought and not *just* for th'Esar."

"I really don't know what to make of all this," Balfour murmured. He looked pretty unhappy, and I didn't blame him one whit.

"Neither do I if I'm being perfectly honest," I said. "Never asked to get a letter like that one, and I hope I never do again. Brought me nothing but indigestion and too many sleepless nights, so if you're thinking of looking to *me* for a solution to this mess, you'd be looking in the wrong place."

"But you must have some leaning, one way or another," Luvander said, sitting up a little straighter in his chair, so I could tell he was working his way up to being a cheeky bastard again. "About what we should do for ourselves—for the girls—for the others, too. For example, if I was to suggest we storm th'Esar's palace right now demanding answers and possibly some sort of financial security for milliners along the Rue, you can't tell me you'd have *nothing* to say about that."

"You'd be right," I admitted, ignoring that bit of nonsense

about his hat shop. Different men dealt with the rough shit in their own way, and nothing set Luvander at ease better than cracking wise. "Guess I know what we *shouldn't* do more than I know what we *should*. It's not a position I like any more than you, so you don't have to make that face at me."

"Sorry," Balfour said quickly, even though he wasn't the one I'd been talking to. He'd gone from worrying at his gloves to toying with his fingers, stretching the joints by pressing them against the tabletop, then pulling at each finger just slightly, like Merritt had when he'd cracked his knuckles. Balfour's knuckles didn't make any noise at all, but considering the way Proudmouth's joints had creaked when she stretched out her neck, I was glad they didn't.

"Your hands bothering you?" I asked out of the blue. I knew as I was doing it that it was the wrong move, that it'd make Balfour uncomfortable and probably Luvander, too. But I was sick of all this civilian dancing around the point and sitting on things until they became too big to ignore. That was Roy's style, not mine.

"Beg pardon?" Balfour asked, as Luvander wheeled around in his chair to look at him. "Oh! These. No, they're . . . They're fine, they just stiffen up a bit in the cold, and . . . Well, I had someone to look after them, but it seems she's got more to worry about currently than just me, so actually I've had to see the Esar about a replacement."

"You've met with th'Esar?" I asked, trying not to get ahead of myself. "Recently?"

"Why do I get the feeling I'm being left out *simply* because I'm the only working-class man among a professor and a diplomat?" Luvander asked, while Balfour looked between us like a mouse trying to decide whether he wanted to take his chances with the cat or the barn owl.

"It wasn't anything, not really," Balfour said, his hands falling still. "At least, it didn't turn out to be anything, though as you both know, when the Esar calls a man, he *does* worry. The whole experience was actually just . . . strange."

I folded my arms over my chest, not interrupting; even Luvander looked rapt because this was probably better than all the best gossip he'd heard in weeks.

With nobody to interrupt him, Balfour hesitated, then pressed on. "I received a summons while I was at the bastion, complete with a carriage and no explanation other than that the Esar needed to see me. It reminded me so much of when Rook . . . Anyway, I arrived there and—well, I suppose the first thing you should know is that I think he's been firing his servants. There was barely anyone in the palace proper. He doesn't trust the people around him, at least not to perform the same duties they once did, seeing as my escort into the audience chamber was the Esarina herself. *She* said it was because we were going to be discussing things of a sensitive nature, and the less other people knew about our meeting, the better, which I thought sounded a lot like the last thing a man hears before he's carted off to some nameless prison to spend the rest of his days. But somehow—fortunately— it didn't turn out like that."

"So what *did* he want?" Luvander asked, leaning so far forward in his chair that I was sure he'd topple out of it at any moment.

"He wanted to talk to me about my hands," Balfour said, staring at the table. I expected that was because he found it easier than staring at either of us. "He just . . . wanted to talk. He asked if they *obeyed* me, or if I'd been having any trouble with them. I told him that the most trouble I'd had was the attending magician up and vanishing, the same as I told you only more polite, and he told me he'd assign a replacement. After that he had nothing further to say, and so I was sent home."

"Sounds like there's something you're not telling us. No, that's not how I want to put it," I corrected myself, before Balfour's face could seize up in hurt. "It sounds like there's a missing piece to the story that maybe *you* don't know even though you were there. When you think about it, getting the Esarina involved, that's a whole lot of secrecy to talk about something that might just as well be common knowledge for everyone in Thremedon. You've got those hands. Nothing to be ashamed of, anyway."

Balfour caught himself before he pulled them off the table and folded them, awkward and stiff, one on top of the other.

"They sing songs about you in lower Charlotte, you know," Luvander said, scratching behind his ear. He probably thought that was going to be comforting. "'Balfour Steelhands,' they call you. You wouldn't know, what with being so busy you never visit, but they do. Though sometimes, in the verses, it's not your *hands* that are made of steel. But I assure you, all versions are extremely complimentary to your manhood."

Balfour colored up to his ears. "I don't know what to say," he murmured.

"Don't have to say anything," Luvander replied. "But if you *did* come to visit, you'd never be lonely. That I *can* tell you."

"Luvander," I warned. I could look out for the runt of the litter now because this wasn't wartime and he wouldn't get it even worse from the boys once I turned my back.

Balfour rubbed his thumb against the tabletop. "I suppose my visit with the Esar might have coincided with his receiving news about what happened with Rook and Thom," he said, still not looking at all comforted by the idea that someone out there might or might not've been composing a ditty to his balls. "My hands are made with the same principles in mind as the dragons, I'm told, even if they're not precisely the same materials. I suppose in some ways it was an experiment, since to my knowledge it was the first time they'd ever attempted to create something on this scale, hands being so much smaller, after all. I don't even know how they *work*," he added, with a faint little smile. "Trust Thom to figure it out, though."

"I don't like it," I said, reaching down to take a sip of my tea, mostly lukewarm by now, and all the leaves swirling around in the bottom like a bad omen. "Sounds to me like *someone's* trying to squeeze all the information outta one end without giving anything back, like he thinks he can get our help, then just shut us out of whatever he's planning."

"We don't know he's planning anything," Luvander pointed out, his finger tracing over the pattern on his cup, gold leaf and green. It looked like the kind of thing that might've found its way to Thremedon on a pirate ship, maybe one captained by a mutual acquaintance, but I wasn't about to ask and derail the whole conversation. "You know whose side I fall on should the situation warrant taking sides at all. But I just feel compelled—as a sensitive and sensible-minded creature—to remind you two headstrong louts that, *technically* speaking, we have no proof of anything. We have good common sense, and our instincts are a sight better than anyone else's given word these days, but I believe that for the time being, the safest course of action would be to keep open minds. And perhaps more importantly, we keep our eyes open, as well."

I shifted impatiently, like my girl when I'd told her we had a long night ahead of us, but I knew Luvander was right. I knew *we* were right, too, about th'Esar having something up his ermine sleeve, but moving without proof too soon might mean we'd never get another chance later.

I just couldn't stop thinking about Proudmouth and the others, or what Rook must've seen there in the desert. If th'Esar was thinking he could get someone else to fly my girl . . .

"I'm not good at sitting around on my ass when there's work to be done," I said finally, the sound of my own voice drowning out too much heavy thinking. "I'll be the first to admit it."

Balfour let out a chuckle, then promptly looked horrified when we both looked around at him at the same time, like he hadn't realized we could hear him.

"I'm sorry," he said, still smiling, "that wasn't—I wasn't laughing at you at all. I was just thinking that so much of diplomacy *is* sitting around and waiting to take action. I believe I've inadvertently been training for something like this all along."

"You'll have to share your secrets," I told him, just a little proud in the midst of being irritated as a mule in fly season.

"I think I'll write to Ghislain," Luvander pitched in, tapping his index finger against the table. "I'd been meaning to do it anyway, and this seems like the sort of thing he'd want to be here for. Of course, I haven't any idea where he is or how long it'd take him to haul up the anchor and sail home, but it's worth a shot, isn't it? Who knows where the winds will take him."

"About putting all that stuff in a letter," I started, being sensitive about that particular way of conveying information.

Luvander scoffed, pushing his chair back from the table with a loud scrape. "If *that* was the only way I had of getting Ghislain to come back to Thremedon, do you think I'd ever see him at all? I have considerably more wiles in my arsenal than you give me credit for. I'm going to tell him that Balfour is taking regular meetings with the Esarina and I *think* that they're carrying on an affair, but I need him to come back so we can squeeze the information out of him properly. Can't do that without one man to hold and the other to tickle."

Balfour blanched, the smile wiped clean from his face. I'd caught the boys doing that to him once, though I'd put a stop to it by telling them they were acting like schoolboys in love. At least, that particular torture was ended, anyway.

"Don't you think that might also be considered . . . well, *slightly* provocative information, if someone else should open the letter?" Balfour finally asked.

"You're confusing gossip with treason," Luvander said, tugging his scarf up again. "When people read about an affair, the first thing they do is tell their neighbor, *not* th'Esar. And who wants to be the one to tell th'Esar his wife's been stepping out on him with a younger man? No, thank you! But, if it makes you feel better, I won't use your name."

"Oh, *much* better," Balfour said, with a hint of the brand-new edge he'd shown us earlier.

"Ghislain or no," I said, steering the conversation back around with as much difficulty as I've ever had with Proudmouth when the sky started getting fire-crazy, "we sit on this until th'Esar gives us reason to do otherwise. We keep our eyes open, Luvander rakes in all the gossip, and we don't do anything stupid. At least not straightaway. Agreed?"

"Of course," Luvander agreed, as Balfour nodded beside

him. "In strict confidence, I'm more concerned with what comes after that point."

To be honest, so was I.

TOVERRE

As much as I loathed the entire concept of a physician's checkup—and I did, with both body and soul—I was beginning to feel that there was some personal slight in their choosing to overlook me. I'd had an initial appointment along with several other members of our dormitory floor, but they hadn't even so much as drawn my blood! Rather I'd merely been asked about my medical history and summarily sent on my way. If that was to be the standard of care for those of us at the 'Versity, I was going to be sorely disappointed. It was practically no better than home.

Gaeth had been to at least two by my count, and Laure had returned from *her* first last week, only to be summoned back almost immediately.

"They probably just want to give me my blood back," she'd told me, the image very nearly making me sick. "I'll keep it in a little locket, like a lover's trinket."

All these trips to the physician were leaving me on my own with nothing to do and no one to talk to. I'd given up my trips along the Rue to follow Hal—that affair, it seemed, was doomed before it ever began—and Gaeth was as elusive as marsh fog, which had always disappointed me as a child for its ability to disappear right when you thought you'd caught up to it. I'd stopped by his room on multiple occasions to try to return the gloves he'd given me—surely his "mam" was suffering from very cold hands indeed, by now—but every time I'd knocked, there had only been silence. I'd even had Laure try it once or twice, so I knew he wasn't avoiding me.

In the absence of her *and* Gaeth, there was no one in the first-year dormitory building who warranted any real or prolonged conversation, and not just because none of them seemed interested in talking to me.

If Laure was sick, then I was going to have to write home to my mother for reinforcements just to make sure she was taking care of herself properly. My Laure was the kind of person who'd walk outside in a snowstorm when she was running a fever just to cool down a bit, and she'd end up winning a few snowball fights with the local farmhands in the meantime just because she didn't like staying indoors.

I looked out the window and cast my gaze onto the all-too-familiar and now-quite-dreary sight of the 'Versity Stretch in awful, never-ending winter. It was going to either snow or rain, because gray clouds had gathered above the buildings, casting everything in a miserable light. On the street below, men and women were hurrying to get their business over with before the storm began.

I did hope Laure wasn't caught in it on her way back.

She never took an umbrella with her anywhere she went, much less a parasol, and her new coat would be absolutely soaked in a winter storm. My father and *her* father would both be very distressed indeed if I failed to protect my fiancée from the dangers of city life—even though I'd been doing my best with what little I could, and, though they didn't know this, it was more often Laure who protected me than the other way around.

Lost in my idle thoughts, I didn't hear the knock on the door—at least, I assumed there must have been one I missed—as a moment later Laure burst into the room, hair frazzled and coat undone.

"Don't feel well," she said.

A moment after that, she was sick all over my floor.

In the chaos that followed I managed, most bravely, to keep my wits about me. Nor did I panic, though I wanted to. I moved as in some kind of dream—or some kind of nightmare—guiding Laure from the doorway to my bed, avoiding the site of the mess completely.

I knew, of course, that no one who worked in the building would come to help me clean any of this up because in this place no one ever saw fit to clean anything. It was a losing battle, one that would require constant work and round-the-clock vigilance, and we were only simple students. It was up to me to make this better, as quickly and as quietly as possible.

I didn't want to make Laure feel bad for having done it, now did I? Nor did I want any of it seeping into the floorboards.

Laure curled up in my bed and I closed the door, leaning back against it to gather my strength. Then I put on my two oldest pairs of gloves, one on top of the other—one couldn't be too careful when it came to this sort of thing—and began to clean the floor with a mop and bucket I'd bought from the local bits-and-bats shop on the corner, for exactly this kind of unforeseen tragedy.

"Sorry 'bout the mess," Laure moaned from the bed.

I closed my eyes, resigning myself to opening a window—for the smell, of course—which would let all the cold air in. And it was nearly impossible to build up any kind of warmth in my room, especially after the sun set.

"Don't think about it for a second longer," I said, trying to sound soothing and instead sounding strained. "You aren't feeling well. What did the physicians say? Please take my mind off this awful task."

"Didn't say anything," Laure replied. I heard her shifting in the bed, and when I looked back at her, she'd pulled the covers up over her head. The rest of her reply came out muffled, and I had to strain to hear it. "Didn't tell me I was sick or anything, just sent me on my way and told me to come back next week."

"What incompetents," I said, feeling extremely indignant. "I'll . . . I'll write to your father at once."

"Bastion, Toverre, don't do that," Laure replied. "I don't want him worrying for nothing, or thinking I can't take care of myself."

"Nonsense," I said. "This is hardly nothing."

"Just felt a little dizzy, that's all," Laure insisted. "Bet I don't even have a fever."

With great care, I peeled my gloves off my hands and dropped them into the bucket, along with the rest of the mess I'd managed to clean up. It was all garbage now; I could never look at them again, much less wear them, without being reminded of this awful event. I crossed the room to open the window by the bed just a bare inch, then sat down on the mattress beside Laure, hesitating before I peeled the blanket back.

Her face was flushed, her eyes bright. She looked for all the world as though she'd caught whatever fever Gaeth had been suffering from when last we'd met him. Which, bastion help us all, meant I was bound to catch it next.

I pressed the back of my hand against her brow the way my mother had when I was sick—and I'd been a sickly child, suffering every winter for months without fail. If I was to become ill with this disease, then I'd likely caught it already, and there was no further use in being careful. Besides which, Laure's health was currently more important. She was the one who was suffering.

"You most certainly *do* have a fever," I told her. I managed to gentle myself, as I knew—sometimes—my attitude was what some might consider abrasive. "Is there anything I can get for you? A glass of water, perhaps?"

"Sure," Laure said. "But get that bucket of my stink out of here first. I know you're dying to."

"Dying" being the operative word, I thought but didn't say, as that would have been cruel. Laure was rarely ever sick— I could only remember her having a fever *once,* and we'd known each other practically since birth. It must have been very awful indeed if it managed to catch *her* unawares.

"I'll be right back," I told her, patting her on the shoulder. I cleverly fashioned a mask for myself out of one of her scarves; I also took her gloves, so that I could permit myself to touch the handle of the bucket.

It swayed sickeningly when I picked it up, and I kept my eyes fixed resolutely ahead of me, so that I would not be drawn in by morbid fascination and accidentally look down. This was the stuff of which nightmares were made. I had no desire to torture myself further than I was already being tortured.

To my great relief, the hall in the first-year dormitory was blessedly empty of my raucous peers, each under the impression that his or her importance lay in direct correlation with how much noise they were able to make. While I was attempting to study, or while I was attempting to *sleep,* no one else's comfort seemed to matter much to my fellow dorm mates. Not when they could organize a rousing indoor ball game, with the corridors as grounds, and kicking the ball up the staircases the ultimate goal. Laure thought it good fun, but the first time I'd opened my door to see what all the commotion was, I'd been hit in the head with the puffed-up leather balloon, which was generally how these games always ended—or apparently began—for someone like me.

When all their fun was brought to an end by the inevitable broken neck, I could only hope that the 'Versity authorities would see an opportunity to take the matter in hand. Until then, I would have to suffer bravely through the noise of a leather ball smacking against the walls and sometimes even my door at all hours of the day *and* night.

The temptation to find the bastion-blasted thing and puncture it with a knife was beginning to overwhelm me. I made it down the stairs and to the disposal unit around back without becoming ill, though I tossed the bucket into the garbage whole, choosing to forgo the more thrifty approach of dumping the contents out and keeping the apparatus itself for further use. There was another bucket in my room, which I used to store my cleaning supplies, and if Laure found herself in dire need, I would simply have to sacrifice it to the greater good.

One could always buy another bucket.

On my way to her room, I found myself walking by Gaeth's door—he was two rooms away from mine, the one just above Laure's. I moved past it, then stopped and retraced my steps, staring at the number by the knob.

In addition to his curious elusiveness within the dormitory halls, I hadn't seen him attending lectures alongside the rest of the crowd in at least two days. It was possible that, in certain lectures, my ill-advised infatuation with Hal had given me a kind of tunnel vision, blocking out all distractions for the purpose of my private study, but Gaeth wasn't the easiest person to miss. In fact, he rather stuck out from the crowd though not always for reasons that were particularly flattering. As much as I'd tried to stop myself from noticing him, I'd found it to be a nearly insurmountable task. Since I'd never had such trouble with my focus before, I was forced to assume that it had something to do with *him*. Some stubborn flaw in his nature that was affecting me poorly, like a winter's wind stripping the paint from a house.

He'd had this fever—though mercifully, he'd never vomited in my presence—and as such, he might have some helpful information, perhaps as to what balms would soothe Laure's symptoms and whether there was any medicine I needed to purchase for her at the apothecary to bring the fever down. I'd even have settled for a rough estimation of how *much* vomiting I could expect, if only because I was going to run out of buckets very shortly and would have to purchase more before the shops all closed for the night.

If only another trash pail had been what was jammed into my chimney flue, I thought. It would have made life seem considerably less cruel and random, if only for a moment.

Despite the rising sense of futility I was beginning to associate with dormitory life, I tugged Laure's scarf down from my face and knocked sharply on Gaeth's door. For added effect, I imagined I was rapping on his head. For all his good manners, he didn't seem to understand how rude it was to make someone worry after you this way.

Nothing but silence greeted me.

I even leaned in, as close as I could manage without actually allowing the old door with its gray, flaking paint to touch my cheek. Something creaked, but it was only the stairwell behind me moaning from all its regular abuse. After I'd counted to ten—forward *and* backward—I decided I'd been quite generous enough with my time.

"Ho, Laure's friend," someone called from behind me.

It was a girl, coming up the stairs, and a boy behind her, both of them dark-haired and dressed for walking in the cold. They were carrying shopping bags and had—for reasons that

I couldn't possibly fathom—chosen to engage me instead of passing me by to reach their respective lodgings.

"Are you looking for Gaeth?" the girl asked. It was she who'd called out to me, which was odd, since I hadn't been aware Laure had been cultivating any female friendships. She usually had difficulties with that; they were so often jealous of her attributes.

"Just thought I'd see if he was in," I explained, experiencing a slight moment of panic. I had to fetch Laure's water and give it to her, then head to the apothecary and write to Mother—and what was more, I was certain that I had nothing at all to say to these people, who clearly didn't even know me by name. Idle conversation would be a waste of time, and an awkward one.

"He hasn't been in for *days*," the boy said, scratching his head underneath the wool cap he wore. His hair poked out from under the brim in stiff peaks. "Been looking for him to get a bit of a ball game going, but I haven't been able to find him. Not in the morning *or* at night, which just seems rude, don't it?"

"Maybe he has a girlfriend in the city," the girl said, tugging at the boy's scarf. It seemed a very stupid suggestion to me, but I thought of Laure and their friendship and managed to keep my mouth firmly shut.

"Not likely," the boy snorted. He looked past me toward Gaeth's door and shrugged. "Bet he went home or something. Couldn't take the city. All those fevers, all the time. You wouldn't *think* a guy with that many physicians' appointments would end up sick, but there ya go. Thought he'd last a little longer, but I guess I was wrong."

"Oh, *don't* talk about it. I've got mine next week," the girl said, shivering dramatically for her companion's sake. He stepped closer to her. If he hadn't been carrying so many bags, I would have wagered he'd have put an arm around her, as well.

"It's just a little needle," the boy said, shaking his head.

"It is really very large," I blurted out, because it seemed like the proper time for a contribution to the conversation.

"It's not that bad," the boy said.

"He says that, but he fainted *clean away* once he got back to the dorms," the girl confided in me, lowering her voice, even though it was impossible to imagine he wouldn't overhear her. "I couldn't wake him up at all until dinner."

"Did he vomit?" I asked.

The girl shook her head. "But he looked like he was going to."

"That's enough outta you," the boy said, scowling and starting off down the hall once again, dragging his friend along with him. "Lemme know if you see Gaeth, though. Tell him the sides are all uneven without him and Thib's looking for him. Okay?"

"I shall certainly do so," I assured him, offering a small wave.

Under different circumstances, I'd have returned to Laure *immediately* to tell her of my adventure in the hall, but with matters currently as they were, I first retreated to the kitchens to pour her a cold glass of water.

My conversation with the couple in the hall had left me feeling uneasy, for reasons I couldn't quite place. My worry for Laure—not to mention cleaning up her mess—had jolted my mood off center, but I found myself thinking of other things, ones that had nothing at all to do with Laure: Gaeth's vague, preoccupied air when we'd met him in the Amazement; his apparent return home to the country; and the girl's tale of not being able to rouse her friend once he'd arrived back at the dormitory from his own appointment.

That line of thinking did lead back to Laure, since her sudden illness coincided with her return from the physician. I knew a great deal about fevers simply from having suffered through more than my share, and it seemed impossible to me that Laure's physicians wouldn't have noticed anything out of the ordinary with her during either of her visits.

Perhaps the city physicians were—as my father had put it before we left—incompetent jackasses, like every other jacked-up charlatan living in the city, but I was unwilling to subscribe to my father's beliefs just yet. Not even my doctors in the countryside had ever done so much harm, and they still subscribed to the outdated belief that leeches could actually cure a man of his *cough*.

My room was cold when I returned, but at least the smell seemed to have dissipated somewhat. I could see a cloud of red hair above the blankets that indicated Laure hadn't moved at all since I'd left her. I set her water down on the bedside table and moved quickly to close the window, since despite how she might have felt about it, bracing herself in winter air was *not* what her constitution required.

The window made rather a loud noise when I closed it, and I heard the rustle of the covers as she began to stir beneath them.

"Toverre?" she rasped, sounding a great deal like my great-aunt Bernadette, who'd smoked clove cigarettes for much of her youth.

"I am here at last," I told her, turning the lock on the window and making sure it caught before I returned to her side. "And I've brought water, just like I promised."

"M'mouth tastes like pig slop," Laure said, and she pulled the covers down enough for me to see her bright red face. "I probably *look* like pig slop, too. Don't even look at me. Don't tell me if I do."

"You have never looked like pig slop," I said, holding out the water and helping her to sit up. "Not even when you were actually covered in it."

Laure leaned on me instead of the headboard as I held the cup to her lips. Some of it spilled onto my blankets, but at least it was only water. If she was sick in my bed, now that would be a different matter.

"'M sorry about making you clean all that up," Laure mumbled, after she'd had something to drink. "Thought for sure you weren't coming back. You'd gone off to scrub yourself clean, or something, then ask for a change of rooms because this one's no good anymore."

"I'll do all that later," I assured her. "I'll get clean eventually. With a steel brush and everything."

"I *hate* being sick," Laure said, leaning her head on my shoulder.

"I'm sure it will pass quite soon," I told her, stroking her hair with my free hand. "And at your next physician's appointment—to which I will accompany you—you will beat the attending severely around the head for allowing you to leave in this state."

Laure chuckled, then let out a small sigh. "You know," she said, "they didn't even give me my blood back. I *wanted* it, too, because it doesn't do to have it running around out there without me. *They* said they were sorry, but that wasn't possible. Well 's my blood, isn't it? That's like stealing."

"You're delirious," I told her, gently patting her head. "Get some sleep, and we'll talk about everything in the morning."

"Can't sleep *here*," Laure said. She hid an overly scandalized gasp behind a clumped-up handful of coverlet. "What will everyone say? What will they *think*?"

"Now," I said, trying to be reasonable, though I did realize it would injure both our prospects if people were to think we were engaged in *that* kind of behavior together. "I'll tell everyone you were sick, and there's no need to worry—no one would believe someone like you would ever spend that . . . kind of night with someone like *me,* anyway."

"But we're going to be married," Laure said. "We're going to have to spend that kind of a night together someday."

Laure had a fever, I told myself, and could not possibly know she was bringing up such a delicate subject. If I was lucky, she wouldn't remember having asked it at all, and I could also put the difficulty right out of my mind.

Truth be told, I had worried about the same matter myself enough times in the past. Our families would be expecting additions to the fold, little boys and girls they could train better than they'd trained me, and I shuddered at the idea.

"You're grimacing," Laure said. "I'm talking about sleeping with you, and you're grimacing. Makes a girl feel . . . Makes a girl feel . . ."

"That's just the fever talking," I said, tucking her in. "Don't worry about your work; I'll see to it. And we'll worry about all the rest in the morning."

"Grimacing," Laure mumbled, but she buried her face

against the pillow and burrowed in deep. I had a long night ahead of me, finishing up one of her essays—she probably hadn't even started it yet—and sleeping in the chair beside her, in case she needed anything.

I checked to make sure she was sleeping soundly, which she was, then went to gather the books I needed. My thoughts were troubling me, but until Laure was in a more lucid state, I would have to shelve them. And what better way to avoid thinking than by composing an essay?

BALFOUR

I'd started the letter at least ten times already and scrapped just as many pieces of paper since. No matter how I phrased it, the words sounded too needful—as though I somehow didn't realize Thom had troubles of his own to deal with on his travels, and with him so far from the city, there was nothing in particular he could even do for me.

It was just my luck to find someone at last in whom I felt comfortable confiding, only to see him leave Thremedon almost immediately after we'd been introduced. If it hadn't been so sad, it would have made an excellent joke.

Dear Thom, my current missive read, *I really would appreciate your advice . . .*

But that was too abrupt, I thought, without any mention of his health, or Rook's health, or how they were both holding up after their unexpected and nearly fatal adventure. I crumpled the eleventh page swiftly and tossed it into the corner with the rest of them, then pinched my brow too hard with my clumsy fingers.

Since we were friends, I tried to reason with myself, a simple task like this one really shouldn't have been so difficult. He overthought things himself, to some extent—one of the many points of personality on which we came together— but he did manage to write letters despite it, asking for help or simply wishing to hear my opinion on matters both important and trivial. His latest letter, however, had made all my little woes seem relatively insignificant, and I hadn't known how to reply to him.

Until now—now that I needed something.

It seemed greedy to me, like some fatal flaw in my manners, but I had no one else to speak to.

Dear Thom, I tried again, holding the pen stiffly. *I heard from Luvander yesterday that there is a song in the bars of lower Charlotte dedicated to my hands, but also, to my ba . . .*

That was completely ridiculous, I told myself, and tore that one up before I tossed it, so no one going through the garbage might be able to read it.

In warmer weather, I'd confided in the statues, like the old tale of a lonely boy whispering all his problems into a hole in the ground.

The crowds around the memorial generally left at night, and I was able to lean against the sturdy foot of Jeannot or Compagnon and tell them, without feeling as though I were in some way complaining, that my wrists pained me, and that the metal was cold—although I did conclude all my confessions with an apology. It seemed rude to complain to dead men that my situation while living was troubling me, since I had the very good luck of still being alive. Apparently, though everyone believed differently, it seemed that I had *no* manners to speak of whatsoever when it came to dealing with my friends, former or current.

It was a thought that gave me much unrest. Adamo would've been quite disappointed if he'd known.

But it was too cold for that kind of trip now, especially with my hands in their current state. And anyway, the more I did it, the more foolish I felt. These men were gone, and they'd left their petty problems behind them when they left. I had no place burdening them with mine where others came with gifts, flower wreaths, and the like. Had I no real respect for the dead?

There'd also been a chance I'd have run into Adamo or Luvander while lingering at the site, and I'd wanted to avoid that at all costs—and the questions concerning my health especially. What answer should I have given them? Perhaps simply showing them what remained of me would be enough, but I couldn't bear the idea of their pity.

I much preferred Luvander's gossip and his jokes, as though nothing at all had changed. Uncomfortable as they might have made me, the discomfort was at least a familiar one.

Dear Thom, I began again, *I wonder if you might be amused by the promise that upon your return to Thremedon, I will invite you to accompany me to lower Charlotte, so that we may learn the tune to the song praising my genitals and sing it together as a welcome-home present.*

At least this false start made me laugh. It even brought a few tears to my eyes.

If my current accommodations had come with a fireplace, it would have been getting an awful lot of fuel tonight. My mind was just too distracted to compose a letter though I knew the reasons for *that* well enough. My thoughts were currently in a turmoil I couldn't conceive of putting into a letter, even if it was Thom who'd written about the matter first, to Adamo. He, at least, had the excuse of being far away from home, adventuring through the desert with only Rook's moods to worry about. I didn't blame him for being rash. He'd probably thought that the information was important enough to risk everyone's getting into a little trouble, and in strictest truth there *was* nothing illegal about what he'd sent.

By the way Adamo told it, Thom's story had been a recounting of a very sad and disturbing experience that had begun and ended in the desert. But it did make me wonder how Rook had been able to deal with everything—he'd *been* there, right in the thick of it, seeing a resurrection none of us had thought possible. While I knew I would never be able to extract anything from him that resembled the truth of his feelings on the matter, I felt like I surely had some idea—the hope and longing, and eventual despair, he'd felt.

Like it or not, we'd all been tarred with the same brush, and now we were connected in ways I didn't think any of us had ever considered before.

Privately, it made me wonder what I might've done had I

been in Rook's place at the time. Certainly I felt the twinge—the same as any man might have—at the promise of being given back someone I'd thought lost forever. But, just like Rook, neither did I believe in that kind of easy solution.

The Esar was a different matter. He'd never been close to the dragons, as we were. They'd been weapons to him, and nothing more.

Adamo and Luvander had both seemed willing to bet that the Esar wouldn't experience my misgivings, and however much I tried to look at it in a different way, I was beginning to share their opinion. My meeting at the palace seemed all too suspicious in the light of Thom's information—though what it meant for Margrave Ginette and the fate of my hands, I'd been too stubborn to bring up at the meeting. There was more to be discussed than my problems, which affected no one *other* than me.

I was suffering for it, though, my hands too stiff to write another letter even if I'd wanted to. I could still move them enough to accomplish all my daily tasks, but the result was stiffness quite similar to that suffered by my extremely arthritic grandfather, and it made me self-conscious to be seen in public.

The clumsiness, too, might have had some part in my frustration. I could no longer write quickly enough to keep up with my thoughts, and the cramps in my wrists shot all the way up my arms to the elbows.

Even though I'd stopped writing, my hand was still firmly wrapped around the pen, and I knew that I'd have to use the other to pry it off. It was becoming inconvenient, not to mention painful, and I had to check the date again just to make sure I hadn't gotten it wrong.

Some help was coming, at long last.

With timing that could only be called ironic—or impeccable—it had been only after my meeting with the remnants of the Dragon Corps that the Esar had finally contacted me. His letter—to which I hadn't even been able to reply—informed me that he'd set up an appointment for me with one of the *finest* magicians for technical work, his own personal recommendation, and I must accept his apologies for not arranging something sooner but he'd been quite busy with this and that.

I'd been relieved just to realize that his letter had nothing at all to do with my shadowy meeting of peers. *That* was an act the Esar was bound to find suspicious if his present state of mind was as bad as some seemed to believe.

All this living while constantly looking over my shoulder *did* remind me, in some ways, of what it'd been like at the Airman, but it had all of the downsides with none of the brief, momentary upswings that had come alongside it. And, what was worse, Ghislain was not there to stand sentinel at the door.

Knowing that a man like that was keeping watch helped me sleep more deeply at night. I pitied whatever poor pirates crossed paths with him and wondered if they'd be singing about *those* exploits in Charlotte soon enough.

The knock at the door startled me out of any further brooding thoughts I might've had, and I willed my fingers to flex with such force that I heard the metal creak in protest. This appointment was coming none too soon—for me *or* them.

I took the gloves from my desk and struggled with getting them on before I answered the door, while my visitor knocked impatiently for the second time.

They could wait, I thought stubbornly. The last thing I needed was for my hands to be seen by anyone other than a Margrave in *this* state. It reflected poorly on Ginette's work, not to mention how I felt about them personally. Not everyone needed to know my private suffering—not even when it appeared to have become a matter of state.

"Good afternoon," said the man in the Esar's uniform who awaited me, tipping his hat. "Sorry for making you wait. I got all turned around by the Basquiat, then couldn't seem to straighten things out. I've got it now, though. All filed away in my head. Once I take a route, I *know* it. Like the back of my hand," he added, showing me the hand in question. It was pink and chapped with cold, a little split around the thumbnail.

"That's quite all right," I said quickly, pulling on my coat and pressing *my* hands into the pockets. It was to keep them warm as much as it was to hide them. "Is the appointed place very far from here?"

"Won't take us all day, if that's what you're asking," the man said, glancing at me curiously. "You *are* him, right? Steelhands—no offense meant, that's just what they call you in my part of town. I mean, we all heard what happened in the war, but I never . . . None of us up at the palace could even agree about what they'd look like, let alone how something like that'd even work."

"They work very poorly at the moment," I told him, being somewhat short because of how uncomfortable the question made me. Though some of my comrades in the corps had always gone out of their way to be at the center of attention at all times, such scrutiny made me twitch. The tavern songs a drunken mind composed in the dead of night were one thing, but I'd never wished to be famous in the first place, let alone for something I hadn't even *done.*

"Right. Like I said, no offense meant," the driver told me, stepping back so that I could lock the door and follow him down the stairs. He seemed appropriately sheepish, but I was too distracted even to apologize to him.

Dear Thom, I began composing mentally, as I got into the carriage and the driver hopped up on top. *Today I took out my bad mood on someone who made the mistake of trying to engage me in friendly conversation. I doubt it's a mistake he'll be making again anytime soon, and if word spreads of my behavior, I'm sure you'll hear tales of Balfour the Terrible— worse than any dragon—as far as you've traveled. Wherever that place may be.*

The journey passed quickly enough, me writing my imaginary letters and the driver no doubt working out the best way to tell his friends that Balfour Steelhands was a rude little bastard.

It was possible that I was exaggerating, but the stiffness in my hands left me little room for optimism.

I was so lost in my own thoughts that I didn't follow the narrow twists and turns of the streets as we rode through Thremedon—something none of my old friends would have ever allowed—and when the carriage began slowing to a halt, I realized that we were actually back at the palace, though not at the entrance I'd taken last time. The more I looked at it, I realized I'd never seen the palace from behind, and though the shape of the building was unmistakable, I wondered at being allowed to use this entrance, which clearly wasn't meant for the common visitor.

They'd built walls to cordon off the area for a reason—to keep almost everyone *out*—and I marveled at how the gilding around the minarets was faded from the salty wind, and the colors of the turrets seemed somehow less bright.

"Not much to look at, is it?" my driver asked in a low whisper. "That's 'cause the good parts face the rest of the city; but in the back here, it's all shadow."

I'd have to tell Thom about this, I thought, if I could ever manage to write a decent letter again.

There was a woman waiting for me at the door, so that I couldn't very well hang back and ask the driver where in bastion's name he'd taken me. I'd already made enough bad first impressions for one day, surely.

"Good day to you," the driver called after me, taking his hands off the reins to give me a wave-off. "Good luck with them hands. Do wish I'd got a chance to see 'em, though!"

"Perhaps next time," I told him, left with a strange feeling of abandonment as he rode off around the side of the palace, the carriage soon obscured by the wall and a group of ornamental trees.

There was nothing left but to approach the woman, who looked more like a physician than a magician to me, but then, I was hardly an expert. She had a kindly look about her though her attitude was brusque, and she was holding a clipboard with various notes and pieces of paper pinned to it. A pair of spectacles perched on her nose, dwarfed almost comically by her broad face.

"Hello," she said, not holding out her hand—a small fact for which I was incredibly grateful. "My apologies if any of this runaround is an inconvenience for you, but I don't have the same private collection of supplies as my predecessor, and all the best materials *are* here at the palace."

"I'm Balfour. Balfour Vallet," I told her, bowing just slightly. "And I'm glad to meet wherever you feel most comfortable working."

She smiled at that, approval plain on her face. "I'm so glad to hear that, Balfour," she said, stepping aside to welcome me in. "Please, follow me."

CHAPTER SIX

LAURE

When I finally awoke, I felt like I'd been dragged behind my da's plow for a full day during harvest. All my muscles were aching, and my eyes didn't much appreciate all the sudden light, but it was still better than the way I'd felt the day before, because at least I felt like myself—mashed or no.

The worst part had been that voice I was hearing. I couldn't tell Toverre about it because he'd've assumed I'd gone crazy, and I'd wake up after the fever'd passed in some kind of institution, arms bound up so I couldn't hurt myself. But the voice had definitely been there, seeming more real than just a simple hallucination. It sounded like a low whisper, sliding right between my temples—the kind of voice you'd expect a cat would have. And there was a part of it that made me think of fire and metal, too—a distant clang like those that came from the blacksmith's workshop back home.

Thinking about it, while I lay in bed and waited for my head to stop pounding, sure did make me feel crazy. Maybe I deserved to be in an institution, after all.

Must've been a bad fever, in any case; I was sweating like a racehorse now that I was awake. The sweat was cold and sticky, and I was tangled up in so many blankets I thought I was going to melt.

It took a lot of concentration, but I finally got my limbs to move. In a burst of inspiration, I shoved all the covers off me and onto the floor, though one was tangled around my leg and it almost took me down with it.

"Oh, how marvelous," Toverre said beside me, his voice a little too loud for my headache to bear. "In thanks for my hospitality, you throw all my covers onto the floor. Well, I suppose I'd have needed to wash them anyway. *Still,* Laure, I . . ."

He paused, and I wished I could open my eyes just a crack so I could get a peek at him. But I wasn't ready yet—maybe in a minute—so I just turned my face toward the sound of his voice, hoping it looked like I was paying attention. "Huh?" I asked, quite elegantly.

"I see you *are* feeling better," Toverre muttered stiffly. "Just as eloquent as always. You really should never allow yourself to be sick like that, Laure. It is *so* unseemly."

I guessed that meant he'd been worried, so I tried not to get angry at him for being so rude. I also remembered what I'd done—right there, in his room, on his clean floor—and it was hard to be mad at him at all, especially because I *couldn't* remember him yelling at me for it.

"Nngh," I said. I had to clear an enormous, raspy frog out of my throat before I could manage actually talking, but at least I refrained from spitting something gross onto his floor. "Didn't mean to worry you, Toverre."

"You have a hardy constitution," Toverre replied, sounding brusque. "At no point did I believe you were anything other than . . . mildly incapacitated. You were mumbling in your sleep, however, and you missed your lecture today, which means you're going to have to speak with *both* the professors. Are you hungry? I brought you some clear broth."

"Whoa," I said, like I was soothing a spooked foal. "Slow down for a moment, let me make sure I've got all that."

"I merely wanted to answer all possible questions you might have," Toverre said. "Also, it seems your friend Gaeth is missing. I thought that perhaps the fever—*this* fever—was so bad it sent him home. I wrote your father—"

"Oh, shit, Toverre," I said, finally opening my eyes; I had to shield them with my hands, because he'd opened the curtains and all this bright sunshine was pouring in, like a full-frontal offensive. "You didn't have to go and do *that.*"

"Gaeth might be *dead*!" Toverre shouted at me suddenly. "You—*You* might have been—"

"Now, don't," I said quickly. My stomach let out a rumble, and I realized the broth Toverre was holding smelled pretty delicious. He saw me eyeing it and brought it over to me, setting it down on the chair by his bed. "It wasn't anything more serious than a little fever. But . . . I'm sorry I said you did wrong. I guess I'd've done the same, if you were the one taken ill. I didn't mean to sound ungrateful, and I'm glad you were here to take care of me."

"Well," Toverre sniffed, looking away from me. The tips of his ears turned pink, and his cheeks had gone all blotchy, which I guessed meant I'd pleased him a little with my gratitude.

"I'll just have to write Da myself and tell him everything's fine," I soothed, reaching a pale hand over to the bowl. "I'm feeling a lot better. Just a bit shaky, but I'll be back to looking after *you* in no time."

Toverre didn't reply but lifted the bowl and sat in the chair, himself, holding it out to me.

For someone who never could tell how a person was feeling, he had his moments of knowing exactly what to do.

"Guess I've been giving you a lot of trouble, huh?" I asked sheepishly. "I really am lucky you're here with me. But what's all this about Gaeth?"

I should've asked it sooner, I thought, but the fever'd left my brain a little bit stupid, and nothing was working as quickly as it should've been.

Toverre lifted a spoonful of hot broth to my lips and I sipped it without remembering to blow on it first, wincing when it burned my tongue.

"He's missing," Toverre said, not even bothering to be sharp with me about my carelessness. I must've looked like the back end of a sow because he was being so gentle with me. "At least, whenever *I* look for him, he's gone, and at first I assumed it was nothing, just a matter of coincidence. Only it turns out that others—his friends—have noted his disappearance, as well. Someone named Thib, in particular, who requires him for that beastly game you all play in the hallway, but I know that he hasn't been to class, either, and I . . . *well,* considering your condition, and his, and the time I had to think without you to tell me I was being too fanciful . . ."

I could tell from the way he was getting huffy again that he was worried, and if I'd been in finer fettle, I would've probably tried to feed *him* the soup to soothe his nerves.

"Kinda just assumed he was taking his time getting to know the city," I said, taking another sip of broth, *after* I'd blown on it this time. At least I learned from some of my mistakes. "But if Thib says he hasn't seen him in days—and I know *we* haven't—then I've got no idea what could've happened to him."

"If he was recalled home, then surely someone would know," Toverre pointed out.

"I hadn't heard *anything* about him moving out," I agreed. "He couldn't just go and leave all his things behind, either."

"You don't think . . ." Toverre held the spoon back, apparently unaware that I was leaning toward it for my next mouthful. "Laure, you *don't* think he's run afoul of anyone rough in the city, do you? Or that he might have even . . . *ventured into Molly?*"

"No, I don't think that," I told him, reaching over to take the spoon for myself now that I felt a little less shaky. I could see that my getting sick was even worse for Toverre—despite how much he complained—because *this* way, Toverre'd had all that time to let his imagination run away with him. "Gaeth's big. He's not stupid, either. Boy like that can take care of himself. Probably even better than me, but you never heard me say that. Might be the fever talking. Gimme that soup bowl."

"Hm," said Toverre, but he didn't look all that convinced.

Not everyone, I thought, was as madcap romance crazy as Toverre. His problem wasn't just being like that, but assuming everyone else was as crazy as he.

"Then let's look for him today," I said. I was eating a bit more quickly now that the soup wasn't quite so piping hot, and my stomach was growling loudly every time I tried to think. "He's got to be *somewhere*. Nobody just disappears like that. He's more careful about where he goes and who he talks to than *we* are. Anyway, we've run into him more than once in the city, so I think we probably have a good idea of what places he likes to go and when he likes to go there. It'll be a little like your stalking, only not as ridiculously creepy."

"I have seen the error of my ways with regard to *that* particular endeavor," Toverre assured me, which meant he'd be back at it in no time the minute another pretty face crossed his path. "And we will not be embarking on any wild-goose chases before you've cleaned yourself up *and* talked to your professors. If you think it's bad when I write home for you, I can imagine you won't want the 'Versity doing it."

"You imagine right," I said, tilting the bowl of soup so I could drain it down to the bottom.

Toverre winced, and I gave him my very best smile, licking my lips.

"Good soup," I said. "Thanks."

"You *are* feeling better, aren't you?" Toverre asked, taking the empty bowl and spoon from me and setting it down on the table instead of immediately spiriting it back to the kitchen to scrub it out. That, more than anything, told me how worried he must have been. It was almost enough to make a girl feel guilty. But it wasn't my fault for being sick, and I shoved those silly thoughts aside.

"Well, enough to do all the things you said, and look for Gaeth on top of that," I said, oozing out of bed. "If he's sick like I was, and he didn't have you to look after him, who knows what might've happened? Could've passed out on the Rue or something, and with nobody here to check up on him all the time . . ." I shook my head, feeling sorry for him. Being sick like that had been no fun at all, and I suspected even someone as stalwart as Gaeth must've had trouble with it.

Standing up made the world seem a little less dire, and even though I wasn't about to go dancing through the streets or start up a game with Thib in the halls, I was happy to be feeling more like myself again.

Unfortunately, I didn't look like myself. There were big bags under my eyes, and my skin was pale, and when I made a face at Toverre's mirror, I looked like the ghoul from a children's story.

"I really think some inquiries ought to be made into the

reputation of that physician," Toverre said, standing along with me—presumably in case I toppled over, and so he could catch me before I fell on my ass. I'd've liked to see him try to catch me. "The things I've heard indicate a severe lack of care for one's patients. I am *extremely* displeased by her behavior."

"Don't worry; I think I'll be giving her an earful myself, next time I go," I said, stretching out my arms before I plodded over to the door. I needed to get back to my own room, change these fever-stinking clothes, and maybe comb my hair a little bit, so I looked slightly less deranged. Maybe I didn't care about my appearances as much as Toverre thought I should, but I had to draw a line somewhere.

Toverre paused only to fold up the blankets I'd knocked onto the floor, then followed after me.

My room was stuffy and hot, and I immediately opened a window to let some fresh, cold air in.

"Your friend Thib lost consciousness after his appointment," Toverre informed me, as I dug into my dresser for a fresh change of clothes I could take to the ladies' while I bathed. "His lady friend told me, though she hadn't yet had her appointment, so *she* was just fit as a fiddle. And we both saw what Gaeth looked like after he came back from his. You don't think it's another plague, do you? Something to do with the magicians? It's possible they didn't cure it— Oh bastion, Laure, why have we come here?"

"Stop that," I told him. "I don't think that's it at all." I had one black sock in my hand, but I couldn't for the life of me dig up the other. Being turned away also meant that Toverre couldn't see how worried he was making *me* with all this fearful talk, which normally I didn't fall for, but he'd finally gotten to me.

One of us had to be the calm one, and it wasn't ever going to be Toverre.

Privately, I didn't like the sound of it: people fainting dead away in the physic's chair and coming back with all these fevers. I'd just assumed I'd caught it from Gaeth, but Toverre'd seen him more times than I had *and* he had the constitution of a newborn baby in wintertime. It didn't make much sense for me to get sick ahead of him. There was also a chance I'd caught it from Thib. But if by "lady friend" Toverre meant Eveline, and she was still in fine health, then once again it didn't make sense for me to be the one who got stuck under the weather. I knew how much Eveline liked Thib, and how much Thib liked Eveline, and how *unlikely* me catching Thib's fever before Eveline was.

As much as Toverre liked his crazy theories, I was starting to think he wasn't so off base with this one. Not that it was a theory so much as it was a group of nasty suspicions. But once we had the chance to talk to Gaeth, I told myself, there was bound to be some simple explanation. Then I could have a good hearty chuckle at myself, and save the mystery solving to the pay-by-hour detectives.

"Here," Toverre said finally, elbowing me out of the way with his pointy little limbs. "I can't bear to watch this miserable attempt a minute longer."

Quick as you please, and without throwing anything on the floor the way I usually did, he put together an outfit that passed both his approval and mine, though it involved stockings instead of socks, and one of my newer dresses instead of the plain cotton shift I'd been holding.

"The green will give you some color," he explained, all but pushing me out the door, "and it'll make your eyes stand out wonderfully; you'll see. And even if you don't," he added, with what appeared to me to be just a slight hint of jealousy, "everyone else will."

"We're just going to lecture," I protested.

"You've been *sick*," Toverre said, as if that explained itself. "If you don't put your best foot forward and make an effort not to look like a pickled herring, I guarantee you Professor Adamo will write you off as weak stock and that will be the end for us. Of course, if what you desire is to cultivate the impression that you're about to drop dead at the foot of his desk, then by all means, the outfit you'd picked out was a marvelous choice."

Somehow, he managed to compliment a girl and gravely insult her at the same time. He was lucky he was attached to me because nobody else in all of Volstov would *ever* have put up with it.

I stopped him just short of entering the ladies' with me, though for a moment there it was a very near thing.

"You really did miss me," I said, trying not to sound too smug. "The sound of my voice, my witty discussions, my inability to dress myself—"

"Do *not* scare me like that again," Toverre snapped, looking quite serious for a minute. "It's so . . . impolite. Not to mention that I have a crick in my back from sleeping in that chair all night."

"I'll do my best," I promised him.

"See that you do," Toverre said with a sniff. "I'm going to clean my room now."

We'd both feel better after all our necessaries had been washed out. As much as I figured Professor Adamo didn't give a hoot what I was wearing or whether I'd washed myself that day, it always made me feel more human to sluice off after I'd been sick. It seemed to me like I was washing the sickness off, and even Da had always told me that you could do half a physician's job for 'em just by using soap and water.

Well, ex–Chief Sergeant Adamo was probably used to men showing up in fighting condition, too. Toverre was right, and a little bit of preparation wouldn't hurt.

I bathed and dressed without any of the other girls needing to use the facilities, which on a regular day would've seemed like a real piece of luck, but today just seemed a little eerie. Much as I hated to admit it, Toverre'd kind of gotten to me with all his talk about people getting sick and Gaeth disappearing. He was good at blending in, for a country boy. It was something I'd noticed right in the beginning, but there was a difference between being some trouble to track down and clean vanishing off the face of the earth.

Which he hadn't done, I reminded myself. Coincidence was going to explain everything, and we were going to have a good laugh together later.

But I wanted to find him for more reasons than one. First of all, because he was my friend; and second of all, because

I was starting to get the feeling like he could've been Toverre's friend, too, and you didn't find someone like that on every street corner. He was good to Toverre—even gave him an extra pair of gloves one time to warm his hands—and no one other than me had ever done something like that for Toverre before. It was important to keep this poor idiot around, and Toverre never had to be the wiser for how I'd helped him.

I tied my hair back with the ribbon Toverre'd picked out, hoping he wasn't going to make a fuss about me hopping over to the 'Versity with wet hair. It was only a short little jaunt, and it wasn't even snowing.

Toverre's door was open when I reached his hallway, and he was on his hands and knees, scrubbing parts of the floor I was fairly certain I'd never been sick on.

"I'm ready to go," I told him, just so he wouldn't think I'd snuck out behind his back or anything like that. "Can I dump my laundry in with yours?"

"*Please* do," Toverre said, straightening up and wringing out his little sponge into a brand-shining-new bucket. "I can't stand the sight of your clothes when you do them. They come back all wrinkled, and then it's so many hours I have to spend on ironing them."

"You don't have to bother with that," I told him, feeling somewhat guilty as I dumped my clothes on top of the bed linens I'd mussed. "Then again, you're you, so I guess you kinda do."

"Stop stalling," Toverre said, checking his watch. "Professor Adamo's latest lecture should be letting out at any minute; if you talk to him straightaway and don't waste too much time, you'll still have time to make Professor Ducante's general consultation hours."

We heard the peal of the bells as we were crossing the grounds, which made Toverre pick up his pace. I had to do the same just to keep up with him; for someone with such skinny legs, he sure could run. I found myself looking for Gaeth's face in the crowd, and occasionally I caught sight of a flash of golden hair, but it only ever let my hopes down when I craned to see a face that wasn't his. Gray coats seemed to be "in" this year, as Toverre would have said, and eventually I gave up looking.

Where was he? And more importantly than that, was he all right?

"There he is," Toverre hissed in my ear.

My heart jumped, and I jerked my head around. "Where?" I asked.

Toverre nudged me in the right direction, and I realized at once he hadn't been talking about Gaeth but Professor Adamo. My thoughts were way too scrambled, as evidenced by my inability to concentrate, and I wished I'd had some better plan—one might even say "strategy"—laid out before I came to speak with him.

At least the professor was a fan of improvisation, I told myself. That might earn me some points if I didn't choke on my own foot first.

"Now go talk to him before he's surrounded," Toverre instructed, still poking me in the back. Bastion, but it was annoying, and I swatted his hands away as I made my *own* way into the hall.

Professor Adamo—hard to think of a war-hardened man like him with a "Professor" tacked on in front of his family name, and I didn't think he could much fathom the title, either—didn't seem like he was swarmed by students to me. He was having some kind of argument with his assistant—a prissy little prancer if ever I saw one—and no one was even trying to get close to them.

I should've taken that as my cue, but Toverre was hissing what must have been his idea of encouragement behind me, and there was no turning back. Instead, I catapulted myself forward, before I could lose my guts, and landed right in the middle of what Adamo would've described as a "preexisting skirmish."

"Ahem," I said.

Both of them whirled on me; if they'd been wearing weapons, I suspected, right about then was when they'd've been drawn. Thankfully, they weren't—although if it'd been that kind of fight, my money would've been on Adamo, no question. His skinny little note-taker was the worst kind of know-it-all; I doubted he could apply even a fraction of what he knew to real life.

"Well?" Adamo demanded. "What is it?"

"I . . ." I began.

As ever, I was reminded of how very *solid* Adamo was. He wasn't even that tall—barely a few inches over me—but he was the squarest and most-sturdily built person I'd ever known, reminding me more of a brick storehouse than a man. His chest was particularly wide, which I imagined helped while he was shouting out orders to everyone; and, now and then, when he forgot himself in the middle of a lecture, he'd use that voice without any warning. Now, *that* woke all the sleepyheads up, and made some of 'em piss their trousers, too.

I loved it, which was why his was my favorite lecture class. You never knew when he was going to start shouting like the war was back on, and it gave me a feeling of genuine excitement.

Toverre just said it made him hyperventilate. Now, *there* were two men so completely different it was impossible to imagine they were both the same species, I thought, and rubbed at the back of my neck to keep from smiling.

"I believe you've intimidated her," Adamo's assistant said. I'd actually forgotten about him—which was what I usually did with people I didn't care for, so that they wouldn't annoy me. I wasn't like Toverre; I didn't like to let these things fester. Instead, I just cut them out. "Do you see what you've done? She can barely speak. Come with me, that's a good girl, and I'll get you some tea, or perhaps a cup of coffee, and we can speak like civilized people, without—"

"I don't think so," I replied, jerking away the moment he tried to touch me. "I came to talk to the Chief Sergeant— to *the professor*—to tell him where I was yesterday's lecture, *and* today's."

"That's right," Adamo said, looking pleased for some reason. I had my suspicions that he had no use for his weasel of an assistant, either, but then again, what man in his right mind would? "I didn't think I saw you. We were discussing battle tactics of the Ke-Han hordes."

"Damn it," I said, knowing that Toverre—wherever he'd hidden himself to eavesdrop—had probably lost consciousness over my language by now. "I was looking forward to that."

"Well, then," Adamo replied. "You probably should've come."

"I was sick," I explained, hoping he wouldn't think I was one of those slack-jawed shirkers. And I *had* been looking forward to how the Hordes conquered the Xi'an peninsula. Apparently it wasn't just to do with their special horses, but now I'd never know, since I'd gone and slept through the one lecture I was most looking forward to. "With the fever."

"Yeah, I've heard a lot about this 'fever' the past few days," Adamo said a little skeptically. "Lots of kids been out with that one lately. Guess it's really becoming an epidemic."

"I don't like what your tone's implying," I replied. Somewhere above me, on the stairs, I heard a strangled groan. That was Toverre, on the verge of collapse. "You can ask my physician—Margrave Germaine—whether or not I was in her offices yesterday. If I *wanted* to skip out on one of your lectures, it probably would've been the one you spent getting sidetracked about how pointless naval battles are these days. And I wouldn't've come up to tell you about it afterward, either. I'm no liar. But if I *was,* I wouldn't be a bad one."

Adamo blinked, so that for a second I almost thought I'd gotten one in past all his defenses. I hoped not. What kind of Chief Sergeant—ex or no—would he be if I could win a round with him? He was probably just trying to decide the best way to kick me out of the 'Versity, now that I'd gone and let my mouth get the better of me again.

"Margrave Germaine, you say," Adamo said at last, just as I was about to offer to escort myself off the premises for him. "I'm gonna remember that."

"You can, if you like," I said, making a concentrated effort now to keep from banging the final nail into Toverre's coffin all by myself. "And all you'll find out is that I'm telling you the truth."

"You'll have to forgive my skepticism," Adamo replied, not sounding like he wanted my forgiveness at all.

"Oh, will I?" I asked.

"And naval battles *are* pointless if there's no water between you," Adamo added. He crossed his big arms over his chest, like he couldn't quite let that one rest. "Even worse if you're going after a string of islands like the Kirils, since it's costing you all that money to go forth and back, and meanwhile they're just sitting on their dockyards laughing at you as you waste good fuel."

I wanted to laugh at the thought, but I felt like Toverre might've taken it as the last straw, so I smiled instead.

"Sounds to me like you don't much like the water," I pointed out.

"Ever been down to the Mollydocks?" Adamo asked, before he stopped, looking cross with himself. "No. 'Course you haven't. And you shouldn't go down there, either. And if you do go down there, don't say *I* sent you. My point is, anyone who takes to *that* water's been landed one too many blows to the head. Me, I'll stick to the ground."

"Well, not entirely," I ventured. Adamo hmmphed. "I guess after having been up in the air, nothing else seems quite as good?"

"Nah," Adamo said, scratching the back of his neck. "You can say that again."

It felt like a moment to be quiet, so I somehow managed to button my lip for the pause, giving him a minute to remember whatever it was he was thinking about.

Da said the war did all kinds of things to people before it was over, and I'd seen some of the effects firsthand when a few of the boys came back and weren't quite able to look anyone in the eyes. I figured that if I'd been the one riding a dragon every day for years only to wake up and be told I couldn't do it anymore, I'd've been a little out of sorts, too. No wonder the man was so ornery all the time, like his britches were bunched up too tight.

The Chief Sergeant's horrible little assistant cleared his throat, which I was probably meant to take as a sign to curtsy and get out. Either that, or he was real keen to get back to the debate I'd saved him from losing. Some people just didn't know how to show gratitude.

"Look, if you're really interested in hearing about Ke-Han strategies, you can come by my office sometime," Adamo suggested, snapping to all at once. "At least, if I have one of those. They said something about me having an office. Radomir, where's my office?"

"It's Cathery 306," Radomir said, looking greatly put-upon. "That's *this* building," he added, for my benefit.

"Could I really?" I asked, momentarily in too good a mood to even feel irritated about Radomir acting like my brain worked too slowly to figure things out for itself. "I wouldn't be interrupting important business or anything?"

"If I had important business, I wouldn't be there," Adamo said. He looked surprised I wanted to take him up on his offer, and maybe even a little pleased that I'd shown some interest, which was a new one for me. Usually the only looks I got from professors were more in the range of resigned disappointment. My tutor back home had quit fifteen times before he finally left the countryside altogether. "Come by sometime next week, and if I can find the place, I'll be in it."

"It's Cathery 306," I told him. "Just ask Radomir; he knows all about it."

"And maybe wear a hat the next time you go out," Adamo said, as a parting shot. "Scarf, too. Pair of gloves. A little common sense keeps a soldier from getting sick."

I decided to let him have the final word. He seemed like a good sort, and he was probably just trying to look out for me in his own way.

Toverre came scrambling down at me like a human avalanche as I passed the staircase, his face red and mottled. He probably thought *he* was the one who'd just had to talk it out with a professor. But, I thought, I'd been pretty convincing. At least I'd managed to end things on an up note, *and* I hadn't been kicked out of the 'Versity.

Seemed like I was good at being diplomatic after all—despite what everyone said about me.

"Now, Toverre, that wasn't so bad," I told him, feeling victorious. I'd held my ground pretty well with a master tactician, even though my *own* strategy had consisted of nothing more than just telling the truth over and over again until it stuck. The simple tactics were always the best, or so ex–Chief Sergeant Professor Adamo was always reminding us.

"'Wasn't so bad?'" Toverre repeated, like I'd just started jabbering in foreign tongues and he was trying to piece together what I was saying. Poor thing needed a little more sleep to be in a better mood. "Not *bad*? I thought he was going to start breathing fire himself when you said that about not liking his tone! And it's not as though *you* can repel fire—I certainly didn't buy you *that* kind of dress. Do you have a death wish, Laure, or are you simply confusing brave with stupid?" He paused to draw in a deep breath, and I braced myself for round two. "Do you know, I think he actually *likes* you?"

I'd been expecting everything except that last bit, and it threw me for a loop as surely as if I'd been riding a dragon myself. Of course, I *supposed* that if I had been riding a dragon, I'd have been looking to make the Chief Sergeant proud of me. I'd just never really thought about it in those terms before. If you were gonna dream about something, it made sense to dream about the big beauties rather than the men that rode them.

Wish I could've been, I thought wistfully. It was probably way better than riding a horse, and that was one of the things I loved most in the world.

"He'd like anyone who told him what they were thinking up front like that," I insisted, feeling a little warm all of a sudden. It was because of the damn heat they pumped into these buildings, so that a girl couldn't bundle up for the weather outside without shedding her layers like a wet, newborn butterfly when she came in from the cold. Was it any wonder all of us were getting fevers? "He's a simple man who likes some honesty, that's all."

"I'm sure that's what he likes," Toverre said, with one of those all-knowing looks that really got on my nerves.

This was the sort of thing Toverre liked to read too much into; I knew that from his own affairs. He'd turn a simple glance or turn of phrase into something more meaningful, just like magic.

"Come on," I said, taking him by the arm. This time, it was *my* turn to drag *him* out the door. "If we hurry, we can still make Professor Fussbudget's special what'd you call 'em? 'Consultation hours.' Then we gotta look for Gaeth."

By the sound of things, he wasn't the only one who was missing classes.

BALFOUR

Germaine's workspace was much larger than Margrave Ginette's, and she had a variety of exotic tools that I'd never seen before, even in Ginette's extensive collection.

I supposed it made sense since she was a specialist hired by the Esar personally, but I found myself first surprised and then fascinated by the selection: slender pliers wrought in gold and steel, and drivers for the smallest screws I'd ever seen—so small that she required magnifying lenses in order to work with them.

She didn't like to talk, I realized quickly enough, and after she'd given me her name I fell silent so as not to distract her any further. The room was overwhelmingly bright, though I suppose that made it easier to see all the more intricate parts of my hands, and she made a noise of displeasure when I took off my gloves.

My fingers were stiff and frozen into place; try though I might, I couldn't even move them when she told me to, save for the twitching of my right forefinger.

"They do this often?" Margrave Germaine asked, prodding at them with a thin metal instrument.

"Never before, as long as I've had them," I told her.

"So they perform best with regular upkeep," Germaine said, scribbling something down on a chart. "Well, don't you worry your pretty little head, my friend. I'll have these babies in proper working order by the time you leave here. *Better* than new; that's a promise. And intervals between checkups'll be longer, too, I'd wager. Here I go."

She delved in with her clever tools, rooting around in a way that looked as though it *should* have hurt, when in reality I felt nothing. It made me slightly squeamish to watch as she pried apart fastenings and loosened catches and even drew out a gear or two, setting them neatly on the table beside her. She unscrewed my left palm, setting the thin metal plate aside, and I could see there was rust along the bottom and around the site of one of the screws.

Just as I was about to look away, she seized upon something with her pliers and pulled it out with the utmost care. The look on her face was strange, almost tender, and she held the thing up for me to see.

It was a vial of pearlescent liquid, no bigger than my thumbnail. It shimmered in the bright light like a precious jewel, and I found myself rather taken with the thing despite not knowing what it was.

"This here's the key to your hands," Germaine said, reading my mind as though she were a *velikaia*. "Isn't it beautiful?"

"Quite," I agreed readily, though its removal had cut off all communication with my hand, and the resulting feeling of cold, foreign steel against my wrist was eerie.

She didn't place the vial on the tray, but rather somewhere behind her, out of my sight entirely. After that, she pried the little vial loose from the left hand as well, so that I was left with nothing else but to sit there while she worked, arms tense, feeling disturbed and helpless. I supposed it was something I should've been used to, but Margrave Ginette had always left that part in place, leaving me full use of my hands even as she worked on them.

Everyone did have a different method, and at least Germaine was here to help me. It wasn't for me to complain, no matter how long it took.

The time always passed slowly, but this session seemed longer than usual. Perhaps it was nothing more than my own impatience—that, and I was used to being able to watch the clock while Ginette saw to my hands' upkeep.

"Stay put," Margrave Germaine said at long last—her first words after what must have been hours of silently working on my hands. "I have to calibrate some tools to suit your needs, but we're almost done here; just be patient. If you feel like you have to take a nap, I won't judge you any, either. I'm told the lights have that effect on people, and you look like a wreck. No offense."

I hadn't noticed anything other than a curious warmth in my face and chest, but now that she mentioned it, I *did* feel somewhat drowsy. It probably had something to do with sitting for so long in one place. *It couldn't hurt to sleep,* I thought. I'd caught a rest in stranger places before, thanks to my time at the Airman.

Once, I'd spent the night in the bathroom—the only room I'd found with a door that locked.

I leaned my head back in the chair, allowing my eyes to slip shut as Margrave Germaine rolled her chair away from her workstation. The last thing I saw were those shimmering vials, like miniature stars in the palm of her hand, and I thought for a moment I might even have heard voices. A consulting physician, maybe?

But I would never know the answer, as I allowed sleep to overtake me.

I awoke to a furious thumping sound, so loud that my heart began to hammer. It took me a moment to realize I was back in my own apartment, laid out in my own bed, and the sound was nothing more than my upstairs neighbors returning home. The entire building shook with the force of their steps, and I wondered to myself if they made a habit of wearing solid stone boots.

My head was pounding, and I lifted my hand without thinking to rub at the temple.

Quick, polished fingers—in perfect working order—obeyed my command. The metal was cold against my skin, but it soothed my pulse, and I started into a sitting position at once, holding both hands out in front of me.

They even had back plates, I realized. They were smooth and complete, and when I wanted to make a fist, I could. I did so far more than was necessary out of sheer relief, flexing and curling my fingers, then attempting one of the more difficult tasks I faced daily: undoing one of my buttons. It slid from the loop easily, then back into it, and I could almost feel the press of the metal button against my metal fingertips. It was an incredible sensation.

A small shaft of sunlight was spilling through the window onto my lap, and I found it suddenly impossible to remember any of my present troubles. The job Germaine had done was beautiful; she was truly an expert in her field.

A small, sudden pang of guilt ran through me, as though Ginette would somehow hear me comparing her unfavorably with someone else, but I pushed the thoughts to the back of my mind, allowing myself—for the first time in a very long while—to savor the pleasure of a good mood.

Also, for the first time in a very long while, I intended to make myself breakfast.

I had the skillet ready and was preparing myself for the delicate—yet now somehow manageable—prospect of cracking eggs, when a knock at the door broke into my reverie.

"Coming," I called, hurrying over and opening it. I wasn't expecting anyone, and I did hope it wasn't one of the Esar's men, come to take me back for another consultation. I couldn't complain about the Esar taking special interest in my situation, either—not after all he *had* done for me—but I wanted to enjoy the moment uninterrupted. I also wanted to formulate my thanks so that they would show how much I truly appreciated the interference.

However, I was shocked to see as I pulled the door open, a familiar face I wouldn't have expected, not in a thousand years.

"Luvander," I said, forgetting my manners and staring openly at him.

"Balfour," he replied, staring back at me. I realized he was making fun of my expression, mouth hanging open like a dead fish's, and I colored, closing my mouth at once.

"What are you doing here?" I managed finally—not at all the "do come in" that would have been more welcoming.

"I could ask you the same thing," Luvander admitted, surveying my humble lodgings from over my shoulder. "What sort of place is this for a hero of war, I wonder? Such wealth! Such riches! Such personality."

"It's close to the bastion," I explained. "Anything more extravagant, *and* centrally located, would be far out of my price range."

"Ah, Balfour," Luvander said. "Dreaming big, as always. We flew once, remember?"

It wasn't enough to bring me crashing down from my good mood, but it *almost* managed. I stepped aside, beckoning for him to come in. "It has a nice kitchen," I added, "and a pretty view."

At that moment, the upstairs neighbors chose to travel from one room to another, and the entire ceiling trembled, shaking a few bits of dust and wood down onto our heads. An excellent first impression, I thought, as Luvander stared at the ceiling in horror. He probably thought it was going to collapse on us both. And he was probably right.

"It seems it also comes with elephants," Luvander said at last. He pulled a white box from behind his back, tied up with string. "Invite the elephants down. I brought you some breakfast."

"You did?" I asked.

"I can see you just woke up," Luvander replied. "Perhaps I'll step into the hallway and we'll try doing this again."

"That won't be necessary. I just— *Why*?"

"Why did I bring you breakfast?" Luvander asked. I nodded, and he pulled out a pocketknife, cutting into the string. "Well, I've finally had enough to hire a shop assistant, first of all. And I assumed, with your hands the way they were, you might have trouble cooking. I'm a bleeding heart, what can I say, and our little talk the other day made me realize how much I missed having company from the good old days. You remember those, don't you, Balfour?"

"All too clearly," I said with a mixture of relief and longing.

"So that's them, then?" Luvander asked, nodding toward my hands.

I realized in that moment that I hadn't thought to put on gloves before I'd answered the door, and now they were on grand display. There'd be no hiding them behind my back—Luvander would see through to my embarrassment, and he'd never let me live it down—and so I was trapped, forced to let him look at them until his curiosity was satisfied.

Fortunately, I told myself, they were in working order, polished and new, gleaming when sunlight from my window hit them. I cleared my throat, trying to read Luvander's expression, but it was impossible to tell what he was thinking, as always. For a man with such an expressive face, he rarely—if ever—showed any real emotion. At least, nothing you could tease him with.

"May I?" he asked, gesturing to one of them.

I swallowed, looking away. "Go ahead," I said, refusing to add what I wished: *If you must.* It stood to reason he'd be curious, and he had come all this way. No doubt, if I did protest, he'd tell me there was nothing at all to be ashamed of—recite a few of the verses from "Balfour Steelhands"—and then I'd be further ashamed of having protested in the first place.

The best way to deal with this was to get it over with. I clenched my jaw, bracing myself for whatever came next.

He came forward slowly, as though he knew I wanted to run away, and delicately took my arm by the sleeve. I was forced to look back at him, searching his face warily for his impressions, as he turned my hand over, inspecting every detail, down to my pinky finger. I could feel his touch, but it was so careful that it was only the faintest ghost of pressure, moving from the metal to the flesh.

"Now, isn't that something," he said at last, shaking his head and puffing out a whistle. "Looks as good as new, too."

"I just had them fixed," I admitted. "They're working very well today."

"Bet they get cold," Luvander added.

"They do," I said.

He took the other one, comparing them, noting all the

places where screws approximated joints, then he sighed heavily, letting go of me completely. "You remind me of someone," he said, "but I can't quite put my finger on it."

It took me a moment to figure out it was meant to be a joke about Yesfir, because it lacked his usual good cheer. "Yes," I agreed, pressing the metal palms together. "I know exactly what you mean."

"It's no wonder you wear those gloves all the time," Luvander added. "You probably don't want to depress us. Or yourself."

"And yet I manage that anyway, somehow," I said quietly.

"You should send a note to Adamo," Luvander said. "Nothing too fancy, just to let him know you got yourself fixed up so he doesn't beat down the Provost's door and demand a search party for that other Margrave of yours. He *would* do that, you know. He's always looked out for you. And besides, a man like that misses having a cause to throw his considerable weight behind, mark my words."

"I suppose I could write to him," I acknowledged, since it was slightly less embarrassing than making a special visit just to talk about my hands. I was lucky Adamo hadn't asked about them yet. He'd given me my privacy out of respect, but I knew it was likely that sensitivity wouldn't last long.

"At least it'll let him know the Esar made good on his word about *something*," Luvander said with a little wink. "I'm not saying you have to give Adamo her references or her life's story or anything like that, just let him know you're being looked after by a real woman who actually exists. It'll help him to sleep better at night."

"I had no idea that I was causing you both such worry," I said, wrestling with the urge to hide my hands behind my back and have done with it.

"Well, it's not your fault anyway," Luvander said, patting me on the back in a way that *didn't* feel like a sudden or violent assault. "Some of us were born to be miserable bastards; nothing you can do about that. Do you eat brioche? I realize I probably ought to have asked you that before I tracked your house down, but if I'd asked first, it might've spoiled the surprise, do you see?"

"I'll eat anything as long as it's cooked properly," I admitted, not even bothered by the abrupt change in topic, even though I could tell it was for my sake.

"You're in luck, then," Luvander said, "since it just so happens that *these* are baked to perfection. They're from a dear little place two doors down from my shop, in fact. The baker's daughter likes me, so I get them for free, and she gets a discount on any purchase of a hat or gloves she might care to make."

"That sounds like a very fair arrangement," I said, turning down the heat on my stove and putting the eggs away for another day.

"I'm becoming positively established there now; one day you won't be able to imagine the old Rue without me," Luvander added, returning to his box and flipping it open. Inside it were two enormous brioche buns, glazed and studded with what looked like chips of dark chocolate. Upon seeing them, my mouth immediately began to water. It was certainly much better than any omelet I'd been about to make.

"That's breakfast?" I asked, unable to help myself. "It seems more like dessert."

"And yet it goes down perfect with some tea," Luvander said, grinning. "I could put them on plates if you've got 'em, but I'm not so fancy that I can't eat out of a box, either. We've both seen worse, and any *further* elaboration on that point will cause me to lose my appetite entirely."

We paused for a moment to remember the time Compagnon had made us all soup in Merritt's boots—mushroom barley, if I recalled correctly, though some of the lumps were neither mushroom *nor* barley, but more like lint from his socks.

"I'll make some tea," I said at last since that seemed to be what Luvander was hinting at. "But I do hope you don't mind if I decline to invite my upstairs neighbors."

"Not at all," Luvander said with an airy wave of his hand. "It's cozier this way, and I plan to entertain myself by going through your personal things. Couldn't do that in front of company, now could I?"

"I'm told elephants have excellent manners," I said, filling the kettle and placing it on the stove to warm.

Behind me, I could hear Luvander making good on his word, rustling around the room and tossing things aside more like a trained hunter's dog than a person. I felt the familiar thrum of anxiety and nervous energy running through me, as it always did when my private life was under assault, but it wasn't nearly so unpleasant as it had once been. Perhaps I'd just forgotten how embarrassing it could be.

Then again, Luvander was only one person—he could hardly gang up on me with the force of the entire corps.

My fingers slipped against the plates before I managed to get a firm grasp on them, but that was a characteristic of the metal and nothing to do with my own clumsiness. I caught them, putting them to right, and coming back into the sitting room feeling nearly triumphant. At the very least, Luvander wasn't just over my shoulder, hawking my every move to make sure I was capable of setting a table—which I hadn't been a day ago.

"I see now that you've only come in order to spy on me," I told Luvander, setting the plates down as he pulled aside my curtains, examining the view for himself. "This business of brioche is all a ruse."

"A very delicious ruse, though, you must admit," Luvander said, peeling away from the window and folding himself neatly into one of my chairs. "Well, I suppose you can't admit that since you haven't tried it yet, but trust me, it is divine. You're right about your view, by the way. Very pretty."

"Are you humoring me now? I really can't tell."

"A true gentleman *never* jokes about beauty," Luvander said, getting up as soon as he'd sat to fetch the kettle. I hadn't even heard it whistling.

From where I sat, I could see the thick purple scar on his throat, hooked like a fisherman's lure where it disappeared beneath his shirt collar. It made me wonder if any of us had truly managed to escape unscathed and whether I wasn't being a little foolish about my hands after all, feeling so sorry for myself all the time without any regard for the way the others must have been feeling.

It was a sobering thought, especially as I was someone who had once suffered extremely selfish and insensitive behavior. Perhaps I wasn't *as* different from the others as I'd always believed.

"This mug has a chip in it," Luvander said, scuttling about in my kitchen while I allowed myself to get lost in thought. "Good gracious, were you trying to start a fire in that wastepaper basket?"

"What?" I asked. A horrible sense of foreboding crept over me before I'd even followed his gaze. It was too late for me to stop him, since by the time I'd realized what was happening, he'd already charged over to the bin, where I'd crumpled and left the remains of several of my unfinished letters to Thom.

I should have burned them, even though I hadn't been expecting guests. This was all my fault, and it was going to be unbearable.

"'Dear Thom,'" Luvander began, in a voice I could only assume he believed resembled my own, "'I hope you will take this with the spirit it is intended when I tell you that in lower Charlotte they are singing a song about my—' *Balfour!* Really? You had only to tell me that you needed help composing a love letter; one must never mention their manhood in such a vulgar manner. It is *entirely* unromantic."

"I thought it would be funny," I said, feeling hot under the collar. Since it seemed Luvander wouldn't be joining me anytime soon, I began to cut into my own brioche, eating it to hide some of my humiliation.

"Well, true, but then what about *this* letter? 'Dear Thom, I no longer recall the name, but you wrote last that you'd been enjoying some variety of exotic wrinkled nuts—'"

Before Luvander could read any further, I'd launched myself at him—rather bravely, since I usually took my lumps without protest—from the kitchen table, doing what I could to reclaim what little remained of my dignity. If I'd allowed him to go on, I might never have been able to write another letter to my friend without feeling as though everything had some sort of double meaning.

The papers tore, Luvander nearly knocked a cup of hot tea into his own lap, and the sound of my neighbors thundering down the staircase suddenly filled the halls. It was the closest I'd ever felt to living at the Airman again, and just like that it seemed that my good mood for the day hadn't been ruined after all.

CHAPTER SEVEN

TOVERRE

In the end, it was Laure who'd come up with the daring next step to solve the mystery of Gaeth's unannounced disappearance. It was dangerous—and not in the romantic sense—and initially I was completely against it. While it had taken her a while to talk me around to it, once I'd had time to think it over, I found it a rather inevitable choice.

Simply put, we were going to break into his room. Like common thieves, I'd said, which only seemed to excite Laure even further.

I couldn't call it the more sensible option, since when was there ever sense at all in breaking and entering? But after two days of searching what felt like *all* of Miranda and Charlotte, and even the Mollyedge under Laure's insistence, we both felt crabby and utterly inefficient, not to mention hopeless.

I was angry with Gaeth for disappearing—and so close to exams, as well—but mostly I was angry with myself for letting it get to me the way it had. In my distraction, I'd gone so far as to forget about my infatuation with Hal entirely, though that was one result that was probably for the best. In the country, *all* my crushes had been hopeless, but the knowledge that in Thremedon such relationships were not strictly looked down on forced me to consider the real potential of every suitor.

It was an uncomfortable position to be in, even worse than the troubling resilience of Gaeth's continued presence in my thoughts.

Every time that it grew cold in my room, I was forced to think about him and his curious involvement in whether or not I kept my hands warm. It bothered me to have the gloves and not have Gaeth himself; I wanted to return them before someone assumed I'd stolen them. And, if Gaeth *were* present, I would have been able to twist an explanation from him that would solve once and for all my question as to why he was so peculiar all the time. The gloves, while sturdily made, explained nothing, and I resented them for how warm they kept my hands, how rough-looking and simple they were on the outside, and how soft within.

I'd told none of this to Laure. I didn't know how to describe it, and I knew enough to realize that these were bizarre thoughts, strange even for *me*. Laure had enough to occupy her mind with trying to find Gaeth in the first place, and this latest plan especially required our full concentration.

There was no need to distract her with my peculiarities. At least, not for the time being.

After some argument over the best time to stage our petty crime—my feelings were that this should be done in the dead of night, as was proper; Laure, on the other hand, thought that was foolish and would make it difficult to see what we were doing, besides—we'd finally come to an agreement. We had arranged that I would meet her at Gaeth's door around noontime, when most of the dormitory staff, and its inhabitants, would be out eating lunch.

Despite Laure's very fluid sense of time—and timing, not to mention—she was there before I was, shifting from foot to foot and doing her best not to look suspicious. She was so beautiful that it was impossible to think of anyone finding offense in her presence, but then it was just like Laure not to take that into consideration.

"Bet you were scrubbing all the banisters on your way here," she hissed in a gargantuan stage whisper.

"It was only the doorknob," I told her, honestly offended. "Now give me one of your hairpins."

"One of my hairpins?" Laure asked, staring at me as though I'd just spoken in gibberish. I nodded, holding my hand out to her. "Toverre, you know as well as I do that I don't *wear* hairpins."

That was right, I realized with a start. They were always

getting lost, and she'd find them in the night by rolling over onto one and stabbing herself in the head.

And yet in all the books I'd read, whenever there was a necessary break-in, the intrepid hero borrowed a hairpin from his heroine. What would we use to pick the lock on his door without one?

"Do you have anything similar to a hairpin?" I asked. "Oh! I have it. Lend me your brooch."

Laure unclasped it with some trepidation, still looking at me as though she thought I had taken leave of my senses. "What're you gonna do with it?" she asked. "That's my mother's old brooch, Toverre. I don't want you breaking it."

"I do not intend to *break* it," I told her.

"I don't care what you *intend* to do," she replied.

"Your lack of confidence in me at this moment is extremely distracting," I said, inspecting my tools. The brooch was one of the few pieces of jewelry Laure owned—she had inherited it from her mother after she'd died—but I wasn't looking at the carving on the front, or inspecting the fine green stone. Instead, I turned it over, looking at the pin on the back. It could have been longer—it could have been a hairpin—yet it would have to do, despite its shortcomings.

I knelt beside the door, pressing the pin into the lock. Absolutely nothing happened. After a moment's pause, with Laure's disapproving eyes burning holes into the back of my head, I began to wriggle the pin around inside, hoping to catch the mechanism and spring the lock.

No such luck, though I did manage to slip the pin out of the keyhole and stab myself in the finger.

"Bastion," I hissed, bringing it up to my lips to suck the blood out. "I should have sterilized it before I began."

"Oh, get away from there," Laure said. "And give me my brooch back."

She snatched the item in question away from me, sticking it through the bodice of her dress and doing up the clasp before she shoved me unceremoniously to one side.

"You might be more polite," I suggested, around my finger. "Or at least more constructive."

"No," she replied, "what I've got to be is more *de*structive."

I hadn't the time to ask her what she meant, as without warning she stepped back from the door and gave it a single, violent kick.

The sound reverberated through the halls, and in my surprise I hushed her equally loudly—though to what effect, I had no idea. The damage was already done, and the door swung open with a gentle creak. Everyone was used to ignoring loud noises in this place, and no one poked his head out to inquire after the commotion.

"The lock's weak," Laure explained to me. "Gaeth told me that one time when we were visiting him. You weren't listening because you were cleaning his windowsill. But I remembered."

I recalled the occasion—the windowsill had been covered in at least half a year's amount of thick, gray grime, and a piece of notepaper had been stuck to it with a melted candy. I had been doing Gaeth a favor by getting rid of it, and myself one, as well, since who would want to take tea while looking at something so disgusting?

Laure and I had our different areas of expertise, and neither was more or less useful than the other.

"After you," I murmured, sufficiently bested.

Laure patted me on the shoulder. "No worries, eh?" she said. "You can learn how to pick the lock next time. And I'll even buy a few hairpins."

"No need," I sighed, as she entered the room in front of me. "You'll only lose them, anyway."

It was clear once we were inside that no one had been in Gaeth's room for quite a few days. The strangest smell assaulted me all at once—I realized too late it was the scent of rotting food—and I quickly brought my handkerchief to my nose in order to block the worst of it out. After a brief search, I found the culprit on the bedside table: a half-eaten sandwich that appeared to have been abandoned midbite.

There were also boots by the bed, with socks dangling from them, and a vest hung over the back of his single wooden chair. A fire had gone out in the fireplace some time ago, but the ashes hadn't been cleaned; and a book, held open with an inkwell and with a pen lying beside it, was on his desk.

All in all, the place gave the impression of someone being called away quite suddenly, in the middle of his work—in the middle of his supper, even. This was not the way someone left a room when they were *planning* on leaving it; even someone less thoughtful than I would never have done such a thing. For their own benefit if no one else's.

"Creepy," Laure said.

"Quite so," I agreed.

She moved out of the doorway and deeper into the room, hesitating before she lifted a piece of parchment from his desk. "Don't know whether or not I should read this," she said. I nodded—what point was there in respecting his privacy when we'd kicked down the door to his room? She glanced over the lines, and her face softened. "He's not very good at spelling," she explained.

"What does it say?" I demanded, since I knew that if I gave her time to think about it, she might decide we were being too intrusive and give up entirely. Laure was very sensible and was able to kick doors down when called upon, but she had an unexpectedly kind heart for someone with such strong legs.

"It's a letter home," Laure said quietly. "What you might expect, really. It says he's been feeling a bit poorly lately, but his mam's not to worry because he's weathered worse winters than what the city has to throw at him."

I took the letter from her to see it for myself. He'd spelled city with an "s" and two "t"s—*sitty*—and I felt a kind of affection stir within me; immediately, I sought to overpower it with a more logical sentiment: irritation at the sight of such ghastly penmanship, not to mention his spelling. If I'd known he'd been having such difficulties, I might have offered to write his letters for him in thanks for the loan of those gloves. Then we would have been even. But there was nothing that I could do to help him now that he'd up and disappeared on us.

"I don't like this," Laure said, looking around the room as though she were mad at it. I could tell when she wanted to hit something—I only had to hope that I wasn't nearby when she finally decided to release some of her frustration. "Something's happened to him; it's obvious. People don't just drop off the face of the map like this, Toverre."

"Now, don't jump to any conclusions," I told her, looking over the letter as carefully as I could. Try as I might, I couldn't divine any hidden patterns or code in the writing—there were too many dreadful misspellings for that. "We've barely started looking, and we might yet find some further clue to his whereabouts in all this."

Whatever had happened to Gaeth, I couldn't imagine he'd seen it coming. Otherwise, it was more likely that he'd have tried to tell *us* about it rather than cramming his worries into a badly spelled letter home about his health and the weather.

"I just feel guilty, that's all," Laure admitted, going over to examine the fire. "Like I should've paid more attention when he was sick, tried to talk to him more. Should've come by with some of that soup you got for me, or *something*."

"You couldn't have known," I told her, placing the letter back where she'd found it. "A person's illness is normally a cause to speak with them less, not more—at least until it goes away."

Laure tested the window, but the lock was still firmly in place, and there were no broken pieces anywhere to be found.

"Well, he must've gone out the front door," she said, looking sheepish when she saw the look on my face. "I was only checking—it's possible *someone* could've climbed up here and snatched him. The door still would've been locked, and no one outside would've known a thing. You don't know what happened. Anyway, it's not a completely unreasonable assumption."

"No, I suppose not," I agreed, moving the inkwell from Gaeth's book so that I could flip through it. Gaeth, it seemed, was in the habit of making notes with his pen in the margin—a tactic Laure found useful as well though I personally found it abhorrent. *So* messy, and it made the pages of the book stick together, smearing the ink all over and ruining the neat pages.

There was another piece of parchment, folded up into a square and wedged between the pages like a bookmark. I plucked it out carefully, smoothing the creases and holding it up to the light of the window. It appeared to be another letter, though this one shorter, more disjointed than the first. It was evident to me that he'd never intended to send the thing in the first place, so I had even less compunction about reading it than I had for the first. Of course, I would never have wanted someone going through my private documents and diaries this way—but that was why I kept them so well hidden.

The letter began with the same pleasantries as the first letter had, well-wishes to the family—*famly*—and assurances that he was doing fine here in the big city.

After that, it turned rather strange.

> *Bin having stranj dreems of late, and heering stranj sounds as well. Sumtimes wen I wake I heer noyses like I am in sum jiant macheen. They sound like hissing and metal, like the inside of a blaksmithy. The room advizers tell me that ther is no such macheen in the dormatry, and that I must be dreeming, but I know when I am awake and when I am assleep.*

There was an addition at the bottom that had been crossed out, and I brought my nose nearly up to the page in order to be able to read it.

> *I think I hav been heering a voyse in my head, but it does not sound like mine.*

"Laure," I said as calmly as I could manage. "Would you please come and read this?"

She pulled herself out of the chimney where she'd been examining the flue and—rather blackened, ash smudging her pert little nose—came over to take the letter from me. I sat down on Gaeth's bed, not even mustering the will to be properly horrified at Laure covered in chimney soot. My mind was too occupied with what I'd read.

It took Laure a longer time to read than it had taken me, and as I waited I looked around the room for any clearer signs of Gaeth's mind slowly unraveling. The trouble was, everything else seemed to be very much in order—at least, in as much order as someone could expect from someone like Gaeth. There were no curses written on the walls in ink or blood—which was the first marker for insanity that anyone could expect if the stories were to be believed—and there weren't any diagrams or secret messages or blasphemous calendars, either. I nudged the round rug in the center of the room with my toe, and saw only dust beneath, not demented symbols. The most outrageous thing about that room was the sandwich—and, of course, that madman's letter.

And he had seemed so wholesome, I thought. *What a tragedy.*

"Well, what in bastion's name is this last bit?" Laure asked, in a tone like she wasn't at all certain she wanted the answer.

"He heard a voice," I told her. "A voice in his head, apparently, sounding like a 'macheen'—though I'm *willing* to bet that perhaps it was just someone from the room over. I hope the explanation is this simple: that, in his delirium from the fever, he assumed it was coming from within, as opposed to without."

Laure studied the letter again. She looked somewhat green around the edges, and I didn't blame her. All of this was very disturbing—especially when I considered that we could be living in a building alongside all kinds of madmen and -women. Clearly the 'Versity bureaucracy had no psychological screenings in place, doubtless because they didn't care to, and no protection for their students, save for locks that were easily kicked in, should the paranoia of one of our fellows turn suddenly violent.

"I think," Laure began slowly, so that I could see her mentally girding her loins, "and don't take this the wrong way, Toverre, because I know you already believe this is crazy, but . . . But I thought that *I* heard a voice, too, when the fever was bad. It came to me right as I was drifting out. After I was sick, remember? Didn't think much of it until now—guess I just shrugged it off—but reading this, it all came back to me.

He describes it exactly. Like having someone else crammed right inside your head, whispering things to you, in a voice like—well, exactly like it's coming from the blacksmithy."

I didn't want to hear that, and I opened my mouth to tell her so.

"What on *earth* do you two think you're doing here?" demanded a voice I didn't recognize, from just outside the doorway.

Laure spun around, and I leapt up from the bed as though I'd met the business end of a cattle brand. We'd both been caught, I thought dramatically, and perhaps we'd meet a fate *worse* than the business end of a cattle brand because of it.

There was a man standing at the door—older than us, but not by a considerable amount. He was wearing silver-rimmed spectacles and looking at us like a cook who'd discovered rats in her larder.

Back home, my father always had the cooks club the rats with the flat side of a shovel. I swallowed, wondering how Laure and I could have been so stupid as to sit in Gaeth's room, just waiting to be caught.

"I . . ." Laure said, but she trailed off. There really was no excuse, I thought, and had no words with which to aid her.

How ironic that, when we needed him least, someone assigned to protect the dormitory finally appeared, like a spirit summoned from the ether.

"I happen to know this room was let to Gaeth, a young man with blond hair, who I'll point out is *neither* of you two," the man said, glancing between the two of us suspiciously.

"Oh yeah, Gaeth," Laure said, finding her voice before I did. "He's our friend, and we . . . We haven't seen him for *weeks* now. Neither has anyone else. We knew he took ill with the fever, so we were just—"

"I don't see how that's any concern of mine," the man said, crossing his arms. Then he did a double take toward Laure—as men so often did—and I felt the smallest sliver of hope wedge its way into my chest. Perhaps we might be able to use her assets, hideous as it made me feel to exploit her.

Behind her back, she thrust the letter into my hand, and I took it, folding it up and sticking it into my pocket.

We could use it—somehow—if only to send home to Gaeth's poor parents as evidence of his final, lunatic ramblings. It might bring some comfort to them.

"I know it was wrong to break in like this," Laure added, taking a step forward with some hesitance, as though she was nervous. She was a born actress, though she used her skills sparingly, and she'd never even had a single lesson. "We would *never* have done it except as a very last resort, and then only because we were so worried about our friend."

"It's quite illegal," the man said with a sniff. If he was one of the room advisors, I'd never seen him. Where had he been hiding himself all this time? I doubted he even lived on the premises. "You should have come to me first with your questions."

"I know that now," Laure said, reaching up to twine a piece of her hair around her fingers. "And I feel just . . . *silly* about it, believe me. When there was someone right here all along who could help me. I don't know why we were so foolish."

Ever so slowly—not wishing to draw attention away from my leading lady—I began to inch my way to the door. Gaeth's disturbing letter was secured within my pocket, my hand covering it as an extra precaution. Though I had no idea yet of what we might use it for, it was the best piece of evidence we'd managed to uncover. I just hoped *madness* wasn't catching.

I didn't like what Laure had been trying to say before we'd been so rudely interrupted, but we'd try to sort that out later.

"Now, normally, I'd have to write the pair of you up for safety violations," the man said, some indecision in his voice. The closer we came, the younger he seemed—and not quite as terrifying as the *real* authorities might have been. I'd been certain he'd been one of the Provost's wolves come to arrest us, and now I saw he was merely a shabby little man. "But if—and that's *if*—you leave here right now, I might be able to let you go with no more than a warning, and a promise not to do it again next time."

"Could you *really* do all that?" Laure asked, her voice

pitched to a frequency I'd never heard before. It was ghastly, and my sides were starting to hurt from holding in my laughter. "How perfectly dear of you. We'd be ever so grateful. All we really wanted to see was if he was all right. I know someone like you would understand. You'd do the same for a friend, I'm sure."

The man shifted his weight, looking uncomfortable. He was starting to turn pink—just a natural side effect of being so close to Laure while she turned on the full effects of her charm. Sometimes she didn't even have to turn it on—it just worked naturally—but this was a special case, and I was in awe of her abilities. The older she got, the better the ruse worked. If only I had been born with such a lucky gift.

"Look," the dorm manager said finally, "I have it on good authority that Gaeth went home. I wouldn't look for him anymore if I were you; it'll only lead to disappointment."

"You've put our minds at ease," Laure said, moving closer to him, as though she were about to thank him in some other way. I saw the pink in his cheeks turn to red, but Laure only moved past him suddenly, out into the hallway. I managed to squeeze by him as well, murmuring a few pleasantries before bolting after her.

"At least he'll have fine dreams tonight," I whispered, once we were out of earshot. My heart was racing, and we weren't in the clear just yet—the man could always change his mind and, at the slightest infraction, I was certain my father could have me pulled from this program *despite* how prestigious everyone back home thought it was.

Laure made a disgusted face at me, her cheeks bright red. "Don't want anyone dreaming about me," she snapped, "and you could've helped, so I didn't have to do that."

I stared at her. "What more would you have me do?" I asked. "Should *I* have flirted with him?"

"I've seen you flirt before," she told me, "and just because I'm the girl of the two of us doesn't mean I should have to do such *things*."

"It's because you're the pretty one of the two of us," I told her. "It doesn't have anything to do with anything else."

"That's what you think," Laure shot back, shouldering the

door to her room open. "We're not done talking about that letter," she added hotly, "but I want to be alone for a bit, so scram. And I'd better see you at dinner."

She slammed the door shut behind her, and I winced at the sound, as well as at the little splinters of wood knocked loose onto the floor. I bent down to clean them up, wondering what had gotten into her. Perhaps, I thought, it was that time of the month, then immediately banished the thought from my mind—as she'd been able to hear me thinking that before, and the results were never pretty.

Gaeth's letter burning a hole in my pocket and the splinters bundled neatly in my kerchief, I headed back to my room. There was a great deal to think about now—one mystery solved, but a new one had immediately taken its place.

It would be a miracle if we managed to study for our exams at all.

ADAMO

Nothing wasn't the worst thing that could happen, but nothing happening when you were expecting *something* to happen was one of the worst feelings life had to offer. Mad as it might have sounded, I would've taken the routine of wartime over all this bastion-damned peace and quiet any day.

Of course, I wasn't so selfish that I'd rather have had people dying in battle than everybody going about their daily business without anything to worry over. I was just on edge because I wanted th'Esar to make his move. All this waiting around felt like wasting time, and when I didn't have any information to go on, I couldn't very well make *mine*.

There was some chance our illustrious highness wasn't going to do anything at all. He could do whatever he pleased, like pick his nose with a dragon claw, or sit on the information for the rest of his cushy life. And maybe I was just as worried about that happening as anything because I actually wanted him to give my girl another go. She'd done good work and didn't deserve ending up in pieces.

I wished I hadn't known about any of this. It was making

me jump at shadows and shout at students—even more than usual—and the take-home exam I was making up had questions that forced even Radomir to admit he was stumped.

Good, I thought. Sometimes, there weren't any easy answers. If the idiots in the class could figure out there *was* no right way to solve a problem—and you were damned no matter what tactic you took—that'd be one strong life lesson learned. I'd pass whoever figured it out and send the others to a different class, where the questions would follow a formula and their heads wouldn't get too turned around with possibilities.

"Owen, you are the most miserable and gloomy companion I have ever had," Roy had told me on more than one occasion. "I am going to be forced to find myself a new best friend—and after I worked so hard at breaking you in."

"Go right ahead," I'd replied. "I hope he likes big noses."

I was on my way to see him again—because he hadn't made good on his threat, for whatever reason—passing by the statues because I liked to take the long way to the Crescents. The walk helped me clear my head, and maybe I hoped I'd be a better man by the time I knocked on Royston's door.

Luvander's shop was open, I noted, and a young girl and her father—at least, I hoped it was her father—were just leaving. Luvander himself was seeing them out, and we caught sight of each other at the same time, him waving me over and me unable to avoid the social visit.

"Small city, isn't it?" Luvander asked. "Care to come in for some tea, entertain the crowds, sell a few hats?"

"I'm on my way to meet someone, actually," I said.

"And it's a good thing, too," Luvander replied. "You'd probably sell all the wrong fashions and start some terrible new trend."

"What's it matter to you, if you're the one making money off it?" I asked.

"Principles," Luvander replied. "If I don't have those, what am I left with?"

"A lot of hats," I said.

He stared at me before bursting into peals of laughter that seemed largely inappropriate to the situation.

"You do surprise me every now and then, I must say," Luvander said at last, wiping a tear from his eye. He was wearing a blue scarf, made out of some fancy material that looked softer than wool. "I was just saying to Balfour the other day that you had hidden depths, and here you are exhibiting them."

"Balfour's come out of hiding, then?" I asked.

"Now that he's seen my little establishment is well and truly a shop, and not some elaborate trap to snare him once and for all, you mean?" Luvander asked. "Poor young man. I think we may have been too hard on him, don't you agree?"

"Always said so, myself," I replied, folding my arms over my chest. A bit of a brisk wind picked up, and I stamped my feet impatiently.

"In any case, he didn't come to me," Luvander explained. "That's going to take some more coaxing, probably because I once put fire ants in his— Well, anyway, if they're calling him Steelballs these days, they should really credit *me* for that, that's all I'm saying."

"Luvander," I said, with a note of warning.

"Spoilsport," Luvander said. He sighed, adjusting his scarf, tucking a bunched-up pouf of it under his collar. "I ferreted him out of his little rabbit hole myself. And let me tell you that 'rabbit hole' is *entirely* too accurate a term for that place he's living. Never you worry, though; he was in extraordinarily blithe spirits when I dropped by. Apparently all it took was th'Esar's sponsored tune-up, administered by one Margrave Germaine, if I recall correctly. They were polished like mirrors, and working very well, it seemed."

"Margrave Germaine," I repeated, because something in my head was telling me I already knew that name. Somebody Royston had told me about, maybe, because he never could remember I didn't care much for gossip.

"Now, I know what you're thinking, and unfortunately I *don't* have her references on hand," Luvander said, offering an exuberant wave to someone walking down the Rue over my shoulder. They called out to him, and he performed a grand bow. "You'll simply have to accept my word—or rather, Balfour's word—that she's a whiz with mechanical parts. You should have seen the look on his face; it was simply extraordinary. It was just like the time—well, I can't actually think of a time when we went out of our way to make Balfour happy. Isn't that depressing?"

"Seems accurate to me," I said.

"You're just in a foul mood because you haven't seen them for yourself yet," Luvander said, patting my arm in a way that probably seemed thoughtful to him and not condescending in the slightest. Or maybe he did know exactly how he was coming off, and that was the whole point of how he was acting. "Off with you, then, or you'll be late for your appointment—unless that was just an excuse you made up to get out of having tea with me. You know how I chew your ear off."

"Sure," I said, distracted by that horsefly of a name buzzing around inside my big, empty head. What good was it knowing a thing if you couldn't even remember what you needed it for in the first place?

Royston would've said this was another sign of my getting older, which was only fair since I wouldn't let the issue of his nose go, despite how many years it had been. At least I wasn't going gray the way he was, but I was certainly forgetful enough, with all those student names to keep track of cluttering up valuable space inside my brain.

"And *don't* be a stranger," Luvander said sternly. "I'll look you up, too, if I have to. I have ways and means. I might even show up at your next class and cause a sensation. I can see it now: 'Reunion of the Old Flyboys Causes Riot in the Lecture Hall.' They might even ask for autographs for their collections. All those young, impressionable little minds; the things I could teach them . . . Wouldn't that be exciting?"

"Good-bye, Luvander," I said, putting my hands in my pockets and moving along down the Rue. He was only excited because he didn't know these country kids like I did. A little excitement was okay every now and then, but too much was bad for their digestion.

It wasn't me being prejudiced against the young or the countryside or anything like that, either. You only had to look at the facts: How many students had up and vanished like a good mood on a hot day? There was talk of some winter fever going around, but that all seemed like a steaming load of horse pat to me.

Then, just like that, I had it.

Margrave Germaine was the name that hotheaded girl Laurence had given me when she'd come to see me about missing lecture. I'd even cracked some fool joke about making it stick in my head so I'd remember down the road if I ever caught her lying.

That'd worked out real well for me.

I thought about it for a few more blocks, trying to figure out why someone who was working on Balfour's hands, with a background in mechanics *and* prosthetics, would be wasting valuable time looking after schoolkids with runny noses. The magicians' plague had been devastating, sure, but as far as I knew it hadn't left the Basquiat so strapped for helping hands that those with specializations were forced to do two jobs at once.

If this Margrave Germaine was looking after my boy's hands, it meant she was good enough with metal to turn it into something that nearly lived and breathed, just like our dragons. To me, that seemed like the kind of study you'd have to devote your life to in order to be any good at it. Didn't leave much time for learning medicine to treat 'Versity students.

I wasn't an expert, though, and I wasn't going to go jumping to conclusions like my fool students. I'd wait and see what Royston thought about it—if he knew the woman, and had anything to say about her—and then I'd just have to do my best not to call *him* an idiot if the answer wasn't the one I wanted to hear.

That was one of my most bothersome habits—according to Roy, at least.

The walk down to the Crescents gave me time at least to sort myself out, so I wasn't blustering about like a dragon breathing fire once I finally did find myself on Royston's street. There were dark clouds gathering overhead—the kind that'd soak you to the bone if you tried to fly through 'em— and I wondered if we were due for rain this time, or more snow.

Either way, I was getting my boots wet.

I made my way to Royston's door—not too early this time, thanks to my unexpected run-in with Luvander. At least I didn't have to worry about walking in on something nobody wanted me to see—and me least of all—since the last I'd seen him, Hal was still at the 'Versity, helping his professor come up with exam questions. I couldn't imagine what it was like to have a lecturing assistant who wasn't a thorny pain in my ass, but I guess Hal was proof that they existed somewhere.

I knocked on the door, rubbing my hands together and blowing on them for good measure. I hadn't had a good pair of gloves since the ones I'd worn for riding. Maybe I was going to have to do something about that soon, though I already knew I wouldn't be doing my shopping at Yesfir. I wanted something sensible that'd keep my hands warm and that smelled like real leather, not a flower shop.

"Just a minute!" I heard from beyond the door. Roy operated better when he had someone to greet people for him. I was sure he found it all too taxing to have to actually *go* to the front door and let people in before they froze off what made 'em men in the first place.

"You're late," Roy said. "You're never late. I was almost about to summon the Provost's wolves and have them drag the Mollydocks for your corpse."

"Too cold for swimming," I told him. "Can I come in?"

Apparently my being late meant all sorts of terrible things, like Roy actually resorting to making the coffee himself instead of having me do it for him. The whole kitchen smelled like the darkest, most vile brew I could fathom; it couldn't've been worse than if he'd made it out of stale piss and seaweed. The stench was making Roy's eyes water, which made it the perfect strength as far as I was concerned, but it also smelled like he might've burned the grounds.

Roy'd also had time to do away with the fancy delivery boxes and actually arrange the food on plates like a human. If this was why civilians were always going out of their way to be fashionably late, then I guessed I'd take it.

If I hadn't known him as well as I did, I might even have

been duped into thinking he'd made the sandwiches. But they didn't look like they were still alive, and the bread had been sliced evenly, so it was clear Royston couldn't have had a hand in their creation.

"Well," Royston said, settling in at the table. "What *have* you been up to, aside from making students cry and causing me to go gray with worry?"

"Hal told you about the weeper, huh?" I asked, making a grab for a sandwich.

"He said that a young man left your class sobbing. Sobbing *profusely*," Roy confirmed. "He didn't go into the details, so I was able to imagine them for myself."

"Damn kid's lucky he didn't start leaking out of other places once I'd finished with him," I said, tugging some of the unnecessary foliage out of my sandwich. Roy didn't wait to ask me if he could take it before he relocated it onto his plate. "Tried to lecture *me* on political correctness, and how the Ke-Han were really just poor misunderstood bastards, with the only difference between us and them being *they* were born on the wrong side of the mountains, and now that the war's over, *our* prejudice is the only thing keeping us from thinking of them as allies."

"Oh dear," Roy said, taking a sip of his coffee and grimacing elaborately at the taste. "I imagine he's lucky to have escaped with his life—though you *do* know that you're the one who'll pay for it, in the end. At the very least, you'll have another sternly worded letter from a parent to add to your collection."

"Can't wait," I grunted. At least the sandwich was good, meat and mustard and just a little bit of tomato. It was hard to feel sour about things with a good meal sitting in front of you, and that long walk had made me hungry. "I'll let you keep it with the others."

"They're certainly an exciting read," Royston said. "One day they might even be worth something."

"Sure as shit aren't worth anything now," I agreed.

"Well, I can see that you're not at all in the mood to hear what I have to say, but I feel obligated to tell you that no one's seen hide nor hair of Margrave Ginette at the Basquiat," Royston told me, now stirring liberal amounts of sugar into his coffee in an attempt to make it potable. "It's truly as though someone lifted Thremedon's skirts in the night and shook her out like a mouse. It's unsettling. You know I like a good mystery as much as the next person, Owen, but that's only if I can solve it at the end of the day."

"Rotten business," I agreed. "I hope she doesn't have family looking for her."

"I'm honestly not sure which is worse," Royston said. "If she does, or if she doesn't. I hope your companion is doing all right without her; I'm only sorry I couldn't be of more help to you."

"Well, here's your chance to make it up to me," I told him, knowing well just how much he'd appreciate it. "What can you tell me about a Margrave Germaine?"

"She has no eye at all for colors," Royston said easily. He smiled in that self-deprecating way he was so good at and took an experimental sip of his coffee. I wish I could've framed the face he made after he did so to scare my students into paying attention. "This really is horrendous; I think we should throw it out before it poisons someone. In any case, I take it that's not the kind of information you're looking for?"

"She's the one who ended up seeing to Balfour's hands," I explained, "since Ginette's nowhere to be found."

"Well, I suppose that makes sense," Roy said slowly. "I don't know her personally, but she's one of the *new* Margraves—handpicked by the Esar to replace those *we* lost, so he can be sure that at least *someone* in the Basquiat puts him first. I haven't seen her at the Basquiat since her initiation, actually. I took it as a good sign. It seemed to me that meant she wasn't spying on us."

"Really does like to have his finger in every pie," I said. It was common sense, I guessed, and if I couldn't keep track of a classroom, then I probably wouldn't have been able to keep track of an entire country. All those lords and ladies, magicians and Margraves, diplomats and servants and citizens— the more I thought about it, the more I figured I'd've gone mad long ago, my brain cracked down the middle like a rotten egg.

"He is the Esar," Royston said with a shrug. He stood, crossing to the sink and pouring the coffee out, peering after it as it gurgled down the drain. "Shall I see what I can find out about Germaine? Other than her penchant for wearing brown?"

"She's got a skill for machinery, it seems," I explained.

"And so you are suspicious of her sudden appointment," Roy concluded for me. "Since she *is* one of the Esar's, it would make sense that—if he did anything about this new technology—he'd probably have her working on it right this very moment."

I polished off my sandwich, wiping the crumbs on my napkin. "That'd make sense," I agreed. "Except why would he have her doing common physician's appointments with 'Versity students?"

"He wouldn't," Roy replied.

"Well, he is," I told him. "And you'd better watch out for your . . . boy, too, since apparently there's some kind of fever going around."

"It means so much to me when you act concerned," Roy said.

"Doesn't matter to me one way or the other," I explained, "because *I* haven't gotten sick in over fifteen years. But *you*—"

"I don't enjoy the feeling of congestion," Roy replied tartly. "And once, when I sneezed, I exploded the living room."

"I wish I had you in my classroom for practical demonstrations," I said. "If those pansy-sniffers thought they had reason to cry *before,* I'd like to see them after—"

"No thank you," Roy said, though I could see he was regretful. "As much as I enjoy teaching a good lesson, I've been in enough trouble for one lifetime. Still, I'll see what I can do about this Margrave Germaine. Looking after 'Versity students *and* Balfour's hands, you say?"

"For whatever reason," I replied.

"Let's hope I have more luck with this one," Roy said.

At that, we heard the door down the hall swing open and Hal's voice calling for Royston to see if he was in. Something shifted on Roy's face, a change from loneliness to contentment, and he didn't even try to hide it.

If Hal ever did anything to hurt that, I thought, I wasn't just sitting by on the sidelines of Roy's ill-fated love life anymore.

"You look positively gruesome," Roy said, snapping me out of my vengeful thoughts. "Is something else wrong?"

"It's that coffee stink," I told him, and went to dump the contents of my own cup down the drain.

LAURE

Toverre was supposed to meet me for supper, at which point I supposed I'd apologize to him for being sharp-tempered, but only if *he'd* apologize to *me*. Though it was hard to explain—even to myself—what I wanted him to apologize for.

But the more time I spent in the 'Versity, counting up the number of lecturers that were male versus them that were female—and the more time I spent seeing how some of the pretty students flirted with the professors to bring up their marks—the more frustrated I became. Even Toverre, with his picky little self and his barbed words, had a better chance of being who he wanted to be—whatever that was—because no matter which way I looked at it, I was only a girl. And being one of those meant using your tits more than your brains. At least, that was what everybody expected of you.

Back home it hadn't mattered so much. Or maybe I'd just been too busy raking hay and doing everything Da expected of me to notice. But in Thremedon, where the girls did their hair and their rouge just so every day, so few of them coming to classes and those who did spending more time passing notes with the boys than listening, I wondered why I'd even been invited to come in the first place.

It was all just a show, and flirting with that dorm master only served to remind me of what was expected from me. I didn't just want to be Toverre's wife.

What I *did* want to be was harder to decide, but I was still young, wasn't I? The city meant a whole world of options I hadn't even known about before I'd left home, and the idea that I wouldn't get to experience *any* of them was too cruel. I wanted the freedom to be able to decide.

My mood was made worse by everything that had happened with Gaeth, and remembering that dark metal voice echoing through my dreams. Gaeth had heard it, too—he'd put it down on paper, in his own hapless way—and now I couldn't pretend anymore that it hadn't happened.

Of all the ways to wind up equal to a boy, hearing voices definitely wasn't top *or* bottom on my list. So I was in a pretty foul mood for more reasons than one, and at least Toverre had gone against all his natural instincts and somehow refrained from asking me if I was on my monthlies. Which, thankfully, I wasn't.

That was another thing about boys: No one assumed they blew a gasket for any reason other than they were just really upset. They were allowed to be, and nobody blamed where the moon was in its cycle, or whether or not they had the ill fortune of leaking from *their* privates. It was plain unfair.

I heard dainty footsteps coming up behind me in the hall and made up my mind once and for all to be forgiving—or to at least give Toverre a chance by begging for *my* forgiveness.

But it wasn't Toverre at all. Instead, it was one of the little old owl-women who worked in the post center, where I mailed all my letters home and sometimes got a package back, when I actually remembered to check my cubbyhole. I wondered if she was coming to tell me that I'd forgotten to pick up some surprise from Da and the food had all rotted, but she didn't look as mad as I was expecting, so it couldn't have been that.

It'd happened once before, and I'd tried to *tell* Da that you couldn't just send a good cut of meat in the mail and hope it'd come through all right on the other end. He never was that good at listening, though, and he wanted to make sure I was keeping my strength up. Little did he know I'd've had to cook the thing in the fireplace.

"Hello, Laurence," said the woman. She was Barn Owl, because of how the way her hair framed her face reminded me of one. The other two were Snowy Owl and Screech Owl, both for reasons that were pretty obvious if you knew anything about owls. "I hope I'm not interrupting your dinner."

I hadn't gotten anything to eat yet, so I didn't see how she could've been, and I told her so.

"Not at all," I said, as polite as you please. If I'd been standing, it would've gone nicely with a proper curtsy.

"I have this card for you from the physicians' administrator," Barn Owl said, pulling a stiff white card out of her pocket. "Now, you know how we normally don't make deliveries, but post pickup's closed for the evening, and they indicated to me that it was rather urgent. Given past precedent . . . the meat incident . . . well, you understand."

"Sure," I told her, distracted by the appointment card in my hand. I could recognize Margrave Germaine's blocky, thick handwriting by now, though that didn't make it a familiar comfort. I wasn't suspicious like Toverre, and I didn't believe in being afraid of something unless it gave me good reason, but I knew right away that I didn't want anything to do with that physician's appointment.

Maybe I'd been feeling a little homesick, but being sent home for fever just seemed like quitting to me. And, most of all, I didn't want to hear those voices again. Once was a fluke, but twice meant you were definitely going crazy.

"Have a nice evening, Laure," Barn Owl told me.

"You, too," I said, as she turned and went back in the direction she'd come from. With her gliding off through the mess hall, I got the impression she was about to hunt down and feast on some helpless mice.

That thought made me grin, at least, before I turned my attentions back to the card in my hand.

I felt the same way about it as Toverre would've felt about a dead roach. I wished I could just will it out of existence by wishing hard enough.

After everything that'd happened to Gaeth, I didn't want to go back. It was all too eerie, and I didn't want to know any more about it just as much as I didn't want to be a *part* of it. It didn't make sense to keep seeing a doctor who made you sick, not better. Besides which, I was just plain spooked.

That was the truth of it, and I couldn't hide that from myself, let alone anyone else. I might've had fevers before, but I'd *never* heard voices—clanking, whispery things that murmured to me in my dreams, right before I woke up. Despite how skeptical he was, I felt certain even Toverre would've heard voices if he'd been called in for a checkup like the rest of us. Whether or not he'd've been able to sort them out from all the other voices in his head—telling him to pick this up and scrub that stain and make sure those matched—was another matter entirely.

Maybe Margrave Germaine had learned from someone that Toverre's head was too crowded for *another* talker, and that was why they hadn't even bothered calling him in past the first screening.

Like he knew I was thinking about him, Toverre decided to take that exact moment to show up, right before I could drive myself *too* crazy thinking in circles. Sometimes it just helped to talk to someone—or, in Toverre's case, to listen to someone else talk. His was one voice I recognized, and as annoying as it sometimes was, it comforted me because it reminded me of home.

Toverre was carrying a tray that had all my favorites: meat and bread *and* cheese, and he looked a little squirrelly around the eyes, so I could tell he was gearing up to apologize. He was the good kind of sorry—as far as Toverre being sorry went, anyway, coming to say so before he circled back around to being awful again.

"Here," he said, thrusting the tray at me and looking uncomfortable.

I took a piece of cheese, popping it in my mouth and chewing thoughtfully. "All right," I said, accepting the offering. "You can sit down."

He tugged a napkin out of somewhere to clean off the seat across from me, then sat down in it very neatly. "Oh, good," he said. "I thought you were going to be in a snit. I thought maybe you had—"

"Don't say it," I warned him.

Quickly, Toverre switched tactics. "What's that in your

hand?" he asked. "I hope you aren't soliciting men vis-à-vis their business cards?"

Because that sounded so much like me. Sometimes I didn't know where Toverre got his wild ideas from. "Got a summons for another checkup," I told him. No point in mincing words, and making Toverre grovel at my feet for forgiveness had never really been my style to begin with.

Toverre turned white—whiter than usual—leaning closer over the table.

"You aren't *serious,*" he said in a grave whisper.

"Think I'd joke about something like this?" I asked him, shoving the card in his direction. "See for yourself."

"Oh dear," Toverre said, reaching for it, then drawing back quickly, not even willing to touch it. He probably thought he could catch the fever from it, or at least catch himself his own appointment. "Oh, *Laure,* no! I can't have you going. We don't know what . . . what those awful physicians might do to you this time. After the state you returned in from your last visit . . . Not to mention whatever's happened to Gaeth . . ."

"Do you think I don't know all that?" I asked.

"Well then, you mustn't," Toverre replied.

"I can't just not *go,*" I said, though the idea was sounding pretty good to me right about now. "They'd know where to find me; all my information's on some kind of file. What's to stop 'em from just showing up and carting me off? Unless," I added, "you want to run away with me to Molly. But I hear it gets dirty down there."

"There are laws against that sort of thing, I should hope," Toverre said, looking scandalized.

"Bet there aren't *any* rules if they say it's for your own good," I replied, slicing off another piece of cheese and cramming it into my mouth. "I'm just a girl, after all. Nothing more than a simple 'Versity student, too. How'm I supposed to know how to take care of myself? Better I let these fine Thremedon physicians do it for me. Who's anyone going to believe, them or me?"

Toverre bit his lip, looking uncertain of how to answer me. I took advantage of his silence, ripping open a roll and filling it with sliced meat. I hadn't realized how hungry I was until the food was in front of me. And Toverre didn't even have anything to say about my manners, which meant he must've been troubled indeed.

"I'll go with you, then," he said at last, though I knew *just* how he felt about being stuck in a physician's room. It was almost sweet of him to offer, even sweeter still for him to think he was capable of helping me. "I *am* your fiancé, after all. Surely there are some rights I might take advantage of. Perhaps I'll pretend that I'm too simple to understand the particulars of a checkup—I'll assume that your honor is being violated and insist that I *must* be allowed to accompany you. Otherwise, I'll have to write home about this, no matter what you say. Doesn't that sound intimidating?"

It did, but probably not for the same reasons he was imagining.

As much as I appreciated Toverre's offer of self-sacrifice— and I did; it was enough to sweeten my sour-pickled heart— I was pretty sure that the only thing *worse* than being in there by myself would be if Toverre came along.

I could just picture him stopping Margrave Germaine before every step of the procedure, wanting to know if everything'd been sterilized, and if the sterilization'd been done properly, and who'd done it, and could he speak with them, too? They'd remove him by the scruff of the neck like an unwanted kitten, and in the end I'd be grateful, preferring the fever dreams to this new nightmare.

"I'll think about it," I told him around a mouthful of the sandwich I'd made.

"*Think* about it?" Toverre repeated, like I'd decided to take a vacation from my senses.

"It's my appointment, ain't it?" I asked, folding up the rest of my cheese in a napkin for later. I always got peckish around midnight, especially when I was studying. "It's not for another few days. I've got time; I'll think of something."

"You're not *really* considering going by yourself, are you?" Toverre asked. "Not when we still don't know what happened to Gaeth?"

"He went home," I told him, hoping that by saying it, I could convince myself.

"A very likely story," Toverre replied. "Not without all his things, he didn't. I don't think our friend Gaeth was all that well-off, Laure. You could tell by his handwriting he had no kind of education. And the state of that winter coat . . . ! He wouldn't leave all his clothes and his best pair of boots behind."

He was right. Just thinking about that empty room made chills run up and down my spine.

"How about this: I won't do anything without running it by you first," I offered. It wasn't exactly the bargain Toverre'd been looking for, but at least it was the truth. "I'll start right now: I'm going for a walk to eat some cheese and clear my head."

"We do have exams to study for," Toverre cautioned, staying planted in his seat while I stood up. There were crumbs in my skirts, and I shook them out onto the floor, Toverre quickly pulling his boots away so that nothing would get on them.

"I'm horseshit on tests whether I study or not," I said. We both knew it, so there was no point in being polite about it. "And I've got other things to worry about."

"I could always make you up some quick-cards," Toverre said, thinking it over. "They did wonders for your grammar last year."

"Sure, okay," I said, since I knew the only thing he liked better than studying was proving he could teach the same stuff to me, too. "You do that. And I'll come back to get 'em when I'm done with my walk."

"You aren't going to go somewhere dangerous?" Toverre asked, recalling, no doubt, my threat of running away to Molly from before.

"I'll take this butter knife with me," I offered, picking it off the table and making like I was going to hide it in my sleeve. Toverre looked so distressed that it wasn't even any fun, and I dropped the knife back onto my plate. "Just walking along the 'Versity Stretch," I promised. "I'm not that foolish. Not *yet*, anyways."

Toverre'd made me promise just after we'd arrived—just after we'd nearly been robbed blind—that I wouldn't walk around the city at night by myself. It was too dangerous for young women of a certain age, and even though I could take care of my honor just fine, I knew Toverre's delicate constitution wouldn't be able to handle all that worrying. That left the 'Versity grounds for me to roam, however, streets winding in and out of all the mismatched buildings, each one of them looking like it had been built for a different street.

It comforted me to walk routes I already knew, and the cold night air was bracing—not frigid and unbearable the way Toverre said. It was a crowded time of night, with laughter bursting up off every street corner. There were even night classes for the upperclassmen going on in some of the lecture halls, and I found myself standing in front of Cathery without ever having plotted out a real destination.

There was no one in the city I could really talk to, without being careful not to make them worry too much about my sanity. In fact, there was barely anyone I felt comfortable talking to about the weather, except for Toverre. There was only one person I could think of who might listen, and ex–Chief Sergeant Professor Specialpants Adamo'd made the mistake of telling me where his office was. He was double-cursed, since I kind of thought of him as the sort of man who'd clear out a cluttered head in no time.

It had to be him.

Before I'd had time to talk myself out of it, I was inside the building, the door blowing shut behind me with a sudden gust of wind.

"Cold day," said the desk clerk, smiling at me in a familiar way.

Not as cold as me, I thought, brushing past him with a grunt of agreement.

It took me a few tries to find Adamo's office, because I didn't remember the number Radomir'd given me off the top of my head—it was written down in my notes somewhere, but I hadn't thought to bring those with me. Bastion, I hadn't even been planning on coming at all. I should've been discouraged when I opened the door on a private session between a tall professor with graying hair and a young man about four years my senior, both of them coloring all kinds of purple when I barged in and interrupted them.

"Should've locked the door," I said, giving them a salute. I left my own blushing until I got out into the hall.

Maybe Toverre was right about me—and the rest of the world, too, for that matter—and I was just a silly girl who couldn't find her way about a simple lecture building.

But then I told myself *I* wasn't the one who should be embarrassed since I wasn't the one tangled up with a man at least twenty years my senior. They ought to've taken that someplace private if they were going to go for it at all.

By my fourth attempt, I'd at least started knocking, and when I heard Professor Adamo's voice call out to me with a peremptory "Yeah?" I wondered what I was even doing there. What was *he* even doing there, considering he'd gone and said he didn't even know where the place was? Well, maybe he'd made a point of finding it since exam season was coming up. It wasn't for me to parse another man's motivations, though; I had enough to worry about when it came to my own. What'd I plan on saying, I asked myself, and, maybe more importantly, what was the man going to think of me?

And still, I'd come that far. Might as well see it through all the way.

"Not interrupting anything?" I called through the door, a bit suspiciously. The ex–Chief Sergeant Professor didn't seem like that kind of man, but then, I'd been wrong in my judgment before.

"Enter," was his reply.

I turned the knob and pushed my way in to find him just sitting still and quiet behind his desk, hands folded in front of him, staring off into the air. There wasn't anyone else in the room, at least, and I found I was a little relieved that there wasn't anything fishy going on behind his closed door. Try as I might, I just couldn't see Adamo doing *that* with one of the other boys or girls. It made me mad as anything to picture it.

He didn't even seem to like teaching them. Why would he bother with them outside of class on top of that?

"Well?" he asked, when I didn't say anything. "Take a seat. I'm figuring you're worried about the take-home?"

"Not worried at all," I said, since I'd taken a glance at the copy Toverre'd gone and snatched the minute the test had become available. "There's no answer to that first question. You're better off skipping it altogether and spending your time on them that *can* be solved."

Adamo went silent for a second, in a way that made me near certain I'd gone and stepped in it.

"That's exactly right," he said at last, not looking altogether pleased that he had to admit it. "It's not that there's no point to it, mind, but it's the principle behind the question, rather than the question itself that's so important. It's a hard strategy for some to take to—sacrificing a lost cause so you can turn your attention toward the stuff *worth* salvaging. You're the first person to figure it out if I'm not mistaken. Which I'm usually not."

Somewhere along the way his face had shifted from looking sour to downright approving. I couldn't say I minded the change one bit.

"Well, that's something new for me, anyway," I said. "Normally come exam time, I already know I'm not doing well on them."

"Why not?" Adamo asked, as I sat down. The leather chair on the other side of his desk gave out a long, guttural creak when I lowered myself into it; it was the sort of thing Toverre would have been humiliated by, but Adamo didn't seem to notice it. That was a relief. "You're a smart girl."

"Just don't have a head for memorizing things," I said, feeling warm and more than my fair share of proud that he'd called *me* smart. Sneaking a glance at that test was the best decision I'd made yet. "And I never write down what I'm supposed to."

Adamo snorted, the faintest twitch of a smile hiding in the corner of his mouth. "That so," he said. "Well, me neither, when I went through schooling."

"Then I guess there's hope for me," I replied. I toyed with a piece of leather that was peeling off the arm of the chair, revealing cream-white stuffing beneath. "Not that I think I'd be riding dragons anytime soon, though maybe something similar."

"Guess we're all hoping there won't be further need for that," Adamo said.

"Guess so," I agreed. "Though it seems kinda disappointing, doesn't it? All that work on 'em, and then—poof!—nothing."

"It was more of a crash than a poof," Adamo said. "But I take your meaning."

"Not that I'm one of those lunatics who thinks we should be back at war with somebody, not caring who it is," I added quickly, in case he took the wrong meaning. There was one of those in our class. It seemed to me like he'd only taken it so he could try to talk Adamo around to his way of thinking, which was that the entire Ke-Han Empire needed to be wiped off the map. That type of plan didn't have a lot to do with thinking at all, in my opinion, just some kind of dark spite. As I saw it, he wasn't any better than those in the room who acted like the Ke-Han hadn't done any wrong, and we should just leave them alone to build up their forces again and try us a second time.

But those kinds of talks gave me headaches, mostly since nobody seemed to believe they could be of two minds about a thing—didn't have enough to go around to be of *one* mind about something, I suspected—so I tended to stay out of 'em, unless something in particular really got my goat.

"You can appreciate some of the things that came out of the war without disrespecting those who sacrificed themselves during," Adamo said. Unfortunately for me, he didn't have anything interesting on his desk that I could stare at—no trinkets or portraits of any sweethearts or anything like that for me to focus on instead of him—so that I ended up staring right at his face while he was talking. It wasn't the worst thing that could've happened to a girl. He had a nice face, even when he *wasn't* yelling at anyone. "But that depends on who you talk to, and not everyone's gonna agree, of course."

"That'd be nice, but I'm not holding my breath," I said.

"You'd go purple waiting," Adamo agreed.

"And then there's them that'd say I can't understand all of it anyhow, on account of how it's got nothing to do with me," I agreed, picking out a long tuft of the chair's stuffing before I caught myself; he was watching me do it. Even though he hadn't said anything to stop me, I had a feeling Adamo didn't want me to leave his office looking like I'd used it for shearing sheep. "Although there's some lady diplomats, aren't there? Some of 'em famous, even."

"Not too many of 'em, though," Adamo confirmed, leaning back in his chair. "Though it seems to me the grades come out about even between the boys and girls. Only difference between 'em in my experience is that the boys usually smell worse."

"You're just saying that because you've never gotten a whiff of *me* after mucking out our stables," I said, then immediately wished I hadn't. As great as my new boots from Toverre were, they didn't come with magical properties and never stopped me from sticking my foot right in my mouth.

Adamo gave me a hard look, like he was trying to decide whether I was putting one over on him or not.

"Actually, on the grand scale of horrible stink I could live without, horse manure's not as bad as you'd expect," he said, after a moment.

"Yeah, but chicken shit's just *awful,*" I said, before I could stop myself. "For a small animal like that, you wouldn't expect it to be so much worse."

Adamo pressed his hands against his face, but I could tell I'd made him laugh. So talking about these things with people wasn't *always* the big disaster Toverre wanted to pretend it was. Adamo seemed like the kind of man who needed a good laugh every now and then; made his whole face look different. Younger.

"I was always thankful that was one thing we missed out on," Adamo said, once he'd gotten control of himself again. "Stables in the Airman always smelled like metal and fire, though I guess that's its own stink once you get right down to it. But I never had to worry about putting my boot down in fresh dragon spoor, so I guess that's something."

"I bet it'd be huge," I said, then had to clap my hands right *over* my mouth to keep from saying anything more.

Despite what Toverre said, I did have *some* sense of propriety, and sitting up in Adamo's office chatting about shit just wasn't cutting it. Even if we *were* having a grand old time.

Adamo did laugh then, but I didn't know if it was because of what I'd said or just the trapped look on my face.

"So," Adamo said, but he couldn't get past it, and his eyes looked a little leaky, like he was holding a big chuckle in. He had to stop and try again. "Sorry about that, something caught in my throat."

"Wish I could say the same," I said, feeling my cheeks getting all hot for no reason. It was right about then I realized that I'd ripped a hunk of stuffing out of the chair between my finger and thumb, and I quickly went about trying to shove it back into the chair again. "Might keep me from saying the things I shouldn't, if there was."

"Not at all," Adamo said. "Too many people mince words. Gives me a headache trying to figure out what they're saying."

"No wonder you're so suspicious about a simple student's motives," I replied.

"So you're really not here about exams, then," Adamo said, like it'd taken a whole conversation such as this one to convince him I really *wasn't* playing coy.

I had to think about how to answer him since I'd already proved my on-the-spot tactics needed a little polishing. Now that I'd come all the way up there and I was sitting in Adamo's office with its sensible leather chairs and good, hard lighting, I didn't know how to start saying what I needed to say. Even Toverre didn't really believe me about those voices, though I couldn't much blame him for that. That kind of madness was for madmen; some of the beggars Da chased out of our barn in the winter were always yammering on to people who weren't there.

Maybe you were only crazy once you started talking back, but either way I really didn't want to find out.

At the same time, I wasn't the sort to weasel out of something when I could face it head-on, and I didn't want the professor to think I was some delicate winter blossom who couldn't stomach the idea of a physician's visit.

I didn't know how, but it seemed like I'd done something to earn Adamo's good opinion, and I didn't want to up and prove him wrong.

"Just . . . a lot of things been getting under my skin lately," I said, still working out how much I wanted to say, and how much I wanted to keep a lid on. "Guess I don't have so many people here in Thremedon I can talk to. And I know none of that's *your* problem, so I guess you can kick me out if you want—except when I came in, you were just sitting here by yourself not doing anything. So it seems to me like you must not have that many people to talk to, either."

"Did that start out as an apology before it came around to insulting me at the end, there?" Adamo asked.

"Maybe," I said, realizing that was what it must've sounded like. "But I'm pretty sure I didn't mean it like that."

"Doesn't make all that much difference," Adamo said, and just like that I knew he wasn't mad at me. That was a relief. For some reason, the idea made me even more uncomfortable than the idea of sitting crosswise from a dragon as it breathed steam at you. "Shouldn't punish someone when they're right, should you?"

"Just helps me think, having someone to talk to," I said, easing back into the chair again. At least he hadn't kicked me out, but I didn't need Toverre around to tell me I was being impertinent.

"It's Laurence, right?" Adamo asked.

"Laure's fine," I told him. I figured if I'd come to him to talk about my problems, then I could let him be a little more familiar.

"All right, then, Laure," Adamo said, looking the way he did right before he stood up to make a big speech in class. "I'm not gonna pretend that I'm the kind of professor who sits around after lecture just waiting for students to come to me with their troubles, though. Most times I don't even know what to do with my *own* troubles 'cept for make them worse. On top of that, I don't have a lot of what you might call patience for the things these kids consider real trouble, anyway. Do you see what I'm saying? It all adds up to this: I don't like being asked too many questions, and I'm a piss-poor candidate for a mentor."

"So you're crap with advice," I said, once he'd finished. "That's all right. I never said I wanted someone to tell me what to do, just someone to listen when I open my mouth, that's all."

Adamo blinked, looking like I'd cut the wind straight out of his sails. He'd been expecting one thing, and I'd gone and given him another.

"Well, fine," he muttered. "So long as you're forewarned."

"Think my da'd lock me up in the stables if he knew I was bothering someone like you with my problems, anyway," I told him. "So I won't trouble you for too much longer. I think I've already decided what I want to do for now—see? Just talking things through with somebody listening really *can* help."

Even though I hadn't told Adamo about half the stuff I'd wanted to, I wasn't lying when I said I felt more confident about my prospects—rambling on had given me time to clear my head and put all my thoughts in order. I'd told Toverre I couldn't put off the appointment, but I was starting to wonder what exactly might happen if I did. The worst they could do would be show up at school, and then I could ask 'em in front of everyone what'd happened to Gaeth.

The plan still needed a little fine-tuning, but putting it off would at least give me some more time to prepare.

"So I didn't have to do anything at all," Adamo said.

"Except for grunt a reply now and then," I agreed.

"But you've decided what you're gonna do for a problem you didn't even tell me about?" he asked.

"Righto," I said, getting out of my chair. I probably should've given him a curtsy or something, but he seemed like the kind of man who would've preferred a salute. I fixed the uneven buttons on my coat instead. "That's the one. You've been a real help."

"Are you *trying* to be difficult?" Adamo asked. "I mean, this can't all be by accident. Now you've gone and made me curious—so if you were looking to make me feel like a liar, consider your plan successful."

"When I was little, Da's champion racing horse kicked me in the head," I told him, allowing my eyes to cross, just for further effect. "And me? I've been a little funny ever since."

"That explains everything," Adamo said, but I caught him looking at my face like he wasn't quite sure if I'd been joking or not. He got up after me, shouldering into a coat that looked like it'd been made from at least forty cows all dead and stitched together. I didn't ask if he meant to walk me back to my dorms, just did up the collar of my coat and slowly made my way out of his office.

I was pretty relieved when he followed me anyway, turning out the lamp and locking the door behind us. Some dumb joke about me getting kicked in the head was no proper way to say good-bye, even by my standards. Besides, it'd be nice to have the company.

The walk downstairs through Cathery was mostly quiet at that hour, all the classrooms locked up and darkened; even the last of the brown-nosers and stragglers had already gone home. When we passed by the door with that professor and his student I thought about telling Adamo what I'd seen, but something made me stop, and it wasn't because of the delicacy of the situation, either. He just didn't seem like the kind of man who'd enjoy random gossip. I'd have to save that tidbit for Toverre, who'd probably eat it up.

At least the hallway wasn't completely silent, since Adamo kept clearing his throat like he had something to say, but couldn't quite get around to saying it.

"You want a lozenge?" I asked finally, once we got to the bottom of the steps.

"No, thanks," Adamo said.

"'Cause it's possible you might have some kind of cold," I added. "Hot bath with steam in the room'll fix it pretty quick."

"Or a lozenge," Adamo said.

"I don't even have one, anyway," I replied. "I just thought you might know it sounded like you need one."

It was colder than an old stallion's lonely balls outside, and it would've been dark as pitch if it weren't for the lanterns lining the 'Versity Stretch. I wished I'd thought to bring my gloves, or maybe even a hat; at least I could comfort myself that it wasn't a very long walk back to the dorms.

There was even a little kiosk set up along the walkway, selling hot drinks and stale pastries and the like. I couldn't even imagine how frozen the poor bastard inside must've been, with his breath puffing out in front of him like he was having a smoke.

"Hot drink'll help your throat, too," I suggested.

"You wouldn't know this, 'cause you're still young," Adamo told me, "but when you get to a certain age and you have a cup of coffee after sundown, you don't sleep a lick all night."

"What about hot chocolate?" I asked.

Adamo considered it, face looking craggy with all the nighttime shadows. Then he strode away from me. "Two hot chocolates," he said when he returned, handing me a steaming cup.

"Can't accept that," I said, poking around in my own pockets for some of my allowance.

"Why not?" he asked. "It's already done."

"Well," I replied, trying to remember how Toverre had phrased it, "because it's just not proper for a young girl to let a man buy her anything, unless it's with intentions of leading him on. Or something like that, anyway."

"Then maybe I'll have you buy me a coffee some other time," Adamo said.

"When it's still light out," I added, feeling uncharacteristically buoyant. It was strange—I'd spent so much time thinking about the dragons themselves that there'd never been any space in my head for their riders, but now that I was spending time with one of 'em, it was nearly as exhilarating as I'd always imagined it might be to ride a dragon.

Except if I'd had hot chocolate up in the air, I'd probably have gotten the lot of it on my face instead of in my mouth.

"That sounds fine," Adamo agreed. "If it's all right with your ladyship, of course."

I grinned into my cup, blowing on it to let off some of the

steam. Somehow, no matter how long I waited, I ended up too impatient and I always burned my tongue. Despite that, it was delicious, not too sweet but not too bitter, either. Adamo downed half his paper cup in one big swallow, then grimaced.

"Don't like things sweet," he explained, when he caught me staring at him.

"Guess I'll just have to make sure that coffee I buy you doesn't have any milk or sugar," I said.

"Bastion bless," someone said from behind us. "Owen Adamo, what *are* you doing?"

It was a man with a posh kind of voice, though it wasn't *so* snooty that I took an instant dislike to him. He didn't have a look on his face like he was smelling something bad all the time, either, and he had nice eyes above a big nose. My first impression wasn't all bad—just that he was a little too citified for my tastes. Standing next to him, just a shade taller, was someone I did recognize: the lecturer's assistant Toverre'd taken it into his head to fall in love with for no reason other than his sky-blue eyes and glorious freckles, which in my opinion weren't all that glorious, anyway. At least the situation with Gaeth seemed to have distracted him from that nonsense of late, though I had my own private assumptions about why. Hal stamped his feet and puffed into his hands with the cold, offering Adamo a small wave.

"Having a cup of cocoa," Adamo replied. "Why, Roy, what's it look like?"

"You know very well what it looks like," Roy replied, looking back and forth between me and Adamo. "Ah, if I'm not mistaken, this is the same exuberant lass who once inquired as to whether your trousers caught fire in midair, is it not?"

"That's me," I said, feeling a distinct prickling in my cheeks. At least it was cold, so I could probably square away most of the blame on that.

"Royston," Hal said, coming very near to elbowing him in the ribs. "I'm sorry about him. He's always going on about manners, but I think he secretly likes forgetting he has them."

"It would hardly be polite to ignore what's right in front of my eyes, wouldn't you say?" Royston said with a sniff. I knew exactly what he was thinking, and by hiding a sudden giggle in my hot chocolate, I ended up making a sound like I was choking.

"Might be needing spectacles soon," Adamo suggested. "Seems like your eyes are finally going."

"This really is incredible," Roy said, ignoring him completely. "You have no idea, young lady—Owen Adamo has not willingly spoken to someone younger than he is for at least fifteen years. And he does not drink hot chocolate, either."

"We probably shouldn't interrupt him, then," Hal said, looking at me like he thought he recognized me but couldn't quite place it. He looped one arm through Roy's, giving him a gentle tug. After a moment of standing his ground, this Roy fellow allowed himself to give.

"Don't think you've heard the end of this," Roy called to us, as Hal pulled him into the night.

"Never once thought I had, actually," Adamo muttered. He finished off his drink in one more go, then crushed the cup in his hand with a small grunt. "Here's some advice, Laure."

"Thought you didn't like giving it," I said.

"Consider it more of a warning, then," he told me. I nodded, touching the backs of my teeth with my numb tongue—I'd definitely burned it, and now all the taste buds were tingling. "Never keep an old friend around for too long."

"And why's that?" I asked.

"Because they start knowing you too well," Adamo replied.

CHAPTER EIGHT

BALFOUR

We were in the middle of delicate talks with Chanteur—we'd graduated from the laborious task of hammering out land trade rights and finally come to the crux of the Arlemagne visit, which was to establish our mutual desires for alliance during future wars—when I first heard the noise.

It was a low hum, like gears beginning to grind slowly against one another. I looked up to see if anyone else had noticed, but they were all paying attention to the passionate speech Chanteur was giving—about their centuries-old marine difficulties with Verruges, and why it was necessary for Volstov and Arlemagne to crush those seafaring pirates once and for all.

No one but I had noticed, then.

I waited for the sound to fade, or for someone else to glance up and catch my eye. But neither of those things happened; rather, the noise grew louder, and it sounded like a piece of metal being dragged over steel. I pressed my fingers to my temple, wondering why no one else was reacting to it. Chanteur hadn't even paused in the middle of his speech.

Perhaps there was some construction happening in the street and I'd been so immersed in my own business that I'd missed reading the notification posted downstairs. Or perhaps everyone else in the room was simply a more professional diplomat than I, trained to tune out all extraneous noise so that it wouldn't interrupt proceedings. Even Troius didn't show any signs of being disturbed—half-asleep, perhaps, and twiddling a pen between his fingers like he was thinking about taking notes, but also thinking about how nice it would be not to bother. There was nothing in his expression that indicated he was hearing the same frightful noises I was.

I drew in a deep breath, willing myself to be calm. Despite all my best efforts to ignore what I was hearing, the sound itself was slowly intensifying. It was like being caught within the workings of some enormous waterwheel, the metal groaning and creaking all around me.

At the Airman, Ivory had often complained of suffering from headaches so severe that he took to bed and wouldn't speak to anyone for the entire day. He'd said it sounded like all the dragons crowding themselves into his head at once, squeezing and scraping up against one another until he felt like sticking his knife in there just to get them out again.

Fortunately for everyone, not the least Ivory himself, he'd never actually gone through with the plan.

"I think that you're forgetting where Volstov's strengths lie," said Diplomat Auria, one of the more-experienced civil servants attached to our particular case. "It's been years since we fought any kind of naval battle—decades, even. Our resources are exhausted from warring with the Ke-Han for so long—until these past months, that was our main focus—and we've only *just* begun to recover from the economic loss, not to mention the depletion of our soldiers. Surely none of you has forgotten this."

She added this last point with a look around the Volstovic side of the table, as though we'd all managed to fail her once again. It was evident that she was frustrated by her team being comprised of mostly novices. Most of those with more experience, such as Margrave Josette, were working on relations between Volstov and the Ke-Han—and Auria had made it clear on more than one occasion that, should negotiations fall through, she did not expect to catch any of the blame for it. One woman alone could not champion this cause, she'd explained, and also, it seemed immensely humorous to her that after years of being qualified for more than she was given, she'd somehow *gone back* to being a 'Versity lecturer rather than receiving her desired promotion.

"Surely there's no need to be *so* negative," Troius reasoned. "No one's counseling we leap from one war and straight into the next. It's merely a question of support—isn't that right, Chanteur? *If* Verruges should come knocking, we pledge to lend our boots to give them a firm kick in the ass, pardon the expression."

Troius was good with people; even over the roaring between my temples, I saw that Chanteur appreciated the friendly piece of vulgarity and offered us all his first real chuckle that day.

"That *is* what we had been hoping for," Chanteur said.

"I believe it's well established that Verruges *will* and indeed has already been 'knocking,' as you so charmingly put it, for nearly as long as we were at war with the Ke-Han," Auria replied. "I do not believe our country can agree to something that conscripts us into further conflict, and certainly not one with no conceivable end in sight. Simply put, Volstov cannot *afford* to agree, despite our desire to show solidarity."

Chanteur dabbed at his nose, looking drippy but also mortally offended that we hadn't been moved by the passion of his speech alone. I was curious to hear what he'd make of his defense—that is, if that infernal racket would quiet for long enough to let me listen.

Unfortunately, at just that moment, there was a horrible screeching sound, like metal shearing apart, and I buried my face in my hands, attempting to squeeze it out. My hands were somehow cold through the gloves, even though the rest of me was sweating like it was the dead of summer.

Then, just as abruptly as it had started, the noise stopped. After such intensity of sound, I felt for a moment as though I'd actually gone deaf. If it hadn't been for the sound of my own heart pounding in my ears, in fact, I would've assumed I had. Slowly, the regular noises of the day began once more to filter in; I could still hear the sounds of Auria arguing with Troius, and Chanteur blowing his nose in between interjections; but they seemed distant now, as though my head had been plunged into a bucket of water.

Another voice, one I didn't recognize, whispered something in my ear.

I jumped—a perfectly reasonable reaction, I thought, given I hadn't realized anyone was so near to me, but I found I'd been correct in my assumption. There *was* no one close enough to me for that, and yet I still heard, or even felt, the echo of that voice, the sensation of hot breath against my cheek and throat.

My twitching was severe enough to catch Troius's attention. He gave me a strange look and broke away from the argument for a moment to write something down on his collection of blank notes at last. Just as though we were two bored students in the 'Versity, he folded it in half and slid it across the table.

I glanced around to see if anyone had noted the action, but Chanteur and Auria were deeply engaged in a discussion about whether or not we were Verruges's next target if Arlemagne's sea defenses should fall. No one had noticed, so I read Troius's note.

Are you all right? it said.

I smoothed the page out carefully, the fingers on my right hand twitching ever so slightly. It was likely a cause of my nerves, but even the smallest of involuntary spasms made me nervous, as though at any moment my hands would begin to fail me again. Was this to be the way the rest of my life was—my hopes raised by a period of good luck, only to be dashed again when the mechanisms slowly wound down once more?

I am fine, I wrote back, and hurriedly shoved the paper in Troius's direction.

Chanteur was tapping his fingers against the table in irritation now, staring at Auria as if he was pondering declaring a very personal war between the two of them there and then. I mimicked his gesture without thinking, drumming my own gloved fingers quietly against the table's surface. It was a simple enough act, and yet all at once the grinding of metal started up again in my ears. The sound of it was muted now, like the gears of an enormous clock turning to keep time.

Feeling distinctly foolish, I used one of my own sheets of

paper to write a message to Troius. *Do you hear anything strange?* it asked, and I passed it under the table before I could be tempted to elaborate.

"I am of the opinion that we have been very generous in our talks so far," Chanteur was saying; it seemed Auria had gotten out of her chair now, the better to look him in the eye. That was the trouble with women diplomats, Troius had explained to me once over lunch; everyone expected them to be sweet and kind, and when they turned out to be ballbusters, it was double the usual offense. I didn't agree with him, but it did seem to be part of the trouble Chanteur was having at the moment—not Auria's fault, I thought privately, but rather his. "Considering the various indignities visited upon the last envoy—how our nobility suffered at Volstovic hands—I think it very unexpected that you would deem yourself worthy of commanding anything at all, let alone steering the direction of these talks. We are the ones who *deigned* to send a second envoy, after all."

"I will not be bullied into making a decision," Auria said, turning rather red in the face, herself. "I don't care how many times I have to repeat myself, Chanteur. We may continue this discussion in front of the Esar, if we must, as I am but his mouthpiece here. He will tell you, the same as I have, that we are not currently able to donate anything to your cause."

I felt a tapping at my leg and reached down to take the note back from Troius.

The only thing I hear is the sound of our talks being extended another two months, the note read. Under that, crossed out but still legible, was: *Kill me now.*

I smiled, but my skin had turned clammy with sweat, and I was starting to feel suffocated by the still air in our discussion chamber. Underneath those miserable talks remained the faint humming, whirling of cogs, and the occasional clang, like a piece of metal being beaten flat. If I could get out of the room, I hoped, there might be some chance the noise wouldn't follow me. Such an idea didn't seem logical if the sound was in my head—and it had to be, if Troius hadn't made note of it—but then, what *was* logical about hearing things?

Metal groaned, like the beating of enormous wings, and I heard the voice again, just the faintest whisper. It was too quiet to make out. It sounded halfway between the cry of a baby and a lonely moan.

Perhaps I was suffering from some postwar medical condition that hadn't chosen to manifest itself until just then. If so, the timing was excellent. I'd be the latest airman to destroy relations with the Arlemagne, just carrying on tradition— although it didn't seem to me that it would have been entirely my fault. Matters were self-destructing without my assistance.

I'd heard of soldiers who'd been in great battles coming home with shock, dealing with sounds that weren't there, memories of the horrors they'd seen—their minds transforming harmless, everyday noises into something far more sinister. I'd spent the better part of my life surrounded by the very sounds I was hearing now, the creak and groan of organic metal, living machines. It was exactly like stepping into the dragon stables—to speak with Anastasia for a time or hide from the other members of the corps. I didn't know what could possibly have triggered it after so long, but now that I'd recognized the sounds, there seemed to be no other explanation for them.

I would have to seek out a physician, or perhaps consult first with Adamo and Luvander to see if they'd ever suffered anything similar. Maybe in visiting with my fellow airmen, I'd unearthed more than pleasant memories.

Now, that would be an interesting discussion to initiate. It would be harder to begin than any awkward letter, and I could just see myself, invited to tea in the back of Luvander's hat shop, clearing my throat and asking, "So, have you heard any dragons lately, boys?"

My right hand twitched again, and I reached into my coat pocket for a handkerchief to dab some of the perspiration off my face.

"We'll put it to a vote, then," Auria was saying, her jaw clenched tight. "If I find I'm outnumbered, for whatever reasons, then we'll discuss further terms about the specific aid Arlemagne will require. If *not,* then you'll have our answer clearly, without appeal. Perhaps we may still work out some sort of emergency clause with regards to your situation with Verruges. Rest assured, Volstov would never abandon an ally, despite our current position in world affairs."

I flexed my hand, then clenched it beneath the table, practicing until I no longer felt the lingering sensation of that lone, troubling twitch. My hands had been so lifelike since their recent overhaul—and certainly my living hands had also twitched during moments of great anxiety—but I found that I didn't altogether like the feeling of it when it happened to the metal. There were some accuracies that a prosthetic simply shouldn't be able to achieve, and when they moved on their own, it always left me to wonder if they'd simply end up developing a kind of awareness of their own, just the way the dragons had.

The idea was utterly absurd—but no more so, I supposed, than hearing voices.

I glanced up from the table only to find that Auria, Troius, and the other members of our envoy were all staring at me. Their expressions varied from curious to annoyed.

"Is something the matter?" I asked, somewhat mortified. I already knew the answer, but this was the easiest way for me to ascertain in what way I'd just made a hideous blunder.

"We're taking a *vote*, Balfour," Auria said, clearly none too pleased with having to repeat herself. "Are you all right? You've turned white as a sheet."

"You know what?" Troius said. "I think we should all take a recess. This is an important decision, and I for one would welcome the extra time to really *think* on it from both sides. Best not to rush these important matters."

I was grateful to him, though Auria looked for a moment as though she intended to take his head off.

"You seek out that time to confer with your Esar, you mean," Chanteur said, darkly suspicious. He added a bob of the head for etiquette's sake— his version of a bow to our esteemed highness.

I was gripping the edge of the table so hard that I realized I was beginning to make a mark.

"If you wish to have equal time to confer with *your* king," Auria said, "we will give you that opportunity."

"And call talks off for another month while we wait for the messengers to travel back and forth?" Chanteur asked. "Some of us have families we wish to return to and urgent matters at home!"

"In the meantime, we'd show you every glory Volstov has to offer," Troius said smoothly. "For free, of course."

This much postponement of a simple decision was nearly killing me; I was close enough to standing and leaving without being excused and causing further scandal when Chanteur finally grunted, waving one plump hand. "Very well, take your time," he said. "I know what my king would have me do already. If you are not so lucky, then by all means, take conference with him now."

Troius stood quickly, following me out of the room and away from the collective murmurs on both sides of the table. There was some fresh air in the hallway, but it was not enough, and without listening to hear if Troius was following me, I lurched quickly through the halls, desperate to find some means of escape—or, at the very least, a room with an open window in it.

The voice was following me making wordless sounds in what I was forced to assume was an effort to terrify rather than communicate.

If people were staring at me, I would not have blamed them; neither did I have the energy to spend on keeping up appearances.

The more I ran, the more it became clear to me there *was* no outrunning the sounds. They grew louder and quieter as they pleased, the voice fading away only to start up again even closer to my ear.

"Balfour!" Troius called after me.

The current ballad in Charlotte about me would have to be amended, I thought, to account for my tragic descent into madness. I felt Troius catch me by the shoulder, trying to stop me before I went careening down a flight of stairs. For a moment, I fought with him.

Balfour, the voice said in my ear. *Balfour?*

It knew my name, I thought, then promptly lost consciousness.

ADAMO

I didn't have much time to worry about the hell I was going to catch from Roy next time I saw him. A mind like his could turn any innocent encounter into a whole lot more than it actually was, and I knew he'd been waiting for his opportunity to have a go at me ever since he brought Hal back to the city. Probably since even before then. I'd been twitting him all his life about *his* love life—if it could even be called that—since good old Professor Lingual, and now here he'd gone and gotten the impression I suddenly had one of my own. It'd be open season no matter what the truth actually was, and I'd been going out of my way for the past few days to avoid him at all the usual spots.

He had to know by that point I was avoiding him, which would only make it worse when he finally caught me. But all of that seemed like petty, peacetime thinking to me when Luvander showed up in my office.

"Don't tell me *you've* got a problem with the exam, too," I said. It'd been a mistake passing my office hours around in case anyone needed consulting—because it turned out *everybody* did. Even more of a mistake had been letting the eager students—the ones with eyes like starved animals, begging for approval and grades instead of scraps—take the damned thing home early when they'd asked. It was that question that didn't have an answer that had 'em all in such a tizzy, assuming they'd failed the class, a few of 'em even bursting into tears right in front of me.

"No, it's Balfour," Luvander replied, not even bothering to make a joke at my expense. That was how I knew it was serious.

I reached for my coat, putting it on without a word. We could talk while we walked and get wherever we needed to be twice as fast.

"It's only a rumor," Luvander explained, as we pushed past a gaggle of students at the front door of Cathery and into the cold afternoon air, "but I heard it from multiple sources—and you say gossip never helped anyone!—that the ex–airman diplomat named Balfour had a bit of a . . . moment during the talks with Arlemagne yesterday. It's all hush-hush, which means everyone's talking about it, and I knew you'd want to hear immediately in case there's something actually wrong."

"Your gossip any more specific?" I asked. If there was, *then* I'd consider amending my feelings on how useless wagging tongues were, but not before.

"That's the problem, of course," Luvander replied. "In my own personal opinion, he must have been feeling stifled by such endless tedium—the talks aren't going very well, according to my sources, and they've been at it for days trying to work out all the little details—and some are saying our good friend left in the middle of a vote on Arlemagne's dealings with Verruges pirates. Just stood up in the middle of the talks and ran out of the room, then dropped like a lead weight. Fainted or something. Can you imagine the scene?"

"Doesn't sound like our good friend Balfour," I said. "If he didn't run from *you* lot, I don't think a few diplomats'd give him that much trouble. Where's he now?"

"I assumed we would check his apartment first," Luvander said. "And might I suggest you do your best to intimidate his ghastly upstairs neighbors into being a little more quiet? No wonder the poor thing's feeling worked to the bone if he can barely get any sleep at night without them stomping around. Most days I have trouble making it to lunchtime on a full eight hours!"

"Been to visit him a lot, have you?" I asked, privately thinking that the same rule as with his ability to weather diplomats applied. Balfour'd lasted years on less sleep and more noise than he was currently dealing with. Despite giving the impression that he'd blow over in a stiff wind, he could be a tough little bugger when he set his mind to it.

I'd've been less worried if he *was* prone to running out of the room and fainting like a noblewoman. Then I'd know not to pay this embarrassing incident any mind one way or the other.

"Only once," Luvander admitted. "I'm working him up to accepting the company."

Sounded a little like torture to me, I thought, privately glad Luvander hadn't decided *I* needed the company. Once again, Balfour was a sacrificial lamb, but if he wanted to keep Luvander out, all he had to do was pretend he wasn't home. He was a smart one; he'd figure it out.

I let Luvander lead me away from the main thoroughfare of 'Versity Stretch, loping through the crowds on his long legs and not stopping to shoot the shit with anyone we passed, which was how I could tell he was looking to take us there in a hurry.

At least neither of us had to worry about bypassing the crowds at our statues, since it was quickest to go around it altogether, taking the Whitstone Road to the Basquiat, then crossing the square to the bastion and the small apartments around it. Apparently Balfour was living close by to where he was working these days, which sounded pretty convenient to me. If I'd had a chevronet for every time I cursed making the long walk from middle Charlotte to Miranda first thing in the morning, I'd've had enough money to *buy* my own damn place by the 'Versity and eliminate the problem.

Probably for the best that I didn't since I was spending enough time in Miranda as is, and I didn't want to turn into a stuffed shirt on top of being a crankpot.

Besides, the walk was good for me. Kept the old bones moving.

Streets were always crowded this time of day, but for once, I wasn't letting all the gawkers and the millers and the slow movers bother me. I didn't even settle for making angry faces at the backs of the chuckleheads who stopped right in the middle of the street and nearly tripped me up. Royston could say whatever he wanted about me being a mother hen and not knowing when to quit, but the point was I'd been in charge of keeping my boys alive for a long time. That kind of responsibility didn't just pack up and leave easy.

The last time I'd seen Balfour he could barely move his

hands, and now this'd happened. I didn't like it and worst of all I didn't *understand* any of it, which wasn't doing wonders for my mood.

"Thought you said he was doing better," I grunted at Luvander finally, needing someone to direct my thoughts at. Maybe someone to direct my frustration at, too; Luvander'd regret coming to me for help soon enough.

"He was," Luvander said, neatly sidestepping a man carrying a whole stack of packages tied up with twine. "I was ready to go about singing the praises of Margrave Germaine through the streets after I saw him. Send the woman a complimentary hat, maybe, though that's an expensive gift."

"Something must've happened," I said, just missing putting my boot down in a big pile of slush.

"I do wish he wasn't so secretive," Luvander said with a little sigh. "It's all very sweet and coy, I suppose, and I'm sure it drives the women mad, but it makes it absolutely awful trying to get anything out of him."

"Guess I can't make fun of you for stalking him down like a rabbit in tall grass, now can I?" I asked. If it weren't for Luvander, after all, I didn't even know when I'd've caught wind of all this gossip. Looking Balfour up, finding out where he was living these days, would've been difficult, too. I'd probably have started at the bastion, asking everyone I met and causing an international incident just by being there. Balfour might've been the safe, declawed version of an airman that made the Arlemagnes feel more at home—he certainly wasn't the sort who looked like he was going to slap any asses—and after everything that'd happened with Rook back in the day, I guessed that made them feel appeased. But I was a different kind. Just looking at me was bound to remind people of the war.

Especially at present. Part of my ease in getting through the streets was that people were clearing out of my way left and right, without me even asking. It was handy; I'd have to remember the expression I was wearing for later, when I was late for appointments and couldn't afford anyone slowing me down.

"It's just a little farther this way," Luvander said, steering west of the bastion toward a tall clump of apartment houses, all grouped together and built with the same gray stone. The architect had done his best to spruce 'em up with some fancy design work up around the rooftops, but the masonry was starting to crumble. One of these days an unlucky bastard was gonna catch a gargoyle right in the head; I was keeping my eyes up, just to make sure that unlucky bastard wasn't me.

"Are you having a staring contest with your brother up there?" Luvander asked, glancing back over his shoulder. "While the resemblance is uncanny, I would ask that you do *please* try to stay focused. I'm reasonably sure you'd win the match anyway, but it makes you look very peculiar, and you know how people talk. We wouldn't want to damage Balfour's good standing in the neighborhood."

"If you've been visiting him, then it's probably been knocked down a couple of pegs already at least," I said, casting one last stubborn look upward. Luvander was right, though. And if Balfour was feeling poorly, then the last thing he needed was a living gargoyle pounding down his door. I took a deep breath, willing the crags in my face to smooth out.

Luvander surveyed my attempts, cringed, then shrugged.

"I'll have you know that *I* happen to be universally beloved wherever I go. It's as though a magician put a spell on me at a very young age in order to make me happy and successful for the rest of my life. Hello, my dear flower, how are you today?" Luvander directed this last not at me—thank Regina—but at a middle-aged woman in a dark green uniform, who seemed to be the concierge for Balfour's apartment building.

I'd half been expecting him to suggest this was a stealth mission and to surprise Balfour we'd have to pick the locks, so I guessed this moment of sanity was a pleasant surprise.

"So there's two of you this time," the woman said, adjusting her spectacles. They were attached to her face with some kind of jeweled chain—no doubt she thought it very handsome indeed, but it made her look like a cat in a fancy collar to me.

"Two of us," Luvander confirmed, putting on that winning

smile that made him look just a little *too* devious for my liking—like he was about to announce that he'd found Raphael's old books at last, after everyone'd been searching for days, and somehow I always got the feeling *he'd* been the one to hide them. "I hope that won't be a problem. I just happened to pick up another concerned well-wisher on my way here. Some people bring flowers, others bring old friends. Of course, the flowers might've brightened up the place more, so I think at this moment I'm experiencing buyer's remorse."

"All right, that's enough outta you," I said, shrugging my shoulders uncomfortably.

"If you're sure you *want* to visit him," the woman murmured, adjusting her spectacles.

"And why wouldn't we?" I asked.

"Haven't you heard? They're saying he went mad right in the middle of the bastion," the woman said, leaning forward with an air of confidentiality, like she'd been waiting all day to get some proper chin-wagging in. "He just up and left right in the middle of something important. Guess that's one way to show them Arlemagne cunts you mean business, isn't it? Tell you what, though, talks'd never have gone on this long if the dragons were still around. Mark my words, they'd be pissin' in their boots and running back to their cindy king in no time."

"I couldn't agree more," Luvander said carefully, eyeing me like he thought I was going to wade in and tell her what for, and he assumed he was going to have to bodily restrain me.

Like he could even if he wanted to.

Truth was, I had more important things on my plate than educating some lonely gossip. If I started in with every backward-headed civ who didn't know their ass from their ankle, then I wouldn't've had any time for teaching my actual students, not to mention all the other things I really enjoyed doing.

Luvander relaxed slightly when he didn't see me wind up for some kind of wrestling match. "You know, it would be fascinating to see what they *would* do if they came to the rooms one day to find a few dragons waiting for them," he added, getting a faraway look in his eye. "One never could outargue my dear Yesfir—she was much too clever for that, old girl—and if I recall correctly, Cassiopeia never even bothered with conversation. A little too burn-happy, if you ask me, but that certainly would make those talks interesting, wouldn't it? They'd end because there'd really be no one left to talk *to*!"

"Before my friend's swept away by nostalgia," I said, "do we have permission to visit Balfour, or not?"

"You two head on in," the woman said, pausing to polish one of her spectacle lenses. Fortunately, Luvander's wild little story had blown right past her. "I ain't seen him today, but that don't mean much. He's a real quiet fellow, keeps to himself mostly. Last person *I'd* expect to cause a scene in the middle of the bastion, but it just goes to show I ain't got the sense given a mouse."

"You ain't kidding," I muttered, and Luvander gave me a little shove in the back, just to show me he'd heard and I should've been sweeter-tongued while talking to a lady.

It was more than a few flights up, which I guessed was all right for exercise, but I had to wonder how Balfour'd managed it when his hands were troubling him. By the time we finally reached his floor, even I was a little winded. I let Luvander knock, seeing as how *he* never ran out of breath, and then we both stood there, the strangest get-well party I'd ever been a part of. Also, we were probably the first.

"Perhaps I *should* have brought flowers," Luvander said regretfully, "but I think he was allergic to the pollen . . . Do you remember that one time Compagnon collected all those stamens—"

I didn't have time to ask if he'd cracked his head on one of the low-hanging beams coming in, because Balfour was there opening the door.

To put it frankly, he looked like shit.

The thing with someone like Balfour was that he was always so damned tidy and put-together. The minute he didn't bother with it, he ended up looking like he was about to drop dead. He was pale, probably clammy, and his hair looked like something for birds to nest in. There was a neat little pattern of wrinkles on his cheek from a pillow, and when he saw us he looked like he wanted to sink through the floor and disappear.

That, at least, was a familiar look.

"Oh," he said, fidgeting with the doorknob. He wasn't wearing his gloves, but fuck me if I was going to stare and draw attention to something that made him uncomfortable. I focused on his face instead, even if I was curious. "I didn't realize you were coming. I didn't realize anyone was coming . . ."

"We thought we'd surprise you," Luvander said, inviting himself in. He pushed past Balfour into the sitting room and made a noise of despair. "In the nick of time, by the looks of it. Let's get some sunlight in here, shall we?"

That left me and Balfour staring at one another at the door. He wanted us to be elsewhere, and I definitely wanted us to be elsewhere, but neither of us was gonna get what we wanted just by wishing it and staring at each other.

"You eaten yet today?" I asked, giving him my look. If he said no, he was going to regret being so careless, and I'd know if he was lying. That was the look I'd perfected.

Too bad it didn't seem to work with students and their homework. They just didn't have the right amount of shame or common sense for self-preservation.

"A . . . little," Balfour said carefully, glancing over his shoulder as Luvander started making some kind of infernal racket with the window shade. "I suppose you'd better come in."

"Before Luvander gets you slapped with room-destruction charges?" I asked.

It was an okay little place, if sparse, with barely any color on the walls. Either Balfour'd just moved in or he hadn't seen the point in adding something personal to the place. No posters on the walls; no paintings or portraits. There was a settee on the far side of the room and a table with a few chairs in the middle of it; the room opened up into a kitchen the size of a closet, and I noticed the water closet and the bedroom next to it. Sure would've depressed me to live in an empty little place like this, I thought, especially coming from some-place so distinctive.

But maybe, after everything the boys'd put him through, he'd felt like he needed some peace and quiet.

There could be too much of that, though, so much that you didn't notice yourself getting so lonely until it was too late. I cursed myself for not checking up on him sooner and was grateful Luvander had been nosy enough to do it for me.

"I suppose you've heard about the little incident, and that's why you're here?" Balfour asked, sinking down into one of the wooden chairs by the table. "Troius said it wasn't as hu-miliating as I seemed to believe, but I take it he was lying to spare my feelings?"

"Who's Troius?" Luvander asked from the window. I glanced over to see that he'd managed to get himself tangled in the curtains, and I had to wonder if he was acting like a clown on purpose, so that Balfour would crack a smile or something. If that was his intent, then it wasn't working.

Even though it wasn't my style, I had a moment of appre-ciating Luvander's intentions. Not the way he wouldn't shut up when everyone was sick of hearing him talking, but his heart was in the right place, even if his head was up in the clouds.

"One of my . . . friends, another diplomat," Balfour re-plied. He hesitated before the word "friends," then looked guilty after he used it, like he didn't believe he even had friends.

Well, that was where he was wrong, for starters.

"So we're not the first to visit you?" Luvander asked, fi-nally managing to pull one of the drapes aside. Balfour shied away from the shaft of sunlight that flooded the room, shield-ing his eyes. Bright light glinted off metal, even blinding me for a moment.

I cleared my throat and looked away so he'd feel more comfortable. "Wanted to hear what happened, in your own words," I said, keeping it businesslike. "But before that, wanted to make sure you were all right."

"I'm all right," Balfour replied, like a physician'd tapped

his knee with a little mallet and the response was pure reflex. "Thank you for coming. It's very kind."

"Of course we'd come," Luvander huffed, stalking over to the other window. "Do you think we're criminals? Ivory might have been," he added, "but *we* certainly weren't."

"Sit down, Luvander," I said.

"Just trying to liven up the place," Luvander protested.

If I'd been at the top of my game, he wouldn't've had the balls to protest at all. I tried again. "Luvander, sit *down*."

"Oh, all right," Luvander acquiesced, pulling up the third chair and draping himself into it backward.

"Now you're gonna stop talking," I explained, "and Balfour here's gonna start. Whenever he's ready, though; he can take his time."

"Well . . ." Balfour said. "There isn't much *to* say, really. I'm sure that whatever you've heard, it was right. 'Mad Airman Ruins Diplomatic Proceedings; Runs Wild through Bastion Hallways.' Does that sound about right?"

"There was some fainting in there somewhere, too," Luvander said lightly. "Was that also a part of it?"

"Oh, yes," Balfour replied. "How could I forget?"

I didn't like his entire demeanor, I thought; it was pale, like his face, and the dark circles under his eyes made him look like a ghost. He needed a mother of some kind to bring him soup and blankets, in my professional opinion, but the last thing he needed was me telling him that.

"I believe what Adamo is trying to ask, in his own way," Luvander said, gentling as he leaned forward across the table, "is what exactly happened on *your* end of things."

"Like if I had some kind of reason, or if I just went mad?" Balfour asked.

"Exactly," Luvander agreed.

Balfour folded his hands onto his lap, hiding them under the table. It still seemed like the sunlight was bothering him, and every now and then I caught him twitching, head jerking around like he thought he heard something. "I . . ." he began, licking his lips.

"You want something to drink?" I asked.

"No, it's all right," Balfour said. "I'm merely trying to see if there is a way to say this without seeming as if I *did* just go mad that day. It's quite possible there isn't any, because I might well have . . . And yet it does seem embarrassing to admit to it, doesn't it?"

"Saying it helps," I said. "Makes you feel better."

"People've called *me* mad before, not to mention," Luvander added, trying to be supportive. "And I've gotten by just fine, haven't I?"

Balfour caught my eye, and I figured he couldn't've been feeling *that* bad if he was still up for poking a little fun at Luvander's expense.

"I see how it is," Luvander began, about to embark on a meandering tale of sorrow.

"Shut it," I told him. I must've gotten some of my magic back, because this time, he listened right away and did as he was told without protest.

When you were dealing with someone whose natural inclination was to be quiet—like Balfour—it was necessary not to scare him away from talking. You had to make him feel comfortable, let him know it was his turn. Someone like Luvander abhorred a vacuum, and maybe he thought he was helping Balfour by filling up the silence so no one had to be uncomfortable, but in truth, he wasn't doing the man any favors by taking control.

"I began to hear things, on the day of the meeting," Balfour said slowly. I could almost imagine him pulling at his gloves as he worked up the courage to gain some momentum—just like the old days—except that he wasn't wearing any. "At first I thought it was simply my mind growing bored with the proceedings and finding something else with which to occupy itself. I shouldn't say this—I have no real cause to complain—but being a diplomat really is *unbearable* some days. I consider myself a rather patient person, but no one there ever wants to listen to anything but the sound of their own voices and their own solutions. It can be very disheartening, at times. Especially when, day in and day out, the same matters are addressed over and over again, and we never really get anywhere."

"On the bright side, you *do* get all the best gossip first,"

Luvander said, and I realized he was doing his best to be comforting.

"Either that, or you end up a part of it yourself," Balfour agreed somewhat reluctantly.

"So you started hearing things," I said. It wasn't the kind of thing any man wanted to hear repeated, so I figured I'd be the one to do it and get it out of the way real fast. And we had to be sure, when it came to stuff like this.

"The way you say it, I can't tell if I was overreacting or not," Balfour said, looking sheepish. "Sometimes I think it was just the product of an idle brain. It's certainly never happened *before,* anyway. As far as I know, there's no history of such things in my family—not that I could write home to Mother and ask, you understand. The question would worry her."

"No accounts of relatives going screaming out of boring parties?" Luvander asked. When Balfour shook his head, he sighed. "What a pity."

"Don't remember Amery ever doing it," I said, steering us back to topic as best I could. Bastion knew Luvander was trying to be caring in his own mad way, and it was probably helping Balfour to have something to laugh at every now and again, but someone had to keep us focused.

"Perhaps my brother died before it came to that," Balfour pointed out. It was a moment of straightforward grimness I wasn't used to seeing him display, and he quickly looked away.

"Go on," Luvander said softly.

Balfour chewed on a particularly dry part of his lip, hesitating before he spoke again.

"I didn't realize what it was at first," he said at last, in a fearful way that I could tell meant we were coming close to the heart of the matter. "It sounded like metal. Just metal working, machines going, gears grinding up against one another, that kind of thing. And it was quite loud. At first I thought they were doing some kind of repair labors in the street until I realized that no one else was reacting to the sudden noise. Then I assumed they were merely hiding their discomfort—being professional, as it were—but I asked one

of my fellow diplomats and he indicated he didn't hear anything."

"You told someone else you were hearing things first?" I
asked.

"Well, not exactly," Balfour said, with a miserable little
twist to his mouth. "I was as subtle as I could manage without betraying any of the specifics. I simply asked him if he
happened to hear anything strange at all, and when he realized that meant *I* was, he attempted to call off the proceedings. He also bore witness to my subsequent exit, so I
suppose there was no point in being coy about it, after all.
And now that everyone knows *something's* the matter . . ."
Balfour shook his head again. The only color in his cheeks
was a flush of embarrassment. I'd've been uncomfortable,
too, if I knew the whole city was talking about me like that.
"I didn't tell my friend the details of what I'd heard,
though—I didn't really get the chance."

"So it sounded like metal, then," Luvander said, resting his
arms against the table. "That's not so bad, really, Balfour. I'm
sure there are worse things it could be. If Rook were here,
he'd begin naming them all in order: beginning and ending,
I'm sure, with one of the illustrious workers over at the 'Fans
claiming you'd knocked her up. Now *that'd* be something I'd
run away from."

Balfour huffed a quiet laugh and I sat back in my chair,
hoping the damned little thing wouldn't turn into a pile of
kindling under my weight. I didn't like it—not one bit—but
I wasn't a physician, either, and it wasn't my place to make
any diagnosis. Stress did funny things to people, and for all I
knew, this was just another simple case. It didn't make much
sense to me that it'd turn up now of all times, considering the
kind of stress Balfour'd managed to weather *before* the war
ended, but that was luck for you.

"Yes, but there's more," Balfour said quietly, staring hard
at a knot in the tabletop. Whatever it was, I knew we probably weren't going to like it.

"Out with it," Luvander said, reaching across the table to
put his hand where Balfour's would've been if he hadn't been
hiding them under the table. "It's only us, after all. At least

half the men at the Airman could've outdone you with stories of the things their minds conjured up when they weren't paying attention. You *know* that. What's more, despite my penchant for gossip, I'll have you know that I am extremely good at keeping secrets. Once you tell me something, it's gone forever. Locked away like that story about the Margrave's daughter in the tower, only somewhat less gruesome at the end, I hope. Also, you needn't worry about Adamo saying anything because he hasn't any friends to speak of. Just look at him."

"If I did," I said, "meaning if I did say something, it'd be because I want an expert's opinion and not just my own to go on."

I wasn't going to tell a lie for anyone's comfort, and I had a feeling Roy might've been helpful with this one. He wasn't a *velikaia,* but he knew his fair share of them. Besides that, he was smart as a whip and spent so much time learning about everything I was certain he'd have an answer or two about all this.

Maybe Balfour would be able to listen to him since he didn't seem able to trust *me* just yet.

"I realize what this is going to sound like," Balfour said, looking up from the table at last. There was a look of resolve on his face I'd seen only a handful of times, and usually right before he was about to do something stupid, like marching into the belly of the beast to get his favorite pair of gloves back. "Just so you know—before you have me committed to an institution, I suppose. But after a while, I began to recognize the noise. I thought I must have been mistaken, or perhaps that I really had taken leave of my senses and this was the form it had chosen, but I refuse to accept that now. I am *not* mad. I *know* what I heard, and it sounded exactly like a dragon."

Balfour paused, letting that sink in, but not so long that the silence would get too out of hand, forcing Luvander to start talking again.

"It's simply unmistakable," Balfour continued. "I'm sure either of you, or even Ghislain, would have recognized the sound straightaway. It's only that I've spent so much time telling myself *not* to think about it that ... well, I suppose I'd made myself resistant toward that particular conclusion. Yet I've heard it in my dreams enough times that I can't pretend for the sake of avoidance. I knew that if I at least told *you* two, you'd have a better chance of understanding than anyone else. I'm beginning to form a theory of my own, but considering the rumors on just how sound a state of mind I'm in at present, I'd at least like a second opinion."

"You heard a dragon?" Luvander asked, his voice hushed.

"In your head?" I added, just to clarify.

"Well, I am reasonably certain it hadn't landed in the square, if that's what you're asking," Balfour said with the hint of a smile. "The funny thing is, I almost ... I suppose if I have come this far, now I have to tell you the rest. It wasn't just the scraping and the banging or the turning of gears; I also heard a voice, in the barest of whispers at first, and then more clearly just before I fell unconscious. Or fainted, if that's what you wish to call it. It knew who I was; it said my name."

Luvander drew in a sharp breath as quietly as he could manage, and I forced my mind to take stock of things one at a time, instead of shooting in a hundred directions all at once. There was a chance Balfour'd been having a real bad day. Of the survivors, he'd suffered harder than most, and that had to wear on him day in and day out. There was no reason to jump to conclusions or to be thinking about Thom's letter, for example—the one that'd said all kinds of things about bringing a dead dragon back to life.

There was no reason to do it, and yet I was pretty damn sure Luvander and I already were.

"I know what you're thinking," Balfour said, before either of us could gather our wits fast enough to say something—desperate for it to be the right thing, yet without too much hope for that. "I know I *have* been in and out with fever ever since; I think that it's likely what caused me to faint in the first place. But I didn't feel at *all* strange when it first started happening. The voice came when I was at my most lucid—triggering the fever, perhaps. What I mean to say is, it wasn't the product of delirium. It wasn't a feverish hallucination. When I'm ill, I don't hear it at all. And shouldn't it be the other way around?"

A real unwelcome thought occurred to me, and I wrestled with it for a moment before letting it out into the open.

"Are you hearing things right now?" I asked. It made sense, and it'd explain that awful twitching, Balfour's head jerking around from time to time like he thought someone was calling his name somewhere in the distance.

"It comes and goes," Balfour admitted. "I haven't been back to work simply because I'm never certain when it's going to start up again. I even tried making a kind of chart, writing down the times of day it returned, but there's no real pattern. I would say it's driving me mad, but I think that's a rather unfortunate hyperbole given the circumstances, don't you think? Unless it turns out to be true, in which case . . ."

"Fevers make everyone a little funny in the head," Luvander said slowly, looking to me for support. "I had an uncle once who marched down to the lake and threw himself in because he thought my aunt had drawn him a very large bath. It took all us cousins to haul him out again, and all the time him screaming that we should give him his privacy in the lav. The whole town came out to watch, in the end. My second cousin Levent almost drowned, actually, and it's why I have a very personal rule never to visit my relatives in the country ever again."

"Now, let's nobody leap to any conclusions just yet," I said, trying to convince myself as much as either of them. "Fever's going around the 'Versity like wildfire right now, or so I've heard. Stands to reason there'd be a bit of it in the bastion, too. *If* that's what's making you hear things, then it ought to pass as soon as the bug's out of you."

"That *is* what I was hoping," Balfour admitted, twisting his hands in his lap. They looked like little dragon claws from this distance, overhung by the shadow of the table. If he was staring at them every day, I thought, didn't it make sense he'd be hearing dragons not only in his sleep but during waking hours, too? I closed my eyes for a moment to listen—to see if *I* could hear anything, or if it was some of the whirring and clicking from those hands—but they were completely silent, and all I heard was the three of us breathing and a sudden gust of wind howling outside the building.

"Might be best to wait it out," I said finally.

"And not tell anyone about it, either," Luvander added, very practically.

"It doesn't sound so foolish when you say it," Balfour admitted. He almost looked relieved he'd told us, which I guessed meant we'd done our job all right.

"But you're going to have to be very forthright about how you're feeling," Luvander added, tapping his fingers against the table. "No long-suffering silences from you, young man, *and* I'll show up here with soup if I have to just to make sure you're getting well again. If you prove stubborn, I'll have to send another letter by pigeon to Ghislain telling him to return at once, and *believe me,* the last thing you want is him showing up here with his old Ramanthine remedies, not to mention whatever he's picked up on the open seas. He'll have you drinking chicken's blood out of a hollowed-out Ke-Han skull, and you'll do it because, well . . . Because your alternative would be saying no to Ghislain."

Balfour shuddered. "No need to make me worse with talk of things like that. I'll do whatever I can. I'd prefer not to feel this way, myself."

"We'll check up on you," I said. It wasn't a suggestion, and fortunately, nobody spoke up with their idea of a better plan. "I can do mornings, and Luvander can come at nighttime. How's that sound?"

"A little like I'm an outpatient," Balfour replied.

"But you suppose you'll accept it," Luvander said for him.

"However did you know?" Balfour asked.

"Then it's settled," I said firmly. "And, if you don't mind, I'm requesting permission to share your experiences with a friend of mine at the Basquiat who knows a sight more about everything than I do."

"A friend of yours?" Luvander asked, with a look of pure shock. "No—I can't believe it."

Balfour, on the other hand, looked momentarily reluctant, then allowed his shoulders to fall in a shrug of acceptance. "I don't suppose it matters much now one way or another who knows," he admitted quietly. "As long as all this doesn't make its way back to my mother. I wouldn't want to worry her for no reason."

"Despite how much my friend likes to talk," I said, "*almost as much as Luvander here*, he can keep a secret, too, and at least he has common sense for matters that should be kept private. Leastways when those matters don't involve him."

"It offends me that you are intimate with such a fascinating person," Luvander said, "and you haven't introduced us."

"The world'd end," I told him, "with both of you in the same room together. You'd both be trying to outtalk each other so hard your tongues'd fall out. Actually, he'd probably end up blasting you from here to Nevers, now that I think about it. You free Sunday?"

"Unfortunately, I'm busy bringing soup to my old friend Balfour, who isn't feeling well at the moment," Luvander replied. "But perhaps I could get a rain check on the introduction?"

Balfour's laughter at that served to make us all feel better, I suspected, and somehow Luvander and I managed to join in. But it was a serious matter—one that was going to demand a whole lot more thinking and not something a simple chuckle'd be able to solve. When I left Balfour's apartment it was with a heavy heart, and I wasn't looking forward to any answers I could possibly get. None of 'em made for a promising future for any of us.

CHAPTER NINE

TOVERRE

Unbeknownst to Laure, who had enough difficulties of her own these days and often disapproved of my more intricate plans, I had embarked on my own private investigation, delving more deeply into the mystery of the missing Gaeth by taking matters—and a pen—into my own hands.

To begin with, I wished to resolve the issue of his mother's gloves once and for all. In order to get them off my hands—a pun that made me very proud indeed—I would have to write directly to the source herself, the good woman to whom they truly belonged. I had been in possession of them for long enough, and, as Gaeth showed no signs of returning to reclaim them, I had only one other option: I would send them back to her forthwith.

This topic, however, was merely a small ruse upon which the rest of my plan hinged. By writing to Gaeth's mother explaining the situation with the gloves, I would surely be able to glean some information about Gaeth's current health. If he had truly returned home, then my inquiries after his well-being would bring a certain manner of response—but if he was *not* with his family in the countryside, then all our suspicions of his disappearance would prove to be well founded. The question of where he was would still be unanswered, but we would know for certain whether or not there was something darker afoot.

Laure was always telling me not to become carried away by my own imagination. The trouble with this particular scenario was that I simply *couldn't* imagine what was happening. I hadn't been carried away at all.

Because of this, I would have to make my inquiries subtle. I did not wish to embroil myself in something too dangerous—it was possible Gaeth had been caught up deep in some seedy business with Molly and, having offended the wrong person, had been taken to task in a sudden, gruesome fashion. But truly, that did not seem like him—even though I did not know him well enough to quash all my sordid suspicions.

Writing to the mother was the best first step—and made easy because we had absconded with a letter he'd been ready to send to her, including proper postage, as well as her name and address. She was Jetta with no surname, and she lived in Borland. The place itself wasn't even on any maps, and because of that I knew of it, as it was famous for being one of the smallest towns on the Volstovic side of Locque Nevers. Borland seemed an apt name for a place known throughout the countryside as being comprised of mud and cows. It was no wonder to me that Gaeth's coat was so shabby and his writing so poor; and, more than ever, it seemed necessary for me to send these gloves to his mother, for who could tell what she was wearing without them? In all likelihood, she didn't have anything.

And so I had written to her a very simple letter, inquiring after her son's health and remarking upon his goodness in lending the items to me, then stating I was returning them to her, and I did hope she would offer her son my thanks since they had kept my hands very warm indeed.

I was in agony over waiting for a response, but I knew the post took ages in the backcountry. It was possible they wouldn't be able to find Borland at all, and the package would be returned to me without any reply as thanks for all my cleverness.

Under normal circumstances, I would have Laure to complain to, but she seemed curiously elusive these days. I wondered if she hadn't been taken with the fever again, since—much to my horror—it seemed to be making another sweep through the dormitories. Now more than ever, I considered myself lucky to have eluded the process altogether after the initial appointment. What sort of horror had I managed to dodge, precisely? I'd spotted both Thib and Laure's lady friend wandering the hall at odd hours, and though I would normally have suspected some other kind of foul play, it was clear from their tousled hair and glassy looks they weren't sneaking off just to be with one another, else they would have been better groomed. Had they no shame when it came to being so unkempt? More importantly, did they wish to spread their vile disease among as many fellow students as possible? It was clear I would never understand the motives of some people, nor their lack of concern for the well-being of others.

Yet another clue was that our lectures the past week had been half-full even at the best of times, and I could tell poor attendance was irritating some of our professors, all of whom were busily outlining the various helpful strategies for self-paced research. Laure would have said the lack of attendance was due to how boring these lectures were, but I'd noticed that even some of the students who spent the first few weeks kissing up to the professors were missing, and so I was deeply suspicious.

It was also possible that Laure was avoiding me because she didn't want me to force her to go to the library archives, but I'd gone to the trouble of making her up a set of quick-cards for each class, not to mention a handful of sample outlines for the essay topics I thought most likely to suit her interests. It was the nearest I could get to actually *doing* all her work for her—something which neither her pride nor my faith in her would allow.

If it turned out that she was still cross with me about the incident with the dorm leader, then I was going to become very cross with *her* in return. I had managed my best apology; the very least she could do was accept my sincerity, permitting us both to move on.

Weighted down with my study materials, I knocked at Laure's door. The numbers screwed into the wood were badly tarnished, and I did my best not to look at them while I waited. Perhaps I'd return later with some polish, when my hands weren't full of lecture notes. Briefly, I wondered if I had time to do it now, but my polishing handkerchief was somewhere deep in my pocket. I didn't have time to pull it out before Laure wrenched her door open, eliminating the need for a decision one way or the other.

"Oh," she said, looking me over, her eyes stopping on my notes like they were a pile of horse filth deposited onto her doorstep. "You're studying already?"

I could have informed her that I'd begun my attempts at research a week ago, but that might have made her feel insecure about her own efforts. "Am I interrupting something?" I asked instead, not sure if I wanted to hear the answer. At least her eyes were focused. That was a good sign.

"Not really," Laure said, scratching at the back of her neck. "Suppose I forgot we were supposed to work together. Come in, then. I was just having a snack."

I might have divined that last piece of information for myself since there were crumbs in her hair and a smudge of what must have been chocolate at the corner of her mouth. On top of that—now that I could have a better look at her— she *was* looking a little peaked and unusually pale, with twin spots of color high in her cheeks, as though she'd just returned from a bracing walk in the cold. I stared at her, trying to discern whether or not she was exhibiting symptoms of another fever, but she was doing her stubborn best not to meet my eyes.

"Are you feeling quite all right, my dear?" I asked finally.

"'M fine," she said, waving her hand in irritation. "It's been warm in the room, so it's getting me down. Do you think someone shoved something up the chimney again while I wasn't looking?"

"I feel that if anyone was going to begin a campaign of ruining chimneys, they most certainly wouldn't begin with yours," I assured her, looking about for a clean place to put my studying materials. "They'd pick an easier target, certainly. One that belonged to someone less terrifying. Like mine."

"You can be plenty terrifying when you want," Laure said, stretching her arms up over her head and letting out a huge yawn. "I'd be terrified myself right now if I wasn't so tired."

"That's just the studying you're afraid of."

I glanced around the room, taking in the mess but managing to limit my visible discomfort quite commendably. Laure had allowed the fire to go out, I noticed, and despite her complaint about the temperature, I found it rather chilly. And, of course, the rest of the room was a disaster—there was simply no other word for it—her desk absolutely covered in sheets of notepaper and her clothes strewn about on the floor and over one chair. Laure had a habit of taking things off, then leaving them where they landed. She found it more convenient at home, since her room was too small to fit a proper wardrobe, but she *had* one here.

Habit was no excuse for all the clutter, nor were her usual protests that there was a method to her madness.

"Sorry 'bout the mess," Laure mumbled, sensing my distress. Perhaps I hadn't hidden it as well as I'd thought. "Meant to see to it before you came around, but I guess I lost track of time. You ever feel like that sometimes? Like you wake up and all of a sudden it's getting dark and it's time for bed already? I got no idea what's happening to all my free time. Guess it's just how short the days are."

"I believe everyone feels that way when it comes time for exams," I told her, placing my things on the lone empty chair while I cleared off the desk proper.

Despite my hopes, the papers strewn about were not our class notes. Rather, they were scraps of parchment covered in what appeared to be little drawings, a few of them charming illustrations in the style I'd come to expect from Laure— men with tall hats and women with triangular dresses, the better to distinguish them as the fairer sex. There were some, however, that looked much stranger than anything I'd ever seen her draw before—enormous black beasts with hooked claws and cruel snouts. I stared at one for a moment, attempting to make sense of it, until all the pieces came together in my head.

"Laure, have you been drawing dragons?" I asked her.

"Give me those," Laure said, in a tone of voice that I knew meant I should acquiesce at once to avoid the trouble of being beaten soundly. "I was just having a bit of fun."

"Perhaps you could turn these in to Professor Adamo as

extra credit," I said, with a touch of slyness. Laure really *would* hit me if I implied anything outright, but I'd heard them talking the day she'd gone to apologize.

Even if my suspicions about *her* feelings were wrong, it was evident he liked her better than any of the other students.

"Perhaps I could put my boot up your ass," Laure said, pulling the papers out of my hands and folding them up—not, I noted, crumpling them. "Be sort of poetic justice, don't you think, since you gave them to me?"

"Now, Laure, be reasonable," I said. "You know as well as I that there are several different schools of etiquette when it comes to returning a gift, and not one of them would recommend *that.*"

"Just stay out of my things," Laure huffed, shoving the drawings inside one of the boots in question. I hadn't meant to embarrass her, but her face was curiously red. I wanted to put my palm against her brow to check for warmth, but now didn't seem to be the time. "You don't always have to be cleaning up behind a person in their own room. You came here to study, and that's all we should do."

"If I've offended you *again* . . ." I began, then trailed off, not sure of where to finish. The floor was still littered with skirts and stockings, but I was doing my best not to pay attention to them. "Should I come back some other time?"

Laure stared at me for a moment. The light from the window reflected off her eyes, making her irises appear far paler than usual.

"I'm sorry," Laure said, turning away. "I didn't mean to be a beast. It's just this physician's appointment's got me feeling all out of sorts lately. Like I told you, I decided to dodge it, but they sent another reminder, and I don't want 'em to mail Da or anything and tell him his little girl's gone rogue in the city. Knowing him, he'll want to pull me straight out of the program for not following orders."

"We certainly can't have that," I said as mildly as I could manage. "You know as well as I do the only reason *my* father allowed me to come was because I'd have you to chaperone me in the city."

"I know," Laure said, twisting her hair back and off her

neck, making a transient bun held up only by her fingers, which she dropped a moment later, waves of orange hair tumbling around her face. "I'll think of something better eventually. I mean it. And I'm probably just making too much of things anyway. We don't *know* that those appointments had anything to do with what happened to Gaeth, do we? Lots of people've gone and come back and haven't had anything wrong with them."

"Except for that awful fever," I said.

"It was only a couple of days," Laure pointed out, looking perturbed. "Not even bad, by a fever's standards. I can handle a lot worse than that, now can't I? I have and I will."

There was no arguing with her when she was being so stubborn, I thought, and gave up for the time being.

Instead of squabbling pointlessly, I reached over to pick up my note cards, not sure of how to proceed. If she truly wished to get this physician's appointment over with, and deal with it in her usual, indomitable fashion, then I supposed there wasn't much I could do to stop her. I certainly wasn't capable of physically restraining her—not with the disparate nature of our strengths—and she was bullheaded enough that sometimes even the best-reasoned argument might as well have fallen on deaf ears. I found myself wishing irrationally for a third party—even simple Gaeth would've done—to help me reason with her. I was only one person, after all, and as a result it seemed my opinion tended to matter very little.

"I want you to think very carefully before you do make a decision, one way or the other," I said, running the pads of my thumbs over the smooth surface of the note cards. The clean simplicity of their crisp edges and neat handwriting soothed me. A terrible thought occurred to me, and I hesitated before bringing it up. "But, Laure, you're *not* planning to tell them you've been hearing voices . . . Are you?"

Laure sat down on the end of her bed with a flounce, skirts bunching up underneath her. I could see she was wearing the green stockings I'd bought her; they didn't match at all with the dress she was wearing, but I kept that small detail to myself, touched that she'd made the attempt in the first place.

"I don't want to get bundled off to some women's hospital

for raving idiots, if that's what you're asking," Laure said, rubbing the back of her neck again. "But I don't like feeling out of sorts and lying to a doctor when she asks me how I'm doing, either. I just want someone to fix all this—and isn't that what a physician's job is? Make me one of them nasty-smelling herbal teas, crush up some dried rats' bones. I'll take whatever she's willing to give me, so long as it works."

"I wouldn't ask for the rats' bones up front," I suggested. "Just a thought."

At least I managed to make her laugh, and her concentration was better that night than I'd been expecting, given her disposition when I'd first arrived. But there was nothing more I could do for her mood than distract her, and my ability to do that was only going to last for so long.

And so it was just when I was beginning to give up hope—and assume the gloves had been lost by an errant postman—that I went to check for new deliveries the next morning and found the flag in my postbox up. There was a letter waiting for me in the box, the corner smudged with what appeared to be a thumbprint of mud. I wrapped it with a kerchief and slid it into my pocket. And because of the time, I was forced to read it in the lecture hall, just before Ducante began our first lecture that day. It burned against my side the entire walk along 'Versity Stretch. By the time I arrived at Cathery, the excitement and impatience had nearly given me apoplexy.

As the poor professor surveyed the small number of attendees in his room with a look of offended displeasure, I neatly slipped one of my pens underneath the blobby wax seal to break it. My name had been spelled wrong on the front—Tovere, with only one "r"—but the address itself was correct, and I supposed that was all that mattered for those in charge of 'Versity post.

"What's that you've got there?" Laure hissed, peering curiously over my shoulder. "Something wrong at home?"

"Does this look like my father's handwriting to you?" I asked, briefly showing her the letter before I hid it once again from any prying eyes that might have been lurking about. "I believe this was written by the only soul in Borland *able* to write—if one considers this 'able.'"

"Borland?" Laure snorted. "What're you corresponding with that place for?"

"Be quiet for a moment, and let me read it," I told her. I felt her breath on my ear, which meant she was reading along with me.

Sir Tovere, it read, and I felt a pang of tenderness and pity, *Thank ya for yer writing. The gloves are nice of ya. I will be wearing them. If only ma son should wear some himself. May be he will buy some. I know ya asked for his health, but he ent heer. He has schooling now in Versity. May ya be well. Jetta.*

"You wrote to Gaeth's family," Laure whispered.

"I wrote to his mother, yes," I replied. I had a strange, chill feeling creeping through my chest, and I glanced at Laure to see if she felt the same way. "I had gloves that belonged to her—I thought I should send them back . . ."

"You thought you'd meddle, is what you thought," Laure snapped.

"And it's a good thing I did, isn't it?" I asked. "Since now we know Gaeth never *did* go home."

"Fat lot of good it does us," Laure said miserably. "We still don't know anything. This just makes it worse."

"Now, be sensible," I began, but Ducante cleared his throat, signaling a start to the lecture—and an end to all idle chatting.

Needless to say, I was incapable of paying attention to what he had to say. I managed somehow to copy down word for word what he was dictating, but without properly listening to the sound of his voice. It all passed from my ear straight to my pen, without once passing through my brain. *That* part of me was full of dark and nervous thoughts.

If Gaeth had not gone home, yet those in charge of our dormitory believed he had, then he truly *was* missing. And with no one aware of it save Laure and me, the chance that he was in danger somewhere seemed greater than ever.

This was too large a matter for the two of us to take care of on our own—and yet I had no one in the city I felt I was able to confide in. If I took this quaint letter to the authorities—I supposed the Provost would be the most likely candidate—I knew without question I would only be laughed at. What evidence did I have? Who was Gaeth to them? Could I explain that the boy had been hearing voices before he disappeared—and back up that evidence with Laure's situation? I most certainly could not.

The more I went over my suspicions in my head, the more dangerous they seemed to me, yet the sillier I knew they'd seem to someone else. And still, I felt the keen sense of responsibility driving me to find *some* solution—for Gaeth's sake.

Where in Regina's name *was* he?

I was tangled up in my thoughts when I heard the bell chime. My hand was cramping with how quickly I'd been taking notes, and I managed to ease my grip on my pen just as Hal took over speaking for Ducante.

". . . if there's anything you need help with," he said in his kind, easy voice, "don't hesitate to ask. Even if it's not about the research or the studying—I'm here to talk, if need be."

I felt as though a lamp had been lit suddenly over my head. In all the time I'd spent watching him—and with how carefully I had conducted my study of his behavior and his habits—I knew he would not be the sort of person to laugh at someone when they felt their companion was in need. If I took my concerns to him, perhaps *he* might know—from official class roster—whether or not Gaeth had withdrawn or made some excuse to the professor regarding his prolonged absence.

I rose at once from my seat, ignoring Laure's questions as I pushed past the crowd of students desperate to escape the lecture hall.

This, I realized just before I arrived at Hal's desk, would mark the very first occasion I had actually convinced myself to speak with him. It seemed easier somehow to do it because it was not on my own behalf but someone else's.

He was in the middle of stacking a few heavy books, and his back was facing me; I could have cleared my throat to let him know I was there, but suddenly I was seized with uncertainty and panic, and by the time I managed to wrestle control of myself, he had already turned around.

"Hello there," he said, offering me a quizzical smile. I stared back at him, aware my mouth was hanging open. "Is there something I can do for you?"

Gaeth had saved me, I recalled, on that fateful day when I'd had my heart irreversibly crushed by the impossibility of ever getting to know Hal as I'd once wished. Now it seemed it was my duty to do something for Gaeth in return.

"I . . ." I managed, quite sure I felt Laure's eyes boring holes into me. She was no longer in the room, but knowing her as well as I did, I was certain she was lurking just outside the door and watching me like a hawk. "That is, I heard what you said just now. About if anyone needed to talk."

"Oh, really?" Hal asked, brightening. Once, that expression might have had my knees buckling, but today I was all business. "Don't tell anyone, but you're actually the first person who's ever actually taken me up on that offer. There's another class coming in about fifteen minutes from now that I'd wanted to sit in on, but I'm sure we could use the professor's office in the meantime. Would that be all right?"

"That would be more than adequate," I said, clutching my books stiffly to my chest as though shielding myself from a dragon. "Thank you."

"It's no trouble at all. *Really*," Hal added, leading me out the door with a smile.

I was nearly certain I saw the top of a fiery red head disappearing behind the doorframe just as we passed through. Dear Laure never had been all that gifted with matters of subtlety, and I wondered if she intended to follow us all the way to the office, too.

Because of my own pragmatism—it made little sense to fall in love with someone whose affections lay elsewhere— my heart no longer jumped each time he spoke, and I could appreciate the slight bits of humor in my current situation. It was slightly jarring to come to such a realization when faced so immediately with the former object of my affections, but there it was: simply another thing Gaeth had gone and ruined for me. Hal had the same complete lack of guile that Laure did, which caused him to sound almost excited by the prospect of someone else's problems. Since I was doing this for Gaeth's sake as well as to satisfy my own curiosity, I did my best not to say anything at all until I'd been spirited away to the upstairs offices, at which point Hal's attentions could be fully focused.

Ducante's rooms were blessedly clean, if slightly cluttered by scrolls of dusty parchment, and there was a large plant in the corner that badly wanted watering. I restrained myself from wiping down one of the bookshelves as I passed, even though I was certain Hal wouldn't have noticed and everyone would have breathed a little better because of it.

He didn't sit behind the desk but rather leaned back against it. I expected he was probably anxious to show me that we were peers, and that I could feel comfortable sharing all my deepest anxieties with him not as though he were a professor but a fellow student. It was a sweet gesture, yet due to the bizarre nature of my request, it was suddenly very tempting to clam up entirely or to invent something out of thin air.

Somehow—reminding myself of Gaeth in order to maintain my focus—I forced myself to sit down, lowering myself slowly into the leather chair so that it wouldn't creak embarrassingly.

"So, are you worried about the exams?" Hal asked, bracing his arms back against the desk. "I know there've been a lot of students in about that lately. And it doesn't help that some professors have been drawing up practice exams with all sorts of trick questions on them. They think it'll help if the first-years overprepare, which I suppose is one strategy . . . But I'm sorry, I'm getting ahead of myself here. You're . . . Toverre, aren't you?"

"How did you know that?" I asked, instantly suspicious, the color rising high in my cheeks and no doubt making me look as though I had the pox. Had he known I was following him all along?

"I'm sorry," Hal said, tucking a piece of hair behind his ear. He gestured toward the neat stack of notes and textbooks in my lap. "I didn't mean to unsettle you. It's just that you have very distinctive handwriting. I have to read your essays out loud to Professor Ducante; he claims it's going to drive him blind."

I couldn't hide my papers now without feeling self-conscious, but I rather desperately wished to. Also, I was going to have to be more careful when I answered Laure's homework for her, in the future. It was a lucky thing I knew her handwriting so well.

"I hope his eyes don't fail him before the end of semester," I said, realizing it was my turn to speak again. I wished I had thought to grab Laure when we'd passed her by—these things were always so much easier with her along to make a joke and break the ice. Also, whenever she was in the room, no one so much as looked twice at me. Hal's gaze—with his cloudy gray eyes—was unwavering, and I found it difficult to sit still without staring back at him.

"They're very good essays," Hal added, to soften the blow. "I suppose I shouldn't have told you that, about the handwriting."

I felt even more uncomfortable with the unexpected praise and cleared my throat quickly to distract him. "It's not exams I wanted to talk to you about; I have organized a very precise system of studying, and I'm feeling extremely confident. No worries at all *there*. This is more of a personal problem."

"I see," Hal said, nodding once to show he was listening. He hesitated, then spoke again. "Is it that girl I always see you with? Not to pry, of course."

"Laure?" I said, momentarily horrified out of my deep concentration.

"I guess I was wrong," Hal said, looking as though he was trying to keep from laughing. "My intuition's all off today. Didn't sleep very well last night. Perhaps you'd better just tell me, before I embarrass myself any further."

He was not the one who needed to be embarrassed, I thought, but I took his suggestion gratefully.

"It's about a . . . friend of mine," I began, staring at an empty space on the desk just next to Hal's wrist. I had to say it all at once, or else my doubts would get the better of me and keep me from speaking entirely. "By the name of Gaeth. He's gone missing. Actually, he's *been* missing for some time now, long enough that I'm *sure* it's not just my imagination running wild. The redhead you always see me with—Laure—and I came here together with him, and so we became friends. We'd have lunch with him at the beginning of the semester, even dinner sometimes. And then, one day, he stopped coming to classes, to the dining hall . . . No one else he knew could tell us where he'd gone. I will admit right away that we did something inadvisable—we were even caught in the act, so I believe it isn't too incriminating to tell you now that Laure and I ended up breaking into his room just to see if he was there. Which he wasn't, much to our dismay. We'd been told he went home, you see, only all his things were still in his room. There was even a half-eaten sandwich, though if I speak about it too long I'll be ill. The point is, everyone here seems to be under the impression that he's gone back home to Borland. We even spoke to the dormitory authorities, and that's what they told us. Only then I *wrote* his mother, inquiring after his health, and she as much as told me to ask him myself since she believes him to still to be here!"

The whole thing had become quite the tale when I finally paused to catch my breath. It was the most I'd said to anyone other than Laure since Gaeth had gone missing, and I was nearly trembling by the time I'd come to the end. I wanted to add that a gentle, hopelessly simple creature such as Gaeth could get into all sorts of trouble without someone cleverer there to get him out of it again, and that I should have realized it sooner and kept a better eye on him to begin with. But none of that concerned Hal, and I held my tongue.

Hal drew in a breath, crossing his arms. I could tell I'd upset him from the sudden tension in his face. The poor man had clearly been expecting something about a tender youth's love life, or perhaps the typical sob story from a student waking from their stupor to realize exams were coming up.

To be fair, that was all the trouble I had expected from the city when I'd first arrived. The dreams I'd harbored were of first love and proving myself capable of every challenge the 'Versity saw fit to throw at me. All the rest had come quite out of nowhere—first Gaeth, then Laure's own strange behavior. And as committed as I *was* to my own independence, I couldn't solve it all by myself.

I was sorry to have to share my disillusionment with Hal, but there was no one else with whom I'd be able to talk.

"The reason I am so concerned," I added, as Hal continued to think with knitted brow, "is that he was exhibiting some signs of the fever when last we spoke with him. I worry for his health, not only his whereabouts."

"Well," Hal said at last, letting out his breath, "I can't say that was what I was expecting at all. Do you think it's something to bring to the Provost's attention?"

"I wasn't sure," I admitted, clasping my hands tightly together. "Perhaps I should have filed some official report, but I didn't wish to do anything so drastic until we knew for certain he *hadn't* gone back home. I only just heard from his mother today."

"The post does tend to get stuck up around Borland," Hal agreed, plucking at the elbow of his sleeve. "I lived around there—just across the river, actually, in Nevers. We used to say it was because of all the mud, with the postmen getting stuck in it."

"I wouldn't be at all surprised," I said, attempting to feel lighthearted and failing spectacularly. My skin felt hot and itchy, and I dug my nails into the soft skin on my palm. "I really do apologize if this is inappropriate. I understand that none of this is your jurisdiction. It's just difficult to . . . to find . . ."

"It's difficult to find someone to talk to in the city, sometimes," Hal said, leaning forward just slightly. It was easy to forget he'd been from the country, just like Laure and I were—at least it had been for me. The difference between him and the people I'd known back home stretched wide as Locque Nevers itself. "I felt that way, too, when I first came. If it wasn't for . . . well, I understand what it's like, anyway. I've adapted, but it took a while, and lots of feeling uncomfortable at parties in the meantime."

I smiled, and it wasn't even the fake smile Laure had forced me to master so I wouldn't frighten all her school friends away with what she called my "grimacing." "I am doing my best," I told him, just so that he wouldn't worry.

"As for the matter of your friend," Hal said, sitting back again, "I really don't know what to say. You're right that it isn't my jurisdiction—not at all—but I'm glad you came to me about it. You said you spoke to someone, and they told you he'd gone home?"

"Yes," I said, the smile slipping off my face as easily as it'd appeared. "That *is* the part I don't understand. I was wondering if you'd have any more information about it, or if Professor Ducante had some official note?"

"Nothing that I've heard of," Hal admitted. "There have been a few because of this fever, but . . . Gaeth, you said?"

"Yes," I replied. "From Borland. I don't know his surname."

"Doesn't ring a bell," Hal said, "but I suppose I could do some asking around. See if the dean knows anything." He tapped his chin while he thought; the dreamy countenance he usually wore in class had been stripped away, replaced by an expression of sharper intelligence. It was easier now to see him as the hero who'd saved Thremedon in its hour of need, and I quickly looked away in order to avoid more vulgar staring. "I've been living in the Crescents while doing my own studies, so my knowledge of the dorms isn't that extensive. I could find some things out for you, though. At the very least, what someone would have to do to withdraw in the middle of the semester. I'm betting there's all kinds of paperwork to fill out, at the very least. Not to mention some kind of room inspection—which is strange, considering what you told me about the state you found his quarters in. Best to have all the information before we go to the Provost, or else they'll waste time doing it themselves, and I'm afraid with the time it takes them to get that kind of business looked after, you won't get your answers very fast."

"If there's paperwork, I don't think he could have filled it out by himself," I said, trying not to feel as though I was betraying Gaeth's confidence by admitting his failings to someone as smart as Hal. "Perhaps Ducante might have had something to say about *his* essays."

"Like I said, I don't remember the name," Hal said apologetically. "It's possible he never turned in anything at all."

"I wouldn't be surprised to hear that," I said.

"No? I'll be sure to keep that in mind," Hal said, sliding off the desk to get a bottle of ink, a pen, and some paper. "How do you spell his name?"

I dictated the letters for him, ashamed at the relief I felt washing over me now that I'd unloaded my difficulties on someone else. But not only had I survived the conversation, it seemed that something good might even come of it, as well. Surely, someone who'd once saved the lives of countless magicians would be an enormous aid to Laure and me in saving one rather large citizen of Borland.

"I'll let you know if anything comes of this," Hal said, waiting for the ink to dry. "And I'm glad you came to me, Toverre."

He reached out to give me some comfort—his hand upon my shoulder, giving it a gentle squeeze—and I felt a combination of feelings, including elation *and* despair. He was smiling at me again, for encouragement, which clearly revealed the blue flecks in his eyes.

"So am I," I mumbled, and I stood quickly from the chair, bolting out the door without further word.

BALFOUR

The fever broke early in the morning on the fourth day. I knew the exact time, because I woke with a start, feeling as though someone had been calling my name. But the apartment was ghostly still, not even the pounding of boots overhead or the faint sound of carriage wheels upon cobblestones from outside to indicate I was anything but alone in the world.

Then the clock on my bedside table chimed dully. It was five in the morning exactly, just before dawn, and I was so drenched in my own sweat that I was in dire need of a bath.

I could tell the fever was gone because I felt lucid—and completely in control of myself—for the first time in four days. The first emotion I experienced was acute embarrassment. Then, overwhelmed by my gratitude at being well again, I ignored those pettier feelings.

At least, at that hour, the hot water wouldn't have been all used up by the other residents of the building. I ran myself a bath, sitting in the steam and reveling in the silence, broken only by the rushing of water through the pipes.

There was no voice. I waited, straining to hear it, surprised but tentatively relieved when nothing came. I had grown so used to the sound that to be without it now seemed surreal.

By the time I was finished with my bath, and the sun was rising, casting dim light through the room, I had begun to remember what it was like to live my life normally.

It was a good feeling.

I made myself breakfast, with time to spare before Adamo appeared for his daily appraisal of my condition. The stomping had begun upstairs as my neighbors stirred to start their day, but since that was a familiar pounding—and not the quickened rhythm of my heart laboring in my chest, or the sultry, metallic whisper of a voice just inside my ear—I felt less resentful that morning than on any others. Even my breakfast tasted delicious, and I finished it a little too quickly; it seemed my appetite had returned to me tenfold, and I hoped Luvander would bring some kind of snack with him when he visited me after work hours. He always did, despite my protests. Both he and Adamo felt the need to look after me—and, in light of my recent behavior, I supposed they were right to worry. I had been worrying myself, after all, and I knew I would have done the same for them if they'd been in my shoes.

My hands, in contrast to the rest of me, remained nimble and dexterous—I'd half expected them to slip back into stiffness as quickly as they had after prior appointments, but they were operating as good as new, if not somehow better than ever. The more I worked with them, the better attuned to my thoughts they became, until they almost felt like *real* hands, despite their appearances. I even caught myself in a moment of surprise when I glanced down at the sink and saw water bouncing off metal.

I did remember to dry them more carefully than I would have simple flesh and skin. Feeling like a newborn child did not mean I had to act as foolishly as one.

Perhaps, if I continued to feel so hale when noontime rolled around, I would be able to go to the bastion and make my apologies. I hoped that Chanteur would look at the incident as a piece of entertainment rather than a grievous insult, and I also hoped that I hadn't caused Auria too much suffering because of my ridiculous behavior.

I wouldn't blame myself for it, but that didn't mean I could avoid all culpability. With everything she had on her plate, Auria's situation should have made anyone feel terrible. I often cringed at the idea of shouldering all her responsibilities— it seemed worse to me than piloting a dragon into the middle of a battlefield, because it was so much less straightforward yet equally dangerous.

Don't be foolish, Balfour, I told myself. Auria already blamed me as much as she blamed all the other new diplomats who had no idea what they were doing and whose inexperience undermined her authority on a daily basis.

Rather than sit about with my thoughts plaguing me, I turned my attentions to the mess my apartment had become, gathering up dishes in one arm and blankets in the other. There was a fine layer of dust on the bookshelves, and the house smelled musty and stale, just like fever. If I cracked open a window, that would be gone soon enough, and I was finally feeling up to the task of building a fire in the fireplace.

It was invigorating to be well again; after so much lying around, the sudden energy I experienced was like a jolt of adrenaline. I wanted to go out, but Adamo would be visiting— and, just as if I'd summoned him, there was a rap on the door.

He was early—which wasn't so unlike him—but I opened the door with more vigor than usual, almost as excited as a little child to see what he'd make of my recovery.

"Not at all suffering, like the landlady said," Troius said, sweeping inside while I stared at him in surprise. "You look healthier than ever, Balfour. And here everyone was worrying themselves sick over you! Though I have to admit," he added, as I shut the door and turned to face him, "if you were trying to get out of service for a few days, that *was* a clever little trick."

It took me a moment to realize what he was implying, and when I did, I was filled with horror. "You don't think I was putting all that on?" I asked.

"Of course not," Troius replied. "You're not nearly a good enough actor for it, are you?"

"I suppose I'm not," I admitted.

Troius looked around the room, taking it all in curiously. "Aren't you going to ask me to sit down or have a bite to eat?" he asked finally.

"Of course," I said, eager to hide how his sudden appearance had thrown me off-balance. Troius had never come around before; I hadn't even known he'd been aware of where I was living.

Perhaps I'd mentioned it when I'd first moved in and discovered I was living beneath a foreign race of people who regularly employed cinder blocks as shoes, but it had been a long time since then. I didn't even know why I was letting that detail bother me. Since Luvander had tracked me down easily enough, it stood to reason that Troius could do the same.

He was staring at me, and I realized I hadn't begun to make good on my offer. Instead, I was standing before him like an uncouth fool who never entertained visitors, or knew how it was done.

In some ways, that would be a correct assessment. Even some of the other airmen—though they delighted in putting bugs in one's laundry and buckets of ice water over one's door—had better manners than this when it came to entertaining.

"*Would* you like to sit down?" I asked him, sweeping off a chair compulsively even though there wasn't anything on it save for a thin layer of dust. My illness hadn't left me much energy for cleaning, and though the general state of my apartment was still exemplary compared to the state of *every* room in the Airman, that wasn't saying much.

"Honestly, I'd prefer to be in bed, at this hour," Troius

said, but he took the seat gladly, throwing his boots up on the couch-side table. He was, I noticed, wearing gloves, though whether it had to do with the cold or a misplaced sense of fellowship, I wasn't yet certain. "I don't think I'm cut out for all these morning sessions. If you want my opinion, I think the Arlemagne are waging some kind of psychological warfare on us, booking up all the earliest slots, then talking circles around us while we yawn into our sleeves and try to pretend we're not falling back asleep. How are we supposed to argue a point when we're barely conscious? Between that and Auria yapping in my ear, it's enough to make a man feel like he's landed in a proper nightmare. If I *wanted* to work on Arlemagne time, I'd move to damned Chastenay and have done with it."

"I rather like it, actually," I admitted, drawing aside the shades to let in the faint morning light. The sun glinted off my hands, and I realized once again that I hadn't put on my gloves. It hadn't occurred to me, because I'd thought it was Adamo at the door, and he'd already seen me at my worst— not just lately, but also during my time at the Airman. He didn't question it, and for that reason alone I'd allowed myself to let down my guard a little. "Doesn't it give you a little satisfaction to be finished with work just as some people are *beginning* their day?"

"Why, Balfour, that's positively vindictive of you," Troius said, leaning in his chair so that it tipped back onto two legs. It creaked dangerously, one of the old pieces I'd taken from the Airman before it was cleaned out; it was the chair Ivory used to sit in at the piano, but it had seen better days. "Though to answer your question, I have no room for satisfaction once the talks start dragging on well past the point of lunch. Bastion, your hands are a sight, aren't they?"

I clenched them into fists, fighting the urge to slide them into my sleeves. Such behavior was very childish, and—as I'd insisted to my mother when she'd begged me to come home after the war—I was no longer a child, now twenty years of age and perfectly capable of taking care of myself. There came a point in a man's life where he was forced to confront his anxieties head-on, so I held up my hands, spreading my fingers wide.

"I suppose you haven't seen them since I've had them repaired," I said, flexing them for show. "They're a much neater job now; at least, I think so. There wasn't any paneling over the back before at all, if you remember that mess of cogs and gears, and little pieces of dust and lint were always getting caught up in the works. They look a great deal more finished now, not to mention far more serviceable."

Troius stared, even dragging his chair across the floor to peer at them more closely. I found myself wishing however irrationally for my old room in the Airman—equipped with a chute in the floor for a quick escape. Perhaps I'd have one installed here, but I'd have to get to know my downstairs neighbors much better before I started dropping into their apartment unexpectedly whenever some awkward situation arose.

"Not stiff like your old ones, are they?" Troius asked, thankfully not trying to touch them. That was still beyond my zone of comfort. "I remember you complaining about that. Well, not complaining, because it's you, but the equivalent."

"They haven't been, thus far," I said. It was the smallest of details, perhaps, but the one I was most grateful for. Even when my own body let me down or grew weak, as it had during the fever, my hands remained in perfect working condition. The stark silver outline of them was almost a comfort, something I could focus on, and I stared at them so I wouldn't have to think about Troius's scrutiny.

"Sorry to catch you off guard," Troius said, picking up on my discomfort too late for anyone's benefit. "Funny, me talking about Auria's big mouth when I've got my own to contend with. I didn't mean anything by it, Balfour—just never seen anything like them before. Most people haven't. You *do* know what they're calling you down in Charlotte, don't you?"

"Certain variations, yes," I admitted, taking the distraction as an excuse to hide my hands behind my back, where the sunlight warmed them.

"They really *are* a keen piece of work, though," Troius

said, stretching his arms over his head with a yawn. "Guess that's what the dragoneers are doing with their time, now that there's no more use for them *actually* building dragons."

"I really have no idea," I told him, crossing into the kitchen to see if I had anything to present as a snack. Perhaps some food would distract him—fill his mouth for a time—and not offering anything just seemed like bad manners. "Margrave Ginette, the woman first assigned to work on my hands, never really worked on any dragons, as far as I know. She was trained in the theory of it, but her experience was chiefly mechanical. Originally a clockmaker, I think. I didn't ask that many questions at first, but it was my understanding that whatever makes the hands 'come alive,' so to speak, came from somewhere else, and she knew as much about it as I did—which is to say, very little."

"Maybe that's why you were having so much trouble with them," Troius suggested. "Sounds like she didn't *really* know what she was doing."

"I wouldn't call it that," I said, in absent Ginette's defense.

"All that aside," Troius said, waving his hand, "you *are* coming back into the Arlemagne fray with me, aren't you? I mean, you do look well. Not like you're about to go tearing out of the room and fainting again."

"I feel much better," I said a little too rigidly.

There was cheese and bread in the larder, and that would have to do. I'd gotten into the bad habit of not keeping my rooms well stocked once Luvander had started bringing food by. I was going to have to work on that since it hardly seemed logical to expect someone who didn't even live with me to provide my daily sustenance—even if what Luvander brought by was regularly mouthwatering and at a discounted price from the bakery.

"You can't blame a man for asking," Troius said, in the same tone he used to placate Chanteur. "It's been lonely. No one to pass notes with. I tried with Auria, but that vein in her head nearly burst." He sighed before his voice turned somewhat keener. "You *were* behaving awfully strangely, you have to admit. Didn't you say you were hearing things?"

"Did I?" I asked, slicing the cheese as neatly as I could

manage, cutting out a spot that appeared to have gone green. Despite my distress, my hands remained blessedly steady, further proof that they weren't really a part of me. If they'd been more natural, they would have been trembling just slightly with the effort it took to be deceiving. Yet, now that I'd told Adamo and Luvander the truth about what had happened to me—what I'd really heard—I knew that I didn't want to be discussing it with Troius. In fact, I didn't want to be discussing it with anyone.

The fewer people gossiping about Balfour Steelhands and his imaginary voices, the better.

"Yes, you did," Troius said, leaning forward in his chair. "I assumed later it was just the fever, of course. Was it?"

"I must have been delirious," I told him in true diplomatic form.

"Oh, good," Troius said. When I turned around, I could see that he even looked relieved. Perhaps he really had been worried about me, and my own defensiveness over the subject had me acting irrationally suspicious. "Because if you *were* experiencing something more serious, as your friend, I'd have to—"

A knock at the door interrupted him, sending him twisting around in surprise. I set the bread and sliced cheese down on my table and went to answer it, brushing the crumbs off my palms. This, surely, had to be Adamo. I was only sorry we wouldn't be able to speak as candidly as he might have liked—especially in light of my recovery.

"Sorry I'm late," Adamo grunted, as soon as I'd opened the door. "Got caught battling the beast that guards your lair again. Damned doorkeeper wanted to know about the weather, and how we managed with all this cold when we were up in the sky. She's got a mouth on her that could've replaced the raid bells, and no mistake. We'd all be running to the girls just to get away from her yabbering."

"Did you tell her about the time Niall went through a storm cloud?" I asked, ushering him in.

"Told her he came out the other end crackling like a live wire," Adamo confirmed, with the ghost of a chuckle. "Not to mention Erdeni smelling like a broken bulb for weeks afterward. He's damned lucky he didn't lose part of her to melting or worse."

"Goodness," Troius said from the kitchen, halfway into a cheese sandwich. "That sounds awfully uncomfortable. Is something wrong with this cheese?"

Adamo stiffened, glancing at me after he'd taken in the sight of Troius. Adamo had a keen eye and never missed a detail; just then I could almost tell exactly what he was thinking about this ruffian, who was speaking with his mouth full and spraying pieces of cheese onto the floor with every word. Troius saved all his good manners for the diplomats—and, under regular circumstances, I was always relieved to find him so relaxed with me.

This was different. He had no idea what kind of trouble bad manners could get him into, in front of a stickler like ex–Chief Sergeant Adamo.

"The cheese *is* a little old," I said, in an attempt to defuse the situation. "I haven't been able to go out much lately."

"So who's this?" Adamo grunted, folding his arms over his chest. That was pure Adamo for making it clear he didn't like someone. Sometimes, depending on the person, he'd actually state it out loud. No one ever tried to argue with him.

"I was going to ask the same thing," Troius replied, "but the cheese distracted me. The name's Troius, son of Lyosha. Might have heard of my father, actually, he's a little famous for the original treaty with Arlemagne. No? Well, in any case, it's a pleasure to meet you, ah . . ."

Troius trailed off, proffering his left hand for a shake; his right was still holding on to the sandwich he'd made. Adamo stared at him like he thought he was a weasel, and I decided to do the honors of introducing my two friends to each other, all while hoping they never had cause to meet again.

"This is Adamo," I told Troius, standing between them like no more than a messenger. "He's—he *was*—the Chief Sergeant of the Dragon Corps, which is obviously how I know him. Adamo, Troius is another member of Auria's group; we've been working on the Arlemagne matter together."

"Take it you haven't been as lucky as your father," Adamo replied.

If Troius was wounded by the comment—as Adamo no doubt intended—he gave no indication of it. Instead, he shrugged. "What can I say? Those Arlemagnes drive a difficult bargain."

"Feh," Adamo said. *"Arlemagne."*

"There's something we can agree on, at least," Troius said cheerfully, retracting his hand at last and wiping a few crumbs off on the front of his waistcoat.

Adamo grunted again—not even willing to muster so much as a "feh" that time—and turned to me. "Take it you're feeling better?" he asked. "Color's back in your face. Don't look so much like a ghost anymore, either."

"It's like he was never sick at all," Troius added. "I'm trying to convince him to come back to the bastion with me today. Getting out of the house might do him some good. What do you say, Chief Sergeant?"

Tension crackled in the air like lightning, and I was reminded again of Niall's brush with death during the thunderstorm and the static electricity that had clung to him for weeks afterward, making his hair stand on end when he dragged himself from bed to have lunch with the rest of us.

"Would you like something to eat, Adamo?" I asked.

"Yes, would you?" Troius added. "There's some ancient cheese that might kill you, and some stale bread."

"Luvander'll be by with something this afternoon," Adamo said, voice clipped, as though he were doling out working orders. He was already on his way to the door. "I should get going. I don't have time for dawdling, much less eating someone else's food, then insulting it. But maybe I'll stop by when Luvander does to talk more about how you're feeling. Good to see you up again, Balfour."

He was leaving, I realized, so that he would not commit some kind of criminal offense in my apartment. Of all the types of people in the world, flippant ones like Troius were Adamo's least favorite, and I knew how he felt wasting his time on people he thought were idiots.

Troius was a lucky man—though from the expression on his face, he had no idea about the terrible fate he'd just dodged.

I locked Adamo out, with appropriate thanks, then turned to face my remaining guest.

"Wow," Troius said, letting out a low whistle. "Would you believe it? *The* Adamo. Chief Sergeant of the Dragon Corps, the big statue himself. He's about the same size as his memorial, unlike you. Pretty impressive. Does he stop by often?"

"Because of the fever," I explained, moving to stand by him, so I could try some of the bread for myself. Troius was right; it was so stale I nearly chipped a tooth.

"Looking after you, just like a mother," Troius said. "Isn't that thoughtful? He doesn't seem the type. Did he say Luvander was coming, too?"

"Another of my fellow airmen," I said.

"Of course," Troius replied. "Naturally. You all get together regularly, then? I suppose they were worried about you, and those voices you were hearing. *I* would be, anyway, if I were them."

For a moment, I was too taken aback to say anything. In that instant, Troius's face changed from one of curiosity to sheepishness, and he slapped himself on the forehead. "I really *am* sorry," he said. "I might as well skip work myself, today, at the rate I'm going. Some days you always step in it, don't you? And here I am, still chewing your ear off, when you're trying to recuperate. I just thought you might like a little distraction—but I've probably been *too* distracting, chasing your friend off and eating your cheese. If it can still be called that," he added, with a quiet laugh. "Sorry about that, Balfour. Really."

"It's all right," I told him. "Adamo's like that with practically everyone. And the bread *is* stale. I can't even imagine what the cheese tastes like."

"I'll get out of your hair, leave you to recover on your own," Troius said, clapping me on the shoulder. "Don't think twice about me—suffering all alone with Auria and Chanteur, the lone brave soldier left on a bleak frontier—and no, don't follow me; I'll see myself out." He paused by the door, one hand on the knob. "It's just good to know you're feeling better," he said earnestly. "I always worry about you."

"That's really not necessary," I murmured, staring at the floor. "I haven't even written home about it."

"No need to worry Mother, eh?" Troius asked, his cheeky grin returning, before he disappeared out the door.

At least, I told myself when he was gone, I wasn't cleaning up the stain he left behind on the floor when Adamo was through with him. And it would make a fabulous story for Luvander when he arrived. Finally, I had something with which to repay him after all he'd done for me.

CHAPTER TEN

LAURE

I'd managed to put the appointment off for two weeks, but I woke that morning with a feeling of dread after not sleeping too well—my dreams were full of anxious noise and not much else—knowing for certain they weren't going to let themselves be brushed off any longer. The nervous fog followed me out of bed while I got dressed and trudged downstairs, shrugging off Toverre the way I'd been doing lately—making his face scrunch up in hurt though he didn't say anything about it.

My suspicions were confirmed when I found the summons in my mailbox, printed in capital letters. It told me just what I'd been expecting—and I didn't have to be some prophetic Margrave with well water in my veins to have predicted it coming.

If I missed another appointment, then I was in deep dung.

Those weren't the exact words, of course, but I knew when someone was fuming mad and trying to be nice about it, holding off on the curses because they thought honey'd catch more flies than vinegar. Professional or not, these physicians sure were persistent, and there wasn't much point in saying no to them any longer. My appointment was tomorrow afternoon and I'd better turn up. *Or else.*

But there was no way on Regina's green earth that I was telling Toverre.

It was strange not to share everything with him—we always did, and this problem marked the first I hadn't run to him with at the very start. First of all, he'd be no good with it. He'd want to write Da, or go to the Provost, or go with me to the appointment. The first would make Da upset; the second would have all of Thremedon thinking Toverre was crazy; and the third was just plain pointless. What did Toverre plan on doing to protect me—talk a few ears off until Germaine and her assistant begged for mercy?

As funny as the image was, the whole thing was too serious to joke around about. And I wasn't letting Toverre get himself involved. I didn't want him getting into trouble just because I wasn't able to handle it.

But I couldn't go back, I told myself, shoving the note card in my pocket with a feeling of dread. No matter which way I looked at it, I felt like the fever'd been Germaine's doing in the first place.

And I never wanted to hear that voice whispering to me again.

"I see you have a letter of some kind," Toverre said, doing his best not to snoop.

"Nothing worth mentioning," I replied. The look on his face told me he hadn't already read it over my shoulder, and I was glad for it, if a little guilty, too.

It wasn't something I could talk to Toverre about because I could tell how much it upset him. It was like a big blotch of mud that he couldn't wipe away, and if there was nothing he could do to help, then why get him all worked up in the first place? Maybe it wasn't altogether fair of me to have decided that for him, but it was a chance I was going to have to take. It was my job to take care of him, and that meant not burdening him with stuff that was bound to make him crazier than he already was.

I felt bad about it because I could tell I was hurting his feelings not letting him in on everything like I always did, but we'd get past that soon enough. *He'd* been the one who always talked about how things were going to change once we got to the city, and now he'd got what he wanted. Just came in a different package than he was expecting.

The way things'd shaken down for me so far in the city, there was only one person I could really talk to about any of this horseshit. I also knew he wasn't going to like it, so I was gonna have to be sneaky and butter him up some first, just so he wouldn't think I was going to make a habit of running to him every time I got a hangnail.

Part of me was pretty disappointed, since I was pretty sure ex–Chief Sergeant Professor Owen Adamo almost thought well of me. And now I was gonna go and make him think I was one wheel short of a carriage—or one wing shy of a dragon, you might say.

No getting around that, though. Someone with problems too big for her to tackle on her own couldn't afford to be too proud to ask for help. As much as I wanted to prove to everyone that I could handle myself *just fine* in Thremedon without a man to lend a hand, all I wanted was someone to talk to. Someone like a friend, only smarter and more important than the friends I already had.

Maybe if the 'Versity'd had any female professors teaching us first-years, I might've gone to one of them instead. But if they *were* lurking around in the woodwork, I'd never had 'em for any of *my* classes, and I didn't want to speak to some stranger who didn't know I had a good head on my shoulders before I told 'em it was coming loose.

My mind made up, I made my excuses to Toverre and bundled my scarf around my neck, checking to make sure I had a little money in my pockets before I stepped out into the cold. I hadn't memorized the ex–Chief Sergeant Professor's schedule or anything like that—I wasn't Toverre, and I wasn't going to stalk him after hours through the streets of Thremedon—but the bell for class was about to ring, and I knew that he usually only taught half a day's worth of lectures before retreating to his offices like a bear in hibernation. I guess once he'd figured out where they were, he'd figured out he liked spending time there.

Also, if I stopped to think too much about my plan, then I'd probably chicken out, but as long as I kept my feet moving and my courage screwed up, then I could see it done.

Even if Adamo *didn't* have any solutions for me, I'd feel better once I got everything off my chest. And maybe all I needed was for someone to point out how batshit I was acting for me to be able to snap right out of it and start living my life the way I always intended—getting good sleep and not twitching at every shadow.

I stopped by the hot-drinks kiosk on my way from the mail room heading to Cathery, getting a hot chocolate for me and a black coffee for Adamo. As funny a face as he'd made after tasting the sweet stuff, and as much as I might've wanted to see it again, if I was planning to get him in a good mood, I figured I'd better try something that had a real chance of working.

The man behind the counter was the same one who'd been there the other night, looking just as cold as ever. When he tried to give me too much change, I dumped the difference into a little jar for tips.

My experience with the dorm leader was still stinging me, and I wasn't about to start taking *money* just because someone liked the way I looked.

There was a fierce wind kicking up in the courtyard as I made my way across the stone path, and I tucked my head down to protect my face. I nearly rammed into a group of third-year girls, all of them with buttons on their coats that matched the ones on their boots, and hats jammed onto their neatly curled hair.

"'Scuse me," I said, but they were too busy talking to hear my apology, or to make one of their own. I wasn't snoopy like Toverre or anything, but I couldn't help overhearing their conversation.

"He's so *violent*," one of them was saying, tugging at her wool cap. "I don't like the way he shouts at *all*. I think you're mad."

"You just don't have any appreciation for a *real* man, Flora," said one of the others. "I think I'll stop by his office later, ask him what sort of strategy he'd recommend for ensnaring one of the famous airmen."

"You wouldn't *really*," said Flora, covering her mouth with a gloved hand.

"I would, too," the other girl said. "Maybe I'll try it tomorrow, just you watch."

" 'Scuse me," I repeated, louder this time. Without waiting for an answer—in my experience, idle gossips never had any manners—I shoved past the three of them so that I could get in the door.

I never understood why groups of people felt the need to gather *right* in the narrowest part of the street or mill around in doorways, but I was too huffy even to think about that. The nerve of some people really got under my skin—especially those that were older than me, and meant to know better. If I hadn't wanted my hot chocolate so badly, I might've accidentally spilled some of it on one of them—ruining their fancy boots, too—but it wasn't any of my business what other people thought of Adamo, and they'd surely learn for themselves that he didn't have any interest in their silly games.

At least, that was my opinion of him—which was apparently higher than any of *theirs*.

This time, I didn't need to walk into anyone's offices or interrupt any private meetings, seeing as how I already knew which one was Adamo's. A part of me wanted to barge in on purpose and see whether that student and professor were going at it again, but both my hands were full, and I didn't want to spill a hot drink anywhere if I got too much of an eyeful.

I hadn't actually thought about the problem full hands were going to give me until I was standing there in front of Adamo's door, with no way of opening it or even knocking. The paper cups were filled all the way to the top, and just big enough that I couldn't fit both of them in one hand. I could've kicked the door to let him know I was coming, but it seemed disrespectful, and I didn't think Adamo'd appreciate me leaving my mark that way.

I shifted to one side, real slow, to see if I could bang my shoulder up against the door instead. I'd've had to move my whole body to do it, I realized, so I couldn't quite get the leverage, but maybe I could manage it with just my elbow. At least I could be grateful that this corridor was mostly empty—the students were on the lower floors, rushing to their next classes or heading out to lunch and to freedom. I strained, then managed to thump my elbow against the door *without* spilling hot chocolate all over my glove. It might've been only a small victory, but it was a good one, as far as I was concerned.

"What in bastion's name are you doing to my door?" Adamo asked from just behind me.

I turned too fast, nearly dropping both the cups and wishing I knew how to sneak up on a person that quietly.

"What's it look like? I was knocking," I said, holding up his coffee. "Brought you this. On account of last time, just so you know I didn't forget. But it's making it real hard to get into your office."

"Lucky for us both I wasn't in there, then," Adamo said after a second of staring at me like I was a dog that'd suddenly brought its master a dead bird. "Thanks."

He took the coffee from me and unlocked the door, holding it open so I could get by. The office was exactly the same as it'd been the last time I'd dropped in, except that someone'd seen fit to tape over the hole I'd made in his chair, so I couldn't pick at the stuffing anymore.

I took a sip of my cocoa. Since I'd waited this time, carrying it all the way through the cold streets, it didn't even burn my tongue.

"I take it you're not here about exams this time, either?" Adamo asked, crossing around from behind me to get to his desk. The little paper cup I'd given him was already half-empty, which I figured was as good a sign as any. I hoped it was brewed the way he liked it.

"Don't I wish," I said, sitting down in Old Creaky, my chair from before. "If my only problem was a bunch of exams I had to take, wouldn't you think I had a pretty easy life?"

"And that you were complaining for no reason," Adamo said with a shrug. "You wouldn't believe the sob stories some of 'em come in here with, all because I didn't give 'em a check next to their grade. Even worse is when you stick a comment or two in there that's not all praise. You'd think I slaughtered their childhood pets or something."

"Do they cry?" I asked, suddenly interested.

"Like babies," Adamo said, draining the rest of his coffee with a noise of appreciation. I was starting to think *he* was a dragon, the way he guzzled down hot stuff like he couldn't feel it. They could've called *him* Ironmouth.

"Toverre made one of our tutors cry once," I confided, picking at the tape over the hole in the chair. "He corrected everything she said; she couldn't finish a single sentence, much less teach us anything, and he kept at it until she finally lost it. Think she had a few fits and had to move back home."

"I can imagine that," Adamo said, a faraway look in his eyes like he imagined *he* was on the verge of a breakdown any day and was ready to get in a carriage and roll away. "Toverre's that friend of yours, isn't he? The one with all the pens?"

"My fiancé," I corrected automatically, licking at the corner of my mouth to make sure there wasn't chocolate there.

"Huh," Adamo said, sitting back in his chair. For a second he looked confused—I took the engagement for granted, but it tended to surprise other people—but the moment passed quickly enough. "Are you here about the, uh, engagement?"

"What?" I asked. Now it was my turn to look confused. "Of course not. I'd like to kill him sometimes, of course, but he's been all right lately."

Adamo stared at me for a moment longer, then shrugged something off. "Well, since you're not here about exams, and you didn't bring Toverre, your fiancé, to pick at my grammar and make *me* cry, you're gonna have to enlighten me as to why you really came."

"Oh, that," I said, not giving myself time to overthink anything. I'd come all the way here, hadn't I, and I could feel the crisp edges of my latest summons digging into my side through my pocket. "It's not . . . anything to do with school, actually."

"That's a relief," Adamo replied.

"Wish it was," I said. "See, whoever's in charge has been scheduling these checkups for all the new students—I guess to make sure we're all protected from whatever fever's run-

ning through the dormitories and whatnot, or to make sure
we aren't bringing anything into the city with us that we
picked up from the farm. Everyone's had 'em, or at least,
most of us have, but then . . . It started to seem like everyone
who went came back with this mean kind of fever. Like
somehow getting the checkup was making us sick."

"Physician wouldn't be doing his job, if that was the case,"
Adamo said.

"*Her* job," I corrected him. "And that's exactly what I
thought. I've got a healthy constitution—only been sick five
days in my whole life—and after my second visit, all of a
sudden, I've got this awful fever. Sweating, vomiting—no
use coating it with sugar; I was doing a *lot* of things I wish I
wasn't—and having these weird dreams where I kept hearing
things that weren't actually there."

"Hearing things?" Adamo asked, suddenly looking sharp.

"I'm *not* screwy," I told him firmly, suddenly regretting all
the sweet cocoa in my stomach since some amount of being
nervous was finally settling in. "At least, I never was before
I came to the city. And I know how it sounds—like I'm out
of my mind—but maybe I'm half expecting you to tell me
I'm being cracked and all I need is to pull myself out of it.
The thing is, they want me coming again, for another one of
those checkups, but *I* don't want to go and find myself sick
again. It's just a feeling I have, but it doesn't sit right with
me. Goes against my instincts, and I don't like doing that."

"When're you due?" Adamo asked. I pulled the card out of
my pocket, setting it down on the table.

4:00 PM, it read, and under that, **M. GERMAINE.**

"Stands for Margrave Germaine, I'm assuming?" Adamo
asked.

"She's the one," I replied. "Seems all right enough, even
though her place is full of these *instruments*—metal ones, all
of 'em kept out of sight so as not to make us shudder. But I
caught sight of 'em, and damn me if it wasn't eerie."

Adamo picked up the card, turning it back and forth. It
looked small and silly in one of his enormous hands, but I
didn't know what he thought he'd get out of inspecting it so

closely. He must've known something I didn't because he couldn't stop staring at it.

"Didn't lend yourself much time to get out of it," he said finally.

"Sure I did," I said. "The *first* notice was when I came to see you last week."

"But you didn't tell me about it," Adamo added.

I felt myself color and cleared my throat, trying to keep any signs of *blushing* off my face. "Guess I didn't want to tell you," I explained, "because it sounds so loopy."

"You're saying others had this same fever after going to visit her?" Adamo asked.

"Sure did," I said, remembering Gaeth suddenly. A feeling of dread crept through me, and Adamo must've seen some of it on my face because he gave me a sharp look.

"Anything else you want to tell me?" he asked.

"Someone I know, another first-year," I told him. "He got the fever, too. Had his appointment before me and suffered from it for a little while. And then, out of nowhere, he just disappeared."

"Disappeared?" Adamo repeated. His tone wasn't skeptical—at least, not skeptical of the information I was giving him, I didn't think—and it encouraged me.

"I thought maybe he'd gone home, but he left everything behind in his room," I explained. "Like he meant to come back to it. Like something happened to him. And then Toverre—you remember, my fiancé—wrote a letter to his mother back home, and when she replied, she seemed to think he really was still here. But nobody's seen him for over a week now."

"Sounds like he disappeared to me," Adamo replied.

I set my cocoa down on his desk. It was too cold—having passed the perfect point where it wasn't scalding hot but wasn't warm enough, either.

"So," I said. "I'm crazy, right?"

"You shouldn't go to that appointment," Adamo told me. "That's what I think."

It hadn't been what I was expecting, not by a wide mark, and I had to repeat it a few times in my head to make sure I hadn't just misheard him. "I shouldn't?"

"Instincts are there for a reason," Adamo replied. "All this city living tells you to go against 'em a lot of the time, but sometimes they're all you've got to protect you. And I say, why ignore 'em when they're so clear?"

"Well, because they're gonna tell my da, for one thing," I replied, aware of how childish it sounded. "And if I get in too much trouble here, he'll call me back home for sure. But for another, Margrave Germaine's gonna come and get me at this point; had another note from her a few days back that said if I missed *this* appointment, she was gonna be real worried about my health, and she'd have to come see me in the dormitories. Felt like intimidation to me, but what do I do about it? I don't have anywhere else to live."

"Four this afternoon," Adamo said, clearly thinking over something heavy. He turned the note card over in his hand one more time. "You mind if I take this?"

"Go ahead," I told him. "I sure don't want it."

"Guess it wouldn't be looked on as decent if *I* came with you to that appointment," Adamo said, more like thinking out loud than asking me a question.

"Not even one way," I agreed, since it wasn't polite not to answer someone.

"And I'm not sending you in there like a soldier for some answers, either," Adamo added. "Felt bad enough when I had to send one of my *boys* on a mission like that."

"I could go on a mission," I told him, folding my arms over my chest. "Even if I'm *not* one of your boys."

Adamo snapped out of whatever'd taken control of him, looking at me for the first time since I'd shown him Germaine's summons. "Yeah, I guess you could," he admitted. "But that doesn't mean it sits right with me, and I'm not gonna do it that way."

"Guess you just can't trust someone who hasn't been tested in the field," I said, managing to make it only a little sulky. For a second there, I'd almost thought he was starting to think of us as equals.

"Guess I can't," Adamo replied. "But I got another idea for you, though. You ever heard of Yesfir? It's a hat shop."

ADAMO

I had a whole lot of junk in my head that needed sorting out, and for once I didn't have any idea of where to begin.

I didn't know when I'd become some kind of counselor, but first Balfour'd spilled his guts to me, and now I had one of my own students following suit. Both of 'em were equally mad—not in the way they thought, but because they'd decided I'd make a good listener when all signs pointed to how piss-poor I'd be at it.

The problem was that I'd picked up on a few similarities in their separate stories—things that shouldn't and by all rights *couldn't've* been the same, but were anyway—and I was the one putting both sides together. That is, if I could even find a way to make things fit.

I really didn't like it. Sure, everyone at the Airman'd had their own opinions about whether or not Balfour was man enough for the job he'd inherited, but he'd handled the same shit as any of us and then some, on account of all that hazing. He was a tough little bugger underneath it all. This girl Laure I knew less about, but what I did know seemed pretty sturdy to me.

She wasn't one of them fainting flowers, and she wasn't the sort to make up stories for attention, either. At least that was what it seemed like to me, and I was gonna feel real blockheaded if it turned out I was wrong. But I had a few instincts of my own and they were usually good ones. She wasn't a rotten egg. After dealing with all the nutters th'Esar sent my way for airman training, and before that working with my fair share of deserters, I knew a liar when I saw one.

I'd taken her appointment card just to make sure I wasn't imagining things, and I kept staring at it, like *that* would somehow help me make sense of this whole mess. Maybe I was hoping that the next time I looked at the name on the card, it'd be something different and I could unclench.

Royston would've said I was acting like some young schoolboy who'd snagged a trinket from an admirer, but I wasn't going to give him a chance to get that far. Never mind the fact that the thought'd gone and entered my head in the first place. I had a lot more to be concerning myself with than simple nonsense.

Normally we'd have met in a coffee shop, but I was starting to feel kinda paranoid, and the topic was sensitive enough that I didn't want anyone eavesdropping—not an idle café gossip, which Royston was himself sometimes. I'd promised Balfour I'd be discreet, and even if no one knew or cared about a country girl studying at the 'Versity, that didn't mean a man could go blabbing about the condition of *her* mind all over the city, either.

It was only common decency.

As far as I was concerned, the only place where I was comfortable having this discussion was my very own home. It wasn't as fancy as Roy's place in the Crescents, and it didn't serve fancy little vegetable sandwiches with no crust like they did at Piquant—which was "our place," according to Roy—but Royston was just going to have to saddle up and deal with roughing it for an afternoon.

Probably wasn't the exact attitude I wanted to have toward someone I needed to help me, but there it was.

My place was clean, even if it did smell like "dragon and dirty boots and the inside of an old coffeepot."

Roy arrived late, of course, but since I knew his style, I'd told him to come about an hour before I needed him to, and it all worked out. There were certain strategies for dealing with people, same as in battles, and when you had friends as complicated as mine were, you needed to arm yourself in advance.

"I can't say I wasn't intrigued by the message you left for me at the Basquiat," Royston said, peeling off his scarf and hooking it over the rack I never used. Why have one of those at all when the back of a chair served your purpose just fine? "All this secrecy! The messenger told me you threatened to find him and do him bodily harm if he went 'flapping his mouth' to anyone else. That's *one* way to make *everyone* paranoid, you know. You really should be more discreet sometimes."

"I said that?" I grunted. It wasn't because I was playing coy but because I honestly didn't remember.

Royston gave me one of his long-nosed looks. "It does sound like you," he said.

"Guess it does," I admitted.

"You *are* going to tell me what's bothering you, I hope?" he asked. "There's only so much I can take of you stalking the streets like a wild bear in search of prey. I never know when you'll claim your next victim, and I can't handle the responsibility."

"Bastion," I said, momentarily distracted. "You really would get on with Luvander. Or else you'd kill each other; I'm not really sure."

"I'll pretend that's a statement I understand, shall I?" Royston asked, folding his coat neatly over the rack and heading off ahead of me down the hall. "It's not some sort of code, is it? If you've resorted to code, I'm leaving right now. The tiger strikes when the moon is full; the lion leaps at midnight; you really would get on with Luvander. Et cetera."

"Have some coffee," I said, following him into the kitchen. "And shut up."

"Such ambiance," Royston said, settling down into one of my chairs, wasting no time in making himself feel at home. "You wonder why I don't come here more often. Why *am* I here, by the way?"

I still had Laure's card in my pocket, and I pulled it out, setting it down on the table. Not that it meant anything by itself; I just wanted to have it there. Serving as a reminder, maybe. "Got a few more things to talk to you about. Remember Margrave Germaine?"

"The woman who dresses like a mushroom," Royston said, leaning across the table to peer at the card. "Quite distinctly. You *could* have told me that's what this was about. I've been making my own discreet inquiries into the matter already. You'd be shocked—or perhaps you wouldn't—at how quickly my fellow Margraves and Wildgraves in the Basquiat are willing to gossip about someone they consider to be a spy. Her well-known liaison with the Esar did her no services among us, fortunately for you. Everyone has some little bit of dirt or another, though it's slow going when you have to piece together something useful from all that idle chatter."

"Lucky me," I said, doing my best not to look like an eager schoolboy at lecture. "So what'd you find?"

"Well, your hunch was right," Royston said. "If the Esar *was* going to capitalize on the new information about the dragons, it seems likely that her services would be the ones he'd use. She was an assistant on the original dragon project, though they never used her Talent outright; I'd assume she was simply too young at the time to participate, but she must have learned a great deal from the original magicians. I'm not saying for certain that's what she's doing now, however—if she is, she's smart enough not to leave anything so helpful as a speck of proof lying around—but it *would* make sense for Germaine to see to your man's hands first, if that's the case. According to anyone who knows anything, the principles of dragons and Balfour's steel hands are essentially the same, and observing him might very well help her to fine-tune the process of *other* endeavors. I must stress again," he added, looking at me sharply, "that this is speculation based on what information I *did* suss out. We still don't know that the Esar—meticulous as he is—is planning anything."

"So you believe that?" I asked him.

"Not for an instant," Roy told me.

"Better not go shoveling that shit in my direction, then," I said, thinking over what he'd said. It all made sense, but there was still a piece missing. Why the *hell* was a woman like that doing routine checkups on 'Versity students, and why had Laure and Balfour both come away from seeing this woman feeling feverish and hearing voices?

A dragon's voice, in Balfour's case, I reminded myself. I wasn't prone to the shivers, but I got the faintest sliver of one right then, like someone was dripping ice water down my back.

"Best let those thoughts out, whatever they are," Royston said, peering at me from across the table. "You'll give yourself an ulcer otherwise."

"With all your chatting around, did you find out anything about why Germaine's playing physician to the new 'Versity kids?" I managed finally, spitting the words out like bad food. "If she's such a high-end Talent, you'd think th'Esar'd put her to better use than wiping snotty noses. But one of my students told me they've *all* been coming back feverish— and I'm sure, what with you being so caught up on your bastion gossip, you've already heard about what happened with Balfour."

"There might've been a murmur or two about that poor gosling floating around the Basquiat," Royston said, pressing the tips of his fingers together. "Nothing too undignified. I believe most sympathized with the poor man for having to deal with the Arlemagne emissaries day in and day out. No one enjoys that. I'm simply lucky enough that I've been forbidden to speak with any of them, on pain of death. You know how it is."

"Well, fever's not all that's been going on," I said, coming around to the real point at last. As much as I could and did give Royston shit about dancing around a topic, I was as guilty as anyone right then. Sometimes, a man knew he wasn't gonna like the answers he was about to get and avoided asking the question for as long as possible.

"Oh?" Roy asked, his attention immediately focusing. He was pretty sensitive to mysterious illnesses at the moment, and I could tell the idea that it might've had anything to do with another Margrave was getting under his skin.

"Balfour said he was hearing voices," I said, not feeling guilty because I'd gotten his permission to talk about it. Still, it felt a little strange telling someone else without him being there to supervise us or make sure I wasn't misrepresenting it. "And before you ask—yeah, I believe him. He's the worst liar I've ever met, so I know he wasn't spinning some story to cover his ass after making a fool of himself in front of the diplomats. The symptom came alongside the fever, and that *fever* came after he had his damned checkup with Margrave Germaine."

Royston sighed, glancing away from me to look out the

window for a long moment. He was gathering his thoughts, sorting them out, and putting them in order, but sometimes he could get too caught up in the flourishes and the embellishments. I could only hope I wasn't in for three, four minutes of contemplative silence, at least not today.

"When magic gets into someone without a Talent, it *can* cause a slight fever," Roy said at last, right when I was about to reach across the table and drag the words out of his mouth. "Their bodies aren't used to the sudden change—the water gets into the blood, you see, where it's treated almost like an infection until the body becomes accustomed to it. Hence the reaction. I didn't think anything of it before, since, as you said, it *is* winter, and fevers always spread like wildfire through the 'Versity dorms the moment the weather changes. But you say Balfour fell ill, too, and that this woman's been providing the care for all those first-year students when her specialties *clearly* lie elsewhere. You *know* how I hate to leap at shadows; it wastes good energy. But I would be remiss to decide I could ignore this uneasy feeling entirely in favor of my own personal comfort."

"Shit," I said, rubbing my hands over my face. I hadn't shaved long past the point where I'd meant to; waking up early to see Balfour before work had taken up most of my free time, and I was closer to growing a beard than I had been in about fifteen years. Pretty soon I was gonna have a nice winter goatee to match Roy's if I wasn't careful. "One of those kids went missing, you know."

"I can only hope he proves easier to locate than Margrave Ginette," Royston said, looking grim. "I wonder . . ."

"You wonder what?" I prompted.

Roy was so lost in thought he wasn't even complaining that I was pacing back and forth, or that my stomping around was distracting him. "Hal heard a similar sort of rumor," Roy explained. "About a missing student. I wonder if it's the same one, or if they're being spirited away right and left. How embarrassing for the dean if that's the case."

"Ain't funny," I said.

"No, of course not," Roy agreed. "It's very grave indeed. It

leads me to believe something I don't want to contemplate—
and yet all the clues do point directly toward it, making the
conclusion inevitable."

"And that is?" I asked, hoping he wouldn't confirm my
suspicions.

"That Margrave Germaine is conducting experiments in
magic on children," Roy replied simply. He pressed his fore-
fingers to his temples, closing his eyes for a moment, then
relaxed. "And if her specialty is in dragonmaking . . ."

"This is a fucking mess," I said.

"Very well put," Roy said.

We were quiet after that, giving our thoughts the gravity
they deserved. It wasn't as though we could go to the Provost
about everything—him being th'Esar's bastard son made it
clear where *his* loyalties were—and I felt like I was going to
be arrested myself just for having these thoughts. They *were*
treason, sure enough—and I'd feel like the madman, not Balfour, if it turned out I was believing His Highness capable of
something so fucking drastic.

"I gotta meet with the boys," I said finally. "We'll stand
together, same as always, but if it's about dragons, then it's
not your fight. You get your large nose out of this and stop
asking around before you're exiled again, or worse."

"How cheerful you sound," Roy replied, but his voice was
without any humor; it was a sorry day indeed when he got no
pleasure from teasing me. "The Esar *has* been desperate to
regain full control over the city. And with so many of the
magicians dead after the war, now is the perfect time to
strike. It wouldn't be so difficult to rearrange the balance of
power completely, so that there *is* no balance—perhaps even
no Basquiat. It *all* lines up perfectly, doesn't it? With everything we know?"

"We don't actually *know* anything," I told him. "And I'd
suggest keeping thoughts like those to yourself before the
wrong person overhears 'em."

"I do know how to be discreet," Roy said.

"I'm talking about Hal, too," I said—not a pleasant topic
to get into with a friend, and surely one that wouldn't make

him too happy with me, but I had to make him aware of the dangers all the same. "You don't know who that boy trusts or what kind of people he talks to. Could be working for th'Esar himself after everything that went down at the end of the war. You watch out for yourself."

"I'm surprised at you, Owen," Roy replied, sounding genuinely hurt.

"I'm just saying you don't exactly have the best track record," I said, which was nothing but the truth.

"I find it unfortunate that you are so tainted by my past relationships you refuse to see any goodness in a truly good person," Roy told me. "Hal should hardly suffer because of *my* failings." He sounded caustic now—probably embarrassed he'd shown any kind of real emotion—and I wondered if I'd done the wrong thing by bringing up my concerns.

But the shit we were discussing *was* treason. Just talking about it was grounds for imprisonment, or worse. And with all the *velikaia* hanging around th'Esar these days, maybe even *thinking* about it could mean the end.

I should've been smart, like Rook and Ghislain, and gotten the hell out of the city while I still could.

Yet, a dry voice—sounding a lot like Royston's, once I thought about it—told me that would never have worked. I might've hated the responsibility of being in charge most of the time, but I needed it, too. Why else would I have taken the damn lecturer position in the first place? It sure as shit wasn't because I loved teaching.

I was the kind of person who needed to be looking after someone—a whole lot of someones, more like. It was the only thing I was halfway good at, and the feeling like I was going to fail and let 'em all down was usually the kick in the ass I needed to get my brain working.

"If something is happening," Royston said at last, voice tight, "then the Basquiat needs to be forewarned. We can't simply have something sprung on us when we're at our weakest. Though I am loath to accept the idea, and though I have no clue as to what the Esar could possibly be planning, a little dose of mistrust at present does not seem particularly unwise."

"He's building the dragons again," I said because I knew it was true. It was the one thing he'd done that'd won him the war—or so the people felt—and it'd made him a hero along with the airmen. It'd been his idea, when he was a much younger man and had much larger vision. But now all his thoughts had turned inward, to Thremedon. Without an enemy outside to focus on, he needed to find one somewhere else, and the Basquiat was his next target.

The dragons had been his weapons against magicians in the first place—albeit Ke-Han ones, not Volstovic. But to him, the principle would be the same; he'd always had trouble with the restrictions presented by a rival group for his loyal bastion.

It all just made sense in my gut, and if I was wrong, then I'd allow myself to feel pie-faced.

"I don't know whether you're angrier that he's doing this or that he's doing it without you," Roy said, somewhat sharp-tongued. "But I'll let you sort that personal matter out—if you leave me in charge of *mine*."

"I gotta call the boys together," I told him again. "We can talk about the rest later, and you can wrangle some apology outta me if it makes you feel better."

"Perhaps," Roy replied lightly. "We'll see how I'm feeling. We'll see if I'm still around; if I haven't decided to abscond with my life to some other, less difficult city."

I didn't want to leave things so uncomfortable with him, but I wouldn't've done a good job of making my case to him just then. It was a bad idea to let Roy stew over a slight—but we both had more important things to worry about, and I just hoped he'd understand I had *his* best interests in mind when I'd stuck my nose into a place it didn't belong.

"I suppose I'll have to cross-examine you about that young girl with whom I saw you enjoying sweet drinks at another, more appropriate time," Roy said as I was showing him out the door.

"I'll hold you to it," I said.

"Just see that you're careful," Royston said, tugging on one glove and then the other. His voice was clipped—I knew things were bad when he wasn't even getting any enjoyment out of teasing me. "It can be . . . difficult for someone from the countryside to adjust to city life. I don't mean to sound crass, but it's the truth. You should keep it in mind."

I was surprised enough that I came close to shutting the door in his face. Somehow, good sense kept me from making too many mistakes in a short period of time, though, and I refrained.

"Okay," I said instead, though it stuck in my throat. "Thanks. I'll keep that in mind." Things'd work out with us since they always did; neither of us was the kind of person who had so many friends we could afford to lose the few who managed to stick around.

The door closed behind him, and I just hoped he wasn't going to do anything stupid, like unburden himself to someone who might be unburdening *themselves* right in th'Esar's private confidence.

For now, I knew I couldn't let Laure see Margrave Germaine, no matter how many angry letters they sent. The rest, like what it meant—and me looking out for her this way—I'd deal with later.

TOVERRE

Somehow, without my knowledge, Laure had been fraternizing with our Professor Adamo again.

The only reason I'd learned the truth at all was not due to my own innate skills of deduction but the fact that she'd come to see me at last, as a gesture of peace between us, and told me outright.

After I got over the initial slap in the face that she had been confiding in someone other than me, I was at least grateful she'd found someone with any kind of standing who was willing to help her, though I sincerely hoped her good looks had nothing to do with that man's eagerness. Hero of Volstov or no, there were some things that were never acceptable, and I did not care if he had twenty statues dedicated to him throughout the city. Laure's honor was far more important than anyone else's reputation.

In private, I was actually relieved she had unburdened herself to me. We had never gone for very long without speaking to one another, and I wasn't at all certain how to mend relations if too much time passed. Quite fortunately for both of us, they never had yet.

At first, I was too hurt to absorb a great deal of what Laure had to say, but I perked up when I realized what she'd told Professor Adamo—namely *everything*—and what Adamo had told her in return.

In other words, he intended for her to seek the help of one of his fellow airmen.

"One of 'em works in a hat shop—or he owns it, I guess; I'm not real sure," Laure had told me, looking as though the information didn't much matter to her one way or the other. She said it so casually that I wondered if she even understood just how impressive this was. Given her interest in the dragons, I would have thought she'd be far more excited. "Name's Luvander, and that's where Professor Adamo says I'm supposed to meet him. Never been, but I thought maybe . . . Do *you* know where Yesfir is?"

I'd been pacing the room, but at that I whipped around so quickly that it was clear I'd startled her.

"You mean that popular little boutique along the Rue—the one using peacock feathers in its display?" I asked.

I *had* heard of it—I knew exactly where it was—but I'd never set foot inside. All the most fashionable hats were for women, though I'd seen that Yesfir also had an immaculate collection of gloves on display. The detail work, the stitching, and the differently colored leather, not to mention the caliber of customers I saw within, were enough to make me burn with desire every time I passed by.

It was like a dream, deposited onto the Rue for my very own enjoyment. *And* it was run by an airman.

This was what I'd waited for, the culmination of all my time in the city, wandering through the Amazement and—admittedly—spying on the glamorous citizens traveling in and out of the theaters. On our very first day in Thremedon, we'd all been deposited like so many bales of hay in front of the statues of the airmen. They were Volstov's heroes, but more specifically, they belonged to the city, no matter how much some people in the countryside were fascinated with them. Thremedon herself had adopted the Dragon Corps, and now they were as much a symbol of city life as the Basquiat or the Esar's palace. I had admired their sharp stone noses and their square-cut jaws from afar, the same as everyone else, and I had been lucky enough thus far to have even met one of them, despite how grim and crass he tended to be.

Laure had been drawn into his confidences, and invited to meet his friends. I wondered—as I unquestioningly invited myself along—if I might even be able to speak with this Luvander the way I'd never dared to do with Professor Adamo. At least it was clear he had far better taste than his ex–Chief Sergeant.

The idol worship I'd felt when I had first arrived in the city—staring up at those noble faces, imagining all their exploits—had returned tenfold. At last, there might be something in Thremedon that lived up to my wildest expectations.

If I thought about it too long, I was bound to be sick with excitement—especially considering Laure hadn't even suggested I would be accompanying her.

By contrast, Laure seemed neither to understand nor care about the enormity of our situation. It was as though she had received a gilded invitation to dine with the Esar and Esarina, and here she was, behaving as though it didn't mean anything.

She was a smart girl, infinitely more capable than I was when it came to all sorts of things, and yet I had to wonder over her priorities.

There was a sobering element amidst all my excitement, however, and one that made it easy for me to keep my feet firmly planted on the ground. Laure had told Professor Adamo about everything, and he had believed her enough to offer her his protection—which made the matter very serious indeed. Whatever was happening to the students in the first-year dormitories was a grave enough matter that some-one like Adamo hadn't simply brushed it off as hogwash. And, since he appeared above all things to be an extremely pragmatic man, this gesture surprised me. He hadn't scoffed at Laure, as I had assumed someone in a position of his authority would have done, having seen all the dangers of war firsthand.

And while I had my own personal opinions on the subject of Adamo's feelings toward my dear fiancée, he did not seem the type to chase after flights of fancy simply because he liked the person doing the fancying.

"So . . ." Laure said slowly. "You're being awful quiet."

"I'm picking out what to wear," I explained, which was partly true. "And what *you* should wear, for that matter."

"I don't even know where to start," Laure said.

"Don't you want to make a good impression?" I asked. "They *are* airmen, after all. And one of them owns a hat shop, which means he has some knowledge of fashions."

"Figured you'd want to come with me," Laure said, playing with a loose thread at her sleeve.

"Did you also figure there would be no talking me out of it?" I asked, readying myself to argue my position. "I can hardly send you—a beautiful young woman—to consort with *two* rugged ex-airmen all on your own. You are my fiancée, and even if you were not, such a rendezvous would hardly be proper—"

"I'm agreeing," Laure told me, "because I'm not in the mood for arguing."

And, I suspected, because she might have been intimidated after all. Bastion only knew I was. Even if she did not show such things the same as I did, the tight set of her jaw and the dark look around her eyes made it clear to me that she really did know what an incredible honor this was—and also, the gravity of the situation was weighing upon her more than she let on.

I was glad she'd seen my side of things so quickly. I couldn't very well allow her to go barreling into the belly of the beast without *some* manner of masculine protection.

Even if all that protection amounted to was someone like me, it was my duty as her betrothed—but more importantly, as her friend—to stand up for her best interests, no matter the consequences.

I knew she trusted Professor Adamo, and I supposed I had to as well, but things were progressing far too quickly for my liking. I didn't have any control over it happening, either, which only made the impression of impending drama that much more intense.

One good thing *had* come out of it, at least: Laure had finally decided once and for all not to return to that beastly physician. We still couldn't say for certain whether that had been the cause of everyone's fever, but it didn't seem prudent to take the chance. I still got the shivers whenever I thought about Gaeth's room, and not just because of the half-eaten sandwich we'd left behind. No doubt it was well on its way to becoming a sentient organism by now. At the very least, it was a homing device for all kinds of vermin. The dormitories would soon be crawling with bugs and mice.

Yet that did not frighten me as much as my wicked imagination, which ran in every direction the moment I thought of Gaeth—wherever he was. *However* he was. All my feelings for hats, pestilence, and airmen aside, this was a serious matter.

Gaeth's disappearance had been hard enough; I couldn't imagine what I would do if the same thing happened to Laure.

"What are the conditions for my attendance?" I asked, searching her face to see if the same worries plagued her. She looked tired, I realized, but in relatively good spirits. I gave her arm a little squeeze, and she patted my hand.

"Don't spend too long figuring out what to wear," she said. "And don't make me change, either. I don't wanna waste any more time than I have to."

As a favor to her, I didn't spend nearly enough time choosing a scarf and gloves. But I knew how she hated waiting around when she could be stomping purposefully through the streets like one of the proud horses I'd seen drawing carriages—though, she always informed me, these Thremedon show beasts weren't nearly as fine as the ones she'd helped to raise back home.

"I wonder if he's called *all* the airmen together," I said, checking myself one last time in the mirror. Despite all my preparations, Laure was still more striking than I was—and she hadn't even brushed her hair.

"As far as I know, it's just Luvander," Laure told me, taking my arm as we passed through the door outside. "At least I think that's it. You know all their names, don't you? You *must*."

"Luvander *is* the owner of the hat shop," I told her, choosing to be helpful instead of goggling in shock at her lack of knowledge. Obviously, in true Laure fashion, she'd paid far more attention to the dragons than to the men who'd been their pilots. Everyone knew only five of the corps had survived past the end of the war. One of them was our professor, the only one Laure seemed to have much interest in, and two had quit the city after the war—I'd learned a few useful things listening to city gossip, alongside all the rest. The fourth was Luvander, proprietor of the famed Yesfir haberdashery, and the fifth was that poor creature with the metal hands, a favorite topic among current city playwrights.

"I can remember a few of the names," Laure admitted sheepishly. "Adamo, of course, and Luvander—though to be fair, he's the one I always used to forget. And Rook, of course. And someone that started with a 'B' . . ."

"Are you thinking of Balfour?" I asked her, as we made our way down the familiar path of the 'Versity Stretch. The air was cold enough that it was bound to snow, and I hid a series of loud sneezes behind my handkerchief.

"*That's* the one!" Laure said, snapping her fingers. "I knew it couldn't be Bald-something."

I gave her a look of horror, then quickly pulled her to one side of the street before she could step in the steaming yellow puddle we passed.

Not everything in the city was as glamorous as I'd hoped, but I'd come to appreciate its shortcomings all the same. As long as you looked before you leapt, you could avoid most of her unpleasantness.

And, as I understood it, this part of the city was far cleaner than Molly. I shivered when I imagined what it must have been like living there, and Laure—bless her heart—put an arm around me, as though *I* were the one who needed comforting.

Yesfir was just a little way down the Rue, past the square where the airmen's statues stood, and a few shops down from the hat shop in front of which Laure and I had nearly been robbed. It seemed like ages ago, but it had only been a bare few months. Despite that, the memory was still fresh in my mind, and I suspected the same was true of Laure. I even caught her looking suspiciously up and down the street—either for fear we'd meet our thief or out of desire for revenge. One could never be certain with Laure, and I didn't envy the poor fool his position if she ever did catch sight of him.

"Ah, this is it, I believe," I said, to get her attention.

She tore her eyes away from a man innocently shoveling a pile of old snow, turning instead to gawp at the store windows with her mouth wide-open.

"How many birds you think went into that display?" she asked, tsking in awe. "Do they slaughter 'em, or do you think Luvander's got a whole bunch of naked Ke-Han peacocks in the back?"

"I give them little scarves and hats in the winter, actually," said a blond man standing in the doorway of the shop. He appeared more amused than offended by Laure's question, which was fortunate, and I appraised him from the corner of my eye so as not to be rude. He was wearing a handsome vest with a green scarf wrapped around his neck. However, he was *not* wearing a coat, so I assumed he must have come from inside the shop, perhaps to grab a breath of fresh air.

There was no question in my mind: This man was obviously *the* Luvander. My brain helpfully provided that very obvious slice of information before it shut down completely.

"What about boots?" Laure said stubbornly.

"*You* try finding boots to fit those little claws," Luvander said, shaking his head. "And oh, how they scratch!"

"Maybe they're mad about being naked," Laure replied.

"I personally would be *delighted* to end up as a hat," Luvander said. "You'd make a very fine one, with that coloring. I take it you're Laurence? Please don't let me scare you off; I'm frightened of what Adamo will do to me."

"Laure works fine," Laure said. "And I'm not scared."

"You certainly don't look scared," Luvander agreed.

"As long as you don't keep me in the back with the naked peacocks," Laure warned.

"My word, this conversation has turned very fresh very quickly," Luvander said, blue eyes lighting up with wicked delight. "If Adamo overhears us, he'll keep *me* in the back with the naked peacocks."

I couldn't allow the conversation to continue any longer as it was going. While Laure might have enjoyed the banter, this was no way to go about making a first impression—despite how odd this airman was.

There was another one who hadn't quite lived up to my expectations. At least he dressed impeccably, though I wished suddenly I could have had some of Laure's brazen disregard for common courtesy, so that I might have asked him why he'd chosen to open a hat shop after piloting a dragon. The two things seemed quite incongruous.

In any case, I cleared my throat, and Laure turned to look at me, almost like she'd forgotten I was there. She was actually craning her neck for some reason—I suspected privately she *might* have been trying to discern if Professor Adamo had already arrived—and to my shock she actually blushed.

"Oh yeah," she said. "This is Toverre."

"Your bodyguard, I hope," Luvander said, with a wry tone I wasn't entirely sure I appreciated. It wasn't an insult outright, but it certainly had the implications of being one.

"Her fiancé, actually," I replied.

"*No,*" Luvander said. "Really?"

It was what I assumed most people must have thought when they learned that little detail—wondering how someone like me had managed to find myself so lucky, no doubt—yet none of them had ever actually vocalized their surprise quite so blatantly.

I felt myself begin to color. "Really," I told him, mumbling a bit.

"You lucky little man," Luvander said. "You'll have to tell me your secret sometime. I am extremely interested in learning your techniques. Well, no more standing around freezing our feet off; *I* don't have a coat, and I'm more than ready to go inside."

Exchanging a look with Laure, I followed him into the shop, where it was thankfully much warmer. There were no customers within, and Luvander hung up a *Closed* sign behind the glass window, between a red and purple display. It smelled of new felt and soft leather, and I breathed in deeply, reveling for a moment in how pristine everything was, how organized.

"So I've heard from Adamo that you're interested in buying some hats," Luvander said, gesturing for us to follow him deeper into the shop. There was a little door behind the counter, which he opened, and I reluctantly left the shop itself behind. "How awkward; redheads are notoriously difficult to work with."

"Green or blue suits them very well, I find," I said instinctively.

"Of course," Luvander agreed. "I meant their dispositions, which are notoriously dreadful. Ace was a redhead, and *how* he carried on! Merritt, too. Both of them crazy as—well, as naked peacocks, I suppose. Mean little bastards. Wouldn't want to fit either of them for hats. This is Balfour, by the way. You make your introductions while I make some tea."

Privately, I wondered if Luvander himself wasn't a natural redhead—considering, in his own words, "how he carried on." Then he stepped aside, letting us enter the back room, which was a little kitchen with a white stove and sink set, and a table in the middle, at which a young man—not much older than Laure or I, I suspected—was sitting, gloved hands on the tabletop.

"Hullo," Laure said.

I had intended to make my own introductions right away, but I was momentarily fascinated by the ghoulish mask hanging on the wall directly over Balfour's head. It looked like something pilfered from a barbarian land, though from what I'd read for classes and my own personal edification, it didn't appear to be Ke-Han in origin.

"That thing looks like me in the morning, doesn't it," Laure murmured, nudging me with her elbow.

"Hello," said Balfour, passing a hand through his hair and standing. I might have told him that there was no need to stand on *our* account—since he far outranked us in terms of importance—but I was so soothed by the unexpected display of good manners that I could hardly speak up and tell him to stop. "I'm . . . Well, I suppose Luvander already told you, didn't he? I'm Balfour."

"I am Toverre," I said, much comforted by the sight of his gloves, as well. They were made of crisp kid leather, an off-white color, with dark buttons at the wrists, though they fit him a little stiffly. "And this is my fiancée Laurence, but she prefers to be called Laure. It is a pleasure to meet you."

Balfour was an extremely pale creature, who looked like one good winter storm would finish him off once and for all—but then, that was what everyone often said about me back home. Since Balfour was an airman, I could only assume he'd proven his own resilience ten times over, and that gave me hope for my own prospects during future trials.

And it was nice to meet someone with some knowledge of etiquette—a handsome, thoughtful, *young* city gentleman, who just so happened to be a noble ex-member of the Dragon Corps.

Laure nudged me in the side, presumably to remind me *not* to get any ideas. She needn't have worried; we were there strictly on business, and business was my sole focus of the hour.

Whatever came later entirely depended on how our business went.

"Laure's the reason for this little meeting, Balfour," Luvander called, from where he was busying himself with a tin of tea and five separate mugs. Not one of them matched, but they were all clean enough to suit my standards. One even came with a dear little saucer. I watched him to make sure he washed his hands before he began, then turned my attentions back to Balfour. "She's one of Adamo's *students,* you know."

"Don't have to talk about me like I'm not here," Laure grumbled, going over to the table and picking out a seat. I knew she was only put out because Adamo hadn't arrived yet—try as she might to conceal it from me, I had a feeling my suspicions were proving all too prophetic. I didn't know how I felt about this, to be perfectly frank; one could not have called my misgivings jealous, merely pragmatic. How *would* Professor ex–Chief Sergeant Adamo take to Laure's engagement if things grew serious between them? Might he attempt to get rid of the impediment—namely me—once and for all? I had no delusions of being able to best him man-to-man. I could only hope he'd been honorable with Laure thus far.

"Don't get the wrong idea," Luvander said. "We're bound to go on talking about you after you've left, too. That's just my nature. Don't you find this preferable, though? Gives you a little sense of what we'll say when you aren't here to know about it. That always makes me feel a little less paranoid."

"I'm beginning to understand why them other redheads had horrible dispositions," Laure muttered darkly, smoothing out her skirts.

Balfour waited for her to settle and for me to take my place beside her before he finally reclaimed his own seat.

"Somehow, he doesn't mean anything by it," he confided, not bothering to lower his voice for Luvander's benefit. "Sometimes—quite often, actually—he says things without thinking. He's very interested in gossip, you see, and prone to flights of fancy, but there's no real malice in it."

"Why, Balfour, are you conspiring to give away all my secrets at once?" Luvander asked, striking a match to turn on the heat beneath the kettle. From the way it began to steam almost immediately, I could tell he'd been preparing in advance for our arrival. "And here you had me thinking that you were the only one of us with manners, but at last you reveal your true colors."

Balfour flushed, but I thought I caught him rolling his eyes, as well.

"We're not offended," I assured him quickly, moving my chair closer to Laure's. The position was a precaution, in case I needed to kick her under the table. "In truth, we're both quite honored to be taken into your confidences this way."

"*I* was, anyway," Laure said, recovering a bit of her charm. "This one invited himself along for my protection. Said it wasn't decent, me meeting a group of men in the city all alone, with no chaperone to speak of."

"And he was quite right," Luvander said, coming up behind us with a lacquered tray filled with all the accoutrements for a proper tea. The napkins were clean and neatly folded, and I had to keep myself from snatching one up to brush away a spot of loose tea leaves on the table before me. "I don't know how many wild stories you've heard, but we were quite notorious back in the day. Not at all proper company for a young lady. Speaking of which, let's all take a minute to thank bastion Rook isn't here. In fact, I'm rather shocked Adamo didn't *insist* on accompanying you down here himself in order to limit our terrible influence on you. Perhaps he assumed that Balfour would take charge of the situation, thereby mitigating any damage I might cause to your *lovely* person. Now, would you be a dear and take a moment from your stalwart defense of the girl's honor to help me with this tray, Balfour? It's incredibly heavy."

"Of course," Balfour said, reaching above my head to set the tray onto the table.

Thankfully, there were no disasters.

Of all the things I'd expected from a lunch meeting with some of the few surviving airmen, drinking tea hadn't even entered into the equation. I supposed I'd imagined they drank liquid fire at all times, and breathed it, too; not being city-born, I'd allowed myself to be swayed by some of the more outlandish rumors about the corps.

I could see now that my assumptions had been greatly un-just; Luvander was evidently in the habit of entertaining fine guests. Despite the mismatched china, the pot, milk pitcher, and sugar bowl were all clearly from the same set—painted a lovely shade of green and decorated with a scrolling gold detail I'd seen imitated in a lady's frock just last week as I was walking down the Rue.

It was all very fashionable indeed. I wondered how long he'd had it, and more importantly, where he'd bought the thing. It certainly wasn't traditional Volstovic ware.

"It seems rude to start without him," Luvander said, seat-ing himself backward in a chair and casting a curious glance at the clock on the wall. It was wooden, carved in the shape of some enormous sea beast with sharp teeth; the claws overhung the face of the clock, and it appeared the hands were made of wood and not metal. Perhaps it had come from the same place as the mask—I was beginning to be slightly overwhelmed by all the curious details in back of Luvander's shop. Attempting to take them all in at once to paint a portrait of the man's tastes was making my head whirl. I wished I'd thought to bring a notebook so that I might write them down, to ponder them more methodically at a later date.

"He's never late," Balfour said, adjusting one of his gloves at the wrist. "At least, not unless my concierge got him in her claws again. I'm starting to think she likes him, actually. It's the only possible explanati— Ow!"

Luvander cleared his throat innocently, and turned to smile at Laure. "I imagine the matter must be something very seri-ous, for him to go to all the trouble of gathering us here and exposing you to our considerable charms," he said, tugging at the scarf around his throat to tighten it, but not before I caught a glimpse of the purple scar curving up from the base of his collarbone over the bob of his Adam's apple. Perhaps the scarf wasn't so much fashionable as it was a necessity; with a gruesome scar like that, it would probably be difficult to sell fripperies. "He wouldn't tell me anything—not even a peep—without getting your okay first, but since you're *here* now, perhaps you might fill the two of us in, just so we don't have to go over everything again when Adamo arrives? He likes to streamline communications. Quite frankly, I don't think he'd speak at all if he didn't have to."

"Some people sure do like talking an awful lot more than others," Laure agreed in a way that somehow managed to compliment Adamo and insult Luvander at the very same time. I hadn't known her to be such an adept study at double-speak, and I was unexpectedly proud.

"Then allow me to be the first to capitulate," Luvander murmured. "I cede the floor to you, my bonny redhead. If you're comfortable, please do proceed."

Laure reached forward to take a gulp of tea, then looked around the table.

"I've got an appointment with one of them physicians they hired to look over the new students," Laure said, glancing toward me as though she meant to ask if that was the best place to begin. "It's kind of a long story, with a lot of boring ins and outs, but what it shakes down to is that everyone who's gone to see this physician comes back sick, and one of our friends didn't come back at all. I know it sounds loopy, and that's part of why I waited so long to ever say anything, only now it's my turn to go back and I didn't want to risk it. You all can think I'm crazy—I'm giving you permission right now—but I *know* that Germaine woman made me hear voices. Never had delusions before."

"Voices?" Luvander asked, his expression suddenly sharper than it'd been only seconds ago.

Laure reached for her tea but collided with Balfour—who was doing the same thing—and one of them spilled the cup all over the table, splashing against his hand.

"Shit!" she said, leaping up and casting about for a napkin. "I'm sorry. If you get it under cold water quick, the burn shouldn't be that bad."

"It's all right," Balfour said, surprisingly mild. Luvander had already produced a number of cloth napkins from the tray, and I took some myself to help sop up the tea before it ran over the edge of the table and stained anyone's lap.

I was so focused on my task that I nearly missed Balfour removing his right glove, the pale fabric stained with a dark brown blotch of tea. But for once it wasn't the mess that really caught my attention. Rather, it was the sudden flash of silver—I'd assumed it was a bracelet when I saw it earlier—but once I'd looked, I found I couldn't tear my eyes away. It was one thing having heard about it and quite another to see it for oneself—what those "Steelhands" looked like in person.

Balfour's entire hand was crafted from the finest metal I'd ever seen—brighter somehow than silver, and much more flexible. I was fascinated by its movements, which were fluid and not at all stiff, perfectly mimicking the joints and curves of a real hand. Gradually, I became aware of the napkin growing damp beneath my own fir ;ers. Luvander and Laure had both stopped cleaning.

"Ah," Balfour said, clearing his throat uncertainly. "I don't suppose the two of you have heard a little song they're singing in Charlotte, now?"

"They're students," Luvander replied. "Adamo's students. I doubt they have much chance for hearing anything other than the echoes of his displeasure in their little student heads."

"We are from the country," I said, at last managing to look away. I could tell that my scrutiny was making Balfour uncomfortable—I didn't blame him for that—and I nudged Laure's foot delicately with my own until she, too, managed to turn her gaze elsewhere. "We aren't 'up' on current gossip."

"Lost his hands in the final battle," Luvander said simply. "It was all *very* heroic, and the people of Thremedon are mad about him because of it. You should listen to the songs one day; they're quite good."

"I can't even imagine," Balfour murmured.

"How'd you lose 'em?" Laure asked.

I cringed, and even Luvander flinched; Balfour merely looked surprised at the question, as though no one had ever really asked him *that* before. Leave it to Laure to ignore all sense of propriety in order to satisfy her curiosity—and leave it to me to allow it because of my *own* curiosity.

"I'd assume the details are a little too grisly to share with such delicate company," Luvander supplied, when Balfour seemed unable to reply.

"I'm not that delicate," Laure said.

"I, of course, meant your companion," Luvander explained. "I'm not sure how prepared he is to hear the details. Don't take it too personally. I'm not even sure *I'm* prepared, and I was there, myself."

"We held tight to the reins," Balfour said suddenly, our heads whipping round in unison to look at him. "One of the many precautions we took to keep from falling off should we have to dodge a missile attack. They were made of metal, because leather would have burned too quickly, and I'd wrapped them round my wrists. When Anastasia—my dragon—was hit the final time, her neck snapped. My mistake was trying to hold on to her; she moved in such a way that pulled the harness too far, and the reins sliced clean through."

We were all silent for a moment, each of us falling prey to our own ghastly thoughts. I couldn't imagine the pain, or what it must have felt like in that moment to realize his hands were gone—what it must have *been* like to realize that it wasn't all some terrible mistake, a nightmare from which he could disconnect himself.

"Now we've done it," Luvander said finally, the cheerful tone in his voice wavering only for an instant. "We've become sidetracked—just the kind of thing Adamo hates—and where *is* the old man, anyway? If one of *us* showed up late, he'd grab us by the ear and dangle us out the window himself!"

"You said you heard voices?" Balfour asked. The moment of recollection had passed, and though he was now as white as a sheet, the faraway look in his eyes had diminished almost completely. He no longer looked like a ghost. "After visiting Margrave Germaine?"

"Yeah," Laure said, shrugging uncomfortably. "I know it doesn't sound right, but I *swear*—"

"Did they say anything?" Balfour asked. Apparently, he was interested enough that good manners no longer applied.

"Nothing, really," Laure began. She bit her lip, staring up at the mask over Balfour's head like it was challenging her somehow, then sighed, shoulders slumping. "Maybe a few things. Most I could pick out was my name. Just kept saying it over and over again in the night."

"I've seen Margrave Germaine for these," Balfour said, lifting his hands to us. I could see some of the gears were still visible at the junction between his thumb and forefinger, breaking the illusion of metallic skin. "I also . . . heard things."

"Bastion," Luvander said. "What a merry, strange crowd this one is."

"Gaeth heard voices, too," I said. On instinct or habit, I touched his letter through the fabric of my vest pocket, which was where I always kept it—in case someone should be snooping through my things and find it by accident. It seemed necessary somehow for me to protect him this way from those who would believe he was a madman *and* a simpleton, when I knew he was neither.

"And who is Gaeth?" Luvander asked. "Your other fiancée?"

"The student who went missing," I replied. "He left behind a letter—it described the same phenomenon."

"I wonder if this is the way the magicians felt, during the fever," Balfour mused, looking distant again. Memories of the war could have been nothing but painful for him, I assumed, and here there was no hiding from them.

"Yes, but where in bastion's name *is* Adamo?" Luvander asked. He checked the clock for the hundredth time, fiddling with the knot in his scarf. All at once, the clock began to chime—a horrible, squawking noise that sounded like a bird being murdered. Even Laure jumped a little. I could feel my heart move in my throat, and Balfour's hands gripped the lip of the table so tightly that, when his fingers came away, they'd left little indents in the wood.

"Why do you own such a horrible timepiece?" Balfour

asked. "I've kept quiet about it for this long, but it's worse than hearing voices!"

"Ghislain sent it to me," Luvander replied, somewhat sulkily. "It was a gift. I'm certain he murdered pirates for it. You really don't like it?"

Balfour opened his mouth to reply when I heard the faintest of bells ringing somewhere behind me, within the shop.

"Someone's at the door," I said, for that was the only assumption I could draw from the sound.

"The shop is closed," Luvander replied. "I understand that my wares are in high demand, but for once I agree with Adamo—there are more important things than hats. Don't tell anyone I said that."

"Mightn't it *be* Adamo at the door?" Laure asked. "Who knows how long he's been ringing, with us yapping like this."

"I told him to come around back," Luvander said. "But he's getting old, isn't he? Perhaps his memory's failing him. I'll go see to it."

He stood, the chair scraping beneath him, and headed to the door. It swung open without a creak, swinging back and forth on well-oiled hinges. Luvander's disappearance left only Balfour, Laure, and me together—the most awkward of trios. None of us wished to be the first to speak, and so we sat in uncomfortable silence. I could tell that Balfour and Laure wished to question each other in more detail about their similar symptoms, but neither of them felt comfortable doing so in front of me. And so I was the third wheel, I realized. But I could never have left Laure alone with Balfour, impeccable manners or no.

"Well," Balfour said at last. "Do you remember *what* it sounded like?"

"Metal," Laure replied. "All whirs and grinding gears. Kind of what I'd imagine those hands'd sound like, if they were three times as big."

"Incoming," Luvander said from behind the door, and barged in a moment later.

Behind him—in a moment of utter, bizarre coincidence—

was the older man I'd seen with Hal on more than one occasion—the one who I could only assume was his lover. He was alone, without Hal, and I knew immediately from the expression on his face that something was amiss.

"I've come on Owen's behalf," he said, "since the man in question has just been arrested."

CHAPTER ELEVEN

BALFOUR

Once, in the middle of the war, I'd seen Cassiopeia set light to a store of powder. Everything had happened as if in slow motion—the yellow flames arcing through the night, one moment of perfect silence suspended in the air before Ivory's target caught flame. It'd sent explosions ripping fiercely through the battlefield, nearly knocking me off Anastasia, since I'd been closer to the ground doing my usual reconnaissance.

The effect Margrave Royston's announcement had on the room was quite similar to that experience. Everything went still and cold. Then, abruptly, the room exploded.

I was very nearly knocked off my perch again, though this time by the young lady Laure, who'd surged to her feet and strode right over to Margrave Royston as though she thought he'd been the one to do the arresting personally.

"What d'you *mean,* 'arrested'?" she demanded.

"Exactly what it sounds like," Margrave Royston replied—without any of the witticisms for which he was so notorious among the diplomatic circles.

"What *for*?" Laure persisted. I couldn't blame her for leaping into action at once, after all. She hadn't been trained to deal with this kind of situation—she was a student, and not an airman, retired though we were. It was always nice to have someone so forceful among our numbers, unafraid of asking the difficult questions. Before, we'd been gifted with rather a surplus of forceful personalities, so that neither Luvander nor I was used to speaking up. Usually that someone was

Adamo; but obviously, under these circumstances, someone else needed to step up and take his place.

"That is a very good question," Royston said, "one which I find I cannot answer officially. I have my suspicions, though, if you'll hear them."

Laure didn't seem impressed by the diplomatic answer. I folded my hands to keep them steady while privately wondering whether the young woman had ever been told it was bad luck to behead the messenger. "What kind of city *is* this, anyhow, where you can go around arresting people like that—just willy-nilly?" Laure demanded. "And what sort of friend are *you* that you didn't *stop* 'em?"

It was a great deal to absorb all at once. The girl's companion—young Toverre, who'd been clinging to a napkin through the entire thing as though it were a life raft—practically leapt up from his seat to try to calm her, elbows and knees everywhere, while I myself glanced to Luvander to see what he made of this mess. While my responsibility toward him was considerably different from that of a fiancé, I'd spent quite enough time hiding in the bastion, away from old friends. Now, more than ever, it was important to show solidarity—especially if what Royston said was true.

He was sitting very still, hair falling tousled over his knitted brow, and he hadn't even reacted to the revelation of Adamo's first name, which I myself hadn't been aware of until just then.

Surely I must have known it at one point—perhaps when I'd first joined the corps, during a whirlwind of preparations and paperwork—but that was feeling as distant a memory as my early childhood. Adamo had always been *Adamo* to us, just as we'd known each other by single names. It evened us out when we entered the Airman, where no one was a country lord or a petty thief. We were all just Dragon Corps.

"Young woman, please restrain yourself before you do both of us physical harm," Margrave Royston said. He looked troubled, and I couldn't exactly blame him. Adamo was untouchable, or so I'd always thought; I couldn't imagine him allowing this, nor could anyone else in the room, it seemed. Even the war had never managed to faze him. We were all shaken. "Trust me when I assure you—I attempted to do the very thing you have suggested, and I was informed that this was no happenstance arrest but rather was being carried out on the orders of the Esar himself. I don't know how much comprehension you have of Thremedon's particular politics, but a magician trying to argue against the Esar has almost no chance at all of overturning his ruling. In fact, if he became aware that *I* was making a fuss over things, he might just make things worse for Owen in order to make a point. He likes magicians very little, but he likes *me* even less. The quieter I was, the less *messy* things would become."

"That's horrible!" Laure said. Her face was turning red the same way Merritt's always did when he inevitably discovered the latest indignity to be visited upon his poor boots.

Toverre was standing beside her, attempting to calm her down, though he seemed reluctant to actually touch her, thereby risking the full force of her wrath turning in his direction. A wise move, I thought, and I was shamefully grateful that Luvander had no such temper to speak of.

"Did they tell you what the charges were?" Luvander asked at last.

"Treason," Margrave Royston said with a blank expression that stirred something dangerously close to fear in the deepest part of me. There was no chance he'd misspoken; I wouldn't lie to myself and hope for something like that. "Conspiring in private with secret information to use against the Esar, more specifically. I came here to warn the rest of you—I half assumed the shop would be crawling with Wolves when I arrived—but perhaps we're still ahead of the pack, so to speak."

"They wouldn't come *here,*" Toverre said, glancing over his shoulder in sudden suspicion, as though he was having second thoughts about having come to the shop.

Perhaps that was the smart reaction to take, but I couldn't have moved even if I wanted to. I felt rooted in place, a curious mixture of guilt and horror doing battle in my stomach. Of all the people I knew, Adamo could take care of himself the best—that was never in question. There had always been the possibility during the war that one or more of us might be taken captive at any time; we'd always been prepared for it. Indeed, after our last flight over the Ke-Han capital, some of us *had* been held in their prisons. It was merely that no one had ever imagined those doing the arresting might be on our side of the Cobalt Mountains, rather than the Ke-Han. Despite that, our course of action was clear: If Adamo was in trouble for something that involved all of us, then it was up to all of us to get him out of it.

It also implicated everyone in the room, including the two young students. What a warm reception they were having in the city.

I hadn't even been given chance enough to ask Laure everything I'd wanted to. Given the gravity of Margrave Royston's news, it seemed unlikely we'd be able to focus on anything other than Adamo's plight—hardly what Adamo had planned for us, I realized. Even in prison, he'd be trying to protect us all, keeping our names out of it.

Perhaps I'd been trained too well by him—I should've been furious, but I found myself coming down closer on the side of admiring.

"It's my fault, isn't it?" Laure asked, suddenly hushed. "I went to him, told him all those things about that Germaine woman. I knew not going was gonna get me in trouble. But it got *him* in trouble instead."

Margrave Royston blinked. He looked completely awful—the way Thom had, sometimes, when the rest of us had been out on a raid and he'd been alone in the Airman, waiting up all night for news. He must have been with Adamo when it happened. Either that, or he'd had exceptionally fortuitous timing to enter the scene at the very last second.

"Are you referring to Margrave Germaine?" he asked Laure.

"Who else?" Laure said, throwing her hands up in the air. "She started all this, mark my words. Ain't nothing good that's ever come of her that *I'm* seeing."

Luvander sighed, rubbing his eyes with his thumb and forefinger. Without its usual lively animation, his face simply looked tired and much older than I remembered. I wondered if I shouldn't be the one bringing *him* lunch every now and then, if only to keep things even between us. Just because I'd suffered the most obvious injury didn't mean the others hadn't. His throat had been stitched up with a needle and thread. And, as he said, he wasn't the sort of man to be taken down by a "wee infection," but he worked hard at his shop, from sunup to well past sunset. Not to mention all the energy he used up with his complicated monologues. It was a wonder he didn't eat like a horse, just to keep up his strength.

"That may well be the connection, now that you mention it," Margrave Royston said, smoothing the hair at his temple as though he needed something to do with his hands. I recognized that impulse; only a moment ago I'd been wishing for my gloves to toy with. "I am *not* saying it's your fault, so please cease looking as though you've not made up your mind whether to strike me or not. All I mean to say is that if Owen *had* been meeting with his fellows previously, at no great detriment to his personal freedoms, then perhaps it *was* his sudden interest in Margrave Germaine's business—which is *the Esar's* business—that suddenly landed him in trouble. If it was his investigation into what Margrave Germaine has been doing and not your little meetings of the minds, then . . . I do detest speculation, but it would explain why Dmitri hasn't turned his sights on this shop yet, and *we* are all safe and sound while *he* is not."

"Isn't *that* a comfort," Luvander said, standing up at once. "Well, dear friends, as they say when mired in the filthy muck that passes for water down by the Mollydocks: We're all in deep shit now."

"Still, better off than Adamo," Laure muttered, looking quite content to start a fight with anyone who disagreed.

No one dared. We veterans could smell a battle coming and knew how to avoid it altogether.

"I looked into Germaine's business, myself," Royston said thoughtfully. "But I suppose the gossiping of the Basquiat doesn't concern him as much at present. It's more what Adamo *represents,* I believe. There isn't any statue of *me* in the middle of the most popular street in Thremedon."

"Do you think we might at least be able to see him?" I

asked; someone had to be the man to get his hopes up, after all. "Perhaps the Esar—he *must* see reason. We've done nothing wrong. As far as any rational man is concerned, we've done nothing at all."

We'd all agreed to let the Esar act first for this very reason. I didn't think anyone had ever dreamed *this* would be the first action he'd take—especially when the most Adamo could be accused of was forcing me to eat breakfast when I wasn't hungry. Some mornings it seemed like a crime, but it was hardly an arresting offense.

"You're assuming this is a man with whom one can reason at all, by this point," Margrave Royston said, still looking grim. "After the war—not to mention what happened to our diplomats in Xi'an—his state of mind has been increasingly . . . fragile. No; that isn't the word. *Suspicious.* Antoinette can barely get him to agree to see her these days, and all because she practically runs the Basquiat. He doesn't want her to know his thoughts; I doubt he wants anyone to know them. He doesn't *trust* anyone anymore, and like it or not, Owen cuts a rather threatening figure."

"That he does," Luvander agreed, tugging at his scarf. "What's more, he's *our* threatening figure. Surely you don't mean to suggest we do nothing at all? As much gossip as we've heard about you, I'm sure one or two stories about the Dragon Corps and its complete lack of common sense must've reached your ears in return. That's not exactly how we play it, diminished numbers or no."

"When did I insinuate that? Such a course of action is hardly what I'm counseling," Margrave Royston said. If the reminder of his past stung, he didn't mention it. Thremedon rarely forgot its scandals, but at least it did stop caring about them after a while. "All I meant was that we have to be cautious, for Owen's sake. And to remind impetuous youth that, according to law as it stands, the Esar does not *technically* need a reason to arrest anyone. People tend to forget that. He is the Esar, and if he wished, he could arrest anyone wearing blue on a Saturday. The people wouldn't like it, and he'd never be so careless with their support, but it *is* possible."

"Someone oughta change that law," Laure said.

"It's in place from the war," I found myself explaining. When I'd been learning all the rules and provisions that comprised Volstov's system of government, in order to be ready to take my place with the other diplomats, I'd found most of the memorization boring, but at least the knowledge had stuck. And now, here it was, proving useful in a most unexpected way. "I . . . suppose that, what with one thing and another, and the continued threats from the Ke-Han, they never got around to rewriting it."

"Rather convenient for the Esar," Toverre murmured, deep in thought.

"And inconvenient for us," Royston agreed. The two seemed similar in some way though I couldn't put a metal finger on it.

I felt indignant all of a sudden, for Adamo most of all, but also for my friends, and lastly for myself. We'd spent so many years fighting against an external threat—fighting for Volstov, our home, in the face of a deadly horde—that it had never even occurred to me Thremedon might one day turn around and betray us, like a favored pet suddenly turned rabid.

Once again, I had to think that Ghislain and Rook had been the smartest, realizing the climate in Thremedon didn't welcome living heroes and getting out while they still could.

"Hm," I said, as something further occurred to me.

"What is it?" Luvander asked.

"Before I realized what any of this meant, I'd been planning on sending a letter to Thom about all this," I explained as quickly as I could, leaving out that it was something of a custom between Thom and me to write each other whenever things got rough. We told each other about the most awkward, embarrassing things that we'd recently undergone, and—through the exchange—they no longer seemed so terrible to either of us. "I was writing a letter to him about all of this, just to get it off my mind. About how I'd run out of the bastion, humiliating myself in front of everyone, and how I had been hearing things—those voices. I'd written about everything, really. I never sent it, but if we *are* coming under suspicion, it seems like it might be a good idea not to leave it lying around."

"You're not thinking of leaving now?" Luvander asked, looking aghast. He glanced about the room, then cleared his throat. For a moment, it seemed as though he'd forgotten he was speaking in front of an audience—and that it was up to us to represent Adamo's training to the best of our abilities. "In fact, allow me to rephrase that: As the senior member of the Dragon Corps in this room, I *forbid* any of you to leave this haberdashery until otherwise notified of your freedom. Do you follow?" To me, he added, "How was that? Did it sound very Adamoesque?"

No matter how grave the danger, at least he was still capable of making *himself* laugh. By now, I knew better than to give him any such encouragement.

"Do those orders apply to all of us?" Laure asked. Her face was slowly losing its angry red coloring, and she seemed somewhat more composed than she had been before. It reminded me of a calm day in the countryside, just before a downpour. "Or only them that actually signed up for the corps in the first place?"

"All of you, I should think," Luvander said with a sniff. "Excepting, of course, the illustrious Margrave Royston, who will no doubt very soon regret having come to inform us of our situation when *he* is implicated in our nefarious dealings. How many exiles will this next one mark, Margrave Royston?"

"At least you didn't call me Mary Margrave," Royston said, rubbing at the back of his neck the way Adamo did when he felt uncomfortable, with a toothy smile that was so far from any of Adamo's habits I had to wonder why they were friends at all. Adamo had never explained the matter to us, and it seemed rude to pry. "So I suppose we're getting friendly, aren't we? Since you are so clearly about to ask a favor of me."

"For Adamo's sake," I said, ever the diplomat these days. "The letter is the stupidest thing I could have written. It implicates all of us, and if for some reason they should search my apartment . . ."

"If I *am* exiled for my pains," Royston said, "and not imprisoned, or worse, I sincerely hope the rest of you are there to suffer along with me."

"Think of it like a vacation in the countryside," Luvander suggested.

Margrave Royston cringed. "Please, do not mention that," he said, voice pained. "Just give me the address and I'll be off on this madcap errand."

I did as he asked, writing the address down on the back of a caterer's business note card he had with him. He left immediately after that, and only the four of us remained in Luvander's kitchen.

"Don't worry too much," I told Laure, as Luvander took off his apron and moved in the direction of his shop. "Where are you going?"

"To open the store, of course," Luvander replied, "so that no one thinks anything is amiss. If you want, you can go upstairs. There's a game Ghislain sent with very dirty illustrated cards, which I'm sure will make the conversation among the three of you quite interesting."

"Well," Toverre said, after Luvander had breezed out of the room.

"He's used to another kind of people," I explained. "Like he said before—we really are lucky Rook isn't here. However uncomfortable you feel now, *that* would make things a thousand times worse."

"So now we just wait, is that the idea?" Laure asked darkly. I could tell by her expression that was her idea of a terrible plan, and while I knew it was our only one, that didn't mean I had to like it, either. Every mission needed a bit of reconnaissance, but since I was usually the man conducting it, I felt all wrong just sitting there.

"I suppose we do," I confirmed.

No one suggested we look into whatever lewd card game Luvander had mentioned. The mean-looking clock that made such awful sounds on the hour chimed unexpectedly, making us all jump again, but other than that, no one spoke. Toverre poured himself another cup of tea, then began to polish the handle of the teapot with his napkin; soon, he moved on to one of the saucers, and he was eyeing my stained gloves with a distressed expression. Finally, before his eyes popped out of his head completely, I forced myself to be the first to say something.

"Are you all right?" I asked, managing not to comment on how the others would've torn him apart if this had been the Airman.

"They're going to stain if you don't soak them," Toverre said all at once. He'd been holding it in for a long time, it seemed. "I know a few tricks. Would you mind terribly if I tried to clean them?"

"I don't see why not," I said. "You couldn't possibly make them any worse."

"Oh, but I could," Toverre told me, sweeping them off the table and heading to the sink. "Not that I *will,* mind you, but it is possible."

"Can't believe you're thinking of a stain at a time like this," Laure muttered.

"What better time to think of a stain?" Toverre asked. He began to pump the water into the basin, and Laure rolled her eyes but chose not to argue with him.

Over the duration of time that followed, I discovered something that might have been perfectly obvious to the others all along: I was complete shit at waiting.

I'd checked the clock at least fifty—probably closer to a hundred—times when the door connecting the shop and the back room finally opened. The sound of Luvander chatting with a group of customers filtered in, then was cut off abruptly when Royston entered, shutting the door behind him.

He held a white box in one hand, wrapped with one of Luvander's garish ribbons, and he looked extremely put out.

"The sly dog made me buy a *hat,*" he explained, dropping the box onto the table and loosening his scarf. "There was a group of customers, and I know *why* he was doing it, but the damn thing cost thirty chevronets and I don't even have a 'lady friend'!"

I wondered if I could have guessed, when we were first introduced, that Luvander would make such a shrewd businessman.

"Never mind my considerably lighter wallet," Royston continued, fishing some papers from his pocket. "I did as you instructed, and I tried not to read your personal correspondence—though if I had, it would be all you deserved for leaving incriminating documents lying around. Apparently there'd been another visitor for you not half an hour earlier. But," Royston added, looking like a satisfied cat, "he wasn't as persuasive with your landlady as I was. She didn't let him in, despite the fact that he threatened to come back with some of the Esar's men. I suppose we're lucky I got there before they did."

"Thank you for retrieving them," I said, somehow not as relieved as I could have been. I didn't like the idea of anyone's returning to my room with the Esar's men. Especially since, if Royston hadn't brought me those letters, I might well have been the next ex-airman arrested.

That, at the very least, would have made for an interesting letter to Thom.

"Something else you want to say?" Laure asked, even though Toverre tried to hush her seconds later. "I don't mean it like an insult. You've just got a look like you're not quite telling us everything. One of my cousins used to get it when he was sick—that was how you knew to clear the room before he spewed."

"Delightful," Royston said, though he did look a little as though he was going to be ill.

I wished Luvander was with us, so that he might conduct the conversation better than I was currently handling it. But I wouldn't get very far on simple hopes, or so the proverb about wishing in one hand and shitting in the other went. It was actually a phrase Rook had told me—see which hand fills up first, he'd said—and, like all things Rook had passed on, it had stuck, in its own way.

"There *is* more," Royston said, after he'd taken a moment to catch his breath. "It's part of the reason for my delay, actually, and I do ask your forgiveness. It seems you've all been very patient in my absence. It's merely that the route to your apartment took me directly past the Basquiat, and there was a dreadful commotion out front. Wolves, carriages parked all around, and Margraves shouting in the streets. Lady Antoinette was there—it was she who caught my attention, though I'm not certain if she meant to. When a *velikaia* is in great distress, she is able to project her thoughts without intending to, and anyone with a Talent will pick up on it. Her voice—her Talent—is particularly distinctive. It has a signature, if you will."

"This a story or a history lesson?" Laure interjected.

"*Laure,*" Toverre hissed, looking scandalized.

"No, she's quite right; I talk too much when under stress," Royston said, taking a moment to collect himself. "I have a habit of getting caught up in my own words; feeble as far as excuses go, but if you'll forgive me once more—it's been an extremely trying day. Shall I get straight to the point?"

"That'd be nice," Laure said. She'd taken the reins of the conversation in exactly the same way Adamo would've done, if he'd been there with us. "Who's Lady Antoinette?"

"Are you serious?" Royston asked.

"She's one of the Esar's closest confidantes in the Basquiat," I explained, to make the potentially long story short. "Until very recently, their friendship was what allowed him to work closely with the magicians at all."

"And yet since the end of the war, we've been on thinner and thinner ice," Royston concluded grimly. "What I managed to glean from Antoinette, once I'd calmed her down enough that I could be assured she wasn't going to injure any of the guards in the middle of the street, was that our Owen wasn't the *only* man arrested today."

Abruptly, I felt my heart begin to pound in my chest. Whatever was happening in Thremedon was a threat I'd never been trained to combat. I'd been raised among the country nobility, and though there had certainly been intrigue and politics enough there, the consequences had never been so dire. You'd lose an extra guest at dinner parties—and that was the extent of your punishment for a bit of gossip that reached the wrong ears. I felt as though I'd been dropped into a game where I knew only half the rules and understood none of the consequences of losing.

In the corps, it had always been my duty to scout ahead, so

that I could recommend the best angle for my comrades to attack. For the first time in a long time, one of my friends was in hot water, and I hadn't the faintest idea about how to approach it. I hadn't even been able to warn him a storm was coming.

"They were arresting Margraves?" I asked finally.

"Two Margraves and a Wildgrave," Royston confirmed. "Normally I'd make a joke about Margrave Holt being taken in for his unconventional style of dog-breeding, but this hardly seems the time and place. Josette—Margrave Josette, you'd know her as one of the diplomats who got caught up in that mess in Xi'an—told me the Esar's men have been questioning Lord Temur all morning. They haven't arrested *him* yet, but I suppose the Esar remembered he was Ke-Han and decided to take some kind of offense at it. I honestly can't tell you what's happening, but I *can* tell you what Antoinette intimated. It's as though he's well and truly lost his mind to paranoia."

"All those people arrested, and us just sitting here," Laure said, shaking her head. Despite the stern quality of her voice, I could tell from her body language that she was frightened. It didn't seem fair for her or young Toverre to be caught up in all this when they were barely more than children. I was sorry for them and for myself, but I was sorriest for Adamo, separated from the rest of us, without the consolation of company and no doubt spitting mad about it.

"If you'd like to charge out into the street and get arrested yourself just for acting mad, you're more than welcome to do so," Royston said sharply. Then he sighed, pinching the bridge of his nose. "I'm sorry. That tone was uncalled-for. You merely reminded me . . . Stubborn heroics tend to bring out the worst in me."

"I don't suppose you have any suggestions of something we *can* do?" I asked. It wasn't an entirely unrelated question, since, from what I'd heard, Margrave Royston was considerably more well versed in dealing with the political dangers of being disliked by the Esar.

Then again, the airmen had been in such trouble before. Only then, we'd had the power of the dragons behind us.

"I do, but I'm not particularly fond of any of them," Royston said, running a hand through his hair. He lowered his voice to barely more than a whisper—reminding me all at once that we *were* in the back of a busy shop, through which all kinds of people passed. Luvander was probably doing his best keeping them away from the door, but with a topic like this one, one could never be too careful. I only hoped some useful gossip was being imparted by his customers. "If it comes to it, I might have to ask *you* to use your position to make a plea with the Arlemagne diplomats, Balfour. I'm sure they'd be only too glad to help us oust our own Esar, wouldn't you agree?"

"Now *that* is most certainly treason," Toverre said, looking quite white around the eyes. He'd been silent the whole time, and I realized he'd taken all the silverware out of Luvander's drawers to polish each piece individually with a napkin. "I may be from the country, but I'm not a total fool."

"It would be a last resort," I reasoned, in part to soothe myself as much as Toverre. Nothing could be so dire that it would come to that—at least, I had to pray it couldn't. "No one's going to turn to the Arlemagne to solve our problems just yet. Especially not when we aren't sure *what* our problems are."

"*I'm* pretty sure," Laure said.

"I believe he meant what official reason will be given," Royston explained.

"Actually, what I'm really wondering is: Why now?" I asked.

No one had an answer for me though everyone was silent for a moment, trying to come up with one.

"Asking the Arlemagne to help would be like sending an invitation to the Ke-Han to march over the mountains and solve our problems for us," Laure said finally, sounding mutinous. "Bet they'd be pretty eager, now that we're all so friendly with each other."

"Here is what I think," Royston said, knotting his scarf about his neck. "No one should do anything until I get back."

"That's funny," Luvander said, passing into the back room. "I wanted to say that, too, but it seemed selfish. Never you worry, my darlings, only an hour left and I'll return to you. I'll see if we have the proper size for you back here!" he added, clearly calling out to one of his customers. "Don't listen to your friend, either! Large heads are a sign of wisdom and sensuality."

He popped a funny little shrug in my direction, then he was gone, being sure to shut the door firmly behind him. In his wake, the horrid clock started chiming the hour. But it was as clear a sign as any that we needed to lower our voices.

Luvander was subtle when he wanted to be; it was only surprising because he was so unsubtle the rest of the time.

"You're leaving?" Laure asked Royston, not allowing herself to be distracted. It seemed to me she hadn't even noticed the clock. "But we haven't decided what to do about Adamo yet."

"That is precisely why I am leaving *now*," Royston explained, "before we come to a decision and I'm locked into whatever mad course of action two students and two airmen can dream up. An interesting alliance, I must say. Bastion help me, I honestly don't know which is worse—if you drag me along with you, or if you don't. I have a few things at home to set in order, no matter what happens. Besides that, I think I can convince someone to throw her lot in with us. Trust me; if things are heading south as quickly as they seem to be, we'll need her on our side. I have to get to her before she formulates her *own* plan and does something rash, however."

"The way you talk, it sounds like everyone you know's a complete idiot," Laure said. At her side, Toverre continued polishing away. I was worried for the spoon in his hand, and for his fingers.

"There is a *very* good reason for that," Royston said.

"Like attracts like, huh?" Laure asked.

"If your friendship with Owen wasn't proof enough of that . . ." Royston began.

"Then I suppose we'll be here," I said, flexing my hands anxiously. One of the metal knuckles cracked loudly, and everyone looked in my direction. It was obvious—to me, at least—that I couldn't return to my apartment. I didn't know why anyone would want to bring the Esar's men to my shabby little room beneath the elephants; it certainly wouldn't be for them to get a decent night's sleep.

My not knowing *why* someone wanted to arrest me, however, wouldn't make much of a difference when they *did*.

Dear Thom, I began in my head. *It would seem that I am writing to you from prison . . .*

"We will set this to rights," Royston said, glancing in Laure's direction. "I don't make a habit of promising things I can't deliver, but Owen's tough, as I'm sure you know. He's weathered worse than this before."

"Just don't be gone so long this time," Laure said, pressing her lips together tightly after she'd spoken.

Toverre looked up as though he wanted to say something, then stopped himself.

"I'm going to find out *who* has been taken, and *why*," Royston concluded. "And it is going to be enlightening, I'm sure. Then I will—bastion help me—return to you lot and give you what information I've managed to gather. That is, unless *I* am arrested first."

"Sounds like a solid plan," Laure said. I couldn't tell if she was joking or not, because her face was so grim.

"I don't suppose this is a very good introduction to Thremedon," I said.

"Nonsense," Royston said, heading in the direction of the back door. He'd left his newly purchased hat behind, but then I supposed he *was* coming back for it later. "The only time Thremedon is truly herself is when she's boiling over with political scandal. The two of you are getting the authentic experience. If you live through this, then you can take anything she'll throw at you."

"And if we don't live through it?" Laure asked.

"It will make an excellent story," Royston replied.

He took the rear exit, not braving the public side of the shop, and though his words were glib, I sensed he was worried.

For a man who'd already been on the wrong side of the Esar's graces to be so shaken, it was clear everyone else had good reason to watch their backs.

And for a man like Adamo to be arrested, it was clear the whole city had been turned upside down.

ADAMO

There was one thing I was grateful for, and that was: I hadn't been arrested in front of my students.

It would've made their little lives to see the cruel taskmaster, burdening them with questions that couldn't be answered and battles that couldn't be won, punished for all his injustices, just like they'd always dreamed of. It'd give 'em a skewed view of the world, too—one in which somebody actually got his just deserts in as grand and embarrassing a way as possible.

The second thing I thought was, didn't I merit being taken in by Dmitri himself and not some green little squadron?

Then I realized these weren't the Provost's Wolves at all.

On the downside of being taken away quiet—followed back to my office like it was a meeting they were after, the enemy let through the gate by my own damned lecturer's assistant—was not knowing how long it'd take before anyone knew I was missing. And a whole lot of shit could happen to a man in a short amount of time. *Especially* when Dmitri wasn't involved, because at least I knew *he* was a fair lot who liked to ask a man questions before beating his head in.

But it'd been four and a half full hours—I'd developed a system for telling time in case I was ever taken captive by the enemy, locked up in a dark little cell like this one—and my head was still in the same shape as ever.

No one had even come to see me; I'd just been put out of the way like an out-of-fashion hat, stored somewhere dark until somebody had use for me.

There *was* noise coming from other parts of the prison, which could only mean one thing: I wasn't the only one who'd been arrested.

I had to hope that they hadn't taken one of my boys—that they'd gone after me because of all the snooping I'd been

doing on my own and not because I was calling secret meetings of the ex–Dragon Corps in Luvander's hat shop. If the
latter was true, then I'd sent one of my students—someone
I'd been trying to look after, and keep safe—straight into the
eye of the storm. I cursed myself for that misstep, but I hadn't
figured the situation was dire enough.

Yet here I was, suffering the consequences of letting my
guard down just because it wasn't wartime anymore. I had to
hope my other inmates were strangers, and that someone'd
come along eventually who'd slip up and give me the information I needed to know even though I was likely going to
be the man being questioned.

I'd heard the sound of footsteps three hours after my arrest,
and then again at the four-and-a-half-hour mark.

Only half an hour later—give or take a few minutes—at
the five-hour mark, I heard footsteps again. These came
closer than the others; it took me only a few moments to realize they were coming for me.

The way I was being kept wasn't too uncomfortable. I
wasn't even chained up properly, just a shackle around one
ankle. There was a chair in the corner of the cell, but no bed,
which meant I probably wasn't meant to stay there long. It
was more likely a holding cell than anything else—an
in-between prison, before the serious shit happened. I sat on
the chair, folded my arms over my chest, and got all questions off my face.

Barely a moment later, the door to my cell opened.

"Good evening, Adamo," said a familiar young man. I recognized his face, but it took his name a couple more seconds
to come to me. That piss-pot in Balfour's apartment—Troius.
"I told you I had connections, didn't I? Try not to look surprised on my account."

I hadn't looked surprised, and we both knew it. I resettled
in the chair, not giving him the satisfaction of answering
him.

"Well, all right," he said. "Suit yourself."

He was dressed different than before, wearing some kind
of uniform, all black. There was a familiar smell on him, too,

something that brought back *good* memories rather than bad ones. Dragonsmoke, mostly; the stink of hot metal.

"It doesn't have to be this way between us, you know," Troius said, folding his arms. "I actually respect you enormously. I was *excited* to see you in Balfour's apartment that day, though of course I was saddened to realize what it meant—that you were conducting meetings behind the Esar's back, no doubt about a little matter concerning his hands? You couldn't be content with your status as heroes, could you? Some people never *can* appreciate their good luck. They just have to *press* it."

"So is this my sentence?" I asked, shifting around in my chair. "You gonna stand there and talk me to death?"

"Death?" Troius asked, shaking his head. "I'll never understand why you men of war always leap to that dire conclusion without pausing to consider any of the steps in between. He's like that, too, you know—the Esar. It's why he needs someone like me. I believe I told you before that I come from a very long line of diplomats. It didn't impress you then, but perhaps once you realize how my skills can come in handy for your own benefit, you'll show a little more appreciation."

"Doubt it," I said. I was being—as Roy would've said—a stubborn ox, but the way I saw it was that men like Troius liked to hear themselves talk more than anything else. If he had something to say, he'd end up saying it whether I kowtowed or not. This way, I wouldn't have to abase myself and feel dirty afterward.

Plus, I wasn't exactly feeling generous after being hauled down to prison and all. Since he was definitely a clever kid, Troius would figure it out quick enough.

"Yes, well," Troius said, looking annoyed for a second, which satisfied me more than it should've and definitely more than I let on. Sure, I was in a bad mood, but things hadn't gotten so bad I was feeling suicidal—whether this little shit-eater told me death was in my future or not. "I suppose I can't blame you for your lack of imagination. The Esar was the same way. He wanted the lot of you executed, but *I* intervened on your behalf. The truth of the matter is that it'd be a criminal waste to kill someone of your Talents. I prefer to recruit my betters rather than massacring them in the streets as an example to my peers."

"You got one part right, at least," I said, listening for the sound of more footsteps. There weren't any, so at least I knew this wasn't some kind of distraction to keep me talking so I wouldn't be prepared when the real guard came to haul me off. "As one of your betters, let me give you a little tip: It doesn't exactly put people in a good mood when you throw 'em in a cell. Their first thought usually ain't 'sign me up!'"

"You're very funny," Troius said. "I wish I'd been the one to know you, instead of Balfour. I tried out for the same position, you know, and yet somehow he actually won the heart of a dragon. Sometimes they really *are* just like women. Totally unpredictable. And nonsensical in their choices, too."

"They don't call Balfour 'Steelballs' for nothing," I pointed out, leaning sideways to spit on the floor. Him talking that way made me mad, but there was no point in letting him see it. "I doubt you'd measure up. No offense meant, and all. Just not much room for diplomacy in the skies."

"I can see that I'm going to have to use stronger methods of persuasion on you," Troius said, lacing his fingers together to crack them. He was wearing gloves, too, I saw, black like the rest of his uniform, but with a stripe of bright green down each seam.

Here it comes, I thought, bracing myself for whatever screwy-minded torturer they kept down there to get his jollies out on prisoners because he couldn't get it up with a woman, or a man, or even a barn animal. But instead of calling someone in, Troius walked out of my cell door, leaving it open.

Now, that was one kind of torture, I guessed, staring at freedom while my leg was chained up.

But before I had time to get too confused by the tactic, he returned with a few guards in tow. One of them bent down to unshackle me while the other two stood on either side of Troius. They must've thought I'd been kept in solitary for long enough to go mad and that I just might be crazy enough to rush him, frothing at the mouth like a wild dog. But I wouldn't break that quickly—even if I did want to snap the little whelp's neck in two. I was smart enough to wait for the right time to do it.

"That will be all, thank you," Troius said with a smug look on his face. I *did* want to rush him, maybe knock that look *and* his head off along with it; unfortunately I had a brain rattling around in my skull, and it was telling me not to make a move until I knew the lay of the land.

Keep it patient, Owen, I thought. This wasn't all-out war—not yet, anyhow.

It'd been a long time since I'd played chess with one of my boys, and most of the corps save for Ivory and Jeannot had been shit at the game, making me complacent with winning. But at least a man never forgot the basics.

"Quite effective, aren't they?" Troius said, once the big lugs'd filed out again. I didn't like how they were all dressed, in uniforms the same as the Dragon Corps had, like a private force the purpose of which I could only start guessing at.

"Depends on what they're supposed to be," I said, standing up. It felt good not to be shackled to that chair anymore, but I wasn't about to admit to how grateful I was. "You been hoping to make an army? Because I got news for you; the Esar already *has* an army and they wear red, not green."

Troius looked smug again, and I instantly knew I'd brought up something he'd been trying to goad me into saying. Playing right into his hands—or so he thought—and even if it rankled my pride, I guessed I had to keep letting him think that was exactly what I was doing.

"I want to show you something," he said, affecting a little bow that made me want to knock him over like a ninepin so he'd learn some humility. He started out of the cell again, then paused by the door. "If you're thinking of doing anything foolish, I really *would* counsel you against it—I wasn't exaggerating when I said I made your case singlehandedly. It wouldn't be very . . . strategic, shall we say, to attack your only ally in this place."

"Duly noted," I grunted, since that seemed to be what he wanted to hear. But if he thought we were allies, then not only was he conceited, but he was as mired in dreams of shit as a dung beetle.

"Excellent," Troius said, turning smartly on his heel and—I guessed—expecting me to follow.

It was real hilarious to have a guy like this thinking he belonged in the same sentence as Balfour. None of my boys would've ever turned their backs on a prisoner, even one who'd promised nice and mild not to pull anything stupid. Apparently he thought my word meant something to him, but I never gave it to someone I didn't respect.

Maybe he was just expecting, because he had all the power and I had none, that I'd have to admire him. The poor thing really did believe whatever his doting mother had told him all his life: that he was a special, precious boy.

The hallway was lit up with flickering track lights, same as the Airman had been, though that was about the only similarity. The prison was much quieter, for starters, no boys whooping it up from behind closed doors.

Since Troius had turned his back on me, I took my chance to look around. There were fewer guards than I'd expected roaming around—just enough to keep me from making a move—and the cell next to mine was empty, despite Troius's insinuations that there were others in my position.

I just hoped he hadn't laid a hand on one of my boys. I'd have to kill him for that.

The next cell, however, housed a redheaded woman in a blue dress. I almost panicked at the color before I realized she was older than Laure; her hair was cut shorter and her face was all wrong. I knew her from somewhere, though. She was sitting on a sagging bed, hands folded in her lap, looking utterly hopeless. Though she wasn't a soldier and didn't have my training, I could still tell by her air of defeat that she'd been there for a long time. She kind of reminded me of the look Rook's brother'd got when he felt he was making progress, only to wake up the next morning with beetles in his hair.

Strangely enough, it was thinking about that cracked-nut professor that gave my brain the jump start it needed. I was nearly past her cell entirely before I realized that I'd met her working on Balfour's hands in the common room—a couple weeks before we'd all moved out of the Airman for good and into our own places, so day in and day out we weren't forced to look at each other.

So Margrave Ginette wasn't dead after all. She'd been scooped up, whisper-quiet, the same as me. That didn't exactly bode well for my own situation, seeing as how she'd been missing for weeks, and nobody *I'd* talked to had guessed to look in prison.

I wondered what she'd done to get hauled in. If she was anything like me, then the answer was "next to nothing."

Up ahead and around a bend in the hall, there was another woman, shouting blue murder in Ramanthine. My cell had been far enough removed that I hadn't heard her earlier but I could hear her muffled voice echoing off the walls. Troius didn't seem particularly bothered by it. Maybe he was just used to the noise by now.

I recognized the voice before I saw her face through the barred window: a dark, smoky accent I'd heard at countless parties, mostly events Royston dragged me to before abandoning me. It was his associate and occasional companion, Lady Antoinette.

She was th'Esar's occasional companion, too. They'd been lovers once, or so Roy said, but it didn't seem that could possibly still be the case unless th'Esar was up to something weird in the bedroom.

Antoinette was pacing the floor like a caged panther, stalking back and forth in a fine dress the color of blood-dark Ke-Han wine. Troius paused in front of her cell, and she ceased shouting long enough to give him a glare so cold I half expected him to turn to stone on the spot.

Just my luck that he didn't.

"I take it you're enjoying your stay," Troius said.

"Insignificant worm," Antoinette said, spitting on the floor of her cell. "I'll crush your skull."

Attagirl, I thought but didn't say.

"Still out of sorts because you can't get into our heads?" Troius asked, tapping the side of his temple. "You're only going to tire yourself out trying. Best to quit while you're ahead. That way, no one gets hurt."

"How very droll," Antoinette said, drawing close to the

bars of the cage. "Because I was going to say *precisely* the same thing about your little revolution."

"It's hardly a revolution if the man in charge condones it," Troius said.

"It's amusing that you assume it is that *man* who controls Thremedon," Antoinette snarled. She hadn't noticed me until that point, but I saw a brief look of confusion pass over her face when she did.

"A pleasure, as always, my lady," Troius said, bowing.

Antoinette reached her arm out between the bars so quickly that I acted on instinct, putting myself between her and Troius. One of her nails caught me on the back of the neck, so sharp it drew blood.

"Just like an angry cat," Troius said. "Did she hurt you? How embarrassing."

"Wasn't even a scratch," I said, wiping the blood off—without him noticing—before we continued on our way.

I'd heard all about this kind of thing from Royston, and I braced myself for things to get freaky.

Sure enough, they did.

Royston is coming to help us, murmured a smoky voice in my head. In one of my proudest moments, I somehow managed not to twitch like a fly'd landed on my neck. Troius was watching me for signs of that very communication, and I scratched my cheek, keeping a surly look on my face with my eyes focused straight ahead.

Oh, great, I thought, hoping she could hear me, because I sure as shit didn't know if I was doing this thing right. *We're fucked now.*

Don't be absurd, Antoinette replied, her voice growing more distant the farther I moved from her. *I cannot communicate with him directly—he is very far away—but we can still sense each other. It will be the way he finds us, once he realizes I've been taken as well.*

Why can't you read this idiot's thoughts? I asked, trying to make it quick, before our connection was severed completely. *Not enough thoughts in there to read?*

Because of the . . . Antoinette replied. True to my luck, she faded out before I could hear the key piece of information I needed, but we'd already passed through a door and were ascending a flight of stairs, and I assumed it meant we just weren't close enough anymore.

Maybe when I was back in my cell, then we could talk a little. That is, if I was even taken back there at all.

Troius took me through a small door, which led directly out onto a narrow stone bridge. We were still underground, I suspected; the bridge crossed over a dark body of deep water, and everything smelled like ancient, wet rock. The prison was behind us, and there was another door ahead, with the bridge connecting them.

"It's just this way," Troius said, turning to look at me over his shoulder. "She doesn't like prisons, you see. She's finicky about that."

I wondered if I had another—less friendly—*velikaia* to contend with at the end of my journey, one who'd do a lot more to me than scratch my neck. It'd make the most sense for them to pry through my head to see what my treasonous self had been up to, but I was shocked I was even getting such just treatment. Part of what Troius had planned for me, most likely; his warped idea of what constituted "fair play" among his "allies."

"I've been looking forward to your reaction for a long time," Troius said, stopping short in front of this new door to remove one of his gloves. I saw a flash of metal against the palm of his hand—probably a key—but he just wrapped his fingers around the steel knob, palm flat against it. I heard the turning of heavy gears, the sound of them grinding as some mechanism was unlocked, then the door swung open.

We were standing on the threshold of a large room with high ceilings and fine tiles, with a few other young men— and women, too—dressed in the same style as Troius, wearing all black like they were attending Thremedon's funeral.

But I wasn't looking at them, not after the first moment. Not with the dragon in the room.

She was little, looking like barely more than a baby, and built with all streamlined silver metals. Her eyes were smoky and pale. There were smaller differences between her and the girls I was used to seeing, but the most important one was size. There was no way a grown man could ride her; she was only about the height of a grown man herself, with a narrower wingspan and no carved place for a harness and saddle.

The moment Troius stepped into the room, closing the door behind him, she came forward with her talons scraping the floor, stinking the way the old girls used to, of forges and fire on metal.

"Very handy to have an army you don't need to feed, isn't it?" Troius asked. "Although the cost of making just one could feed an army itself. A good thing the Ke-Han Empire needed to pay us *so much* tribute. And a good thing we had so much scrap metal left over from the first round."

So this was one of ours, I realized, melted down and re-formed. It would've felt as wrong as if I'd seen a baby made out of Roy's and Luvander's and Balfour's body parts all sewn together, but Troius had achieved his life's dream and I was rendered speechless.

"Adamo, meet Ironjaw," Troius said, holding his hand out for the dragon to press her sharp muzzle directly into it, like a dog rooting around for a treat. I could see there was a round piece of metal actually implanted in the center of his palm; there was a jewel the color of blood right in the middle. "She was the first, and I was a suitable match for her. Can you imagine? Just when I thought I'd never have my chance to be a member of the Dragon Corps—a new Dragon Guard was built, and I the premier member."

I didn't ask the obvious question—the one he clearly wanted me to ask, about whether or not he was king of Dragonland, and all that horseshit. "'A suitable match?'" I repeated instead.

"A great deal of blood was tested," Troius explained, momentarily disappointed by what'd piqued my interest. "The Esar couldn't have anyone from the city join these ranks, not with their biases. They could be too easily manipulated by members of the Basquiat, you see. But as it turned out, there were more Talentless bastards in the countryside than in the city anyway, so he brought them all in, myself included. A few were tested before me; Ironjaw rejected all the other potential matches. The fever even killed two of them. But not me."

"How many did she go through?" I asked. Troius would probably like answering that.

"Ten," he replied proudly.

"And what about the others she rejected? The ones that didn't die?" I pressed.

Ironjaw was coming closer to me—though I, despite everything, had been trying to keep my distance. The floor was all cut up with talon marks, just from her taking her daily walks, and her metal-lined nostrils were enormous, bigger than Proudmouth's had been. She was scenting me out, I realized, and I held still.

If there was anything of Proudmouth left inside her, I wondered if she'd recognize me. But there was nothing recognizable about Proudmouth as far as I could see.

Holding it together, talking about business, making sure I got some answers—doing all that with a dragon circling me and not letting on to the way my heart was beating—was one of the hardest things I'd ever done. And I'd fought Ke-Han magicians in my time. Head-fucking-on.

"A few of them are my assistants," Troius replied. "Some work on the other two."

I couldn't keep the surprise from my voice. "There are *more*?" I asked. I really was feeding into the drama Troius wanted, but I would've dared any other man in my shoes not to react the same way as I had.

"Well, yes," Troius said, sounding slightly distressed. "One of them, unfortunately, chose a very simple country boy, and he named her Cornflower. After one of his cows, apparently."

My head was swirling. "And the third?" I asked.

Troius's lips twitched. "The young woman she chose has not yet presented herself," he replied.

"Sounds sensible to me," I said, talking to try to keep my head above water, at this point. "Maybe you scared her off."

"She's being tracked down as we speak," Troius said. "With the massive expenses involved, you can't very well just *let someone go* if one of the dragons takes a liking to her.

We're still ironing out all the kinks." He flexed his palm idly; the metal in the center looked stiff, like it was bothering him. Something about it reminded me of Balfour, and I remembered what Troius had said about that fever killing people. He was lucky it hadn't done the same to Balfour—though I had to wonder why Balfour'd fallen ill in the first place. Th'Esar wanted fresh blood, obviously, and young fools whose minds he could shape any way he wanted, so they'd always agree with him on how the wind was blowing. That was why he hadn't brought this plan to me or the other boys, despite the pain in the ass it'd be training new recruits. We were probably too opinionated for him.

So why had Balfour gotten sick? Some kinda mix-up with his hands, or something worse?

I didn't have enough information yet, so I was gonna have to keep this conversation going.

"Never did any of this stuff with the old dragons," I muttered, hoping I was pandering to Troius's idea of me as the gruff old Chief Sergeant who just needed a push to let go of his outdated, preconceived notions. To him, I was a stodgy old man who needed to be shown the light of progress. It'd give him a charge to think he was teaching his mother to suck eggs, and I'd have to swallow my pride and let him believe it.

"Well, that's not *entirely* true," Troius said. At his feet, Ironjaw was still staring at me. It was real difficult not to hold my hand out or something—just like Troius had—the way I'd do for a friendly dog, or even for my girl, back in the day. "Part of the problem with the initial run of dragons was that the Esar himself had very little control over them. They chose who pleased them at will, and that gave you a little *too much* power, don't you think? Power over a very expensive and personal endeavor put forward *by* the Esar. Does that seem fair to you? It's no wonder he wanted to try again—and this time, be able to actually control the experiment."

"So what makes these ones so special, then?" I asked, like I was real skeptical. "Other than them being pint-size, and probably house-trained." I knew men like Troius. All I had to do was convince him he already had me all figured out and he'd let down his guard.

'Course, what I was gonna do *after* that was anyone's guess, but at least I had a starting point.

"I'm so glad you asked," Troius said, and he really did look pleased—with himself, mostly. "I must say, I *did* hope that once you saw our progress for yourself, it would put you in a more compliant state of mind. That being said, well, I'm sure my particular . . . situation didn't escape your sharp eyes?"

He held out his hand, giving me a better look at it this time. The metal in his palm was about the size of a watch's face, silver like the dragon's knobby spine, and the red jewel bigger than I'd thought at first glance. There was also something moving inside, like a liquid, though the gem was too dark for me to be able to see it too clearly.

Lucky for me, Troius was the kind of idiot who liked talking about himself more than anything else.

"Never seen anything like it before," I grunted, 'cause he'd *love* that.

Sure enough, he brightened like I'd told him he was the son I'd never had and we were gonna go berry-picking in the fields together, just us and his pet dragon.

"I'm honored to be the man who gets to show it to you," Troius said, passing his good hand through his hair. "Truly, I know that to you it must sound as though I'm repeating myself, but . . . I've admired you for a long time, Adamo. Well, anyway, *this* little gem solves the problem of loyalty quite handily. Once the dragon makes her selection, our Margrave takes the accepted donor's blood and mixes it with the dragonsoul material. She obeys my commands, true enough, but our relationship goes deeper than that. I hate to throw philosophy in where it doesn't belong, but you *could* say we're one being. I hear her now and then, but unlike your 'girls,' she doesn't have complete independence. She can't act on her own; she *needs* me to approve or disapprove of her decisions. In turn, I issue the commands, and she fulfills them."

I was starting to feel a little too much like a teacup in a tempest for my comfort. Even though I'd joked about

Royston being the last person you'd want to come and bust you out of jail, I sure wished I had him there, to listen to all this, and not forget a single detail. He was an ace at sorting through shit piles of information real quick—not to mention he had a lot more experience in dealing with pompous jack-asses than I did. My jackasses tended to be the regular type—the snotty ones that cried when you blew too hard in their direction.

I was just trying not to stare at Ironjaw.

She had begun pacing between me and Troius, sharp claws digging into the floor for purchase. Our girls had never done a lot of walking; I guess now I knew why. They'd practically been caged up, only let out on rare occasions; they definitely didn't make good house pets.

This one could probably have slept curled up on a kiddie bed, having the whole run of an apartment without her tail slapping against any walls. That is, if nobody minded ruining the floorboards.

"So what you're saying is th'Esar doesn't need to worry about losing control of his dragons *this* time since he's got 'em hooked up to some of his most loyal citizens," I summarized. If I were ever to get out of there, I needed to make the story short, sweet, and scary enough that it'd be able to mobilize people to *do* something instead of just wag their tongues.

Th'Esar was crazy for trying to pull a stunt like this, and Troius so glory-hounded he would've gone along with any-thing to see a piece of the action.

"Something like that," Troius admitted. "The Esar trusts *me* of course, but some of the others can hardly be called loyal. Or even citizens, for that matter. While we made a con-siderable number of improvements to the arrangement this time around, what we *weren't* able to change was that pesky side effect of dragons needing to choose their riders. Or their owners, I suppose, given the circumstances and allowances made for size. We presented vials of each candidate's blood, and wouldn't you know it—I was the only member of the Esar's *trusted* guard to be chosen at all. The others didn't pass the test. I'm not sure whether that makes me lucky—I'm inclined to believe it makes me special. In any case, we mixed that blood with the well water in each dragon's soul, binding machine and man together; part of that mixture resides in the dragons, and part is kept with the Esar. You see, in the absence of working with those he can *trust,* the Esar had to resort to a contingency plan. He has the power to destroy both dragon and guard if he sees fit should they attempt to betray him. Considering what occurred during the run of the *first* Dragon Corps, we thought it best to do things this way."

I rubbed my hands over my eyes. My first thought was, *At least there aren't more of them,* but I couldn't deny that part of me almost wanted to see it. Maybe even have one of my own, like I really was lonely enough that I'd trade in the real deal for a toy version.

There was no bastion-damned way I was gonna be happy with it, though. I was just pissed because of how cockeyed the plan was—and also how I'd been left out of a system I'd once considered, however foolishly, *mine.*

"So what do you need me for?" I asked. "Sounds like you're all set. Three dragons, three people, and a bunch of lackeys to spit and polish. Th'Esar's brand-new Dragon Guard. You're all set."

"Well, we *are* currently working on a fourth," Troius said shrewdly. And where was all this damn coin coming from? "But no, I can't mislead you in all good conscience—were you to sign on with us, you wouldn't be granted a dragon of your own. Of course, *I* trust you, but the Esar . . . Well, he's his own matter entirely. He made certain provisions in order to avoid the mess that happened with *your* era. What we would like—what *I* would like—would be for you to join as an advisor. A mentor, really. Your experience is invaluable. No magician's experiment can replicate *that,* no matter how hard they may try. You know the old guard in and out. In my opinion, from my studies, I believe that any Dragon Corps *or* Dragon Guard would be in need of its Chief Sergeant."

"Chief Sergeants fight alongside their men," I explained.

He'd probably read about that part, too—or had he conveniently forgotten it?

"That wouldn't be possible," Troius replied, looking disappointed himself. "Unfortunately."

"So, I'd be a mascot," I said, rubbing at my jaw. I'd been clenching it so tight that *it* felt like iron. "Someone to ride in carriages at parades and let all of Thremedon know this ain't just some upstart's idea of throwing his predecessors to the dogs. That this has history; that all they have to do is take a look at the statue to know they can trust their good old hero."

"I wouldn't put it exactly like that," Troius said. "I know it's a lot to take in at once."

"Yeah, and I need some time to think it over," I replied, because it was what he'd been expecting. If Antoinette turned out to be right, then there was gonna be some kind of rescue headed our way, and I needed to be in my cell in order to get rescued.

Then again, knowing what I knew, I didn't want anyone coming for us. I could only assume these new girls were weapons; those talons looked mighty sharp, and I could tell by Ironjaw's stink that she was a fire-breather. Whether or not she was a smaller version than the one I was intimate with, I knew firsthand how dangerous she could be.

"Of course you need some time," Troius said, looking mighty relieved. "I hope you won't take it personally when I return you to your cell. Proper protocols must be observed, even in these times of upheaval. And you can't imagine I'd be able to let you go free now after everything I've showed you."

"Not at all," I said.

Being thrown in a cell wasn't something I'd chosen to take personally. But having everything I'd stood for resurrected, torn apart, and stitched back together like every nightmare I'd ever had after the war'd ended—that was a different story.

Still, I let Troius usher me out, real polite-like, stopping only to pat his dragon on the head like she was his pet cat. She looked after him, expression unreadable, but she met my eyes when I finally allowed myself to *really* look at her. I couldn't tell if she was happy or sad, or even if she felt anything.

I didn't look back again, but the image of her stuck in my mind like a well-aimed dart. It wasn't until we'd made it back across the bridge that I realized what'd been bothering me about Ironjaw: All that time in the room, and she'd never said a word.

CHAPTER TWELVE

LAURE

Ex–Chief Sergeant Professor Adamo had been arrested, and I was starting to think it was a miracle we'd won the war at all considering how the rest of the Dragon Corps chose to respond. By doing absolutely nothing.

That wasn't exactly fair of me—better they come up with some sort of a plan than charge in and make an already bad situation ten times worse—not to mention we didn't know whether Adamo was being kept in the regular prison or, more likely, somewhere else. But I was feeling so mixed up that being fair was the least of my worries. I was spitting mad, sure, but there was something else going on that made my chest feel tight—and for once it wasn't an old bodice I'd squeezed myself into. Every man there was feeling turned on his head, but I could tell from a glance around the room that none of 'em was feeling like *I* was. It was part responsible and part awful, and another part I wasn't willing to examine too closely just yet. It was gonna mean a heap of trouble once the dust'd gone and settled, but it looked like I wasn't going to have to worry about that for a long time yet. I didn't even have it in me to stop Toverre from polishing all the spoons in Luvander's kitchen, though I'd stopped him short of starting on the cupboard handles.

"Now isn't the time," I told him a little too sharply.

"It won't take long," he hissed back, but he did drop his hands. After that, with nothing to do, he looked like a wilted marsh reed.

But if he got started, I was afraid I'd join him. It was getting that bad, just sitting crammed in Luvander's upstairs apartment, which was at least more comfortable than waiting in the stockroom of the hat shop. Only none of us deserved to be feeling comfortable.

I felt like a traitor and a deserter—like we'd all abandoned our captain in the middle of wartime. And he'd taken the heat for us while we sat around polishing spoons and drinking hot cups of tea and talking about the weather.

"It shouldn't be too long now," Balfour'd said, but that'd been two hours ago, going by the shrieking clock downstairs. I was keeping count.

With every hour that passed, I felt more and more hopeless.

It was an hour and a half past sunset. If Germaine had sent anyone looking for me at the dorms, then they were shit out of luck since I was spending tonight with my fiancé and what remained of the Dragon Corps. Now, *there* was something to write home to Da about. I was lucky I was already engaged since no man would marry me if he heard about a night like this one.

It certainly sounded a lot like a dream Toverre'd once had. I could tell he was excited, but he was doing his best to tone it down for my benefit.

I wasn't made for waiting around while somebody else did all the work. Some people got so caught up in worrying about what consequences their actions might have that they never did anything at all, but that wasn't how Da'd taught me to be, even if he *had* wanted to teach those skills to a son, not a daughter. My personality made it so that I had trouble sitting still, especially when someone I cared about was in trouble.

I could tell the others were starting to get worried about my mood from the way they all kept looking at me like I was a kettle about to boil at any second. But nobody said anything, not wanting to set me off.

The problem was, we couldn't do anything until Royston came back. To me, it seemed like the regular dungeons weren't good enough for Adamo, and even if he was there, did I really believe it'd be that easy to get to him? We had to get some information first. The cover of night would be good, too; less conspicuous moving around with a big group in the dark, especially if it turned out our companion Balfour was next on the list of wrongfully arrested.

So it was real nice of Adamo's friend to help us and all, but I was starting to think he was talking to everyone in the city with how long he was taking.

And if anything happened to Adamo because he'd needed to tell every story starting from the date of his birth and what the weather was like that night, I was probably going to hit under the belt, whether he was a Margrave or not.

The clock downstairs shrieked for seven seconds, then cut off.

"I'd say it's time for dinner," Luvander suggested, clasping his hands together. "I'll put something together while we wait—no use going into this on an empty stomach."

I couldn't remember the last time I'd eaten. Breakfast, maybe; I'd gone to speak with Adamo during lunch, so I hadn't had time to eat anything then. It seemed frivolous to worry about eating at a time like this, but then again, people were rash and stupid when they got hungry. I'd put food in my mouth, but only if it meant helping Adamo.

"I'm going to have trouble feeding all of you, I can tell," Luvander added, halfway to the door. "Does anyone here dislike cooked tomato?"

Nobody answered, but that was because I'd heard the sound of a large thud from the room below, and I hushed everyone so fiercely they actually listened.

We were quiet for a few long moments, before Luvander dared to speak up. "Do you suppose that's the Margrave Royston?" he asked.

"Wouldn't he ring the bell?" I retorted, which was only what he'd been thinking and wanted someone to confirm his suspicions by saying it.

There wasn't a single person in the sitting room whose nerves weren't on edge. Everyone was waiting for something awful to happen—whether it was bad news or soldiers finding out our whereabouts and descending on us without any warning.

I looked around the room for something I could use as a weapon, and my eyes landed on the collection of pokers for the fireplace. There were only three of them, but Toverre probably shouldn't be given one anyway. He could stay behind and defend the fortress.

"Excellent thinking," Luvander said, moving quickly and noiselessly to pass them out. "Sorry, young man. It seems you've been left out."

"Too dirty for him anyway," I muttered.

Toverre delicately wiped his palms on the front of his vest. "I will do what I can to help," he whispered.

Just then, there was another thud, louder and closer to us. It was coming from the direction of the stairs, I realized, and I drew myself up to my full height, poker in hand.

"I wish I'd thought to lock the sitting-room door," Luvander said thoughtfully. "How clever that would have been."

"This reminds me of whenever Rook came back from the 'Fans," Balfour added; there was a hint of humor in his grimness that I appreciated in a soldier.

"Now, don't attack all at once, just in case we aren't under siege," Luvander suggested. "Then again, what do I know? The targets were all so much easier once."

"I'll stand in front," Balfour offered.

I was about to tell him not to bother when something slammed into the door, throwing it wide-open.

From first glance, I could tell it wasn't Royston, because whomever it was, he was way too tall. I shouted and Luvander joined me—because he was crazy, I was beginning to suspect—and then I threw myself, with my weapon, at the nearest weak spot. I'd been aiming for the intruder's head, but because of his height, I must've miscalculated, and hit his shoulder instead.

I connected solidly, at least, but the blow merely glanced off the bone.

"See, Raphael?" a deep voice said. "That's why I went first."

"Ghislain?" Luvander asked, still wielding his poker—though I could've told him it wouldn't do any good against a giant like this one. He'd ignored mine like I'd hit him with a stalk of wheat.

"I've gotten warmer welcomes from merchant ships," the man said, looking down at me. "And I *rob* merchant ships."

"You could have rung the bell like a normal person," Luvander huffed, trying to peer around Ghislain's shoulder. It was a tough job, seeing as how he didn't quite come up to it.

"Had a surprise for you," the giant named Ghislain said.

"Did . . ." Balfour trailed off, and when I glanced over toward him, he was pale as a ghost. Or maybe like he'd seen a ghost. "Did you say Raphael?"

"Thank the bastion," came another voice from behind Ghislain's huge body, which was blocking up the door like a live barricade. "I was starting to wonder if you'd all forgotten about me."

"Get out of the *way*," Luvander said, grabbing Ghislain by the arm and pulling him into the room. It looked a lot like a canary trying to move a wolfhound, but to my surprise, Ghislain actually gave way.

Sure enough, there'd been another man standing behind him—like Ghislain needed anyone else for backup, since he was clearly a one-man army. At first glance, the other man reminded me a bit of Toverre, overly thin and pale, with black curly hair that had wiry bits of white in it—the way I'd always imagined Toverre would get someday after a certain amount of time living in the big, dirty world. He cocked his head at me curiously, clearly about to ask who the hell *I* was, then I couldn't see him at all because Luvander had thrown himself across my field of vision, nearly knocking the other man down the stairs.

It looked like a surprise attack more than an embrace, and when Balfour rushed in, I assumed it was to pull Luvander off. Did they have some history together, I wondered, some kind of blood feud?

But despite having seemed like a sensible enough young man before, Balfour joined in, instead—though with a measure more trepidation than Luvander had shown.

Feeling out of place, not to mention confused, I took a step back and nearly tripped over Toverre, who'd come up behind me like a shadow.

"Watch it," I muttered crossly.

"Don't you know who that *is*?" Toverre hissed, eyes on the spectacle by the door.

"Big man called him Raphael," I said, noticing the big man in question standing to one side of the fray. He wasn't showing any signs of joining the party; I figured that was probably a good sign since he was big enough to crush the three of them with one arm, and wouldn't that put a damper on the nice mood? "Guess they know him from somewhere."

"You didn't even *look* at those statues once, did you?" Toverre whispered, giving me a look of intense disappointment. "You spent all your time drawing those dragons, but you never *once* put your mind to the men who flew them! Laure, he's another *airman*. But there were only two more left alive! One of them was Ghislain, and the other—if you'll recall Balfour mentioning his name—was Rook. Arguably the most famous. Which means—"

"Oh," I said, understanding flooding me all at once.

"Ain't polite to gossip about people when they're right here," Ghislain pointed out, not even looking at us when he said it. Nonetheless, I knew it was directed our way, and I elbowed Toverre lightly in the side, shutting him up effectively.

Raphael had managed to fight his way free in the last few seconds, looking at least less deathly pale than he had before, now that he was flushed with exertion. Luvander was grinning like a maniac, and even Balfour looked pleased, if also pink and embarrassed over going wild like that. I didn't blame him for letting loose, though. Seemed to me like people spent too much time in the country *and* in Thremedon on trying to hide what they were really feeling—and so long as it wasn't a *rude* feeling, then what did it matter, letting it show?

I'd've greeted Toverre the same way, probably. Maybe I'd even do the same with Adamo, if we ever got to see him again.

"Honestly, Ghislain, when you said you were looking for 'something,' I never imagined . . ." Luvander trailed off, seeming confused because, probably for the first time in his life, he didn't know what to say. I only hoped Ghislain had a whole cartful of his old companions to render Luvander speechless more often. "I mean I *never* thought . . . Well, would you listen to me? It's a fine state of affairs indeed when I can't even form a complete sentence! No, I've changed my mind; don't listen to me. Everyone pay close attention to Balfour instead."

Balfour looked startled, then resigned himself to the fact that everyone *was* staring at him now, and he was still flushed as a schoolboy caught in a snowstorm.

"Just like old times," Raphael said, looking about the room. "Well, perhaps not *exactly.* There are more hats downstairs, for instance. And this lovely woman is far too young for you, Luvander. I can see I arrived just in time to prevent a crime from taking place."

"How do you know she isn't Balfour's woman?" Luvander asked. "It seems to me an egregious oversight."

"Because she's not Balfour's type," Raphael replied simply.

"You want her for yourself," Luvander huffed. "I'll have you know that she's *spoken for.* Not to mention that if you continue talking about her in this way, I'm quite certain she'll attack us both with a fire poker."

"It's true," I said, twirling it in my hand to show I hadn't forgotten. I appreciated Luvander speaking up for me, though, so some people didn't think I was an object instead of a person.

"New recruits?" Ghislain asked, and Toverre jumped a little, almost like he'd forgotten he was there. Even though Ghislain was three times Luvander's size, he was three hundred times quieter. "One of them's scrawny. Jumps a lot. Like a field mouse."

"We're here because Adamo's been arrested," I said, letting the reminder of what was actually going on sink in for myself as much as everyone else. I didn't blame them for getting caught up in the moment, but just because there was another airman walking around now didn't mean we could afford to forget about the other one, who'd been alive all this time but might *not* be alive for much longer.

"Really? Thought he was teaching," Ghislain said.

"He *was*," I said, while Luvander and Balfour returned their pokers to the fireplace. I held on to mine for a while longer. It was calming me down some to have it in my hand. "That's how I met him."

"Oh, I *see*," Raphael said, settling himself on Luvander's couch. He made a big show of it, but I could tell he was tired and grateful not to be on his feet anymore. "Well, it's a minor infraction at best, and they can't necessarily *prove* the two of you did anything untoward unless you testify against him."

"Beg pardon?" I asked. I was starting to wish Raphael had come in through the door first, so I could've clonked *him* one instead. Might've finished him off, though, the way he was looking.

"It's not exactly like that," Balfour said, sitting down next to Raphael. He couldn't keep his eyes off him—like he thought if he blinked, the man was gonna disappear. "We can explain it all later, but the Esar seems to have taken exception to some of Adamo's actions. He thinks Adamo was plotting against him."

"Seems like I picked a perfect time to drop anchor," Ghislain said. "Could've sailed all the way up to the Kirils and back first, make myself a nest egg, but Raphael here was feeling homesick."

"You'd be feeling homesick, too, if you'd spent every day between the end of the war and now in a fisherman's village," Raphael pointed out. "I'll be smelling tuna in my dreams for the rest of my life."

"Just pretend it's mermaids," Ghislain suggested, lowering himself into one of Luvander's chairs, which creaked ominously under his weight.

"That would ruin all my other dreams," Raphael replied dryly. "The good ones."

"Are you going to tell us where you found him?" Luvander asked, setting an enormous pot on the stove and bringing a few fat, shiny eggplants out of a drawer above the counter. How on earth he could be thinking about dinner at a time like this was beyond me, but I guess that was the difference between me and a trained airman. They knew to eat when the eating was good and probably didn't lose their dinners in the air if the flying got too rough.

Probably. I'd have to ask Adamo about that, too, someday.

"Not to mention how you even . . ." Balfour began, then trailed off as his voice cracked. "I mean, none of us even knew that you were *alive.*"

"Neither did I, for about two weeks after the war ended," Raphael admitted, rubbing at a scar I hadn't noticed before—it curved down from the corner of his mouth, twisting his mouth into a jester's grimace when he wasn't talking. I had to wonder if he'd gotten it during the real fighting, or sometime after, by offending someone in his fishing village. "I got thrown well clear of Natalia in the final battle, which is what might've saved me, come to think of it—especially considering what happened to her when she . . . exploded. I was taken in by a young woman fleeing the capital—returning home to her village by the sea, more accurately, wanting to get out of that mess. And who can really blame her? I *believe* she took pity on me because I reminded her of her brother, and that's . . . about all I managed to gather, really. The Ke-Han language is a terribly difficult one to master. Mostly we signed to get the point across." To illustrate, Raphael made a lewd gesture in the air that caused Luvander to laugh richly, while Balfour looked away and blushed. "Yeah, she got that one all right. So did her father, unfortunately. Apparently it's universal, and he was none too pleased. But when I was brought to the village, suddenly all this good luck started happening to its people. The ocean was full of these giant, silver-scaled fish, practically floating to the top of the water. For a simple little town, they were starting to turn a major profit. And they considered me their good-luck charm. Despite my behavior, they tended my wounds, fed me plenty of horrible food, and put me up. And all I had to do was sit there and babble to them in Volstovic—of which they didn't understand a single word—to secure my position as god of the fishy seas."

"You're making all this up," Luvander accused.

"Only some of it," Raphael replied.

"I was sailing around Tado when I started hearing rumors about a crazed foreigner living as a fisherman near the Seon border," Ghislain interjected, clearly sensing that Raphael was becoming sidetracked. At least one of these ex-airmen knew how to get to the point. "Didn't seem like anything to get excited about. You know how many crazies this country churns out. But I wanted to check it out, just to be sure. Some of the descriptions matched."

"And *some* indicated I had a massive penis," Raphael added cheerfully. "A rumor which my friend the fisherman's daughter must have spread after bathing my naked body with seawater to break my fever. Oh dear, I forgot there was a lady present."

"So you just . . . found him?" Balfour asked, eyes wide like a kid up way past his bedtime. "He was really there?"

"Must've been," Ghislain pointed out.

"Fearsome pirates landed in our village and terrorized its residents first," Raphael corrected, crossing his legs and folding his hands atop his knees, "because of all the extra fish they were exporting and money they were importing. Funny how good luck works that way, isn't it? In any case, I was quite prepared to defend my newfound home—as their foreign benefactor, refusing to abandon them in their time of need—when I realized that I recognized one of the principal threats. Imagine my surprise!"

"Spent the next three days going on and on at those people in sign language, trying to convince them not to burn my boat and hang me," Ghislain said, rolling his eyes.

"I told them it would be bad luck," Raphael explained. "Very, very bad."

Ghislain snorted. "We *could've* taken 'em, though. Little village like that? Would've been easy."

"Yes, well, excuse me for retaining some form of gratitude toward the people who took me in and saved my life," Raphael said with a sniff.

"Wasted time," Ghislain said. "Could've been here sooner; maybe Adamo wouldn't've been hauled off as easily with somebody actually looking after things."

I was starting to like this Ghislain fellow, or at least the way he thought. Judging by the look on Toverre's face, he preferred Raphael—though probably for different reasons.

Life was going to be rough for my husband-to-be.

"At least you returned just in time for our rescue mission," Luvander said. "Whatever it may be."

"Some rescue," Ghislain said, cracking the knuckles on his left hand. "We busting him out with our minds? I sure hope the scrawny one's a *velikaia.*"

"We're using someone else's mind, actually," Luvander said, leaning back against his countertop. "That is, we're waiting for Margrave Royston to return and give us the go-ahead."

"Ah." Raphael sighed. "How strange is fate!"

"Not really," Ghislain grunted. "Just that some things, in some places, never change."

"Well, they're going to have to change," I said, "unless th'Esar's the type of man who *pardons* someone after calling him out as a criminal."

"Only if they're more useful to him alive than dead or behind bars," Luvander said. "But he does do it."

"Margrave Royston being one of them, if I recall correctly," Raphael added. "Sweet Mary Margrave, was it? But we're not allowed to call him that in front of Adamo. The nostalgia is killing me."

"See that it doesn't," Ghislain suggested. "I worked hard bringing you back."

"I get seasick," Raphael explained.

"So do I!" Toverre exclaimed suddenly. Everyone paused to look at him, and he bristled. "It's difficult to break into the conversation," he sniffed. "You all have your own preestablished rapport; it makes outsiders feel somewhat excluded."

"Anyway, while my boat's airing out," Ghislain said, ignoring him completely, "guess it wouldn't hurt to do something about this bad situation."

"We have to wait for Margrave Royston," I told him, though it nearly killed me to admit it. "He's talking to people, gathering information, learning what we need to know about where Adamo is and maybe why he's been taken there."

"And here I'd been hoping it was another Arlemagne scandal." Raphael sighed sadly. "To remind us of the good old days."

"Hear, hear," Luvander said.

"How can you lot joke around when Adamo's in trouble?" I demanded, no longer able to control myself. "Wasn't he your Chief Sergeant? Don't any of you have any respect for him?"

"Of course we do," Luvander said, blinking widely.

"Like he was my own father," Ghislain agreed. "Except better. And not fired from his position as stableboy for sleeping with my mother."

"My fear of the man is equal only to my enormous affection for him," Raphael concluded.

"They cope with their emotions by burying them under their idea of humor," Balfour explained gently. "They've always done it, and, taking everything that's happened since the end of the war into consideration—Ghislain's choice to become a pirate; Raphael's stint as a Ke-Han god of fortune; Luvander and his hat shop—I doubt they'll ever change. Does that answer things for you?"

"Guess it does," I admitted. I supposed it wasn't my place to judge them—not when they'd seen a lot more than I had.

"*Balfour's* changed, at any rate," Raphael said, looking him over with newfound appreciation. "Bastion—if only Rook were here. Then we'd have a real showdown."

"I don't know if I'm ready for that just yet," Balfour admitted. "Someday. We can only hope I'll get the chance."

"If someone else doesn't shut his mouth for you first," Raphael said, indulging in a happy little sigh. "I really have missed this place. Being worshipped was nice, but I'm hoping I can get a little worship here, too. Along with some old-fashioned Volstovic cooking."

"Coming, my dear," Luvander said.

"If they don't arrest you tomorrow," Balfour added darkly, "for the crime of being alive when the Esar thought you were dead."

"Like to see him try that with me here," Ghislain said. He shifted his weight from one side to the other, folding his arms over his chest as he did so. I was pleased as Punch he was here, and not on somebody else's side, either. "So we wait for Margrave Royston to show up, is that it? No wonder we needed Adamo. We're shit at planning."

"He should be here soon," Luvander said. "Unless he's been arrested, too. Which, when you think about everything we've burdened him with doing, is actually entirely possible."

The heroes of the war, I thought, and the most they were capable of so far was sitting around and having a tea-party reunion. It was weird now to think of how safe I used to feel when I imagined them soaring through the clouds on their way to enemy ground.

But I didn't have any better ideas, either.

"In the meantime, make something nice for Raphael," Ghislain suggested. "To fill his empty stomach after he filled my boat with puke."

"He'll never let me live it down, I suspect," Raphael said.

"Not until you're healthy enough to clean it up," Ghislain agreed.

"I think I hear something down below," Balfour murmured. He didn't have to speak up for us all to snap to; I was glad I was still holding that poker.

Th'Esar's men, or someone on our side? I wondered. Soon enough, we'd know the answer.

BALFOUR

One of the first things I'd been taught as a child was not to stare at anyone. It caused others to feel self-conscious, and it was rude, no matter what your intentions were. Curiosity was a feeling best indulged in private, when no one else would take notice, and I knew that I had finally reached adulthood when I was able to keep myself from staring, no matter how much I might have wished to.

Still, I'd have defied any of the others to be sitting on a couch next to Raphael and *not* look at him, just a little, for some evidence that he was actually there.

I wasn't afraid of being teased since I'd weathered all that and more in the past, and there were more important things for everyone to be thinking about than mocking me. What I *was* frightened of was that this would all turn out to be some cruel dream. That in reality, I'd fallen asleep on Luvander's couch while waiting for news, and any second now someone was going to shake me awake and tell me that Margrave Royston had arrived, and also, that I'd missed supper while sleeping like a little lamb.

It was the most wonderful surprise I could ever have asked for, but it hurt, too. Knowing Raphael had been alive this whole time but unable to make some contact with the rest of us, with his *home*, made me feel guilty, as though I ought to have sensed him. His dragon would have been able to if she were still in one piece.

But the worst part about Raphael's resurrection, despite my gratitude, was that it sparked new hope in me. It inspired the foolish—and highly unlikely—possibility that there might be others out there, still alive and not lost forever at all, just living out the past half a year in some other remote fishing village.

It had taken me a long time after the war to convince myself that my fellow airmen were really and truly gone. I would never see them in the streets again or hear them laughing raucously at a stupid joke at someone else's expense. They'd never fill my boots with piss or my gloves with other, less savory liquids. They were dead, and no amount of magic could bring them back.

Except that Ghislain *had* brought Raphael back without using any magic at all.

This was a dilemma, one that I'd be agonizing over for

years to come. The possibility might have been slight, the chances incredibly slim, but now that I had new hope in the form of Raphael, *alive,* I would never be able to stop wondering, *What if?*

If Adamo had been with us, he would've told me—told us all—that there was no point in focusing on the dirty end of the stick when you'd finally turned up some good fortune at last. It was morbid and unnecessary and a waste of time. Whether or not Adamo himself believed that, he would've been able to make *us* believe it. That was something he was uncannily good at.

Still, I wished Adamo *was* here to see this. Despite knowing very little about the man in question's more personal feelings, I did know how much it had bothered him to have so few of us left. Privately, I almost worried he felt responsible, but I'd never been able to broach the topic. Not even with all my shrewd diplomatic training could I find a humane way.

And so, as with most topics, we had all avoided talking about it.

Ghislain, however, hadn't been afraid to look the matter squarely in the eye. He'd chased a rumor of the seas and found one of our fellows, presumed dead—and still looking as though he might keel over at any moment though he was putting on a brave face for the rest of us.

Maybe it was just the rough journey back that made Raphael look so shaky. But the white in his hair made him look like the Esar in the old tale—the one who'd lost his three sons to fever and gone mad the following year.

The noise from downstairs had at least given me an excuse to stop thinking about the whole mess and an excuse to stop staring at poor Raphael as well. He looked as though he needed a full week's sleep, and there we were hauling him along on another calamitous adventure.

He wouldn't have had it any other way, of course, but it hardly seemed decent.

Laure positioned herself by the door, and, with the purposeful, stony weight of a golem, Ghislain stood up. Since

Ghislain bare-handed was more than the equivalent of both Luvander and me and half the Provost's Wolves all armed with pokers, I remained seated on the couch, and Luvander continued chopping eggplant at the counter, though his entire demeanor had sharpened. He'd use that knife as well as Ivory if he had to, covered in slices of vegetable as it was—something Ivory himself would never have allowed.

Light flooded the stairwell from below, and we all held our breath.

"I'm so glad I'm back," Raphael whispered privately to me as Toverre moved quietly over to stand with us. Perhaps he assumed, however falsely, that as members of the ex–Dragon Corps, we'd be able to defend him from any sudden attacks. "This is even better than a welcome-home party."

"Stop yapping," Ghislain suggested from the doorway.

We did as we were told and waited for the intruder to show himself. As my heart pounded in my chest, I thought I could hear the sound of large, metal gears turning—but it was probably just my imagination, the sound of the cogs inside my hands moving, made louder by anticipation.

Then Royston crested the top of the stairs, presumably having found the switch in the storeroom so he wouldn't have to blunder about in the dark.

"You know, I *do* have a bell," Luvander pointed out. "Although since everyone I know seems intent on simply letting themselves in, I wonder why I ever bothered to have it installed in the first place."

"I didn't want to cause a commotion," Royston said, shaking off his coat, the shoulders of which were glistening with melting ice. Sometime between afternoon and nighttime, it had started to snow. When he was finished, he paused, looking at Laure with her poker, Ghislain by the door, and the rest of us, ranged around the room and—speaking mostly for myself—positively vibrating with nervous energy. "Did you multiply while I was gone? I know that children are made during times of duress, but really, this is too much."

"Ghislain just has excellent timing," Luvander said, tasting a sauce he'd been stirring around in a pot. "It seems he brought a friend with him, too. I hope that's all right. We can vouch for him; he was an airman, you know."

Royston gave him a distracted nod, then did a double take, eyes falling on Raphael with more attention than they had before.

"Hello," he said, passing a hand through his hair to shake out the melted snow. "You aren't Rook."

"*Bastion,*" Raphael said, giggling faintly. "Can you imagine if I was? What a life that would be! I don't even think *I* can imagine . . . If the fishermen were shocked by the size of *my* assets, they would have all fainted dead away once they saw Rook's! Actually, I'd rather not think about it. It's too perverted."

"So he's a babbling idiot?" Royston asked, still carefully regarding our newest companion.

"He has always been a babbling idiot," Luvander huffed.

"Found him near Seon," Ghislain said, sitting down now that we'd determined Royston wasn't a threat. "They were worshipping him for being a fish god or something."

"*And* for the size of my—well, no need to anger the lady any further, especially when she's wielding such a fearsome weapon herself," Raphael said, catching himself.

"Now he sounds a little more like Rook to me," Royston said, then smiled. "I'm sorry for staring; my manners aren't usually this atrocious. I was merely thinking about how happy Owen would be to see you . . . But, of course, thinking about him reminds me of this whole rotten situation, and it hasn't found me in the best of states."

"Owen?" Raphael asked, as though someone had just told him it was his birthday and they were giving it away for free at Our Lady of a Thousand Fans, all in his honor. "Ghislain—someone—please tell me I heard that correctly. Who's Owen? Is that who I think it is?"

"Owen's Adamo," Luvander said, sliding the sliced eggplant into the pot. "Or rather, he's Owen Adamo. I'm not sure which is more fun to say, really."

"I'm glad we're all so concerned about him that we're cracking jokes about his name," Laure said, setting her poker down at last. She rounded on Royston, and I didn't envy him his position as sole receiver of her wrath. "Weren't you supposed to come back here with someone?"

"I had intended to, yes," Royston said, looking put out. "I thought I'd left Antoinette in a rather reasonable state of mind; but as it turns out, she lost her temper after I left and ended up being 'hauled in,' as Josette so charmingly put it. Hauled in! Can you imagine? If *my* lover had *me* arrested—"

"Hasn't your lover had you arrested before?" Luvander asked cheekily.

"The scenario was different," Royston replied.

"So that's it, then?" Laure demanded. "We've got no Lady Antoinette, *still* no Adamo, and not even a plan now?"

"It's truly a comfort that even though Owen is not here to badger me, I have you in his stead," Royston said, taking a seat on the arm of the couch. "You'll recall that I said *velikaia* have a way of casting their thoughts outward—like a net from a ship, for catching fish—which makes it difficult for other people with Talent to ignore them. Well, I can still sense her. The projection is faint, but I believe I could follow it to Adamo's location. I don't plan on going *alone,* of course, since I am not the Esar's favorite person to do business with. But if you're willing to follow me, instead of your captive leader, for a little while, I believe I can be of some use to you, at least in guiding you to him."

"And then what?" Laure asked.

"And then . . . something," Royston replied. "I am *not* a Chief Sergeant or even an ex–Chief Sergeant, you know."

"But can't you make things explode just by looking at them?" Ghislain asked.

"I wouldn't call it that, precisely," Royston said. "But yes, I quite take your point. *If* it comes to that—and I really would prefer that it didn't—I can be of more than 'some' use. Though exploding a hole in the wall of the establishment would not be the most subtle choice, and could result in unwanted carnage, some of which might even be our own, depending on how closely Owen is guarded."

"How do we get in?" Laure demanded. Now that she had

some indication of a target—*any* target—she was clearly dying to get out and start swinging at it rather than standing around discussing our next move. It was there that she and Adamo differed, I thought, though Adamo didn't like to dwell on strategy for too long, either.

"I did what I could in terms of research before returning to you," Royston said. "Not to give too much fanfare to my own skills, but you're fortunate that I am the one who can sense her since my knowledge of the city resembles that of an obsessive lover. The direction from which I could sense Antoinette is to the north of Miranda—an out-of-the-way location, but not so remote as you'd think. Unless they've built something new in preparation for this sudden purge—which I don't *think* they've had time to do yet—then the only appropriate building given the location is a prison they once used to hold disagreeable magicians captive. It's underground."

"I don't suppose you have any tunneling equipment?" Luvander asked, his voice hushed, but still unable to keep from making the joke entirely.

"It *is* manned on the surface," Royston said, rubbing his fingers against his jaw, "as it's the location of one of the old Provost's buildings. Not the main one, but there are a few officials there to keep an eye on things. Still, the only real difficulty would be in getting to the actual prison cells underneath the city. I can't communicate with Antoinette directly; otherwise, I'd ask *her* for a more comprehensive layout—that is, if she has one in that head of hers. But since she's always made a point of knowing everything there is to know about the Esar's business, private or no—"

"How scandalous," Raphael said.

"Get to the point, boys," Laure warned.

"Though I'm reluctant to assume anything," Royston continued, "I will tell you what I think, based on what little information I have gathered, from what Antoinette seems to be implying, and from what Josette herself told me. Though neither of them is in the best of mind-sets; the former being imprisoned and the latter dealing with Lord Temur's questioning. What a mess. I suspect the force that took Adamo and Antoinette is *not* the Wolves, since they're being kept elsewhere, and I never once saw Dmitri. Thus—and again, this is merely speculation—I can assume that it's a more private force, one the Esar would trust implicitly not to betray him. They're obviously less concerned with secrecy than they were once since they've arrested people in the streets; but they've managed to assemble without drawing much attention to themselves. That speaks to a rather *small* contingent of personnel, all things considered. Just enough to keep an eye on their dangerous guests."

"So we go down there, you blow up the building, I crack some skulls, and we carry Adamo away," Ghislain said, cracking his knuckles again for emphasis. The way he said it, it almost sounded like a viable plan. But then, Ghislain could be very convincing. "What's the problem?"

"Besides potentially murdering innocents and forcing the Esar to retaliate in a harsh and likely fatal manner? Oh, nothing," Royston said. "No problem at all."

"What if I . . ." Laure began, then stopped herself. When everyone turned to look at her, I saw her gather her considerable mettle, forcing herself to finish the thought. "You think there's a chance that he's in there because of me, right? That Margrave Germaine made me crazy, and she's been trying to hunt me down ever since. What if I went down there, said I'd heard about Adamo, and wanted to know if there was anything I could do to help? They wouldn't be suspicious of me 'cause I'm a girl, and the rest of you could sneak in—though with that big bugger you might want to give up on the idea of being stealthy and skip straight to the exploding part."

"Wonderful, and how did you learn about Adamo's location in the first place?" Luvander said, turning his gaze to me and trying to communicate something to me with his eyes. "More importantly, I don't know how Adamo would feel about us using a civilian as a diversion."

I wasn't as thickheaded as some of the other airmen had always assumed I was, but if what Luvander was attempting to convey was what I thought it was, then I was a little disturbed. Surely this young woman was too young for Adamo—though stranger things *had* happened, I supposed.

"Oh, bastion, not that," Luvander said with a groan, upon seeing my expression change. "What about *you*? Our diplomat? Why don't you go in there and be diplomatic?"

"You mean Balfour?" Royston asked. "They would arrest him on the spot. There *were* people looking for him, according to his landlady."

"Yes," Luvander agreed, "but he's one of us. We send *him* inside, and then he gets in contact with Antoinette, then perhaps some other things happen—and *then* you start with the explosions."

"This is ridiculous," Laure said. She drew herself up to her full height—puffing out her chest the way Adamo did, though it looked less pigeony when she did it—and straightened out the front of her dress. "You lot are an embarrassment, and I, for one, can hardly stand to look at you. Th'Esar's already made his move, and he did it in public. If there's nobody we can go to for help, then we make a stink. Adamo's a hero, isn't he? And don't you think the people of Thremedon would be a mite ticked to learn one of their heroes is locked up without any good reason? They'd be pissed, same as how *we're* pissed. We oughta be able to use that."

"They'd need to hear it from Owen's mouth before they believed anything," Royston said. "But I do agree, that is a sensible way of thinking."

"It's an *Adamo* way of thinking, is what it is," Luvander said.

"So here's what I think," Laure said. "We fake 'em out. You do your explosion bit nearby, just close enough so they think we're making our move but we've got it wrong. Still, they're gonna have to come check it out, or else they'll look real suspicious—and while the place is left mostly unguarded up top, Ghislain here knocks the remaining heads together and the rest of us get inside."

"And once we're inside?" I asked, feeling the same thrill of excitement I always did when Adamo was outlining our new strategies. It wasn't the same as planning for a night in the air, but the amount of risk did come close.

"What was your job?" Laure asked. "When you were flying?"

"Reconnaissance," I replied.

"Then we sneak in there and do some reconnaissance," Laure said. "Get the lay of the land, make sure there are no traps set up, lead the way for the others to come in after us and start unlocking some cell doors. And after that, we have Adamo on our side, not to mention a few pissed-off Margraves—and Antoinette, who by Royston's account knows everything there is to know about what th'Esar's up to."

"And she'll probably be able to enlighten us," Royston concluded, "as to what the hell is going on there."

"Now, I don't want to get too detailed on what's going to happen once we're in there," Laure added, "because we don't know what we're going up against, or even what we're gonna find. If we overthink it, then it's bound to make us panic when it doesn't go according to plan."

"Oh, are we not meant to be panicking already?" Toverre asked. I thought he'd been pale when we met, but he was looking positively white now, if a little green around the edges. It made sense; as an airman, I'd been trained in war, and even I was feeling anxious. This young man was no more than a civilian, a *student*. He was probably hoping our plans wouldn't include him—and, in my opinion, they probably shouldn't. "Silly me, then. Never mind. Carry on."

"Nobody has to come who doesn't want to," Laure said, with a pointed look in his direction. In spite of her attitude toward the rest of us, this seemed almost like an act of kindness—as though she was letting him off the hook.

She was equally unqualified in terms of background, but in terms of her nerve, she might have even been leagues ahead of the rest of us. Excepting, of course, Ghislain.

"Well," Raphael said, slapping his hand against his leg and startling me with the sudden sound. "If I wanted to do a foolish thing like *sleep* after a few days of vomiting, I wouldn't have joined the airmen."

"I'm sure there was a veritable plethora of jobs open to you at the time," Luvander agreed. "Perhaps you could've been a stain-cleaner at the 'Fans. Or the city drunk."

"So long as you save enough energy to muck out my boat after, you can tag along," Ghislain said, standing.

"Well if *everyone's* going," Toverre said, looking distinctly put out about the whole thing. "Perhaps you'll need someone to . . . To stand watch."

"You can always stay here," I said, as it seemed no one else was going to. "It wouldn't be ignoble. Whenever a group of us went out on raids, there were always some who stayed back in case the others didn't . . . Well, that was just how it was done," I amended, realizing that perhaps talking too much about the gravity of the situation would have a sobering effect on our little rescue mission.

"No, it's all right," Toverre said miserably. "Don't try to spare me or my dignity. What kind of wretched creature would I be if I let my fiancée attend this melee without following along to protect her? I merely hope you know, Sir Ghislain, that you are not the *only* one who wishes I was a *velikaia*."

"Sir Ghislain," Raphael repeated. "Do you know, I rather like that? It sounds very impressive, not to mention romantic. Almost like something out of a roman."

"Enough talk," Laure said. I noticed that she'd put on her hat and coat while we'd been talking to one another, and felt the slightest niggling of guilt. We all should have been doing just that.

What we really needed was the air-raid bells to snap us out of it. That'd jump-start the whole crew into action in no time.

"Are my gloves dry yet?" I asked. Toverre handed them to me, pinching them by the thumbs, which weren't stained, and dangling them between us like dead fish rotting on the line. "Thank you," I said.

"You are welcome," he sniffed in reply.

I slipped them on, looking around for something I might have been able to use as a bell. There was nothing in the house, save for a little clockwork timer on the table next to Luvander's stove. Just as I appraised it, wondering how insane I'd have to be to set it off for a certain effect, Luvander seemed to catch my eye, then reached out for it.

It dinged only once, its tone hollow and tinny. But to us, it actually meant something.

"Let me just turn down the stove," Luvander said, putting a lid on his bubbling creation. "If all goes well, perhaps we'll get a chance to eat it. If not . . ."

"If not, it'll soon be able to run the hat shop for you," Laure promised. "Now let's go get the Chief Sergeant."

CHAPTER THIRTEEN

TOVERRE

I'd always known my Laure had a rousing speech or two in her though I'd never dreamed she'd be commanding her own private army.

Even with my incredibly active imagination—not to mention the amount of time I devoted to dreaming up adventures such as this one—I had never dared to imagine something quite at this level of intrigue and excitement.

For me, it was too much. I was well aware that my flights of fancy were just that, and I did not particularly believe I had the constitution for adventure. Yet there I was, with one suddenly dumped unceremoniously into my lap, and the potential consequences of our actions all too real. I could only hope that we weren't all arrested and executed for treason—but no one seemed to be in the mood to contemplate our darkest possible fate just yet, and I couldn't exactly blame them. If we'd thought about it with any depth of foresight, we'd never have left the hat shop at all—a last attempt of our instincts to achieve self-preservation.

Outside, it was dark, the moon obscured by thick clouds, and it was snowing heavily enough that it had discouraged most of the usual foot traffic at this hour. Everyone with a brain in their skull was indoors, not sloshing about through the streets getting slush in their boots. Now and then we passed by an open window, and I could see families within, sitting down to dinner; a young man reading a book; an older woman petting a kitten. They were so caught up in their sensible, everyday routines that no one looked out the window and caught sight of us—if they had, I didn't know that they'd be able to recognize those in our party, wrapped up with scarves and hats and winter coats as we were.

There was simply no telling how fast the rumor would travel once someone realized the airmen were together again, traveling in a group with a single purpose like they hadn't done since the war.

It was bound to cause a scene, and despite my own love of dramatic scenarios, even I understood the need to forgo it, just this once, in favor of keeping to the shadows.

With all the snow, Miranda had fallen hushed and still. Bright windows were illuminated in all the houses, and every now and then a smattering of laughter would spill out from a nearby café or restaurant, but for the most part, the city felt like ours alone. Fat white flakes spiraled down from the clouds, the strong wind blowing them sideways, and I had to very nearly close my eyes entirely to keep from being blinded by them. Ghislain, Royston, and Laure had taken the lead, and I found myself scurrying along in their wake, doing my best to step in the footprints Ghislain had left behind, which were deep and very wide, so as not to become too tired slogging through the snow.

I didn't have the constitution an airman did. And why should I? It wasn't as though I'd been given the same training. Almost from the start, my feet were freezing—I'd have worn thicker socks if I'd known we were going to be tramping through a veritable blizzard—but I kept my hands shoved into my pockets and my head tilted down. We were all going to have fevers come morning—if we even saw morning at all.

But I was hardly the worst off of all of us, even though Raphael had claimed to be in the peak of health. He looked more like a ghost resuscitated after months spent in the grave than anyone seemed willing to acknowledge.

Surely his comrades—who'd known him longer—should have known better and asked him to stay behind? Then it would have been less conspicuous that I remain with him, to see to his needs.

But I had to do this, to stand beside Laure during this important hour. Even if I was not directly involved, *she* was, for a variety of reasons. I would never be able to live with myself afterward if I didn't fight with her despite the fact that I could hardly consider myself an asset to the cause.

For the most part, we didn't talk; the silence was heavier than the snowfall. Yet I knew, given my company, it could hardly last. And, soon enough, I was proven right.

"Let me guess: You're wondering why my statue's so much better-looking than I am," Raphael said.

I hadn't been thinking anything of the sort—for once—but I didn't feel that explaining myself would make it any better. I didn't want my concern to seem like pity, and my lips felt half-frozen in place, too cold for a real protest.

"I much prefer real features to granite ones," I said, with a sniff to keep my nose from running. I cursed my own foolishness in not remembering to bring my handkerchief—I'd left it in Luvander's back room, I realized, after polishing all his silverware. This was the first and only time I'd ever allowed myself to be so careless.

"How very gallant of you to say so," Raphael said. "Though perhaps it's just that you haven't met the *right* feature made of granite, if you don't mind my saying."

I was about to ask him what he meant by that when he slipped on a patch of black ice and I was forced to catch him by the arm to prevent him from falling.

The fact that I was able to catch him *at all,* not to mention support his weight, was a clearer indication than anything else that he could have used a few solid meals—and that we should have eaten some supper before we embarked on our trek across the city.

"All right there?" Luvander asked, looking over his shoulder. "Don't tear my spare jacket, Raphael. It's my second-favorite, and I like it so much better than I like you."

"I had no idea it was such a precious garment," Raphael said, taking care to brush the snow off his shoulders. "Never you mind, everything's fine. Thank you, by the way."

"It's no trouble," I said, releasing him carefully but resolving to keep a closer watch on him.

Laure would certainly be cross with me if I allowed a member of her rescue party to become injured. And considering her mood at present, I wasn't about to do anything to draw her wrath nor lose a member of a group that would soon be devoted to looking after our well-being.

We must've looked like a strange procession to anyone who might've been spying out their window. The seven of us had very little in common—even the airmen, as I'd been surprised to discover, who were as ragtag a group of different personalities as I'd ever seen—but we were *just* the right amount of foolish to go wading through a snowstorm in the middle of the night to break one man out of a royal jail hidden below the city.

After Raphael's brief attempt at conversation, no one else said anything at all. The mood was somber—as though we were heading to a funeral. I didn't know whether it was the sudden realization of the important mission now facing us or simply because no one wanted to get a mouthful of snow. Whatever the reason, I soon lost track of how long we'd been walking, concentrating instead on the heavy rhythm of Ghislain's footfalls in front of me as I hopped from boot print to boot print like a snow rabbit.

"We're nearly there now," Royston said, drawing us down a corner and off the road proper.

Indeed, I could see the shadowed outline of a building up ahead. It looked too small to be a prison, but I remembered what Royston had said about the true facilities lying underground. This, then, was in all likelihood some sort of guardhouse, not to mention part of the cover-up. A modest, simple building housing nefarious deeds done in the deep. This was hardly the city of my dreams.

In any case, that was where we'd be launching our invasion once Margrave Royston began his diversion. I felt a ripple of anxiety run through me and did my best to quell it.

"I suppose it's up to me to go first," Royston said. "I *hate* that. I'll wait for you to get closer—perhaps the building next to it?—so you can see when they vacate the area and make your move."

"I'll go in first," Ghislain said, a certain relish in his voice that made me wonder anew about his character. "Crack some heads to clear the way for team reconnaissance."

"This is just like the old days," Luvander said, breathing on his hands. "Only on the ground, and without Ivory around to set fire to everything in sight."

"It'd come in handy here though, you must admit," Raphael said. To me—because I was standing so close to him and had made such a careful study of him early, in case he should slip again—it seemed to pain him more than the others to talk about his comrade. One of the ones who did not make it back from the final battle, I thought, and bowed my head just briefly in hopes we did not follow him this evening. "Nothing creates a diversion like a whole mess of things bursting into flame. You don't even *need* a dragon for that. Just a match."

"I will go first," Royston confirmed. "And I'll do my best not to catch anything on fire, myself."

"Then me," Ghislain said. "When it's clear on the first level, I'll give a signal."

"How will we know what it is?" I asked, nervously polishing one of my buttons with the fingers of my glove.

"You'll know," Ghislain said.

"And then the rest of us slip in," Laure agreed, rounding on the group. "Are you lot going to be quiet once we're in there? Or am I going to be the one who's gotta explain to Adamo we got pinched because someone wouldn't shut up about his fish-god dick or how much eggplant stew he was gonna eat when he got home?"

"I hardly think that's necessary," Luvander said.

"We *are* trained professionals," Raphael pointed out.

"And professional blabbermouths, too," Laure said, as Luvander made a stitching motion over his lips, then pretended to throw away his invisible needle. "Anything new from Antoinette?"

"Nothing," Royston confirmed. "It's just the same sense of anger, only much louder here. We're in the right place."

"All right," Laure concluded. "Margrave, it's your turn."

"I am so distressed," Royston said, echoing my sentiments exactly. But, unlike me, he was able to square his shoulders and leave the comfort of our company, slipping off into the night. The snow soon obscured him as we slipped silently through the fall to stand in shadows closer to our target.

I hoped that all the snow wouldn't prove a distraction to *our* distraction. Would it be possible to see the explosion Margrave Royston engineered when it was falling so heavily?

If I'd waited but a moment, I wouldn't have had to ask.

I felt it under my feet, the reverberations of the shock rippling over the cobblestones, even though they were buried under so much snow. The noise itself came later—loud enough it nearly knocked me off my feet—and I could see the flash of something bright in the distance. I wondered what Royston had done and whether or not he was all right.

Then I turned my thoughts to myself. I was going to need them.

"Cue mass panic," Raphael murmured, so quiet that I might have been the only one to hear him. Everyone else was too busy focusing on the door to the building in question— as lights came on in the windows, and the door itself opened an instant later, a few men running out into the night.

That, however, was followed immediately by all the lights going on in the building in whose shadows we'd previously been obscured—and all the other buildings nearby, too. With the staggered effect of a row of dominos, all the lights in the city were coming on, while the people on the lower floors of buildings began to flood the streets.

In the commotion, I realized, no one would notice another group of citizens.

With the crowd as his cover, Ghislain slipped away from us. He didn't blend in because of his height and breadth, but he soon disappeared into a doorway, and no one seemed to notice.

I felt momentarily guilty that our actions had disturbed all those people, who wanted no more than I did, when you came right down to it—just to live out their lives in peace and quiet, without being interrupted during their mealtimes. Some weren't even wearing coats.

It seemed that *we* were going to be the cause of more harm to the city than the Esar. We'd certainly be responsible for more fevers in the coming days.

Then Laure grabbed my arm, practically dragging me through the snow, and I realized that the light on the bottom floor of the building we were meant to enter had been snuffed out.

"If that's not our sign," Laure muttered, "then I'll eat my scarf."

We left the uproar in the streets behind—and all that snow, which I was only too glad to see the back end of—and slipped unnoticed into the warm building, just as Ghislain had done earlier. Behind me, I heard Raphael lock the door—those who'd run out probably hadn't thought to take their keys. It would provide a momentary setback, in any case.

"This way," I heard Ghislain whisper in the dark.

We followed him.

I very nearly tripped over something that was not a piece of furniture—it gave too much, and groaned when I kicked it—and I was suddenly grateful Ghislain had not lit a lamp again. First of all, our shadows would be visible from the streets, framed by the windows; second of all, I did not want to see the corpses of our enemies strewn across the floor. At least I didn't step on anyone else, clinging to the back of Laure's jacket in the dark so as not to become lost.

"Watch the stairs," Ghislain said, and I tightened my hold.

"You're gonna knock us both over if you're not careful," Laure muttered, but she didn't shake me off.

The six of us crept slowly down the stairs, Ghislain and Balfour in front this time, presumably because the latter was small enough to get out of the way of the former if we ran into any trouble. Laure was right behind them in the narrow pass, which meant *I* was considerably nearer to the front than I might've liked, with Luvander and Raphael bringing up the rear. They were guarding us, I realized, keeping the two civilians who certainly didn't belong in this kind of operation well flanked on either side. It was very thoughtful of them, but it did little to soothe my nerves.

At least I no longer had to worry about the Dragon Corps's most infirm member slipping on any stray patches of ice. And if there were any troubles on the rickety steps, I had a feeling that Luvander would help him, if only for the sake of his second-favorite jacket.

As we came to the end of the narrow stairwell, Ghislain halted, nearly causing a pileup when Laure didn't take the hint and almost crashed into Balfour, nearly bowling him over like a ninepin. Up ahead, I could see a well-lit hallway with iron doors set into the white walls. The lights lining the ceiling flickered every so often, which gave the impression of candlelight. At least there was some light to see by, though when I glanced down at my fingertips to see how much dust had come away on my hands, I was very nearly ill. Not only was there dust, but there was *grime,* as well, and a slimy streak on my thumb from where I had been forced to guide myself along the uneven wall.

Being too deep underground was one of my private nightmares—I couldn't imagine being buried in all that awful dirt—but I wasn't about to cause a fuss for personal reasons. At least we were in some semblance of a building, no matter how things dripped and dropped in the distant dark. I laid my hand against one of the stones, and it seemed sturdy enough; then I quickly drew my hand away.

I was secretly, guiltily grateful that Margrave Royston hadn't come along with us. After seeing his work firsthand, I knew that I did not want to be anywhere underground with him at my side. It was nothing to do with the man personally, and not a comment on his control over his Talent. I merely had no wish to end up accidentally buried alive should something startle him and force him to cause a cave-in.

After giving us a chance enough to take stock of our surroundings, Ghislain began to move. Balfour, however, had turned his face to the side, squinting, as though trying to hear something. I strained to listen but heard nothing at all.

"Something the matter, Balfour?" Luvander asked, in a bare whisper.

"Pardon?" Balfour asked, shaking his head. "No, I'm fine. It's nothing . . . Just this place; it seems . . ."

"It's *quite* eerie," Raphael cut in. "Though I'm man enough not to be affected, I for one plan on spending as little time as possible here."

"I agree," Balfour said, though he kept peering around Ghislain, as though he was still searching.

"Things could get messy, here," Ghislain said, pitching his voice low, so that I had to crane over Laure's shoulder to hear it. "Helped myself to a few different key rings while I was up there, but I'm not sure what goes where, not to mention none of us knows where we're going yet, so it might take some time. If we run into any guards, I plan on disposing of them. If anyone here's got a problem with that, you can go upstairs and slip out while everyone's still watching Mary Margrave's fireworks display. Got it?"

"Now that you *mention* it, I do love fireworks," Luvander said, tapping his chin, then breaking character immediately when everyone rounded on him. "Honestly, it was just a joke. Pardon *me* for attempting to lighten our spirits before they leave this mortal earth entirely. See if I do you any more favors."

"We'd all be real grateful if you wouldn't," Ghislain said, but he wasn't wearing a frightening expression, so I figured he couldn't be all that upset about it. His sharp features were merely grim and exaggerated by the shadows—looking much like the beastly mask in the back room of the Yesfir hat shop. He reached into his coat pocket, pulling out three separate rings of keys. "Someone take these. I'm gonna want my hands free for other things."

"He means removing heads from bodies," Raphael confided.

"I'll do it," Balfour said, reaching up with gloved hands. He glanced over at Laure, who'd made an impatient move for the keys herself, and offered her a small smile. "Perhaps you can aid Ghislain in giving me cover?"

"Yes, that sounds *much* more dangerous than trying keys in cell doors," I said, patting her arm. "You should absolutely accept."

"Don't have to patronize me," Laure said, shaking me off.

Since the hallway was well lit, and I didn't see myself tripping over the last few steps in the dark, I allowed her to do it.

"Weird place," Ghislain said. "Seems like all the guards were upstairs. Now, why would that be?"

Then, without waiting for the rest of us—not even bothering with a rousing promise of our soon-to-be victory—he rose like the terrifying specter of every bad dream I'd ever had about pirates along the coast or bandits on the main roads and marched deeper into the hall.

Though I'd been holding my breath for some terrific event—another of Margrave Royston's fearsome explosions, perhaps—none came. Ghislain looked left, then right, then back at us, shrugging his big shoulders. Another one of his signs, I supposed.

Laure, Balfour, and I scurried after him; Luvander and Raphael were only seconds behind.

"I don't see any cells," Laure hissed, looking deeply suspicious. "Are you certain we're in the right place?"

"Nope," Ghislain said, heading arbitrarily to the right. "Wish the only man who knew a lick about the blueprints in this place hadn't run off like that. *Hate* flying blind."

"We needed him for our grand distraction," Luvander pointed out. "I *offered* to don a dress and one of my best hats, but no one seemed to like that idea very much."

I found myself giggling—the sort of humor a man embraced before heading to the gallows, I supposed—and did my best to suppress the sound, so that I merely sounded as though I had a bad case of fear hiccups.

We passed by several doors, all of them uniform and perfect—made of iron, with no decorative scrollwork or designs of any kind. I saw Laure peering at a few of them curiously, but when the keys didn't work in their locks, Ghislain hadn't stopped to examine them: nor had he attempted to bust them down with one of his large shoulders, and so we kept moving. It was probably better to do reconnaissance this way—make sure there were no threats lurking nearby before we allowed ourselves to become too engrossed in any one thing.

The largest door was at the end of the hall, crisscrossed with broad strips of steel and fitted with a knob in the center. There was a keyhole beneath it, and Balfour set to work once more, examining the size and shape of the hole in the door, then comparing it against the keys on the three separate rings.

I bent down to help him with them, this kind of detail being something I was drawn to instinctively. Keys were filthy instruments of disease, and I'd spent a great deal of time cleaning them for my father, and Laure's father, and the town's banker—whether they asked me to or not. Rather quickly—for me, at least—I turned up a silver key with the appropriate foot and what seemed like the correct number of wards shaped into it to bypass the lock.

"Try this," I said, handing it over so that Balfour—our key man—might do the honors.

He took it, looking mildly baffled, the metal making a dull sound against his metal fingers beneath the fabric of his gloves and a slight magnetic pull causing the other keys in the rings to be drawn toward his palm. Then he set the key into the lock. I held my breath as he turned it, and sighed with relief when the tumblers shifted, the lock falling open with a *click*.

"Thank you," Balfour said, straightening up and returning the key rings to his pocket.

"We're *sure* this one's not a *velikaia*?" Ghislain asked, peering at me skeptically.

"You would be the first to know," I assured him, quite cheekily for me, but I was privately rather elated with my small success—no doubt the only assistance I would be able to offer for the rest of the night.

The door swung open with a gentle creak, and the six of us stepped inside. Next to me, Laure gasped, and Balfour stopped dead, as though he'd been transformed into his statue—or at least a smaller version of it.

It appeared to me that we had stumbled upon some kind of enormous workroom. Set throughout the room were long, rectangular tables made of stone and framed in wood. They were surrounded by tall stools, likely for whatever workers frequented this factory to sit upon. Against the far wall was the largest assortment of tools I'd ever seen in one place. The sight would've made a man like my father very happy—he imagined himself to be a talented tinkerer—but I couldn't even begin to name half of them. I recognized dozens of pairs of pliers in a variety of sizes, as well as a hammer for sheeting metal and some kind of hacksaw. One of the tables had a dreadful mess on it, large silver and gold machine cogs littered across its surface and a long twisting pipe that looked as though it'd been bent nearly in two.

"This . . . This is the kind of stuff that Germaine woman had in her spare room," Laure said, sounding weak. Slowly, she lowered her hands from her mouth, looking as though she expected the woman in question to leap from the shadows and drag her off to her offices. As if a simple physician was all we had to worry about now. "I knew I was getting a bad feeling from her, I just never . . ."

"I've *been* here," Balfour said, whiter even than Raphael now, which was a feat in and of itself. "I thought it looked familiar before, but I was so distracted—I must've come in a different way, but this room . . . I've been in this room before. It's where Margrave Germaine worked on my hands. Somehow, I'd thought it was part of the palace. But they must have moved me."

Unaffected by our companions' commentary, Luvander strode over to the table with the pieces lying on it, picking up one of the cogs and tracing his fingers thoughtfully over its sharp edges.

"Hard to tell what's what in all this," he said quietly. "I feel as though I've walked in on Yesfir naked."

"It's more than just material for my hands," Balfour admitted.

"Unless the Margrave planned on making you a very *large* pair," Luvander agreed. "With wings."

He held up a finely hammered sheet of metal, about the span of my forearm, which curved in the middle into a sharp hook of metal, reminding me of a talon. The edges were filigreed, and there was a sort of frame to it as well of fine, thin steel, like thick rope wire.

"Should I feel like a proud uncle?" Luvander asked, face red with emotion. It wasn't joy, I realized, but mottled anger. "So many little ones to be."

"It doesn't make any sense for them to be this size," Balfour added. "Does it?"

"Would anyone mind telling me what's going on?" I asked.

"It's clear," Ghislain said flatly. "The Dragon Corps is being rebuilt."

"And th'Esar clearly wishes to play dollhouse with them," Luvander concluded. "He's had them all made in miniature. Isn't that sweet?"

Even I was hit hard enough by this latest discovery to fall gravely silent; I couldn't imagine how these men were feeling, observing what had once been their lives turned into scrap metal upon the table.

But for what purpose was all this gathered here? I wondered, glancing over the collection of gleaming metal parts. Some were clearly recognizable, like Luvander's wing: a claw here, a jaw there, even a curved, ridged tail. The rest was just guts and scrap, I could only assume, thousands of cogs and gears—the human equivalent would be a patient sliced open upon the autopsy table. I shuddered.

"We shouldn't be in here," Laure said. When I turned to look at her—grateful to have something else to focus on other than the grisly sight before me—I saw that there was a faraway look in her eyes. It seemed that she, too, was hearing what Balfour had, earlier in the hallway. "We can't get distracted. We've gotta find Adamo before those bastards upstairs wake up and come looking for who clobbered 'em."

"They won't wake up for a long time," Raphael said cheerfully.

"But," Ghislain added, "I take your meaning."

He left the room quickly—and I had to wonder if it was practicality that impelled him to leave or some deeper compulsion. Balfour was still staring around in horror, and Luvander's face had been transformed by serious emotion. He hadn't yet put the wing down.

"Come on," Raphael said almost gently. "We'll come back later."

"Adamo will know what to do," Balfour agreed, more like he was trying to convince himself than reassure his companions.

Laure touched a rounded piece of metal on the table, then jerked back as though she'd been burned. "Come on," she agreed, and stormed out of the room.

I was forced to scurry after her, the other men somehow able to extricate themselves in order to follow me. Ghislain closed the big door behind us without a sound. "Another stairway out here," he said, knocking gently at the wall in front of him. There was a groaning sound, like stone scraping against stone, and what had appeared moments earlier to be a solid wall swung away from us, revealing an even smaller, darker staircase. "Same formation," Ghislain added.

He had to crouch in order to fit; moments later, he disappeared into the darkness. Balfour moved after him, white around the mouth but with unwavering purpose. Laure looked more than ever like she belonged with them—a stalwart soldier heading off to battle—and I reached out to grab hold of her, wishing she could transfer some of her strength to me.

We left the comforting light behind us and were swallowed up by the cool, deep dark. The sound of dripping water was growing louder—perhaps that was what Balfour and Laure had heard?—and I felt something drop onto the top of my head, causing my stomach to turn over like an omelet in the skillet.

There would be no bath in the world long or cleansing enough to rid me of the crawling feeling all over my skin.

At least the staircase was a short one. I missed my footing, so sure of another step to follow the last one, and Laure steadied me but also clamped a hand over my mouth.

I could hear voices now, though not clearly. They were muffled—coming from around the corner—but the harder I listened, the more clearly I recognized them.

One was the unforgettable bass of Professor ex–Chief Sergeant Owen Adamo, though he was doing his best to speak quietly. The other had a country accent better suited to softer tones, and my eyes widened like teatime saucers. Though I hadn't heard that voice in weeks, I was still able to identify it. Somewhere close by, in this twisted prison compound, was the missing 'Versity student whose mystery had haunted my waking hours.

It was, without question, our friend Gaeth.

ADAMO

Leaving a man to stew with his own thoughts and no one else to talk to was a common tactic in prisons everywhere. Troius probably thought he'd invented it, and wherever he was—having tea parties with his big metal dollies, no doubt—he was probably congratulating himself for a job well done.

What he didn't bank on was the cut on the back of my neck, the scab just now congealing, and my conversational partner in one of the cells a ways down from mine. All that was proving to be a real good distraction.

. . . blood . . . again . . . Antoinette's voice whispered, faint as the wind howling outside a window, only the ghostly noise was right between my ears.

It took me a moment to realize what she wanted, but less time to do her bidding. When someone knew what they were talking about, you didn't stop to ask them stupid questions.

That's better, Antoinette said, once there was blood all over my neck again. *You're much cleverer than Royston would have had me believe.*

He likes to talk me down, I explained. *Doesn't want to raise anyone's expectations.*

Enough small talk, Antoinette replied. *I've done my best to bring a rescue party. Is there anything in your cell you might use as a weapon?*

I glanced around but without high hopes. Troius respected me—though his respect wasn't worth the dirt on the back of a ha'penny—too much to leave me with anything I could use as tool for my own escape. But he'd given me that little chair to sit on. While I wouldn't be able to break any doors down with it, I could sure as shit get a few good blows before the wood splintered.

Not ideal, but I've got something, I told her.

I have a chair as well, Antoinette said. *How inglorious this will be.*

Ain't about the glory, I said, recalling just how often I'd given that same speech to my boys, and a couple of the less practical ones in particular.

How true, Antoinette said. Something about her voice gave me the idea that she might've been smiling. *There is very little glory in being taken captive by someone you once considered an ally. Even worse when it's a friend.*

I sure would've liked to ask her more about *that* one, maybe ascertain whether all that shit Royston'd told me about Antoinette and th'Esar was really true. I wasn't exactly one for gossip, but if she'd been his lover before, something told me *that* relationship was about to get colder than the Cobalts' highest peak. There weren't enough flowers and chocolates and even fine jewelry to make a woman forgive you after this kind of betrayal. But before I could get another thought-word in, I heard footsteps approaching down the hall.

Someone's coming, I told her. *Think that might be your rescue party?*

No, Antoinette said. *It isn't them. All I can sense is the stink of that* woman's *magic.*

I stilled, waiting for Troius to present himself—maybe with his dragon, this time, just to impress upon me one more time who was who in these negotiations. He was probably coming back to see if I'd made my choice yet, thinking he could lean on me a little bit. As if there was any real choice to make. A man needed to be decisive in order to be a good soldier, but that didn't mean his decisions didn't trouble him at all.

I was so focused on Troius and how much I disliked him—and whether or not I could get away with clanging him on the head with my chair straightaway—that I didn't realize until the last second that it *wasn't* Troius coming for me.

Instead, it was some kid I didn't recognize, closer to Laure's age than Troius's. He was tall and a little vacant-looking—and there was just something familiar about his face that I couldn't *quite* peg down. It niggled at me, the way so many things were doing lately, distracting me.

They had the boy dressed all in green like the rest of these Dragon Guard piss-buckets, and I figured maybe that was what was messing with my perception, since the uniform didn't suit him at all.

"Professor Adamo?" he whispered.

All at once, it hit me like shrapnel kicked up during one of Ghislain's crusher-runs. This was one of *my* kids—maybe even the one Laure'd told me was missing. So I'd been wrong about them being shirkers—they hadn't been going out with the fever at all. They'd been "disappearing" and landing in prison, same as I had.

I stood up, getting as close to the cell door as I could without leaving my shackled leg behind.

"Don't suppose you could come in here?" I asked. "Might be more comfortable for the two of us."

"They don't give the likes of us keys to important things," the boy said, shaking his straw-colored head. When he turned back to me a funny light passed over his eyes, too quick for me to study. "I . . . Well, to be blunt, Professor Adamo, I've gotta admit that *I* came to *you* for help. My name's Gaeth. Don't know if you remember me, but I sat in on some of your classes—at least, before I got the fever. They were my favorite, on account of how there wasn't any reading or writing involved."

This time, I didn't have to dig deep into the dried-up, near-senile grounds of my poor mind to place a memory to the name. It *was* the one Laure'd given me, what felt like ages ago now, when we'd met in my office and she'd trusted me to help her. Since I hadn't seen any of my boys around the place, I had to hope I hadn't sent her straight from one trap into another.

Still, now that I knew they were poaching country folk brought to the city under false pretenses, it was anyone's guess what th'Esar would stoop to.

"Sure, I remember you," I said, which wasn't exactly true. I remembered Laure talking about him, which was different. But it didn't matter, since it was what he wanted to hear, and if I was judging him right, he looked comforted. I just had to hope that this wasn't a trap, but that didn't seem like Troius's style at all. If he was gonna use subterfuge, then he'd want to be the one to do it, for the bragging rights—and he'd never send this kid from the country, reminding me in his quiet way of Balfour, though not nearly as well spoken. "Don't know if you've noticed—and I'm sorry to be the one telling you this—but I'm not in much of a position to be helping anyone at the minute."

"I know," Gaeth said, concern flashing over his simple features. "It's awful rude of me—my mam always said you shouldn't ask no one for nothing, 'specially if he's worse off than you, and I've tried to abide by it, even here in the city. But I heard that man talking about how they had you here and I had to come and see you."

"And now you see me," I said, wishing I had higher hopes of being able to help him. "You're not hurt, are you?"

"It ain't that," Gaeth said. "They've had me here for *ages*. I went to see the doctor and must've fallen asleep, 'cause when I woke up, there I was in that big room that looks like a smithy! Couldn't find out where I was, nor if my mam was worried for me. Not to mention . . . well, best not to speak of the beastie."

"Beastie?" I asked, latching onto that last bit. I was getting real predictable in my old age; I just had to hope Gaeth wouldn't hold it against me.

He paled; then his cheeks flooded with color, like he was embarrassed.

"The . . . the *dragons,*" he said, leaning close and whispering nervously, like he was afraid they'd hear him—wherever they were. "They told me I was very lucky—a 'prime candidate,' they said—and they wouldn't let me leave no matter how many times I told 'em I had reading to learn and my mam to write to. Then they locked me in a room with a . . . well, I thought she were a monster at first, but I guess I can't call her that anymore, since in none of the tales can the monsters *talk* so right. She's all over silver and blue, and real gentle, but only once you get to know her. She wanted me to name her so I did—a good name, Cornflower—though the

man in charge didn't seem to like that very much, but I suspect he's got feelings about simple country folk. But she reminded me of my prize milk cow—a real beauty. I *do* miss
home."

Gaeth added this last bit with a deep sigh, and I didn't
blame him in the slightest. Arresting a full-grown man like
me—or a scrapper like Antoinette, who could clearly take
care of herself—was one thing. Not that we'd deserved it,
but we knew the city, and to some extent we understood its
pitfalls and dangers, so that even when th'Esar went off his
rocker and came flying at us sideways, we weren't *too* surprised. But this poor bastard was still a kid, not to mention
simple as sweet cream. He had no way of knowing Thremedon's politics—presumably that's what he'd come to the
city to study in the first place—or what it meant that th'Esar'd
decided to re-create his own miniature army, violating a
pretty important treaty alongside our trust. Far as I could tell,
he just wanted to go home. And I didn't blame him. Hell, I
wanted that, too, and I was a seasoned veteran.

"Where's your dragon now?" I asked.

"I told her to stay put," Gaeth said, peering over his shoulder. He looked nervous, and I couldn't say I blamed him for
that, either. Dragon Corps had been staffed mostly by
volunteers—the problem had been too *many* people wanting
to join, not too few. I couldn't imagine what it'd feel like to
black out and wake up in a stable, with some mean
weasel-faced bastard telling me that I'd been picked to ride
one of th'Esar's finest, without actually having volunteered.
"She doesn't always listen, though. Just like my old Cornflower."

"Troius told me these dragons always listen to orders," I
said.

"Well, sometimes," Gaeth said. "But sometimes Cornflower has a few words to say about orders. And sometimes
she don't follow them at all."

"Interesting," I said, wondering if the reason for the dis-
crepancy was Troius lying to me or Gaeth having a weaker
will. Chances were it was the former—and it made sense
Troius'd *want* to believe everything with the new dragons

was working out peachy, since no one wanted to be the first to tell th'Esar that things weren't running according to plan. Used to be my job. Not anymore. I just hoped Troius would be able to have some real good fun with it.

"I thought maybe I'd try to run away," Gaeth added. "Not that I'm a runner—my da always said, 'Face facts, boy'— but if my mam was worrying about not hearing from me, I figured that was more important than honoring my da's memory. But then I thought, I just don't know what I'll do with Cornflower at the farm. She might set fire to the barn, and then Mam'll have to take her down to the river."

"Don't think they're gonna let you pack up and take her home," I told him before he could get too carried away.

"But I *have* to go home," Gaeth said, concern giving way to plain distress. "I done what they wanted . . . and I miss the sunlight. Without good exercise, I can't even sleep proper. You don't think they mean to keep me here forever, do you?"

"That's exactly what I think," I said, wavering for only a moment before I told him the truth. Why sugarcoat it? Because he was poor and from the country? Because I felt sorry for him? Nah. That kind of shit never flew with me. I'd only had one way of talking to my boys, and this Gaeth had a dragon now, which made him one of my boys just by default. If I didn't toughen him up a little, there was a chance no one would, and he'd end up in pieces somewhere, his fate weighing heavy on my conscience.

Anyway, he took it well, so I knew my instincts hadn't been all off about him. He just stared at me, breathing in deep before he nodded.

"I guessed it," he said.

"Wish I didn't have to confirm your suspicions," I said, starting to lose feeling in my shackled-up leg.

"But will you help me?" Gaeth asked.

"Don't know how much I can do from inside here," I reminded him, clanking the chain a bit for emphasis.

"You could pretend to do what they want, couldn't you?" Gaeth asked. "That's what I did—what I'm doing—not that it's done *me* much good. But if there's two of us . . . And my Cornflower; not forgetting her. One dragon against the other two—there'd be three, but they're having trouble with her. So I'm thinking we'd have better odds. Some even say there's magicians in here now, and I know they're smarter than me—and I'm smart enough to know being locked up ain't good . . . Maybe *they*'d join us."

Well? Antoinette asked, and I was real proud of myself for not jumping when her voice suddenly invaded my head. *Are you being carted off or not?*

Hang on, I told her. *It's a kid. They've got kids down here. Th'Esar's pairing kids up with new dragons and Regina only knows what horseshit plan he's following.*

Silence, from inside my head and outside, too, as Gaeth waited for my answer, all white around the mouth the way Balfour used to get before a raid.

When I'm finished with that man, even the worms will not want to eat him, Antoinette said finally.

Good plan, I replied. *Why poison the worms?*

"Listen, Gaeth," I said, lowering my voice as best I could, so that he'd have to lean in. "Someone's coming to break us out. Friends of mine, I think. If we're lucky—and I'm not saying we will be—can you stick around here to wait for them?"

"*I* could," Gaeth admitted, looking up and down the hall again. "But my Cornflower . . ."

The reluctance in his voice sent a pang through me. If he thought it was bad being nagged by her *now,* try after they'd been together for years, and she knew him well enough to outsmart him *all* the time.

"Where are they keeping the other dragons?" I asked. Not because I was fool enough to think we could go after them but because it seemed like good information to have—for later, maybe, so we didn't stumble into a damn nest.

"There's another building," Gaeth whispered. "Across a bridge—I'm always worried I'll take a tumble straight off the thing. I can swim, but the water's so dark, it ain't natural. No one's fallen in yet, but it makes me sick to look down."

"I've been there," I told him, remembering the metal key in Troius's palm and Ironjaw's claws tearing up the floor.

Just then I heard more footsteps—several pairs this time and all at once, like a team of guards heading toward my cell.

"Is that for you, or me?" I asked, hoping Gaeth wouldn't spook.

"Might be they learned I was coming," Gaeth whispered, holding very still. That might've helped him while dealing with bears in the countryside, but it wouldn't do much good with a trained guard. "I know my Cornflower didn't betray me, though. She doesn't like Troius, and she hates Ironjaw."

Hush the boy, Antoinette said.

Are they friend or foe? I asked.

I'm a mind reader, Antoinette replied, *not an oracle.*

Either way, we'd know soon enough. I tried to indicate to Gaeth that he should hightail it out of there. If he was caught consorting with the enemy, I didn't know how far his precious rare connection to a dragon would go to protect him, and I didn't want him getting hurt on my account.

"It's a big man," Gaeth whispered, eyes fixed not on me, but staring off somewhere down the hall. "*Very* big man."

I could see now why Troius wanted to recruit someone like me to the cause—someone who knew a little something about *actual training.*

Then, an arm—a *very* big arm—reached out to grab Gaeth by the shoulder, managing to lift him clear of the ground.

There was only one person I knew in all of Thremedon who could do that, and I was relieved for a moment to realize my rescue party had come at last. But I didn't want Gaeth panicking and calling his girl to attack. That'd be a surefire way to let everyone know what was happening.

"Put 'im down, Ghislain," I said.

Slowly, Gaeth was lowered to the floor. A moment after that, Ghislain's head loomed into view. "This one's not bothering you?" he asked.

I could hear the jingling of keys, which at least meant that while we were shooting the shit, just casually catching up, somebody was trying to bust me out.

"Not any more than young folk usually do," I replied. "And I *think* he's on our side. Though we've got someone a few cells down who'll be able to tell for certain. In the mean-

time, Gaeth, this is Ghislain. Make your acquaintance on
your own time. You don't want to get on Ghislain's bad side,
now do you, Gaeth?"

"No, Professor Adamo," Gaeth said, not so much wide-
eyed as he was well mannered. I was even starting to like
him, so it'd really chafe my chaps if he turned out to be pulling a fast one on me.

"Good," I said. "What in bastion's name is taking so long
with the keys out there?"

"Keys're getting stuck to Balfour's hands," Ghislain explained.

And, crazy as it might've sounded to anyone else, it made
perfect sense to me. Which just went to show how upside
down my world had become.

"Gaeth?" I heard a familiar voice ask, a little too loud for
my liking, from somewhere outside my cell. It belonged to
that skinny cricket—the one engaged to Laure—though it
seemed I'd forgotten his name outta pure spite.

"*You're* the one who locked him up?" another voice demanded. It was the one I'd been hoping *not* to hear, truth be
told, because it only meant that the girl'd gone and put herself in harm's way—when I'd been trying to put her right out
of it.

But I guessed it was exactly what I would've done, so I
couldn't fault her for it. Still, I certainly wished I'd been less
complacent, so I wouldn't look like the biggest fool this side
of the Cobalts when Balfour finally got the cell door open.

"I didn't know anything about it," Gaeth protested. "Professor Adamo's a hero. He doesn't belong down here."

Your little party could stand to be a little less boisterous,
Antoinette suggested. And she was right, of course. I cleared
my throat, which Ghislain and Balfour would recognize as a
sign for everyone to shut the fuck up. It might've been a
while since we'd all fought together, but some cues triggered
instincts you just never forgot.

Ghislain lifted his hand—I couldn't see his face anymore,
since the opening in my cell door was set too low, but I could
only assume he'd brought his fingers to his lips—and said,
only once but very convincing, "Shh."

Everybody quieted, so all we could hear was the jingling of the keys, and—finally—the sound of the right one sliding deep into the lock, turning with a *click* that was music to my ears.

I couldn't celebrate just yet, but it was step one completed. The door swung open and I saw Ghislain—or the lower half of his body, most of his head cut off by the top of the door—and Balfour crouched beside him. There was Laure, too, standing with her hands on her hips like she needed to be sure I was really in the cell, taking in the details like a natural. Next to her was her fiancé, wringing his hands together, and Gaeth, scratching at the back of his head.

But that wasn't all, I realized, feeling a little overwhelmed. Luvander'd come along, too, and next to him was somebody my eyes wouldn't believe I was seeing.

"We brought a surprise," that someone said, lifting his hand in a wave. "Can you imagine? It's me!"

"Now, Raphael," Luvander cautioned, "Owen Adamo has had a very long day. Let's try not to be unnecessarily wearing."

I had a lot of things to say, but I had to lick my lips a few times and force myself to be their Chief Sergeant, thereby not actually saying any of 'em. "Where's Royston?" I asked finally. "He didn't do anything stupid, did he?"

"That remains to be seen," Balfour said, coming inside the cell and searching for a key to unlock the cuff around my ankle. "He provided the distraction. We don't have much time."

"Then toss Ghislain some keys and get the magicians out," I told him.

"It'll take a minute," Balfour said, trying another key. "I just need to be sure I have the right . . . Ah, there we go."

The manacle opened and I was free. Fortunately it hadn't been on me long enough to do any real damage; though the skin was sensitive, it wasn't yet raw.

Without waiting any longer—so, without wasting any more time—Balfour tossed his keys up to Ghislain.

"There were two in cells that I saw," I told him. "Doesn't mean there aren't more around, so check all of 'em."

"There *are* more now," Laure said, seeming unsure of herself when everyone looked around toward her, then soldiering on. "Margrave Royston said they were making arrests at the Basquiat right after you were taken. Stands to reason they'd be here, too, doesn't it?"

"Let's hope," I muttered. If they were anywhere else, chances were they wouldn't be doing so well. It seemed to me that being *where I was* was actually being *lucky*, 'cause at least it meant nobody was dead. Then again, being dead didn't seem to carry the same finality it used to. What was the world coming to?

"I'll find them," Ghislain said, ducking under the low door of my cell and heading back out into the hall.

With him gone, there wasn't anything standing between me and Raphael anymore. I stared at him, and he stared at me. If we stood around in the cell any longer, I really *was* gonna start spewing all sorts of horseshit—and maybe give him an earful about idiots whose brains went lame in the war and didn't have enough sense in their heads to come *home* after it'd ended, like everybody else.

"Good to see you," I said finally.

"It's good to be seen," Raphael said. "I'll go into detail later, but suffice it to say that I was living on the Seon border, being worshipped as a good-luck charm because of the size of my—"

Am I to assume this very large and handsome man is part of your rescue party? Antoinette asked me suddenly.

Yeah, I told her. *That'd be Ghislain.*

It seems my luck has turned around, Antoinette said. *He looks quite . . . useful. I see that he has Ginette and Wildgrave Ozanne with him.*

Already? I asked.

He moves quickly, and so should you, Chief Sergeant, Antoinette said. *I don't know what sort of distraction Royston cooked up, but I imagine time is not necessarily on our side. Let us value his assistance.*

Got it, I said, drawing myself up to my full height. With Ghislain out of the picture, it'd actually seem impressive.

Luvander and Balfour were both staring at me like they were afraid the sudden shock of seeing Raphael again might've harmed my brain. They were used to me operating faster than this, but I had to take stock of my resources before I could decide where to begin.

In the corner of my cell, Gaeth and that skinny cricket were having a whispered conversation that seemed placid on one side—that was Gaeth—and all kinds of frenzied on the other. I heard the cricket demand, in a stage whisper, where in Regina's name Gaeth had been all this time and something about mother's gloves—probably just some of today's slang I wasn't up on—as Gaeth tried to explain he'd been here the whole time. Meanwhile, the cricket was trying to clean something off his shoulder, using a glove as a kerchief.

Then there was Laure, who didn't look worried, just mad and red in the face, like she was aching to get started. I knew what she was thinking—she didn't know why we were waiting around in a prison for our captors to come back, making rounding us up again real easy—and I wished I had an answer for her, to put her worries to rest.

There were a few magicians I didn't know, though I'd heard gossip about them from Royston, even if I couldn't keep all that horseshit straight in my head for more than two minutes. Antoinette would be a powerful enough ally, and I'd take her word on the rest of the troops.

And then there were my boys. Ghislain would be good for anything; Balfour looked shell-shocked; Luvander could talk any enemy to death; and Raphael looked like you could bowl him over if you tapped him with a stick.

These were the soldiers I had to work with—three of them too young, and totally untrained, to boot. They were *students,* and even if one of them had a dragon, I knew better than anyone that having a dragon didn't all of a sudden transform you into a seasoned warrior. I couldn't compare them to the boys I'd had before—wouldn't be fair to anyone since there was no replacing *that* crowd—but maybe the idea of something new wasn't completely off base. The way th'Esar'd gone about assembling it was all cockeyed, and if I was the first one to see him, Antoinette was gonna have to fight me for the honor of breaking his nose.

I was just gonna have to hope that I could still lead—that after all this time, I hadn't run out of juice.

"All right, men," I said, and Laure cleared her throat. "Troops," I amended, "we've got a bad situation here. Once we get the others rescued, we're gonna convene and see if we can't come to some kind of agreement on what to do next. If Ghislain runs into any trouble, we don't want him to be out there on his own, do we? When a man's flying solo, we've got his back. Ain't that right?"

"Yes, sir," Balfour and Luvander chorused.

Raphael, Gaeth, the cricket, and Laure all stared at them.

"What?" Luvander said, shrugging his shoulders in Raphael's direction. "It isn't *my* fault living among the Ke-Han has destroyed your discipline."

"Let's go," I said, taking point. Just once, Balfour could hang back while I took over position of lead scout.

Someone shoved into place right next to me—a small someone, but looking pretty fierce.

"You're all right, aren't you?" Laure demanded, studying the hall real carefully and not looking at me. If she wanted to ascertain the information for herself, an inspection would've been the smartest choice, but none of us was operating on all burners. "I mean, that Germaine—she didn't do anything to *you,* did she?"

"Nah," I said, shaking my head. Her hair was in her eyes, so I reached over and tucked a piece back behind her left ear. No good setting out on a mission with your visibility compromised. "Guess I'm just not important enough."

"That's not *funny,*" Laure said, then smacked me one on the shoulder. I didn't know who looked more shocked afterward that she'd done it—me or her.

"I'll make it up to you," I said, not bothering to rub my shoulder on account of how we both would've known it was horseshit. "Maybe we can get hot chocolate in one of them real places, not a booth where they're just as liable to sell you sweet brown water."

"Or dinner," Laure suggested, innocent as the country lamb she *wasn't*. "Since I'm missing mine to do this."

"If no one's injured, we move on," Luvander reminded us. I could've hit him myself. Only trouble was, he was completely right.

It wasn't exactly hard to follow Ghislain's trail. Just had to follow the open cell doors, down the simple corridor with its flickering light. To the credit of my new recruits, none of 'em was whispering or muttering anything or—like one poor bastard I'd known—giggling nonsensically every chance he got at things that weren't funny anyway.

We were gonna have to do all this quick, before anyone came to check up on us and realized right away shit wasn't right.

I rounded the first corner, followed by Laure, and nearly ran straight into Antoinette. At least I could be thankful it wasn't Ghislain. I had a hard head, but if anything could crack it, that would've been it.

"I was wondering what was taking you so long," Antoinette said. Her voice sounded a little different now that I was hearing it from outside rather than in. It made me feel like I had water caught in my ears, and I shook my head to wring 'em out.

"Had to wrangle the troops," I said, gesturing around behind me. It was gonna be like herding kittens; a couple of them actually *were* kittens, in my professional opinion.

"*That* one is wearing the uniform of the men who arrested me," Antoinette said, glaring around at Gaeth.

"I never arrested nobody," Gaeth insisted, eyes wide as the sky. "I was raised better than that by a *long* shot. That's the Provost's job, and no one else's."

"I don't suppose I can argue with that," Antoinette said, sharp, scarlet nails drawing a stray piece of hair away from her face.

"He says he's with us," I told her quickly. "He might not be in a cell, but he's a captive. I was hoping you could tell us whether or not he's lying."

Gaeth looked at Antoinette nervously. He had good

instincts—sharp enough to tell he was supposed to be afraid of her. "How's that done?" he asked.

"Just a little scratch," Antoinette said, though it was particularly gentle. "You'll barely notice it."

"If you draw blood, Cornflower's bound to come," Gaeth warned. "It's happened before, and it's never been pretty."

"'Cornflower'?" Antoinette repeated. "Does this boy think his prize *cow* is going to protect him?"

Stranger things had happened before, I thought, but it was time for me to intervene. "She's his dragon," I explained. "I guess we're just gonna have to take his word for it that he's gonna help us get out of here. You wouldn't go back on your word, now, would you, Gaeth?"

"No, sir," Gaeth said. "I'll do what I can."

"Just don't be rash," the cricket hissed. "First Laure, now you . . . I'm surrounded by foolhardy lunatics!"

"Is that Balfour?" asked another woman, standing just behind Antoinette. It was the one I'd seen in her cell earlier—Margrave Ginette. Under the bright lights she looked sickly, too pale. But then again, by my count, she'd been down there far longer than any of the rest of us. "I'm sorry I missed our appointment. I hope it didn't prove too detrimental. How are you feeling?"

"I should ask you the same question," Balfour said, under his breath, like he knew Antoinette and I weren't gonna approve of small talk.

Heavy footsteps sounded along the hall, and I turned around to see Ghislain and three others making their way toward us. One of them was the Wildgrave Ozanne, and one the Margrave Cirse, whom I recognized from a few parties Royston had thrown over the years. The third, of course, was the notorious Margrave Holt, who enjoyed breeding greyhounds—some said he enjoyed breeding them a little *too* much—but he looked normal enough.

Guess it was the normal-looking ones that always got you. Troius himself looked real respectable, right up until the minute he opened his fat yap and started blithering about his ambitions and dreams and sitting next to th'Esar on his throne so the two of them could play dragons all day long with their thumbs up their asses.

I was gonna enjoy spiking *those* plans, sure enough.

"Getting to be a regular army," Ghislain said, sliding the key rings onto his belt. "That's all of 'em. Where to next?"

"I need to speak with the Esarina," Antoinette said, once the newly freed captives had all come within earshot. "I'm told that Nico's scholarship students were a ruse, and that in reality, he's been using them to re-create his lost army of dragons. I'm not sure *how* he got the idea—someone must have given it to him; it's hardly his style to be so clever on his own—but he's violated the provisions that allowed him to build the dragons in the first place."

"You can't be serious," Wildgrave Ozanne said. "Surely he knows the Basquiat would never agree to such measures—and we have treaties in place with the Ke-Han, not to mention! Treaties we went to great pains to hammer out. If they learn we've done this behind their backs . . . Well, *I'm* not going back there for a second round!"

"We've seen the dragons," Luvander said. "Well, pieces of them, anyway. They're in a workroom upstairs, all laid out like clockwork."

"I've seen one completed," I told them. "And I was told there were three more finished up. Might as well get *that* detail out of the way first. They're little bigger than one of your hounds, Margrave Holt, and smaller than a full-grown man like Ghislain—but I'd say they're real enough. Although I haven't heard 'em talking out loud, and it seems like they've been bound to individuals somehow. That kind of magic's out of my league for explaining. I only know what I saw."

"There's Cornflower—she's mine," Gaeth said, sounding troubled. "And Ironjaw, who belongs to Troius. And then there are two more, but they haven't found masters yet. I heard from Cornflower that there's been trouble with the fourth. She picked someone, but they're trying to rewire her so she chooses somebody else. It ain't going so well, from the sounds of it."

"Cornflower," Luvander murmured. "How times have changed."

"It will hardly fit into rousing song," Raphael agreed.

"Hush," Antoinette told them. And, bless her, they actually listened.

"They approached me to help them," Ginette admitted. "I couldn't, in all good conscience—which is how I ended up here. They wouldn't tell me enough of their plan for me to be of any use, I'm afraid."

"It seems simple enough," Ozanne said. "Gather a private force, strike when the Basquiat's weak. There were so few magicians left after the plague, and many of them with useless Talents, for gardening and the like. Without adequate warning, I can only assume he'd have us cornered in no time."

"Which is why I think our best chance would be to speak with Esarina Anastasia," Antoinette repeated, folding her hands in front of her. "She's a sensible woman, and I believe she *will* listen if we plead our case. If the Esar's plan is truly that far along, then our options are few. And I, for one, do not want to see a bloody civil war in the streets over this, which will most certainly be what erupts if we are not *extremely* careful when we act. At the same time, we must act quickly, before the element of surprise is lost. We have to step lightly here, boys—and that means you especially," she added, with a glance in Ghislain's direction.

"That'll be easy," Ghislain said dryly. "No one'll even notice when we walk up to the palace and knock kindly on the front door."

"Permission to speak," Balfour said.

"Granted," I replied, knowing at least *he* wasn't one to waste precious time just to hear the sound of his own voice.

"I have reason to believe the workroom is connected to the palace," Balfour continued; he sounded slightly breathless, like he really hated talking in front of so many people, but he was gonna do it anyway. Good old Balfour. He really did have Steelballs—and while I wasn't the kind of man who took the credit for another man's developments, I did hope I was part of the reason for helping 'em grow. "I'm not certain what kind of opposition we'll face, or whether the passage

will be guarded, but it seemed quite abandoned when I . . .
It's what Margrave Germaine used to escort me from the palace to work on my hands. Margrave Germaine gave me
something, and it made my head unclear, but I don't believe
she counted on my expertise when it comes to memorizing
the lay of the land. I passed through this very hall to get to
the workroom up above; I'm sure of it."

"Ah, *Germaine*," Antoinette said, drawing out the syllables in a way that made me real glad I wasn't the woman in
question, or even a distant relative, for that matter. "We'll
want to deal with her as well, I imagine. Since she was so
eager to take the title of Margrave, then the Basquiat will try
her as one. We should call a meeting."

"Then it seems pretty clear, doesn't it?" Laure asked.
"Who's going where?"

"I think some of us should be going home," the cricket
muttered, but he didn't sound like he had hopes of it.

"Let the girl speak," Antoinette said sharply.

Laure coughed but looked pleased. "Thanks," she said,
straightening out her shoulders. "The way I see it is this:
Magicians go to the Basquiat to call that meeting, and the
rest of us take a delegation to the palace to speak with
th'Esarina. I'm assuming that'd be you," she added, nodding
at Antoinette, "since you're the only one here who knows her
by her first name."

Antoinette smiled, clapping Laure on the shoulder the
same way I would've done for one of my boys, coming back
from a successful raid. "It gives me hope to meet someone
like you," she said. Then, in clearer tones, she delineated the
plan, instructing her fellow magicians to head to the Basquiat at once. If they ran into any trouble, she was clear
enough about what they were to do—just obliterate it by any
means and worry about being called to task for it later. None
of them seemed ready to disagree with her, though Wildgrave Ozanne took a handkerchief from his pocket, dabbing
the hair at his temples, where sweat had begun to bead.

"I really do wish I could stop being arrested for no reason," he said.

Splitting up into two groups made me uncomfortable, but

it was a necessary measure. And knowing that the Basquiat was being gathered was a nice piece of backup. We just had to buy them some time—and since Roy'd done that for me, I figured I could do the same for him.

"Then we're ready," Antoinette said, as the other magicians slipped like shadows down the hall. "Balfour, lead the way."

"He always does," I replied.

CHAPTER FOURTEEN

LAURE

Toverre was wrapped up enough with making sure Gaeth was all right, and that left me free to cast glances at Adamo in the dark—just to make sure he wasn't trying to pull one over on us, telling everybody he was feeling okay when he wasn't. I wasn't the sort to pull a sneaky maneuver like trying to keep an eye on someone without him knowing it, but then I wasn't the sort to go inviting men to dinner, either. I imagined Toverre would have a thing or two to say about *that* once we were out of here, but for once it didn't matter to me what he thought. Or what anyone else thought, really.

For the time being, I was content enough to keep an eye on Adamo. There was being strong-willed, then there was getting your troops into trouble because of your stubbornness, and while I shouldn't've been thinking I needed to tell him how to do his job, I still had to make sure he was feeling all right.

At least he didn't seem to be limping or anything like that. The most I could pick out was that there was a cut on the back of his neck, real shallow, like he'd accidentally broken skin while scratching. If that was the extent of his injuries, then I guessed he was gonna make it, and I could turn my attention back to more important things—like focusing on where I was going, and maybe also what I was gonna do once we got there.

And I wasn't hearing anything anymore, so I could thank whoever was listening for the small favors they were finally granting me.

It'd started out quiet enough, back when we'd first come

down the stairs. I'd heard the voice before, too, though now that it'd disappeared, I wondered if I hadn't been overthinking things, spooked because of how creepy that workroom was, with all those scattered pieces.

It made me feel stupid once I realized what those metal parts'd been for—like I maybe should've thought of it earlier, only how could I have known? It wasn't like the Dragon Corps did parades through the countryside; everyone knew what the dragons were, but I'd never seen one up close, and definitely not enough to know what one would look like broken down into doll-size pieces.

Still, if I'd been smart enough to figure it out right away, then maybe I could've told Adamo sooner, and a big chunk of the mess we'd got into might've been outright avoided.

I hated feeling useless more than anything. It wriggled in deep under my skin and stuck there like milk thistles in cotton.

But if it made *me* mad, then I figured that was barely scraping the surface of what Adamo and the others must've felt like. I'd tried to come up with some kind of comparison, but the only one that even came close was if someone'd gone and dug up White Star, my first pony, from behind the barn. Most people would've told me the comparison was crazy—Toverre, for one—but the more I thought about it, the more it seemed to fit.

She'd been an old girl, but sweet as sugar and gentle as mother's milk when I'd first been learning to ride, and she'd been a fast racing horse in her day. The way I saw it, the only thing harder than saying good-bye to her in the first place would be if some rich neighbor who thought everything in the world belonged to *him,* including my da's property and everything on it, took it into his head to bring her back, just to ride her for fun.

Something like that was impossible, of course, and that was the difference between a beast made of machinery and one made of flesh and bone. But at the same time, I didn't think the two were as separate as most people would've liked to think. The dragons had definitely been alive to them that'd ridden them—I could tell by the way Luvander had

gone all silent, not to mention the way Adamo looked
gut-punched whenever he talked about the new ones.

Compared to that kind of suffering, thinking I'd heard a
few whispers seemed like a minor concern. Guess I felt a
little silly worrying about *myself* when the others had just as
much riding on what happened, and maybe more. I only
wished I could've had a chance to talk to Balfour a bit more
about whether or not he'd been hearing anything—since apparently he was my hearing-things buddy in all this mess,
and I'd noticed him looking around a couple of times like he
thought his mam was calling for him.

I was probably imagining it. Deep dungeons could do
something like that to a soldier, and with all we'd been
through, I supposed I wasn't as immune to flights of fancy as
I'd always thought. It wasn't as loud as it'd been during the
fever, and like I'd said, that workroom had been fucking
eerie. Not to mention we were traveling with a *velikaia* now.
I'd never met one before, but I knew they got right into your
head and stirred everything around like it was a pot of
mashed potatoes. It was possible that had something to do
with it. I sure didn't know how it worked—I just knew
enough not to trust that kind of magic for a second.

No one was saying anything, which made matters worse.
Even Toverre had fallen silent, giving up on telling Gaeth off
to trudge beside him in the dark, casting glances toward him
every so often just like I'd been doing with Adamo. Gaeth'd
been gone a long time; Toverre could've been worried about
his health or whether or not he'd been bathing properly. Either was likely, the latter even more than the former. But then
there was something else I recognized, part of the same concern I felt for Adamo that I'd never felt for Gaeth, though I
had been worried about him.

I didn't want to think about the meaning of that too closely,
and since there were more important things going on, I could
afford not to. We were all on edge, tense as nervous cats, and
while I'd assumed earlier that the corps's babbling was their
way of bleeding off extra energy, apparently they had another stage that came right after that, when a situation got
about as serious as it could.

As much as I'd wanted it before, I found I really didn't care for the silence.

"Ah," Gaeth said, the single syllable bouncing off the passage walls and echoing back at him. He looked nervous when everyone halted and rounded on him—we'd all been thinking we were under attack—but he held his ground all right. "I'm sorry. Didn't mean to interrupt our progress none, I just realized that I've been this way before."

"And?" Antoinette asked, keeping a rein on her impatience but only just. *She* was someone I would've liked to get to know a little better—the kind of person who seemed like she could teach me more than I'd ever learned at the 'Versity if she didn't decide one day that she didn't like me and scrambled my brains like eggs at breakfast. But now wasn't the time to think about that.

Toverre was scowling at her, but only because she'd snapped at Gaeth, and I knew her magic had to make him fighting-anxious.

"There's another tunnel," Gaeth explained, cutting through the group to stand at the front, with Toverre scurrying in his wake like he wasn't about to let him out of his sight for an instant. I didn't blame him. Gaeth was good at disappearing. "Should be right around here. They took me up it once with Cornflower, when I was supposed to meet th'Esar. We came out right in one of his audience chambers—*huge* room, that was. Big hole in the ceiling made of glass. I'd never seen anything like it, and Cornflower neither."

"Cornflower," Luvander repeated, shaking his head faintly. It seemed like he felt the need to remark on the name every time it was brought up. *I* didn't see what was so wrong with it. No need being stuck-up. "I'm sorry, I merely can't reconcile the name with the image in my head. If I get the chance to meet her, I think I'll be expecting a cow."

"I rather like it," Raphael murmured. At least he was making an effort to keep his voice down. "I mean, just think—if we'd been allowed to name our own dragons, there could be worse decisions than a simple flower theme."

"I can't even imagine what some of them might've come

up with," Luvander admitted with a sad nod. "'Titsmercy' would only have been the beginning."

"Would you boys have some fucking sense?" Adamo demanded. He turned to me and cleared his throat. "Pardon," he said.

"Just think of me like one of the boys," I suggested, not wanting any special treatment for any reason.

"Now, that might be difficult," Luvander said with a knowing wink.

"Here it is," Gaeth called in a reckless whisper, having trekked on ahead of us down the tunnel.

He pressed his hand against the wall, and I saw a flash of metal in his palm before the heavy grinding of stone sliding against stone filled my ears.

"Secret tunnel hidden in a secret passageway," Adamo snorted, low enough so that I was the only one who'd hear him. "What a piece of work. The man has an inflated sense of self-worth."

"He *is* th'Esar," I pointed out. "At least it's convenient for us since it'll take us right to him."

"What's that in your hand?" Toverre demanded, pulling at Gaeth's fingers so he could see his palm.

"Dunno what it's called," Gaeth admitted. He looked pretty uncomfortable—especially since Toverre hadn't exactly kept his curiosity quiet, and now everyone was craning around to get a look at what he'd seen. "It's what keeps me and Cornflower together, that's all I know. It means she's supposed to listen to me, even when she doesn't."

"I don't suppose it comes off?" Luvander asked, like he already knew the answer to that.

"No, sir," Gaeth said, shaking his head. "It's planted real good into the skin. Only way to take it off is cutting the hand off, and Cornflower wouldn't like that too much. So I expect they didn't want anyone else to have control of her—excepting th'Esar maybe, but even I ain't sure how he does that."

Far as I could tell, it was a circle of silver metal with a deep red jewel in the center. It looked clean enough, and the skin around it wasn't angry, but the sight of it still made me wince. I didn't like to think about how they'd gotten it in there in the first place, or how much it hurt at first. Poor Gaeth. I could just see Toverre doing his best to keep it polished, though, and came near to laughing despite myself.

"Interesting that Nico should take such an exception to the former Ke-Han emperor's use of blood magic, only to turn to it himself," Antoinette said, studying the jewel. "Or turn it *on* himself, as the case may be." The way she was looking at it reminded me of the way an owl studied a mouse—right before dinnertime.

All at once Gaeth drew in a sharp breath and tugged his hand out of Toverre's grip.

"What is it?" Toverre asked immediately. "Does it hurt?"

"I'm fine," Gaeth said, pressing a hand to his head, like he'd got one of them killer aches my da got, right between the eyes. "It's nothing; well, nothing bad. It's Cornflower. She knows I'm getting farther away, and it makes her restless."

"Can you talk to her?" Adamo asked, coming to the foreground. "Might come in handy if we turn out to need a little backup."

"I can tell her where we're going," Gaeth said, nodding after a minute. His whole body relaxed, so that it didn't look like he was in pain anymore. "Her pen—I mean, the room where they keep them; she doesn't take much to being cooped up like a barn animal—is right below this one. 'Course, if anything happens to me, she'll come running, whether or not we want her to."

"How convenient," Antoinette said. I knew that light in her eyes—she was busy adding everything up, the way Adamo was, making sure she was keeping each piece of the puzzle in mind before she made her next move.

"We should press on," Adamo said, casting a glance back through the tunnel. "Hate to be the one to remind everyone, but time isn't on our side."

"True enough," I said, tearing my eyes away from the jewel in the center. *Ke-Han blood magic,* Antoinette had said; just the sound of it made me feel dirty. That jewel was the same color as the vial of blood Germaine had taken from me. Same color as Gaeth's blood, too, I'd be willing to wager, since it probably *was* his blood.

Was this what Germaine'd been planning to do with me? When I thought about how close I'd come to being trapped underground there myself, I felt like my lungs were being crushed.

"I don't mind going first again," Balfour said, slipping into the tunnel pass.

"Only the two of us will go," Antoinette said, taking Balfour's arm. "The rest of you wait here."

"Now, don't be cruel," Luvander said. "We're not babes in arms. We're seasoned soldiers."

"So you know when to follow orders, don't you?" Antoinette asked. I glanced over at Adamo, who was chewing things over again.

"Antoinette's right," he said finally, making me feel proud. "If an attack comes, I'm betting it'll come through here. So we station our strongest men at the head of the pass, the rest of us standing behind them, and we buy Antoinette and Balfour some time to plead their case with th'Esarina."

"And for us?" Toverre asked, voice shaky.

"Heading back through the tunnel's too dangerous," Adamo replied. "Besides, you made it this far, didn't you? I won't send you away." He glanced at me, and I grinned at him, just to show him I planned on doing all right. So long as I was there, wasn't *nothing* that was gonna be allowed to touch him.

"Come," Antoinette said simply, taking Balfour by the hand. He seemed startled, and I didn't understand why, until I remembered all of a sudden what his hands were made of, and I guessed nobody ever had reason to touch them. Antoinette, to her credit, didn't even flinch.

Then, without any more talking, they disappeared into the tunnel.

Ghislain shifted out to the front, and Adamo followed him. I wanted to go with them, but I knew I'd serve everyone better if I flanked Toverre and protected him.

Staring at Adamo's back made me feel like I was a real part of the battalion. Nobody'd told me to step aside because

I wore skirts over my boots, not trousers. Da would've been proud to see me here—in his own way, after he asked me what in Regina's name I thought I was doing going against th'Esar like this—but more importantly, *I* was proud of me.

Gaeth stood on Toverre's other side, twitching around like Cornflower was probably talking to him.

I'd come *real* close to having a dragon in my head, I thought. I didn't know whether to feel relieved or like I'd missed out on something most people were too meek even to dream of.

Adamo held up his hand suddenly—I knew what it meant even without him having to say anything. Someone was coming.

A moment later, I heard it, too, the sound of feet against stone. Whether it was a few men or a whole damned army, we were ready for them. I swallowed and braced myself.

It was about damn time. All this dillydallying didn't make me too impressed with th'Esar's ability to protect his people. He was so twisted around, busy looking after his own hide, that he'd probably forgotten about everyone else. And considering the Dragon Corps had given their lives to protect him once upon a time, I wasn't too impressed with that kind of self-centered thinking.

I felt sharp fingernails digging into my arm, and I glanced over at Toverre. He was white as a ghost in the darkness, probably scared out of his mind. But he'd come all this way for me, and I was oddly grateful—not as grateful to him as I was to whoever'd decided to let me have Adamo and Ghislain on my side, but it was a different kind of gratitude.

He didn't have to be afraid. Gaeth and I were gonna protect him.

Then, all at once, the opposing force appeared.

They were dressed the same as Gaeth, and I sensed him tensing immediately. Ghislain and Adamo stood between us and them—and there was Luvander and Raphael, too, as the second force, with us as the last resort—but it was too cramped to tell how many of them there were, or get a good sense of our odds and their numbers. That worked in our favor, actually, since it meant they wouldn't be able to come at Ghislain or Adamo too many at a time, and I had a good feeling about whether or not they'd be able to pick off the opposition nice and easy, at a pace that suited them.

"Bastion," the man at the front said, slowing rather than leading the charge, so I knew straightaway what an asshole he was. "What kind of ragtag effort is this? You can't really think you have a chance, do you?"

"Hey there, Troius," Adamo said, like he was checking out dirt underneath his thumbnail. Whatever I'd been thinking about the man, Adamo clearly thought even less. "I was wondering when you'd show. Ain't polite to keep people waiting."

"You'll wish I had kept you waiting longer," Troius replied. "You don't really think you can stand against us? You know firsthand the damage we can do."

"Sure I do," Adamo replied. "And back when the dragons were in testing, and none of us first wave knew if they'd be with us or turn against us, we were prepared to stand against 'em then. They were a damn sight bigger in those days, too."

"I really had thought you'd join us," Troius said, sounding disappointed. "Did the offer not suit you? It gave you a real chance to be who you were again."

"Adamo knows who he is," I said, since none of his other boys seemed prepared to speak up. "But who the hell're you?"

"I'm depressed," Troius replied. "Sad that such a great man has been reduced to leading a depleted army—if it can even be called that—made up of women and children."

"Uh-huh," Ghislain grunted. "And where do you figure me into that?"

Troius didn't have time to answer the question, because Ghislain had struck out to break his nose—fast for a giant and ten times as strong as a regular man.

I recognized the sound from the number of stableboys back home who'd suffered the same fate at the hooves of one of Da's wilder horses. I cringed and Toverre cried out, hiding his face so he wouldn't have to see all the blood.

"Damn it!" Adamo shouted.

"Regina," Gaeth whispered. "That's no good."

"Are we hitting now?" Luvander asked, happily holding up his fists.

I stepped forward—because if it was gonna come to simple brawling, then we were gonna have to show some solidarity—but then the reason for Gaeth's distress became apparent as a metallic scream sounded out from below us. Not even a second later, the floor exploded.

I wondered if this was the way Royston's power manifested itself. Then I didn't have any more time for wondering, as out of the rubble burst a dragon. Smaller than I'd been expecting but no less beautiful. There were a few streaks of dirt on her here and there, and her face was half dog, half horse, with giant nostrils and a rooster's comb made of sharp steel pieces, but all in all she was pristine, the kind of craftsmanship that'd make everyone who knew what they were looking at feel weak in the knees.

"Bastion fuck," I said.

"Now you've done it," Troius added, sounding all wet and pissed from the blood. "Ironjaw! Attack them!"

"We're going to be killed," Toverre practically shrieked, ruining our stalwart moment. Everyone else was just too stunned to react.

At least there wasn't too much room down there for the dragon to maneuver. It took her too long to turn around, claws scraping at chunks of stone, shaking her tail out and nearly bowling over one of her allies. The time that bought us was all Adamo needed, howling at us like the Chief Sergeant he'd always been—even in the lecture room.

"Fall back!" he bellowed, and even Toverre hopped to like a trained soldier, all of us pressing back into the tunnel, where most of the advantage a beast like that had over us would be squandered.

Excepting, of course, if she had firepower.

Then, we were all cooked. Literally.

I was crowded behind Raphael and Luvander, who were, I realized, using their own bodies like shields for Toverre and Gaeth and me. They didn't have to do that, I wanted to tell them, though I'd already put myself between Toverre and the dragon, knowing how delicate his skin was. I guessed we were all just trying to protect each other.

But something was rumbling beneath my feet. An earthquake, I wondered, or the whole place being brought down on top of us from the impact as the dragon broke through foundations to protect Troius?

I was gonna have to stop wondering, because nothing I came up with ever got close to reality. It wasn't any earthquake, but a second dragon. I couldn't see it as well as the first, what with Ghislain blocking my view, but from what I could see, they weren't identical. The new one was patchier all over, made out of different metals, though I was no expert on what dragons were supposed to look like. If there were two dragons against us now, I thought darkly, then we didn't stand a chance.

"Don't worry," I heard Gaeth tell Toverre, as Toverre did his best not to be thrown down onto the dirty floor. "That's just Cornflower."

The second dragon was on *our* side, I realized. Or, at least that's what I thought Gaeth was saying.

Everyone scrambled to get out of her way as she clawed up from the ground like she thought she was a groundhog. There were parts of her that were silver, too, and parts that were another metal with kind of a blue sheen to it. If I hadn't known any better, I'd've assumed that was what'd given Gaeth the idea to name her Cornflower. As she oriented herself in the tunnel, facing our attacker, I could see that all the exposed gears under her belly and her arm and leg joints were bronze, and she had a sharper snout than Ironjaw, with the same enormous nostrils and rows of glittering silver teeth.

Then she lunged forward with a shriek that sounded like metal scraping on rock—or maybe she wasn't screaming, and what we were hearing was just her claws tearing through stone. Gaeth shouted, and Adamo pushed the group by using Ghislain as a shield, moving us clear back through the tunnel while I scrambled to see what was going on.

Cornflower, like any loyal animal worth her salt, had thrown herself in the way of danger, not letting anyone or anything threaten her master. I could see her tail whipping around, scraping at the tunnel walls and sending little showers of sparks and rock down around her. Ironjaw let out a growl and slashed out at her with those mean-looking claws, but Cornflower dodged the blow and held her ground. Likewise, Adamo was holding *our* ground, moving us just out of range of those razor-sharp tails as they whipped back and forth, driving the guards in green back same as us.

The lucky thing about the dragons being between us was it meant that slimy snake Troius couldn't get any closer to us than we could to him. We were trapped on either side of the dragon battle, and I could only hope that man's nose was hurting him something fierce.

Sparks showered up like fireworks around the tunnel as Ironjaw lunged at Cornflower, trying to dart past her. For the second time, Cornflower knocked her back, jaws snapping as she kept her opponent at bay. In a way—though I'd never say this to Toverre, since I could feel him trembling next to me—there was something beautiful about the way they fought, neither one giving quarter but both surging up at once, claws flying and metal gleaming.

Ironjaw rose up on her hind legs and Cornflower sprang at her throat, jaws seizing around the gears there and tugging at one of the cog pieces.

"Attagirl," I heard Adamo mutter, just ahead of me.

But the battle wasn't won, not by a long shot. Ironjaw was slapping at Cornflower with the sharp end of her tail, and it seemed to me like they were pretty much evenly matched, capable of tearing each other to pieces before the fight ended in a draw. I didn't know how much it must've cost to build 'em, but I knew how much of a loss it'd be if they destroyed one another. It didn't seem right to me to be pleased about it, just because of how ticked off th'Esar would be, after all the things he'd sacrificed—his honor chief among them—to build them in the first place.

I heard something else then, real close by, over the clang of metal meeting metal and Toverre's whimpering beside me. It was a funny whispering sound, the likes of which I'd heard before, but I'd never welcomed it. Balfour wasn't even with us anymore, so I couldn't sneak a glance sideways to see if he was twitching around like *he* was hearing things, too.

"Everyone get back," Gaeth said suddenly in a firm voice I'd never heard him use before. He'd already taken Toverre by the arm and started pulling—assuming rightly that he'd gone catatonic on us now that there was so much danger and dirt around. The rock dust was especially thick in the close tunnel air. To Toverre, it probably felt like the end of the world. "Ironjaw breathes fire, and Cornflower says she's about to—just get back!"

None of us asked how a dragon would know something like that.

"You heard the boy!" Adamo roared, tearing his eyes away from the fight and pushing the line back. Ghislain followed suit after a split second, though I could tell it almost killed him not to be watching, to say nothing of giving up more ground. But it wouldn't matter how much ground we held if we all ended up fried to a crisp.

Gaeth's warning hadn't come a moment too soon, either. As we were still scrambling to get clear of the battlefield, orange flames surged around all four walls of the tunnel; they licked hungrily along the stone and swallowed up my sight line of the two dragons. I felt like I'd stuck my head too close to the oven; I couldn't imagine what it must've felt like at the center of the blast, with the tunnel walls so tight and the ceiling so close it practically *was* an oven down there. We were still near enough to the center of action that it made my face feel hot, but I was behind Adamo, so I knew *I* wasn't in any danger.

If he let himself get singed, though, we'd be having some words. No amount of him taking me out to dinner was gonna make it all right for him to go and get hurt.

"*Oh,*" Raphael murmured, sounding like he was attending a meeting of the Brothers and Sisters of Regina, not boiling in the stewpot. "Isn't that just the most beautiful thing you've ever seen in your life?"

"Quiet," Adamo said. Privately—for the very first time—I almost agreed with Raphael. I could be in awe of something and not want it to kill me at the same time.

"I want you all to know that I consider it an honor to die at your sides," Toverre muttered, like he couldn't keep it down anymore. I didn't blame him, really. He'd tried as long as he could; some people just didn't have the stomach for fighting.

"No one's dying here," Gaeth said quietly, patting Toverre on the back. In the dimness of the tunnel, I thought I noticed something strange about his eyes. One of them looked darker than the other. "Don't write my Cornflower off just yet."

Just as he'd said that—like I really needed proof they were connected on the inside—I saw a blue-and-silver head protrude from the flames, which themselves were rapidly petering out. I guess we'd got lucky, and the dragons themselves had to be fireproof, or else what was the point?

Both girls looked singed in the aftermath, but it was the kind of thing that'd polish off in time—that was proof Toverre was rubbing off on me, if nothing else.

As soon as she was clear of the flames, Cornflower lunged again, and I heard something metal go flying, hitting the wall and falling to the ground of the tunnel. I couldn't tell who it'd come from, though, and neither of them seemed particularly injured. I guessed they didn't miss a cog or two the same way people missed limbs. Clearly pissing mad—I don't know how I knew, but I just *did*—Ironjaw whipped her tail around quick, scoring the walls and catching Cornflower across the face, though it only stunned her for a second.

"Deadlocked," Ghislain said, as Cornflower's sinewy body reared up to claw at Ironjaw, who was beating her small wings to try to fan what remained of the flames our way.

"You don't really think you can hide back there forever, do you?" Troius called, so I guess he hadn't choked on his blood *or* burned up. Our luck wasn't perfect, then. "Come, now. My reluctance to kill you right away may have spared you thus far, but do you really imagine that boy can square off against me?"

"Seems to me like he's doing all right," Adamo shouted back. "Seems like your girls are pretty evenly matched, actually, since we've seen that your fire's about as useful as a boat with no oars in this place."

Troius said something else—probably an idiot rejoinder

about how he thought he was only toying with us or some trash; I'd read it a thousand times in my da's old romans—but I couldn't hear him, because the whispering in my head'd just gotten a whole lot louder.

I know that smell, it said, in a woman's voice that reminded me a bit of Antoinette's, though it wasn't exactly the same, either. It was the voice I'd heard during my fever, but a whole lot clearer now, speaking words instead of babbling a whole lot of gibberish. *I've been waiting for you.*

All of a sudden, though I couldn't've said why, I felt like it was drawing nearer. Even though I knew the voice was inside my own noggin, trapped between my ears, I could feel whatever it was coming closer to me over the screech of metal and the sharp scrape of Ironjaw's wings against the cavern wall. I lifted my hands to my head, pushing my thumbs against the temples. Everybody was so busy watching the fight, they didn't notice me. And I was so busy trying to clear my head, I was the only person looking at the ground, which meant I was the one who got to see her first.

Past all the boots, something bright shifted underneath the rubble. I knew what it was before it poked its golden crown through the hole Cornflower had made. It was a dragon, with patches of silver steel around her snout, making her look like a doll that'd been sewn together from a bunch of separate parts. She lifted her head, questing about like a dog scenting its prey; Ironjaw and Cornflower were too busy with one another to pay any attention to her.

But that was okay, because she was too busy looking for something to pay any attention to *them.*

Then she looked straight at me.

At once I felt a roaring in my head, like I was being held under rushing water, and it was impossible to concentrate on anything else—not Raphael and Luvander standing tense in front of us, or Adamo shouting back and forth with Troius, or even the dragons locked in combat, jaws around each other's throats now like wolves going in for the slaughter.

You, said the voice, as the dragon pulled its way out of the hole, standing between us and the fight. *I really have been waiting.*

Toverre tugged at my sleeve. *He'd* noticed. But I shook him off because now wasn't the time, and *yeah,* I'd seen it. Did he think I was blind?

For me? I wondered.

Of course, the voice replied. *I like you. That foolish big man thinks he can call us all to him with* his *blood, but that's not how it works. I want you.*

Ironjaw knocked Cornflower back and metal grated against the tunnel wall, sending up sparks everywhere like we were in the middle of a forge. I didn't know what that damned dragon meant, or why she was talking to me, or if I could even do anything when I didn't have one of those handy circles in my palm like Gaeth did, but if this meant she was my dragon, then I had an obligation to help out.

Even if I didn't know what the fuck I was doing.

"Okay, so help us!" I bellowed, as loud as I could—almost as loud as Adamo managed during class when he caught some poor bastard napping.

Without blinking, the gold dragon whipped around, folding her wings in tight to make use of the small space and launching herself like a sleek, long missile right at Ironjaw's chest. She caught our enemy off-balance and sent Ironjaw over onto her back, giving Cornflower time to get up and shake just to see if anything crucial'd been knocked loose.

"No!" I heard Troius shout. He sounded pretty furious, which made me downright tickled. "This shouldn't be *possible.* The fail-safe—only the Esar should have control over her at this stage! How are you commanding her?"

"Guess you should've asked an expert, Troius," Adamo yelled back. "I could've told you—nothing's as contrary as a dragon!"

"Except maybe a woman," Luvander added, his eyes on my girl.

"You in charge of that one?" Ghislain asked; it took me a second to realize he was talking to me, but only because of how I was staring at the dragons battling it out in front of us. Two on one now; the odds were definitely in our favor, though Ironjaw was clearly the best trained of all three.

"Maybe," I said, which was as honest as I could get without betraying how out-of-my-mind piss-terrified I was.

My girl—if I could call her that—was screeching something fierce, beating her wings and scraping at the rock. All of a sudden it was real hard to tell who was winning and who was losing. I couldn't see Ironjaw anymore, and my heart was about pounding out of my chest when I felt another rumble in the earth—this one coming from somewhere behind us.

"Do they just keep popping up out of the ground like daisies in spring?" Raphael murmured. "If so, I would like one as well."

"Brace yourselves!" Adamo hollered, and everyone grabbed on to somebody else, since the walls didn't exactly seem safe at the minute. The very foundations were shaking with all the excitement, and if this kept up, then eventually the tunnel was gonna collapse around us, and it wouldn't matter who was on whose side when we were all caved in.

Moments later, with a horrible screeching sound like metal being shorn in two, another dragon burst through the ground in an explosive shower of gravel. Gaeth threw himself in front of Toverre, and Ghislain was shielding Luvander *and* Raphael at once, but I could still see—enough to realize that this dragon, too, looked different from the others. She was the dull color of old piping, and her wings looked half-finished, though that didn't seem to be hindering her progress any. She seemed to believe nothing should stop her, and so nothing did.

Oh, her, the voice in my head sighed. *What a show-off. Has to be finished quicker than the rest of us, and now here she is trying to steal all the glory.*

Is she on our side or not? I asked, fighting down the panic I felt.

Who knows? was the cryptic reply. *That's where the big man lives.*

Everyone froze, but the new girl didn't rush us. She didn't even so much as glance in our direction. Instead, with another screech, she launched herself up toward the ceiling, shearing through the rock with her thick iron claws in an attempt to barrel straight through. If she wasn't careful, she was gonna bring the whole tunnel down around us.

It didn't seem like she much cared.

Whatever was up above was more important to her than our little fight. I could see the dragons staring at her for a brief moment, pausing in their fight to wonder at her actions, same as the rest of us. Then they started up again, not distracted for too long.

"That's where th'Esar is," Gaeth said, turning his head to watch her, same as the rest of us.

"Shit," Adamo muttered, looking back toward our dragons. Cornflower and my gold beauty had Ironjaw pinned, and there were terrible tearing sounds coming from that direction; I saw a few silver gears go flying. It was like watching vultures tear apart a corpse.

Just pin her down, I said, feeling sorry all of a sudden. She was only following orders, trying to protect her man. Maybe she didn't know how wrongheaded he was.

Don't worry, my girl said. *I'll teach you to outwit pity.*

CHAPTER FIFTEEN

BALFOUR

The tunnel was a tight fit even for me; it was lucky that we'd decided that just the two of us should press on, since Ghislain would never have made it past the first turn.

We were traveling steeply upward, the rough stone snagging on my sleeves. Antoinette seemed unaffected though it was catching on her skirts, and I was surrounded by the noise of fabric ripping.

It was better than the alternative—the strange, sweet whispers of a distant voice, one I only half recognized. I tried to tell myself that it had been Antoinette calling out to us, but I knew that wasn't the case. There was nothing else it could be but the remains of the voices from the fever. At least now I knew what it was.

All further speculation could be saved for later. I was here to protect Antoinette—though I was certain she didn't need my help, if rumors and my own assessment were true—and help her make her case.

I knew the Esarina though Antoinette clearly knew her better than I did. She knew her well enough to call her by her given name; I was backup, there to snipe in fast and buy the main event some extra time should the negotiations turn to fighting. This was a job I knew well, almost as though I'd been born for it. It had a little to do with diplomacy and a little to do with flight-time reconnaissance—a humorous combination of those things that everyone told me I was suited, both of them as different as different as could be.

And the Esarina's given name being the inspiration, I

could only assume, for *my* dragon, was a strange turn of fate that didn't escape my notice.

"Keep your focus," Antoinette told me. She hadn't been reading my thoughts—that wasn't how a *velikaia*'s powers worked, at least to my understanding—but it was possible I was projecting. I was used to hiding my emotions at the diplomat's round table, but not when the pressure was so high, and this job reminded me more of being in the sky than being trapped in the bastion all day.

I found that source of calm within me and let my nerves go. When I'd been in the air, I liked to imagine bundling them up and throwing them over the side like a ship getting rid of deadweight. This was the same principle.

I was ready then, and Antoinette was satisfied.

Almost immediately after—I wondered somehow if she'd known—we came to a dead end.

"Here we are," Antoinette said simply, tracing the uneven lines on the stone wall with her palm. She was searching for a trigger of some sort, I realized, to open a secret door. It took her a few moments—the first time I'd seen her not know the answer straightaway—though she found it at last after kneeling on the stone and sliding her hand against a lump in the rock. We heard an agonizingly loud creak, then the wall shifted by a few inches, just enough for us to draw in our breaths and squeeze through.

I opened my mouth to offer to lead the way, but Antoinette was already pushing herself into the open space. An instant later, she'd made it through, leaving me to follow behind.

It wasn't sensible—I was there to scout ahead and be the first in the way of danger, presumably so she'd be the one to make it to the Esarina—but I didn't have much hope for my success if I were to argue with her. I was good at following another man's lead, and Antoinette must know her way around the palace better than I.

The secret passageway had led us into a quiet hall. I glanced over at Antoinette, who had a few streaks of black dirt across her dark face. Her expression could only be described as triumphant though she didn't waste time to share what heartening knowledge she had with me. Instead, she turned purposefully to the left, moving as silently as a shadow down the hall.

Again, I followed.

I was careful to keep my focus sharp, my attention on any sounds that would signal disaster. At any moment, we could easily run into a servant or a member of the Esar's personal guard. While Antoinette's presence in the household might not have surprised them, our appearance certainly would. We looked like tunnelers, Antoinette's skirts shredded and rock dust in our hair. When we passed by a brightly polished mirror, I saw that we looked like a pair of lunatics.

If the Esarina did not think us mad, then she would prove to be far more understanding than her husband, for whom presentation had always been a matter of importance.

We were currently traveling through the personal living quarters of the palace, I wagered—and because of that, there were fewer servants to disturb the sense of privacy and peace. However, it also meant I didn't recognize a single door or fork in the hallway, akin to flying blind through unfamiliar skies. Antoinette's knowledge of the place was key, though it made me uncomfortable not knowing how much longer it would take us or even where we were going.

Suddenly, Antoinette stopped in front of a simple door framed by two white tables. "It is late, and the Esarina will be in her study," she explained to me. Then, baffling me completely, she knocked gently on the door.

"You may enter," the Esarina's voice replied, muffled, from the other side.

I supposed it did make sense not to barge in on her—to follow rules of etiquette even though we were intruders in her home—but I marveled at Antoinette's calm demeanor as she smoothed her skirts out before entering the room.

The Esarina was indeed in her study at that late hour, as Antoinette had predicted. She was wearing a simple gown and few jewels, sitting in a window seat with a book on her lap. She was also blessedly alone.

"Close the door, Balfour," Antoinette suggested. I did as I was told.

The Esarina shut her book, making a loud noise in the quiet room. "What has happened?" she asked, not missing the state of our attire. "Is it an attack? My husband once said that you would come for me if Thremedon were to fall."

Antoinette made a pained sound. "Thremedon's under attack," she said bluntly, defying all rules of diplomacy that *I* had ever been taught, "but it's from His Highness this time, and not an outside source."

"I see," the Esarina replied. Her voice betrayed nothing—no worry, no shock. It was as tranquil as her face, which in turn registered no emotion. "What has he done?"

"He's rebuilt the dragons," I said; now that I'd found my voice, there was no time for timidity. "We've seen the pieces, and my fellow . . . ex–Chief Sergeant Adamo's seen the completed versions."

The Esarina lifted a hand to her mouth, bowing her head over her book. She wasn't wearing gloves, as she had been the last time I'd seen her, and I could see that her knuckles were red, as though she made a habit of wringing her hands. I understood that well enough. It was why I'd worn gloves, once—to hide that exact detail.

"I never dreamed he'd go this far," she said at last. "He spoke often, quite passionately, about what the Dragon Corps had meant to him and how he felt that it had been taken away by the circumstances of war, and . . . And by the airmen. Not that I believe he blamed you, necessarily, but I believe he always felt as though the reality never quite lived up to the dream. Their popularity was not his, nor their victories. Not really. But to accomplish all this in secret . . . How did he ever manage to hide their construction?"

"They're significantly smaller than the first dragons," Antoinette explained. "And Nico is gifted in secrecy. You must know that better than anyone."

I wondered if she was referring to something more personal between them—but if the Esarina took that meaning from Antoinette's words, they didn't seem to wound her as they might have wounded a lesser person.

"Still, to break our treaty with the Ke-Han, after all the

trouble we went to in order to get it signed in the first place . . . Did you have any idea what he was up to, Antoinette?" the Esarina asked, raising her head at last. "I know he confided in you more than he ever did in me."

"If I had, Anastasia, rest assured that I would not have allowed things to progress to the point of my arrest," Antoinette said almost wryly. "The facts are simple: Your husband has betrayed his country. You must know what would happen to Volstov if we were shown to be treaty-breakers. I, for one, do not wish my inaction to instigate another war."

"Nor I," the Esarina agreed.

Antoinette pressed on. "We have come to escort you to a place of safety until it can be decided how best to deal with Nico. I speak for the Basquiat when I say that your influence would be welcomed for dealing with the people."

"I must say, I never expected to hear such things from you," the Esarina said. "But then, I cannot imagine I would ever be prepared to hear such things from anyone." She still didn't seem particularly upset, but then I knew better than anyone what diplomatic training could do to help someone obscure her emotions. Surely the Esarina would have been rigidly coached—even more than her husband, so that she could appear soft and pleasing while the Esar appeared to be strong. "Do you believe we must depose my husband?"

"I do," Antoinette replied with a certainty in her voice I didn't share. I agreed with her assessment—but it wouldn't have been so easy for *me* to speak the final words.

"And you have come to take *me* to the Basquiat," the Esarina mused. "That must mean . . ."

"You are the figurehead under which our country must now unite," Antoinette said. "You are a member of royalty; the second-in-command in title. The people will respect your claim to the throne, and it will seem less like a petty rabble has deposed their Esar."

"I always imagined that if this day ever came, you would back Dmitri's claim to the throne," the Esarina said softly.

Antoinette smiled and gathered up the ruins of her skirts to perform a brief curtsy.

"My son is an excellent Provost," she explained. "Would

you have me remove him from that position? I do not imagine Thremedon could find his equal for a replacement, and soon he would be blamed for the lack of order in the streets. The people would resent him. Besides, this country has two rulers for this exact reason, does it not?"

"On its good days," the Esarina said, rising to her feet at last. She didn't seem to know what to do with her book, so I reached out to take it from her. "Thank you."

"You're welcome, Your Highness," I responded automatically. It didn't seem an appropriate response, given the gravity of the situation, and so I added, "I'm sorry." That, too, was weak, but at least the Esarina appeared to have already forgiven me for it.

"It is strange that we should meet here again, Balfour Vallet," the Esarina said. Up close she *did* look sad, but wistfully so, wearing the cryptic expression of a lone noblewoman in an oil painting. "If I am able in the future to write your mother again, I shall have to tell her how her son has proven a hero to his country twice over. Few young men are so remarkable these days."

"Few have such bad luck as I do, you mean," I said.

To be truthful, I was in awe of the Esarina's poise. She could have joined the corps on a raid and fit in perfectly with that measure of calm in the face of her world crumbling around her. Perhaps she'd always known, on some level, that it would come to this, and had been preparing mentally for quite some time. I didn't have enough intimate knowledge of her relationship with her husband to wager a guess, but her strength when presented with her duties was like the other side of the ha'penny to Antoinette's. They were very different women yet equally admirable.

Luvander in particular would have been delighted with certain key bits of gossip to which I'd accidentally been made privy, confirmation of Provost Dmitri's parentage prime among them. But even though I'd memorized every detail of this private meeting, I planned on keeping it just that way—private. It seemed the only decent thing to do.

"Here is your coat," Antoinette said, having gone to the

Esarina's wardrobe while we'd been speaking. She held it for the Esarina while she put it on and I felt my pulse quicken at the reality of what was about to happen. It was inevitable, and we'd been forced to choose this path; nevertheless, it was difficult to believe it. Even in the days when our girls had been going mad and refusing orders and everyone had been too scared to talk to their closest friends about it, we'd never considered rebelling outright against the Esar. We'd gone to him with our concerns—more like demands—but we'd always trusted him to answer them, no matter how mad we'd been that he was keeping secrets from us. This was an entirely different plan.

From this moment on, there was truly no turning back.

I faced Antoinette, meaning to ask her recommendation on the swiftest way out of the palace, when the quiet patter of some distant, gentle noise filled my ears, distracting me from my purpose. It sounded like muffled speech of the sort I heard most days coming from my upstairs neighbors when they chose to shout to one another across the apartment instead of moving from room to room.

"Do you hear that?" I asked in a hushed tone.

Antoinette went still as she listened, and the Esarina shook her head.

"I do not hear anything," she said, pulling the fabric of her coat more tightly around her. It was a beautiful piece of work, deep blue wool with a lining that looked as though it was made of some soft, white fur. I could tell it was the sort of thing Luvander's latest hats drew their inspiration from. Thinking of him drew my thoughts back into the present. I had to retain the hope that those Antoinette and I had abandoned in the tunnels were all right.

It would be especially cruel for Raphael to return from the dead only to end up buried beneath Thremedon after his homecoming—only I truly *couldn't* think about that, or else I'd go mad.

"I thought you might have heard my husband," the Esarina murmured. She didn't balk at speaking of him; she clearly wasn't superstitious enough to believe mentioning him would cause him to appear. I was not so lucky, and I examined the room once more, just to be certain.

"My apologies," I told her. "In my line of work, I've found it better to be safe than sorry."

"Best to get under way," Antoinette said, taking the lead by heading for the door. "Before we *all* start leaping at shadows."

I heard the whispering again when she pulled it open, but it was as inscrutable as a spring breeze, with no form or words that I could catch. The Esarina started after Antoinette, which left me to guard our perimeter from behind. It was a position to which I was unaccustomed, but it seemed most prudent to have the woman with the most knowledge of the palace leading the way, and me behind to keep the Esarina safe should anything threaten our progress.

We traveled to the end of the corridor and turned left, passing by a vaulted stone archway to pause in front of another room.

"The audience chamber has many passages leading to the palace exit," Antoinette explained, opening the door and ushering us in.

"I had guessed this was the way we would travel," the Esarina said.

The audience chamber was an eerie place in the dark, silvery light from the moon shining in through a round window set into the ceiling. Our footsteps were swallowed up by the heavy carpet, so that now I really couldn't ignore the constant whispering in my head. Slowly but surely it was taking shape, forming a language I hadn't recognized before because I'd been listening for speech, not the same word repeated haltingly over and over again.

Balfour, it was saying. Just my name. It wasn't even pronouncing it correctly, as though it was reading the foreign syllables off a sheet of paper.

I didn't know whether I was hallucinating, or if perhaps my fever had returned. Once we got to the Basquiat, I might be able to speak to someone about my problem; the magicians had a great deal of experience with fevers these days. There had to be someone who could help me.

We'd made it halfway across the room when two doors opened on either side of us, and the sound of boots against stone filled the air. I felt my heart leap into my throat, the way it had when Anastasia—the dragon and not the woman, as I now needed to make that distinction—had gone into a steep dive without giving me fair warning. Uniformed guards poured in from both directions; the light of the moon was enough for me to note that they were not dressed as the Esar's usual guards but rather in some formal attire I didn't recognize. Within seconds we were surrounded by men in green uniforms, that resembled very closely what the corps had once worn—epaulettes, tassels, and all. It actually made me irrationally furious to look at them, but now wasn't the time to let my anger get the better of me.

Antoinette drew the Esarina behind her and even bared her teeth. Covered in dirt and ash from the passage, she somehow looked more menacing—like a vengeful spirit that had clawed her way free of the grave.

"Not a *step* closer, any of you," Antoinette said in a tone that reminded me very much of Adamo's when he was pushed to the breaking point. "I am Lady Antoinette, and if you know that name, you know what I can do to the likes of you. If you value your lives—not to mention your minds, if they can be called such—you'll get out of my way."

"*Don't* move," said a voice from within the crowd. I recognized it all too well, but I was still hoping I was hallucinating *that* voice, too.

The men of the guard parted, revealing the Esar behind them. Much like the Esarina, he was dressed casually in simple clothing and his family rings, though there was nothing casual about his gaze as it flicked over the three of us.

There was a madness in his eyes, I realized. Something frenzied that he was only keeping in check by his enormous will. Surely he didn't think he could carry on this way? But then, presumably that was the problem: he believed himself capable when he no longer was. It was our duty—the Esarina's duty—to convince him of the truth. Barring that, it would be our duty to depose him.

"Hello, Antoinette," the Esar said, coming forward through the pathway his guard had opened up for him. "I suppose I shouldn't be surprised to see you. I told Troius he couldn't expect to hold you for long, but he seemed very confident. I suspect he knows what these men do not: that you need blood to work your little Talent. *Clever* bluff, as always. You're very frightening when you want to be. I might even have believed it myself, though I, of course, know better."

"I do not reason with madmen," Antoinette said, turning her face to the side. "Despite how long I have chosen to stay in Thremedon. Your words are wasted on me."

"Then I will speak to the Esarina," the Esar said. "Discover what lies you've poisoned her with. Imagine my mistress and my wife, conspiring together against me."

"It's happened to other men before," Antoinette said darkly. "With some success, even."

"And a member of my old Dragon Corps, I believe," the Esar added, glancing quickly at me. He still had a discerning eye; I would give him that. "It was only a matter of time before you turned against me. You loathed submitting your personal wills to a master. It's why, despite how useful your training was, I could never include you in my new plans."

"Oh, yes," Antoinette said. "It's so wise to surround yourself with agreeable lackeys rather than people willing to tell you when your plans are pigheaded and disastrous. That's how all good empires come to an end, you know."

"She always does this." The Esar sighed. "She says she will not speak to me, then offers her opinions despite her promise. I'm afraid there's no point in arguing, in any case. You know as well as I how this looks. It is my duty to arrest you as traitors to the crown. *Please* do not attempt to resist. I have more than the soldiers you see here at my disposal, and let me make it perfectly clear—the three of you are not their equal in combat."

If only Ghislain had been with me, I thought, then we could have made a proper distraction, while the Esarina and Antoinette used one of the secret tunnels as a getaway. But I was the only member of the Dragon Corps in the room, and

I still knew—because my years of training under Adamo would never leave me—that I had to defend my country, against all odds. Even if it had been just me and Anastasia left fighting over the Lapis capital, I would have done so until the bitter end. Did I consider myself too important to make the same sacrifice the other men had?

Of course not.

"I cannot allow that," I said. Antoinette and I had flanked the Esarina. At least I didn't have to consider myself alone in my efforts.

"Truly," the Esar said, "what do you believe you will accomplish?"

"What we have to accomplish," Antoinette replied.

"I would prefer to hear my wife say this," the Esar said. He took a step closer, and his guard followed suit, closing in on us from both sides. They were blocking all possible exits. I was going to have to make a dent in their ranks somehow, with no weapons, and the odds stacked against me. I only wished I'd been blessed with a more imposing build.

Nonetheless, if I could not *look* as intimidating as Ghislain, then I would have to *act* as intimidating. If I believed myself, perhaps I could convince a few others to believe me.

"We will do what we have to do," the Esarina complied. "They say you kidnapped *children* for this task."

"It was necessary," the Esar said.

"And the treaty with the Ke-Han?" the Esarina asked.

The Esar waved a heavily ringed hand. "Would you have *them* betray *us* first? These are my precautions."

"And these are mine," the Esarina replied.

The Esar sighed; he'd known all along it would come to this, as had we. Even Antoinette had given up reasoning with him. "Arrest them, if you would," he said. "They are too dangerous to allow them their liberty while they await trial."

I steeled myself—I wished I'd had the chance to hear the now-infamous song about me before I died—and saw Antoinette do the same. I didn't want to die with the guilt of implicating the Esarina on my conscience. I didn't want *her* to die because of our pleas for assistance.

Then, without any warning, the floor exploded beneath us.

Is it Royston? I wondered, as I did my best to pull the Esarina away from the epicenter. I placed myself between her and the blast, feeling little bits of stone cut into my back as shouting began among the guards. They didn't seem so well trained now that disaster had struck; they were running every which way, boots trampling anything that tried to stop them. I heard something that sounded like a cry of triumph, cut off abruptly in the rush of falling rock. The Esarina tripped over her skirts—I thought I heard her curse, though it could have been my imagination—then the voice in my head returned, louder than ever.

Balfour! it said. *At last!*

I was startled enough that, this time, it was the Esarina who kept *me* from falling.

We did stumble, my metal hands gripping her sleeve and tearing it as we kept ourselves from toppling over, and I was forced to turn around, to face the direction from which that voice had originated.

I found myself face-to-face with a metal snout, flared nostrils, and sharp teeth. The expression was a familiar one—its owner could have been related to my girl—but the craftsmanship revealed a different aesthetic. This *was* a dragon, unmistakably so, just smaller, as Adamo had warned us the new ones would be. Her jaw was made of darker-colored metal than the rest of her body, and some of her scales were a steely blue color. She looked ragtag but beautiful; her eyes were pale, jeweled orbs, staring straight into mine.

Who are you? I asked. It was only polite.

I don't know yet, she replied quite honestly. *But I think I hurt someone.*

I realized all at once that the shouting had stopped. Those members of the Esar's guard who hadn't fled were all cowering from the dragon, in a corner of the chamber far away from the fissure in the floor, and around a body lying still amidst the debris.

"My husband," the Esarina murmured. Somehow, despite the dragon between them, she hadn't been distracted from what—in her estimation—mattered more.

"Damn it, Nico," Antoinette said.

Neither of them moved to his side; they couldn't, as they had no reason to trust this beast wouldn't attack them the moment they moved. My mouth was dry, but I thought I was beginning to understand what had happened. Slowly, carefully, ready to pull back at a moment's notice, I reached out to close the distance between us, preparing to stroke the dragon's nose with my fingertips.

Then again, it wasn't as though I'd lose any natural part of my body if the dragon were to bite off my hand. She'd find it difficult to chew, at that.

What happened? I asked.

He was in the way, the dragon replied. *He called to me, but it wasn't strong enough. I like your smell better. You were in danger. I couldn't let anyone hurt you.*

I inched closer to her to get a better view of the other side of the room. The body sprawled across the floor did, indeed, belong to the Esar; whether he was dead or merely unconscious wasn't something I could determine from this distance, with my limited expertise.

It was an accident, the dragon explained. *I hit him with my tail. They keep us inside; no room to stretch. Our tails are too long for that. You aren't sad, are you? I didn't like him, but you creatures get so finicky when someone gets hurt. You should know better than anyone, we can* all *be rebuilt.*

As if to drive the point home, she sniffed gently at one of my fingers; or, at least, I felt hot air roll across my fingertips, singeing my gloves.

I was grateful for my training as an airman since I was certain that it was all that was currently keeping me together. I had priorities, but whether or not I could respect them would be a different story. There were actions an airman had to take in a situation like this one, and none of my options had anything to do with standing as still as my statue, staring at a dragon. Then again, no one had planned for these contingencies. Not even Adamo, and he'd been the chief strategist among us.

I have to check the Esar's body, I told the dragon, marveling at how strange it felt. Minutes ago, the Esar had almost certainly been willing to arrest and execute the three of us—his wife and mistress included—and now here I was in the unique position of checking whether or not he was even still alive.

But it was the right thing to do, whether or not he would have done it for us.

Why? the dragon asked, cocking her wide head curiously as I got to my feet. *You're safe now, I think. He won't get up. I hit him hard. It was an accident, but I'm not sorry.*

I know, I told her. *But if he's still breathing . . .*

I trailed off. Not because I didn't know what to say but because I honestly didn't know what would come after that.

He's not dead, the dragon said, peering up at me. *We'd stop working if he were.*

Why's that? I asked, curiosity getting the better of me for a moment.

We're tied to him by blood, the dragon explained. *Just a little. Not enough to wrangle me, but if he broke, then so would we. I think.*

I still have to check on him, I told her.

Even his guards don't seem very worried about that, the dragon said, swishing her tail thoughtfully.

They're scared, I explained.

Sissies, she replied, but she sounded pleased to know I believed they were scared *of her.*

The Esarina sucked in a breath, perhaps still anticipating some further attack. I was acting as though in a vacuum—I was still the only one who knew the dragon was on our side. Or at the very least, she seemed to be on *my* side. But it wasn't kind to keep this to myself any longer.

"It's all right," I said aloud, holding up a hand slowly, so as not to startle anyone. "She isn't going to hurt us. She came to find me."

Balfour! the dragon said, proudly. *I thought I'd bust a gear with all that waiting.*

I probably looked as though *I'd* busted a gear, attempting to have two separate conversations at once. Still, I did my best to apologize to her. *I didn't know you were looking for me,* I explained.

"This . . ." the Esarina faltered, not knowing what words to use. "This creature belongs to you?"

"I wouldn't put it like that, exactly," I said; everything had happened so quickly, I didn't want her to get the wrong idea.

Are you embarrassed of me? the dragon asked.

I wouldn't put it like that, exactly, I repeated, this time for her alone.

"It's one of Nico's dragons, Anastasia," Antoinette said. "Balfour looks as surprised by her appearance as the rest of us—if not more so."

She wasn't wrong about that, I thought. Skirting the edge of the hole my dragon had torn in the floor—while she watched me curiously, wondering why I cared—I knelt near the rubble half covering the Esar's body. His skin was pale, coated in dust from the white stone of the floor beneath the mangled carpet. His condition didn't look promising, but I steeled myself—there was that word again—and leaned in closer, with my head nearly up against his chest, to see if he was breathing. I could have checked his pulse, but I didn't want to trust something as crucial as the Esar's life to the particular sensitivities of my hands. Even after all this time, I was still getting used to them.

Antoinette started across the floor toward us, then stopped herself, standing just short of the dragon behind me. The Esarina herself hadn't budged but was as still as a statue, with her hands clasped tightly together.

A faint, guttural rasp filled my ears, and I felt the Esar's chest rise weakly, then fall.

"He's alive," I said, breathing a considerable sigh of relief myself.

"These damned dragons," Antoinette muttered. She didn't appear to be happy *or* sad about the news, just angry. "He couldn't leave well enough alone."

"We'll take him with us to the Basquiat," the Esarina said, her voice quiet but with an unmistakable undercurrent of iron. "Your healers can see to him, Antoinette."

"Of course," Antoinette said without hesitation. "I'll make arrangements at once."

Just as I was about to ask how we'd make it across Miranda with a dragon in tow—obviously, I could hardly leave her here unsupervised—the sound of shifting rock and dirt broke once more through the silence of the audience chamber.

If it was another dragon, I really didn't know what we'd do. Just one had already caused damage enough, though at the same time, we were all beholden to her for her help.

Antoinette took her place once more beside the Esarina, and I stayed crouched next to the Esar, tensed for whatever might next be thrown our way.

Don't worry, Balfour, the dragon said, apparently having sensed the sudden chill in the room. She hadn't tensed; in fact, it appeared to me as though she was inspecting one of her sharp claws. *It's only a friend. She's awfully cranky, sometimes, and rarely clever, but she means well.*

I barely had time to wonder what she meant by that before another dragon poked its head out of the hole. She was mostly gold, with patches of other metals soldered to her carapace; I barely had time to admire her before she'd squirmed her way into the room with us, followed by Laure, then Adamo, then the rest of our ragtag rescue team, like rabbits being smoked out of a warren. They looked very much the same as I felt— as though they'd been buried, then dug back up again like a dog's prized bone—but no one was missing, and everyone seemed to have their limbs all in the right place.

For a raid, Adamo always said, those were good statistics.

Last to exit the tunnel was the young man in the green uniform, whose name I seemed to have misplaced in the shuffle.

"I wondered if we'd be seeing you again soon," Antoinette said, not looking particularly shaken, though I saw her cast a sharp look over at the new dragon, her lips tight. After all the trouble that'd been caused for their sake, I understood the source of her animosity even if I didn't share it.

I checked the Esar again to make sure he was still breathing. If he was aware of anything that was currently happening, it wasn't apparent. I wondered if what I'd felt hadn't been his last breaths—but then I saw his chest rise and fall a second time. His breathing was shallow, but it was definitely there.

"More dragons," the Esarina murmured. "How many *are* there, exactly?"

"Four," Adamo grunted, looking around. "Appears as if we missed the battle."

"Got caught in one of our own," Ghislain explained.

"Just a small one," Luvander said.

"And we didn't do much," Raphael admitted.

"I told Cornflower to keep watch over the others in the tunnel," the young man in the green uniform explained. "I promised I'd go back for her soon, but we wanted to make sure everything was all right up here first. She'll let me know lightning-quick if anything goes wrong, but Ironjaw was in such a state after them two ganged up on her, and Troius didn't have so many men with him that it'd be a problem for my girl to take care of."

"Forgive me, but I understood so little of what you just said that I fear you might as well have been speaking a foreign language," the Esarina said, wringing her hands together. "And my husband is still in great need of medical care."

I saw Adamo looking around the room, noticing the Esar for the first time, then the guards cowering in the corner, then me and my vigil. My dragon, of course, he'd seen right away—that was one thing he was trying his best *not* to look at, which was a sentiment I could understand. It was difficult for me to look at her as well, but I didn't wish to give offense for a second time.

The rest of the group looked bone-tired. Even Ghislain wasn't standing as straight as he usually did, though that could have been attributed to all that crouching in the small tunnels. But how Raphael was still on his feet, I'd never know. Stubbornness had a great deal to do with it, I'd imagine. Even Laure, who'd been raring to go since the minute we'd learned of Adamo's arrest, looked like she was beginning to wind down.

What we all needed was a hot meal, an even hotter bath, and a good long rest. Sadly, at the minute, all those things seemed so remote as to be almost completely unattainable—far more extraordinary than a dragon.

"I think we'd better call a meeting," Antoinette said at last, brushing the stone dust off her skirts, "before any of this—or any of *those*"—she added, gesturing to the dragons—"gets out."

"Couldn't have said it better myself," Adamo agreed.

CHAPTER SIXTEEN

TOVERRE

Days ago—perhaps even hours ago, though I'd long since lost track of time and its passage—the idea of a clandestine meeting held within a secret chamber of the Basquiat would have delighted me to my core. *How marvelous* and *dangerous,* I would have thought. But a great deal had happened since then, and I was a changed man. I'd been given my marvels and my dangers, my clandestine meeting held within a secret chamber of the Basquiat, and I was ready to see the back side of all these things. Quite simply put, I was sick of them.

It hadn't helped my impression that, for the duration of said meeting, I was exhausted and itchy, not to mention *incredibly* filthy, and no one seemed to share my desperate need to pause the proceedings and take a bath. My own foulness was only a mite more distressing than everyone else's. There'd been no one at the meeting who wasn't caked with dirt and dust. At least our lives had no longer been in explicit danger—though it was difficult to believe even that after having seen what I had.

At least the Esar would not have the chance to arrest me just yet. I had real evidence now that I'd be too delicate for prison—especially if all prisons were so unhygienic.

At the meeting I'd placed myself strategically next to Gaeth, so I could lean on him whenever I began feeling drowsy—he was the cleanest of us all, somehow—and also so I could be certain that he wouldn't disappear once more in the gathered crowd. As soon as this impromptu assembly was over, I was going to have some *incredibly* sharp words with him regarding the etiquette and bad manners involved in leaving your friends high and dry. It seemed to me that the poor fellow really was as hopeless as I'd always imagined him to be; as someone of better standing, not to mention considerably more advanced in the world of knowledge, it was my responsibility to take him under my wing until further notice.

I didn't precisely relish the task, but neither was I dreading it as I might have, once.

We were fortunate Antoinette's hidden chambers were so large, since we'd somehow managed to squeeze so many people into them—Antoinette; the remaining airmen; the Esarina; Laure, Gaeth, and myself; and also Troius, though fortunately we had not attempted to squeeze the rest of his men *and* the Esar's personal guard in with us, as well.

The dragons—all four of them, or three and a half by Laure's count, after the damage done to Ironjaw—appeared to be put out when they'd been told to stay behind and out of sight, banished once more to the tunnels. They'd done terrible damage to the floor at first, forcing all owners to be *quite firm* with the beasts until they did as they were told and curled up, though some managed this with far less metallic rumbling than others.

Laure's in particular seemed to be difficult though I don't know why *that* ought to have surprised me. We were all merely lucky that Laure herself hadn't been born with claws that fierce.

At least the dragons were pleased to be given a job— guarding the guards, as it were, until such a time as we could decide what would be done with them. Because of lack of training, neither Laure nor the ex-airman Balfour could have remained in contact with them from such a distance, but Gaeth was able to, and so he kept tabs on them, telling us at intervals that all was still well and no daring idiot had attempted any mutinies just yet.

Troius, the short-tenured captain of his ill-fated platoon, had posed something of a problem since no one trusted him in the slightest. We'd brought him along as our personal prisoner; though Ironjaw was injured and wouldn't pose a threat with the others also guarding her, it was difficult to communicate with one another freely while he was still a wild card.

There'd been some question—from Professor Adamo in particular—about whether or not Troius should be brought along at all, but Antoinette and the Esarina both felt that it was necessary to include him because of his connection to the dragon. *He* certainly hadn't seemed to appreciate his place in the proceedings, but then he was tied to a chair, with Ghislain standing watch over him. I would have questioned my place if I were in his boots. There'd been dried blood all down his face, staining the front of his uniform, which was also caked in tunnel dirt. The sight of him made me ill; it was a sentiment that seemed to be shared by and large with everyone else in the room, however, though perhaps their reasoning was slightly different from mine.

Ghislain, for example, had looked as though he was just *waiting* for Troius to make his first escape attempt, so that Ghislain could break his nose all over again.

The Esarina—cleaner than Gaeth, I realized quickly, but I couldn't very well presume to stand by her—had appeared distracted, declining the seat offered to her in favor of pacing the room like a lonely ghost. No doubt she'd been concerned about her husband's condition; Antoinette had arranged for a few trusted healers to see to him in secret but I could tell from the way everyone had been acting that no one expected him to live, nor did they know what to do with him given *either* possible outcome.

There was something disturbingly poetic about the Esar having been done in by his own obsession, the very pride of his life that he'd sought to re-create—but I'd done my best to keep that thought private. While everyone else talked business, I'd done my best not to feel as though there were maggots and beetles and worms crawling all over me.

It proved very distracting—making it even more difficult for me to plead my case.

For, given the gravity of the situation, it seemed that the finest minds in the room had all come to the same conclusion. While the rest of us had still been scrabbling at straws, doing our best to make sense of what had already happened, they'd been looking to the future—trying to sort out what step to take next. Immediately it had become very clear to me that no one planned to let the secret of the dragons leave Antoinette's private room.

That realization had made me very uncomfortable indeed. How, I'd wondered, did they intend to swear us *all* to secrecy?

"We destroy the dragons and bury the evidence," Antoinette had suggested firmly. I appreciated that she wished to take charge and had been more than willing to go along with whatever she suggested.

Until, of course, Troius spoke up, giving us all a very grave piece of information. "I'll go mad if you do that," he said. From everyone's reaction, it was clear not too many people cared, and he quickly did his best to clarify his point. "Gaeth as well," he said. "It's possible that the others— Laure, was it? And Balfour—will suffer the same fate. Our blood has been mixed with the dragonsouls. If you break them, our minds will be broken."

I felt a slim shiver of outrage, at which point Luvander gently cleared his throat.

"I don't believe we should destroy them even if such difficulties hadn't presented themselves," he said. "It would be akin to murdering all the witnesses. Unless that is what you intend, in which case, let me inform you, it is a difficult task to slit *my* throat."

"The Ke-Han can't learn of them," Antoinette countered. "Nor any other country, for that matter. They would all take arms against us—the Ke-Han for violating the terms of the treaty, and Arlemagne in particular would assume we intend expansion. We'd make enemies of them, not allies. Do you really want more war?"

"But you can't very well just do that to Gaeth," I said hotly.

Troius cleared his throat. "Nor to the other one, I suppose. And to take that risk with Laure and Balfour—why, we'd be acting no more humanely than the Esar!"

"Nice one," Laure muttered to me under her breath—just like she thought we were whispering together in class.

"Thanks," Gaeth added, scratching the back of his head.

"Don't want to go crazy. Not any more'n I already have, anyway."

"Well, then," Antoinette said, and I felt singled out, like a cutup during a lecture. "What do *you* suggest we do, little man?"

Adamo snorted—I realized it was to cover up a laugh—and with everyone staring at me, and me looking dirtier than one of my father's pigs, I felt very miserable indeed. It wasn't my place to decide these things, I thought. But then again, someone had to do it.

"We'll just have to keep 'em secret, I guess," Laure said, speaking up in my place and rescuing me, as always. "If killing 'em's so bad and we can't let anybody know about 'em either, then that's the only way."

"That won't be easy," Antoinette said.

"With all those guards acting as witness?" Adamo asked. "I don't like our odds. It'll leak, and sooner than later, by my thinking."

"Well," Antoinette murmured very demurely. "I would of course be able to take care of them."

The Esarina stopped her pacing, and we were all drawn to her without her even needing to clear her throat for our attention. Though she was a slim, pale woman, there was something about her that to me indicated vast reserves of strength. "Toying with the minds of others?" she asked. "Erasing information because to us it is inconvenient? This sounds more and more like my husband's reign. And if he is unable to rule after this—and if I am indeed to take his place—that is not the way I would wish to begin. Just because someone else would be doing the dirty work for me, I would not find it easy to turn a blind eye. His Highness used many of his subjects as pawns during the war—Caius Greylace, for example—and I was always distraught that he would play so casually with the lives of others."

"It would be but one memory," Antoinette said, I suspected more gently than she was wont to be. "I would turn it into a shared dream. I would not hurt them, nor would I drive them mad. And the little Greylace now lives quite comfortably in the country, I'm told. More comfortably than *us,* at present."

The Esarina pursed her lips. "And what of this merry band?" she asked finally, with a hint of humor so faint it nearly passed over all our heads.

"I rather enjoyed this experience," Raphael admitted. "I would prefer it if I was allowed to keep the memory."

"The ex-airmen have always been trustworthy," Antoinette said. "Despite how they may behave. And the girl and the boy attached to the dragons can't very well forget about this, now can they?"

That just left me, I thought with a gulp, glancing around as everyone's eyes were drawn to me. Once again, it was Laure to my rescue, as both she and Gaeth stepped closer—as though they were *my* private Dragon Guard.

"I'll see what I am able to do," Antoinette conceded at last. "There may be something I can manage, allowing you to retain your memories yet rendering you unable to speak of this to anyone outside this room. How does that sound?"

"Just great," Adamo replied, in a tone of voice that made it very clear he meant the opposite. It was, however, our best option. As though we were hammering out the terms of our own private treaty, we were forced to make compromises. I was merely glad not to be singled out as the only useless— and expendable—fool there. "Guess it'll be good for my friend Troius over here," Adamo added, after a moment's thought. "'Cause even though I'm planning on watching him day and night 'til one of us dies of old age, I'm also planning on getting some shut-eye, some of the time."

"And what of the dragons?" the Esarina asked shrewdly.

"We wouldn't let the dragons rust," Antoinette replied carefully.

"And you'd *likely* need someone to be Chief Sergeant," Luvander added, glancing at Professor Adamo. "I don't think he enjoys the kind of teaching with which he's currently saddled. But I also don't think."

"Did I ask you to do me any favors?" Adamo asked.

"Not at all," Luvander replied cheerfully.

"I'd feel better with Adamo in charge," Laure spoke up, adding her weight to the scales. "Not that I'm sure whether or not we're planning on becoming *soldiers* or anything that'd *need* a Chief Sergeant, but it seems to me he knows a lot about the dragons. And we're gonna need someone like that."

"I would like to propose a compromise," Antoinette said, with a glance toward the Esarina. "That Adamo and I share equal responsibility in this matter. Not that this is a comment on your abilities to work alone, Adamo, and I hope you aren't offended. But as far as I know, you are no magician. The dragonsouls themselves require someone of Talent to fully understand them—and as I plan on handling the situation with Margrave Germaine *personally,* what we do next will benefit, I believe, from someone with my expertise. It will also help," she added pointedly, "to have someone with whom you are able to share the blame."

"Bleak outlook," Laure murmured, shaking her head.

"Joint Chief Sergeants, huh?" Adamo said, looking uncomfortable but dead certain at the same time. "Well, I can't say it'd harm my ego any. Not to mention, if something goes wrong, two heads are a lot better than one."

"What do you plan on telling the rest of the Basquiat?" the Esarina asked. It seemed that instead of allowing her husband's condition to distract her, she was using her worry as motivation to think—and behave—like a ruler in his stead. I wondered what I would do if Laure was injured so gravely; I would never be able to go on with such grace or dignity. "I hardly think you can trust every Margrave to keep his or her mouth shut—you know how Volstov loves gossip—and you couldn't use the same trick with them as you plan to use on us, surely."

"It'd take a dangerous woman to do all that," Ghislain said appreciatively.

"No," Antoinette said, shaking her head. "There are too many strong minds within the Basquiat—some of them *quite* stubborn, while others have trained to withstand mental attacks. I would not be able to carry out such a feat, even if I wished to—which, I assure you, I do not."

The Esarina's voice was wry. "I assume you have some other plan?" she asked, wringing her hands.

"What I propose is this," Antoinette continued, as though

she'd been expecting that lead-in. "No one has seen these dragons save for us and the Margrave Germaine. Thus, we will tell the Basquiat in strictest confidence that the Esar, with Germaine's assistance, was *planning* on rebuilding the Dragon Corps. That was why he had the students, that was why he made the arrests—and Margrave Ginette is our proof that he was asking other magicians to help him. But none of our fellow arrested magicians ever saw the dragons for themselves; thus, they have no way of knowing how far the plan progressed. As such, no one outside this room ever needs to know that particular detail. And no one *will,* for that matter."

Since it was a solution that didn't involve any further minds being wiped clean—which was a sentiment about which I ultimately found myself unexpectedly calm; certainly, there were aspects of the night I might have been more comfortable forgetting—no one seemed to have any objections.

"Ah," Balfour said suddenly. He looked somewhat startled by the sound of his own voice, but he didn't let that stop him. "We'll have to come up with something to tell the envoy from Arlemagne as well. Both Troius and I were dealing with them . . . before."

"You'll never keep it under wraps," Troius added, reminding us all he was still in the room. "These glorious creations were made to be seen by everyone. They are Volstov's pride and joy."

"No one outside the Basquiat hears even a *whisper* of the word 'dragon,'" Antoinette warned after hushing him. "I imagine that I've been very clear on this point already, but if the Ke-Han were to receive word that there were now *four* new dragons in Volstov, then it will matter very little that none of us *knew* about them in time to halt proceedings. We'll tell the Arlemagnians—not to mention everyone else—that Nico sustained his injuries in an earthquake. Our mutual friend Margrave Royston set the precedent for that to seem plausible, I believe."

"Good old Royston," Adamo said, shaking his head in disbelief. "Never thought I'd be the one getting *him* mixed up in politics."

"You're a terrible influence on us all," Luvander agreed, crossing his arms. "All I wanted was to run my haberdashery in peace."

"Horseshit," Ghislain said, eloquently.

"Where does that leave us?" the Esarina said, gently cutting in before the conversation could become too lively.

"Where does that leave us?" Laure added, echoing the Esarina's words with a more personal touch. Unlike me, she didn't seem embarrassed when everyone turned to look at her. "What I mean is, since the Esar's scholarship program was all just some big ruse to get young bodies who didn't know any better out of the country and test 'em for the dragons, it's not like that program's gonna last now that he's not . . . *You* know what I'm saying. So what do the rest of us do? I don't know about Gaeth, but my da's certain to notice a great dragon following me about, and it's not like I could keep her in the barn. She'd frighten the horses. Maybe burn the whole thing down. And she wouldn't even be happy."

"Obviously, the dragons will have to be kept underground, as they were before," Antoinette replied. "As for the children, I see no reason why they cannot be allowed to continue their education—if that meets with your requirements, Anastasia."

"It does," the Esarina confirmed. "I intend to continue that precedent, in the spirit in which it *should have been* intended."

"Can I say something?" Gaeth asked. Antoinette nodded curtly at him to go on. "I don't mean to interrupt anyone while they're talking and all, but I've spent a long time with Cornflower now. I know you all were talking before about Adamo and his experience, and that seemed to me that something was gonna be done different. And, well, I figure no one else has really had the experience I had, because I was there with 'em while they were kept locked up as a secret, and I know how it made 'em feel. It makes 'em real unhappy. Cornflower was always miserable, with no room to stretch her tail or anything. I know everyone's real concerned about keeping them under wraps and not starting any wars and that it's the most important thing and all, but . . . Well, I just *don't* think it's right to lock 'em back up again."

"The dragon I had dealings with—my dragon—did exhibit a certain jubilation at having enough room to move around at last," Balfour admitted, causing Gaeth to look gratified that someone was agreeing with him. I felt curiously pleased. "Perhaps if we merely moved them somewhere outside the city, where they might be able to stretch their wings? Some of us could even stay with them—though that's easy for me to say, isn't it? It's not as though I have any particular ties to my apartment. Especially considering the noise . . ."

"They'd like that," Gaeth said. "A little fresh air. *I'd* like that, too. Gets musty belowground. It ain't decent."

Antoinette was looking at Gaeth sharply, in a way that I could tell made him somewhat nervous. Despite feeling filthy and exhausted, I stood up straight beside him, so that Antoinette would know that this was a team effort. Laure and I were there for him, even if one of us proved far more useful in such situations than the other. I was simply there to raise the appearance of greater numbers.

"There is an estate to the west of Thremedon," Antoinette said finally, looking somewhat reluctant. It was clear to me how quickly her mind must have been at work, faster than any machine. "It passed into my possession from the Greylaces, and since I conduct my business within the city itself, I've never had cause to use it. The property is extremely isolated—something the Greylaces no doubt found highly amusing, but I've never been one for all that. Needless to say, the house and its grounds are *more* than large enough for a few dragons, not to mention any dragon handlers who might have trouble letting the animals out of their sight. Does this suit your needs? I imagine at least one person would have to stay there at all times in order to keep an eye on our friend Troius."

"Truly, I don't deserve such kindness," Troius said, voice dripping with sarcasm.

"House arrest, huh?" Adamo said, brightening perceptibly. "What do you say, Ghislain?"

"Big house filled with dragons? Sounds familiar," Ghislain replied, cracking his knuckles while eyeing Troius meaningfully. "Guess my boat *does* need some time to air out. Raphael'd have to come along, too. Needs the rest. Country air's good for a man; it's what I was raised on."

"Wonderful," Antoinette said, smoothing her hair back from her face, neatly tucking behind one ear a curl of hair that had been bothering me for at least fifteen minutes. *At last,* I thought, and breathed a sigh of relief. "If no one else has any other concerns to raise, I'd like to suggest we retire for the morning. I, for one, have a great deal of work to do."

"I would like to be able to see my husband," the Esarina added.

The meeting was over at last, I realized, which meant a hot bath was only moments away. Though much had changed, for the time being at least, Laure, Gaeth, and I would not be forced to return to our homes—to the way things were—which, for me, would have been the worst possible ending.

Despite all that had transpired, I was still able to say I preferred this life to the one I had been living before the fateful day I arrived in the city. I had nearly been robbed; I had been assaulted by living conditions far below even the dirtiest urchin's standards; I had been involved in a royal plot against the Basquiat magicians, not to mention the effective usurpation of the throne of Volstov; and, though I felt as though I would never be clean again, I had survived every indignity with only some indignation of my own.

Besides, without me, who would make sure Gaeth did not get himself lost again?

As Laure moved to follow Adamo out of the room, I had a premonition that explaining the dragons to my father would have been the *least* of my worries if I was ever to return to my old home. But I had a good feeling I simply wasn't going to allow that to happen.

ADAMO

After our little secret meeting broke up, everyone'd gone their separate ways to prepare for another long day ahead. Some of us had more work to do than others, and I knew we were gonna be meeting again soon so Antoinette could do what she needed to do to make sure we all kept our mouths shut. Even those of us she could trust to hold our tongues were suspect, and there were some of us she couldn't trust at all.

As much as I wished I could've gone back with my boys, I'd decided to take care of a few things at the 'Versity first, and so I'd ended up walking the kids back to their dorms.

The screwy cricket'd almost passed out on his feet, but Gaeth had claimed he could take care of him and I wasn't one to argue when one of my boys told me he could do something.

Guessed that was how I was going to have to start thinking about him, too—Gaeth *and* Laure, since I'd somehow signed myself up for a second round of Chief Sergeanting faster than you could blink an eye. That was what I got for having secret meetings in the first place, on no sleep, in the middle of the Basquiat. Some things were said without you realizing, and the next thing you knew, you were signing yourself up for the same job that'd given you so much damn grief in the past. I could look forward to singed gloves and the stench of dragonmetal hanging over my clothing; the complaints from Royston that I smelled like a burned-out pot someone'd left on the oven too long. I could also look forward to the same headaches I used to go to sleep with—the same headaches I still had when I woke in the morning, wrangling personalities more stubborn and difficult than dragons themselves.

At least there were less of 'em to work with this time, even if I couldn't quite convince myself that was a good thing.

Laure hadn't seemed that tired, but I could tell it was all will and nerves keeping her awake, same as what'd kept my boys awake during the longest of the late raids, when we'd been hauling ass to race the sunrise back to Thremedon and our soft beds. I'd been able to tell she was chewing on something, trying to come up with the best way to spit it out, and I hadn't wanted to interrupt her, so mostly we'd been walking in silence, past the Whitstone Road and onto 'Versity Stretch itself. It wasn't a half-bad situation, since it'd given me time to try to sort out a few things, too.

Basically, I didn't know how appropriate it was gonna be to take one of my corps out to dinner. For obvious reasons, the situation'd never quite come up before, and I was getting caught on *that* more than I had been on the idea that she'd been my student.

Although that was a sticky little piece of work, and there was no getting around it, either. Roy was gonna have himself a field day no matter what happened, plain and simple. Not that I was planning on letting what Roy said stop me. If I ever let myself go down that road, then I'd never get the chance to do anything fun.

Speaking of Roy, I'd've thought the cricket might've been more like him—talking endlessly no matter how tired he was, just to let the sound of his own voice keep him awake—but somehow he stayed quiet, which I guessed more than anything was a sign of how weary we all were.

It'd been a long twenty-four hours. Not the longest in my life, but closest to. And maybe, just maybe, it'd been the weirdest.

Finally, halfway down 'Versity Stretch, Laure'd cleared her throat.

I almost twitted her about needing a lozenge, but I figured that kind of thing was best saved for another time. "Something to say?" I'd asked instead.

I'd always been better at readying a strategy once I knew exactly the mess I was riding headlong into.

"Just thinking," Laure'd said, puffing her cheeks and blowing out air like a horse. "I feel a little stupid, getting duped like that by th'Esar. Not to mention I've gotta come up with some way of telling my da that I'm staying in Thremedon for good—sure can't go home and leave that beauty here all on her own. Don't think she'd even let me, and like I said, I couldn't keep her in the barn, now could I?"

"Doesn't seem right," I'd agreed.

"So that leaves me in a tight place," she'd explained, glancing over at our walking companions to make sure they weren't paying attention, but they'd been pretty wrapped up in their own thoughts. I'd known right then I was gonna have more trouble with Gaeth than I was gonna have with Laure. Balfour'd be easy 'cause we each already knew how the other one worked, and, in my own way, I was gonna enjoy rebuilding the shit job that was Troius, watching him cry like a baby until he finally manned up. No one wanted to start th'Esarina's reign with more useless killing, and it wasn't as if the poor bastard was evil—he was riddled with ambition and questionable morals, the same way some people carried infectious diseases. It was only a matter of finding him the cure for his stupid ideas. Then I'm sure we'd get along just great, so long as I made sure to have eyes in the back of my head and watch him like an owl watching a barn mouse. Even though none of us had what you might call warm feelings toward the bastard, nobody wanted him to end up as a brainless maniac. That was part of the reason we were having Ironjaw rebuilt; Troius knew it, and I figured that was most of what would be keeping him in line at the Greylace manor. He was the type of man who'd make himself useful in the long run—if I could get him to pull his head out of his ass long enough to see sense.

"At least you've got a place here now," I'd tried to reassure her. "No one else can fill that position but you. Don't think about it like you can't go home. Look at it this way, instead: You're needed in the city. Not many people can say that."

"Also, you owe me a square meal," Laure'd said, giving me one of those sideways looks that women were always giving Roy, poor hopeless chickens. I hadn't even known Laure was *capable* of that kinda look, considering how straightforward she'd always been.

Didn't much mind seeing her use it, though. It wasn't all guile, just an attack from the side route, like I'd been lecturing about a few weeks back.

"Do I strike you as the kind of man to go back on a deal?" I'd asked. I didn't even have to fake sounding put out, since I was still thrown off my kilter by that look.

Magoughin had always said there was something dangerous about a pair of green eyes. It was a shame I couldn't tell that horse's ass how right he'd turned out to be.

"Guess not. I have to sort a few things out a little first," Laure'd concluded, sucking it up and taking it like the perfect soldier.

Yeah, I'd thought. We were gonna get along great.

I even told her as much—private, so Gaeth wouldn't hear it. It was something I'd never even said to one of my boys because they'd all needed *less* encouragement, not more, when they'd come to me.

"Looking forward to working with you," I'd said, then we'd shaken hands on it. There was something about the way she'd held my hand that suggested she might've been interested in a friendlier kind of good-bye, but whatever else I was, I'd never been the sort to go carrying on in the street where you didn't know who was watching. Call me old-fashioned, but some things just belonged behind closed doors where a man couldn't get arrested for it. And besides, I was giving her the same respect as a commanding officer gave a soldier who'd done a job right. Anyway, she was grinning when I'd left her, so I figured she didn't take it the wrong way. It was a first step. And if it turned out we ended up getting more familiar with each other up at the Greylaces' estate, Royston was *never* gonna let up on riding me.

After that, I'd gone back to my office. It was still so early in the morning that there was hardly anybody up; classes wouldn't start for a while yet, and Radomir wouldn't be coming for at least an hour. Maybe, if he'd heard about my arrest, he'd decide to take the day off.

I just had a few things to get in order—not that I'd ever seen fit to spruce the place up or bring anything of my own in, but there were essays and excuse notes and that kind of thing scattered all over the place. I gathered 'em all together and put 'em in a heap for Radomir to sort through, or whatever poor, hapless, miserable bastard inherited *this* job from me now that I was finished with it.

The semester wasn't over yet, so I signed a piece of paper that said I was quitting, and for all I cared my donkey-brained assistant Radomir could be in charge from now on. As far as I was concerned, he could teach the students any way he liked—that is, if there was anyone in the world able to teach 'em anything, now that the only one who was worth her salt probably wasn't going to be attending classes anymore. That alone took away all my reason for staying.

Then, because there wasn't anyone in the world who could fire me now and I'd held it in for too long, I added, *If you want a bunch of half-wits scoring high on essays and going through life thinking they know something, that is. We'd better hope, if there's another war someday, these piss-pants aren't involved with any of the decision-making. And if they are, I ain't fighting.* Then I signed it *ex–Chief Sergeant Owen Adamo,* and left it on my desk.

It felt good, 'cause I was officially free. I'd suffered through this horseshit way too long to respect myself, but I was gonna have to get some of my dignity back now if I wanted to do this job, this *real* job, that actually meant something to me.

Why'd I even put up with this in the first place? I wondered. I guessed I'd been missing my girl so much that I'd figured there wasn't anything I could do that was better, and my life the way I liked it had ended right there in the lapis city, on the other side of the Cobalt Mountains.

I wasn't the sort of man who liked taking pleasure out of other people's misfortunes. It was why I hadn't joined in on all the parades in the streets, whooping it up 'cause the enemy was beat. Now that so many people'd been hurt and so many lives'd been changed just to get these new dragons off the worktable, it was wrong of me to feel so bastion-damn elated.

I guessed I'd have to deal with judgment later, when I finally went to meet my maker.

But I still had one more thing that it was up to *me* to deal with. It was something that wasn't easy for any man, but especially not for me, since I couldn't remember a time when I'd done it.

I reached Royston's place in the Crescents at a little past nine, judging from the sound of city bells pealing in the distance. When I knocked on the door, I knew he wouldn't answer; he was the kind of man who stayed in bed until at least eleven, even when he had a coffee appointment with another man—the sort who was always punctual—at ten thirty.

Hal answered the door, looking tired and worried. He looked more worried when he saw me because I hadn't even bothered to clean up before coming over, and that was wrong of me. I just had to do all this while I was still feeling it, or else I'd never get the balls to do it again.

"You're not . . ." Hal began.

"Arrested anymore?" I asked. "No, it looks like I ain't. And I've got Roy to thank for that, which I guess is why I came here."

"Come in," Hal said, and I did exactly that. I took my boots off in the hallway, so I wouldn't trek mud and snow all over the place, then stood there in my socks, trying to work up what I needed to say. "He's coming down with a cold, actually, so just . . ."

"I know he can be stubborn as an ox, and mean as one, too," I said. "I'm used to dealing with it. Hope you get used to dealing with it, too."

"Well, I was a tutor for very small children," Hal replied, cheeks coloring. "The principles are almost the same."

"Good thing you've got the proper training," I told him. "Thanks for putting up with it. Not many men can."

I left him in the hall like a whirlwind'd just hit him— maybe it had. I knew where the bedroom was, and I'd prefer to do the next step alone, just me and Roy.

He did look like shit when I opened the door, not bothering to knock. I'd already seen everything there was to see, and I knew he wouldn't let me in to look at him like this if I'd given him fair warning: big nose puffy and red, bags under his eyes, dark circles, and everything. He was in the middle of blowing his nose into his handkerchief and he made a sound of horror when he saw me.

"Bastion," he said, doing his best *not* to sound stuffed-up and failing. "Which one of us looks worse?"

"You," I wagered. "Just came by so you wouldn't worry about me."

"And not to see how *I* was doing," Roy replied. "Of course not. That's so very like you. I'll have you know I had to hide in a snowdrift for over an hour before I was able to make my

getaway. I've been sneezing all night and you know how my
Talent gets when *that* happens."

"Yeah," I agreed. "You're missing a special secret meeting
of the Basquiat lying around in bed with your hankie, too."

"No," Royston said. If there was anything that'd get him
out of bed right quick, the idea of missing out on something
that important would probably do the trick. "Hal! Is my coat
dry yet?"

"I'll get your coat," I said. "If it's not dry, you can have
mine."

"I am not showing up at the Basquiat wearing *your* coat,"
Roy told me, then paused in searching his dresser drawer,
looking at me suspiciously. "It's only a cold," he said. "I'm
hardly dying. Why offer to get me my coat? Why not just tell
me to get it myself?"

"'Cause it's easier than the other thing," I replied.

"What other thing?" Roy asked. He really did look like he
was gonna keel over. Funny, 'cause I bet he'd definitely been
expecting the cold to be the thing that did him in, and not me.

"Apologizing," I said, simple as that. It wasn't so hard, now
that I knew I was giving him the vapors. "For what I said
before about Freckles. If he can put up with you while you're
like this, then I guess he can't be half-bad."

"Bastion," Roy said again, staring at me openly. "What did
they *do* to you in there?"

"Some of that you'll find out at the meeting," I said, enjoying that one a little more than I had to. The only thing Roy
hated more than suffering the indignities of a common cold
was the idea that someone somewhere knew more than he
did, *before* he did. I probably shouldn't've teased him about
it at all, since I really couldn't tell him the particulars about
what'd happened to me after I'd been arrested. I trusted him,
but it'd only be putting him in danger—not to mention I'd
already sworn to the rest of the group that we wouldn't be
telling anyone anything. *Everybody* had friends they trusted;
that didn't mean they got to unburden themselves to them
about every little detail.

"Oh, I see," Roy huffed, turning back to his dresser drawer

and pulling out his favorite vest—some black-and-gold piece that, according to him, "never went out of style." According to me, he just liked the damned thing, but you couldn't tell Roy he was doing a thing *sensibly* for once without him taking offense and going to extraordinary lengths just to prove you wrong. "And here I thought I'd get the story from you firsthand. Perhaps, since you've never been involved in a political scandal before, you have a limited understanding of the etiquette involved, *but* it is customary for someone personally implicated to give his closest friend all the pertinent details. Especially when that friend sacrificed his good health and clear sinuses to be of use in the first place."

"I appreciate that," I said, which wasn't quite as hard to get out as the apology had been. "I know how important your sinuses are to you."

Roy gave me one of his sharp looks though the effect probably wasn't quite what he'd hoped since his eyes were all red and watery from blowing his nose. Didn't know how a grown man could make such a big fuss over one little cold, but somehow he managed to wrangle me around into feeling sorry for him anyway.

Or maybe I was feeling guilty since I couldn't tell him about the dragons. And this was gonna pose an interesting obstacle for our friendship.

"Meeting'll be interesting, at least," I offered, with a shrug. I figured I could let him in on that much without giving anything away. And it was the truth. I almost wished I could've been a fly on the wall at the Basquiat when Antoinette let the magicians know what th'Esar'd been planning.

Roy was gonna hit the ceiling. I only hoped he didn't sneeze in the middle of the meeting, right before the dramatic reveal.

"They are *always* interesting," Roy said, with a little sniff I figured was on purpose instead of necessary. He knew I was yanking his chain—probably because I wasn't very good at all that diplomatic subterfuge—but at least he seemed to realize I was being cryptic for a reason since he wasn't threatening to get Antoinette down here to read my thoughts for him.

Little did he know we were on the same side now, the lady and me.

"Well, then, this one'll be especially so," I said, which was where I had to end it. Much as I loved twitting Roy, I was gonna work my way around to having to give *another* apology if I kept at it too long. Silence was what worked best for me most days anyway, so I shut my yap and introduced a little quiet into the room.

With Roy present, I knew it couldn't last long.

"I understand," Roy said finally, resuming with his vest, and searching out a scarf to match it. Bastion help me, but he even had more than one. "You've been sworn to secrecy on some count, and you're a soldier, too good to let a little thing like torture force your tongue. Believe it or not, there are things that even *I* do not wish to know, occasionally. At least that's what I'm trying to tell myself. I think I'm managing to believe it."

"Better be careful," I said, picking out a gray scarf, which he rejected immediately. "That sounds dangerously close to self-improvement."

"That implies I have room to improve," Roy pointed out. He froze all of a sudden, going still all over like he was about to sneeze. I wondered whether I should hit the deck or maybe jam my fingers up his nose—but then his posture relaxed. "False alarm. I accept, by the way."

"Pardon?" I asked, getting the distinct feeling that I'd just been deliberately thrown off my guard.

"Your apology," Roy said; I noticed him tugging the exact damn scarf I'd shown him in the first place out of his drawer and winding it around his neck. Maybe he thought I was too color-blind to notice what he'd done, but I knew what he was trying to pull. "I accept your apology. It seems sincere enough, and I know how it kills you to admit you like anything, not to mention any*one*."

"Just don't chase this one off," I suggested, which was far from what I actually meant, but I figured Roy'd get it anyway.

He knew a lot of languages, and there was no reason "crusty old curmudgeon" couldn't be one of them.

"Indeed," Royston said, examining himself in the mirror and poking at his red nose critically. "Well, if this cold doesn't do it once and for all, I suspect nothing will. What a charming thought."

"You'd better get going," I reminded him, before he could get that lovestruck look on his face and go all moony on me. Even if the Basquiat wasn't getting the full story, I knew he was gonna want his *whole* focus for the meeting. And he was gonna have a lot he'd want to talk to me about after, too.

"It's considered rude to hustle a man out of his own house," Roy said, clearly angling for at least another seventeen minutes to agonize over what he saw in the mirror. As far as I was concerned, there was no chance of it getting any better *or* any worse, and no amount of staring at himself was going to change things. He just wanted to make an entrance, show up a little late and make a big splash, pretending it was all on purpose—but I could've told him this was one meeting where he *didn't* want to miss the beginning.

"Lucky for me, I never cared much what people thought in the first place," I said, getting around behind him and pushing him out of the room like I'd done so many years ago at the 'Versity just to avoid making us both late for exams. It was lucky we'd both been stubborn as bulldogs since I didn't see how our friendship could've lasted so long without us both holding on.

Don't know why I'd even bothered dragging him to exams the way I had since the bastard always marked higher than me no matter what class we'd been attending.

Some people—Laure, Gaeth probably, and me included—weren't meant to succeed in a classroom. All I could do was hope that I'd be able to teach 'em in the way that *had* worked for me, not to mention some of their stubborn predecessors, a few of whom hadn't even been able to sign their own names.

I guess in some ways I was going back to being a teacher, but this time without any pampering 'Versity rules or parents writing angry letters about how the classroom wasn't a situation room and their babies deserved more respect. Roy's collection of complaints would suffer, but I was looking forward to being able to tell people to piss off again. I knew I could count on three of my new pupils to try and get the job done—whatever that job was gonna be—and if the fourth didn't live up to my standards, I wasn't going to hesitate showing him what it felt like to get your nose twice-broken.

Now, there was a style of teaching you couldn't put into practice at the 'Versity, no matter how much you might've wanted to.

Hal was waiting in the hall where I'd left him, still looking befuddled. That was nothing compared to what he looked like when he saw the two of us coming down the stairs, Roy blustering indignantly but somehow never quite seeing his way around to pushing past me so he could get back upstairs.

He could call me a bully all he liked, but we both knew who had the real firepower between us.

Also, there was a mirror in the hallway, so he always had a second chance to make a fuss.

"Is everything all right?" Hal asked, caught someplace between nervous silence and plain laughter. "You're out of bed. I thought you said you were never getting out again. In fact, I believe that was an exact quote."

"Change of plans," I explained, from over Roy's shoulder.

"Are you feeling better?" Hal said, looking suspicious, like he meant to block the door with his body if the answer didn't satisfy him. Guess he was worth some esteem after all, even if it'd taken me a while to come around on the subject. "If you go out and make that cold worse . . ."

"It's Basquiat business," Royston said. Evidently wonders never ceased—he sounded cowed, almost like he was making an apology. "I'll be inside the whole time—perhaps I'll even ask Wildgrave Ozanne to heal me up while I'm there. Doesn't that sound like an appealing solution to this whole business?"

"I'll go with you," Hal said, reaching for his coat and Royston's at the same time. There was a willful set to his jaw that I was beginning to recognize from all the time I'd spent around mulish young people of late—a stubbornness only the vitality of youth could maintain. "I can wait outside, if I have to, but we're coming home straight afterward."

"That's really not necessary," Royston said, looking to me for support.

"Sorry," I told him. "I'm with Freckles on this one."

CHAPTER SEVENTEEN

LAURE

A week after I'd found her, I still didn't know what to name my girl.

It was a small detail, but everyone who knew about it kept bringing it up, like it was the most important thing I had to look after. Not the letter to Da explaining I'd got a job working for Chief Sergeant Adamo—I didn't put "ex" in there, just to keep the whole thing true; I never could lie to my own family—nor all the hassle I went through withdrawing from my place as a student right at the end of the semester. Even though nobody in the 'Versity actually wanted me, much less wanted me to stay, they sure kicked up a stink about me leaving, though the paperwork all went through once they remembered I was a scholarship student and they weren't making money off of my attendance.

I wasn't the only one who'd quit right before the end of the race. Though I was following in ex–Professor Adamo's footsteps, and for me, that was a right noble position.

Neither of us was cut out for it—not like some. Toverre, for example, probably couldn't fail an examination if he tried. Despite the constant bathing—he had four of 'em a day, three after meals and one for good luck or something—and how he was dogging Gaeth's footsteps out of sheer stubbornness, he still found time to study and pull off top marks. I wasn't even jealous of him, just impressed, since Da taught me to give credit where it was due, and it was nice to be reminded that Toverre might be of some use to someone, someday. And not just as Thremedon's finest laundryman.

I was glad I didn't have to study, or even think about studying, since so much was happening all at once. The city itself was in an uproar, distracting most of the *good* students from getting any work done since history was being made right in front of their eyes. I bet they were wondering, *So why in bastion's name am I studying it?* The big thing was th'Esar being as good as dead, out like a light, and those of us who'd been there the only people who knew the truth. Even I didn't rightly understand how they were keeping him alive since it had to do with Talent and I had none, but Antoinette had assured us all that she'd take care of things, and she was the kind of woman who made you believe a thing when she said it. All I understood was your body got weaker the longer you slept, and even though th'Esar had been an ox-looking fellow, it was safer to keep him stabilized with magic. The only thing worse than th'Esar in a coma, after all, was th'Esar suddenly up and dying on us.

It was all people could talk about, and I guess I didn't blame them too much; all they knew was that the man who'd gotten them through the war had been taken out of commission, and I didn't envy th'Esarina one bit having to convince them she'd do just fine in his place. No one knew whether the envoy from Arlemagne would stick around to deal with her or whether they'd consider themselves well shut of Volstov altogether. At least th'Esar hadn't died—since according to my dragon, that would have meant the end of *all* the dragons—but I guess I could sympathize with the people a little. They hadn't been there when it happened, so it had to have come as kind of a shock.

Toverre hadn't wanted to talk about it much though he did mention to me just once that he thought it dreadful that, with all the assistance from the Basquiat's best magicians, th'Esar's conscious mind couldn't have been saved.

But to me, it was pretty obvious why they hadn't—or why they couldn't. Th'Esar'd staked everything on the new dragons; he'd thought they were gonna be devoted to him and him alone, making up for how the first ones weren't. And when one of them betrayed him, going so far as to hurt him in the process, he realized how wrong he'd been and how he'd misplaced all his trust. After that, he'd probably just given up.

You couldn't wake someone when his own dreams turned out better than reality.

I almost felt sorry for him, except it was hard to see my way toward forgiving a man who'd been willing to use me as a pawn.

Meanwhile, I was being called in left and right by Antoinette for private counsel; she wanted to go over all kinds of things with me, even give me advice, like she thought I was her own daughter and I needed the extra guidance. But she had some interesting things to say, and I appreciated it because I knew she had the experience I didn't.

There was also the matter of how I didn't have one of those keys in my hand, while the others—Troius, Gaeth, and even Balfour—did. Even though Balfour was a special case, I had nothing. My girl chose me, so she'd do what I said, but if she was destroyed, I wouldn't go crackers like the others.

"And it's even more difficult to get anything done in Volstov when you start out at a disadvantage," Antoinette'd explained. "For a man as well, I suppose, but especially for us. I've worked three times as hard as my counterparts, and I'm generally disliked for it, even by those who pretend to be my friends. I've weathered gossip and insults, not to mention the disappointment of being passed over by those with fewer qualifications for positions far above their capabilities."

"And is it worth it?" I'd asked.

"I sleep very well at night if that's what you're asking," Antoinette had replied.

She'd been reluctant to use Germaine's services again, and I was even more reluctant, but she'd promised me she'd be looking into it, and in the meantime, I'd just have to work extra hard to make it clear I meant business. It wasn't something I wasn't used to. I was willing to fight for anything if I was sure I wanted it.

And I knew I wanted this.

There was also an individual meeting that all of us who'd been involved in "The Incident" had to attend, during which Antoinette put this spell in our heads that kept us from talking about what'd happened with anyone who *hadn't* been involved. When I tested it—on Wildgrave Ozanne, who was probably always gonna remember me as that bell-cracked ginger—I felt my tongue turn to ice. No matter how hard I tried to say the word "dragon," it dried out before it ever passed my lips.

"Bathroom," I finally managed, and the Wildgrave pointed me in the right direction. I was grateful to escape though I felt him staring at me as I fled.

I didn't like it much, but at least I could talk to Toverre about it still, and Adamo, if I needed to. And I submitted to it because I knew it was a necessary precaution; Antoinette was just doing what she had to. And maybe it'd make her crazy someday the way it'd made the Esar, but I hoped she was too strong to let that happen.

After everything was tied up, and everyone was still walking around like ghosts mourning the end of th'Esar's rule, Gaeth and Toverre and I had one last, late supper in Toverre's room—since it was the cleanest—to celebrate Toverre's success and the end of the only semester of schooling I'd ever be attending. We ate food we brought up from the dining hall, on Toverre's clean little plates, and even though it was supposed to be a party, it felt more like a funeral.

The entire week'd been leading up to something I knew I had to do—but there'd never been a good time for it, or even time for it at all since we'd all been so busy. If I didn't get the chance to do it soon, I was gonna turn chicken. Finally, when everyone was finished eating and no one was talking, I decided it was now or never.

"You mind excusing us for a bit, Gaeth?" I asked.

Despite being a little slow sometimes, like a horse that was bred for racing but turned out placid, Gaeth always picked up on things when you least expected him to, and he never made things uncomfortable by asking too many questions.

"I've been needing to pack, anyway," he said. He folded his napkin—a habit he'd picked up from Toverre—and excused himself from the table.

"But I was going to help him," Toverre protested, already getting twitchy. Now, *he* was someone who could read all the books in all the libraries in *all* of Volstov but never know how to read a room. "Otherwise he'll mix all his socks together."

"It'll be okay," Gaeth assured him. "I'll just be taking them out again, anyway."

"But you'll be taking them out in the wrong order," Toverre said.

"I'll see you both later," Gaeth said with a half-salute and slipped out of the room.

"Well, I hope you're happy," Toverre told me peevishly. "Now he'll be wearing mismatched socks for the rest of his life."

"You won't even be with us at Antoinette's place most of the time," I pointed out. "You'll be here, studying, terrifying professors with your handwriting."

"But I'll *know*," Toverre explained. "And what about when I come out to visit?"

I was surprised he even wanted to—I could tell the dragons made him uncomfortable, though thank bastion he hadn't given me tips yet on how to polish one. I couldn't really blame him since to anyone on the outside, it was impossible to tell what they were thinking because no one else but us connected ones could hear 'em talking. And after the big display in the tunnels, we knew how dangerous they could be. Ironjaw was still recovering, so my girl told me, *and* being tetchy about it to boot. But she didn't have the same constitution my girl had; Troius was probably going crazy from listening to all her complaints.

Still, it was good to know there'd be something familiar amidst everything new, a face I recognized that'd remind me of who I used to be, not who I was changing into. Toverre was my best friend, and I wanted things to stay that way.

One thing, however, had to change.

"Hey," I said, never one to put off what needed to be said, "don't you think maybe we shouldn't get married?"

"Oh," Toverre said, wilting but also looking very relieved. "Yes, I rather think that's an excellent idea."

"All right, then," I replied. "So it's off. That's a relief."

"You could have been a *little* more delicate about it,"

Toverre added, reaching across the table to pile the crumbs from Gaeth's dinner together, swiftly sweeping up the pile with his napkin. "Because I would have been a very *good* husband."

"I wouldn't have been clean enough for you," I replied.

"I would have been clean enough for both of us," Toverre said, but he was smiling wistfully. "This means I will *never* be married, you know."

"Me neither," I told him, bristling. "I mean . . ."

"You never know what could happen," Toverre cautioned. "You'll have thousands of offers—but it will take only one."

"It's not something I wanna think about yet, anyway," I said, wishing this conversation was over with already. Talking about suitors was making me uncomfortable, all the more so because the idea wasn't so fuzzy as it used to be. Had a face attached to it, so to speak, which made it all the more terrifying. "I'm eighteen, and I've got things I want to take care of. I don't wanna be *anybody's* fiancée. No offense. Though it *was* funny since everybody always looked shocked to hear it."

"Much to my embarrassment," Toverre said.

We sat in silence for a little while, and I thought about how free I felt but also how sad. It'd just been a fact of life for so long that being without it made me feel like I was adrift at sea. It *was* important though, mostly because I was positive now that neither of us thought about the other in that way— not even a little—and it didn't seem right to force ourselves. It would've been like making the dragons live underground, when they needed room to stretch and breathe as much as anyone else.

I'd get over it, sure, but I didn't want Toverre to be lonely. Then again, I was doing this for his sake as much as for mine. He had Gaeth, to scare off or—this being the more frightening prospect—to latch onto in his own prickly way. I'd have to come up to the city proper to let 'em both know what'd happen if they messed things up. If Gaeth was worth it, he'd stay the course. But something told me he wasn't the type to spook easy.

"Thank you," Toverre said finally, breaking the silence. "Mother will be so sad, though."

"Da's going to be scandalized." I sighed. "It just doesn't seem fair to anyone else—if there ever *is* anyone else, I mean, so don't get that look, 'cause so far there isn't—to make 'em live with me having a fiancé when we both know that doesn't mean anything to either of us."

"It did mean *something*," Toverre corrected me, a stickler for details, no matter how sensitive the topic. "Just not what anyone else would assume a betrothal meant. I will say that if I had to be engaged to anyone, I count myself incredibly lucky that it was you."

"Well, same to you," I said; I couldn't keep from grinning like a puffed-up pigeon. It wasn't every day Toverre handed out compliments, and he gave them to me least of all on account of how I was the one who knew him best and he didn't *have* to charm me. "Just imagine if you'd been engaged to some skinny little wisp. Who'd've killed all the spiders in your dorm room for you?"

"Please," Toverre said, holding up his hand with a brief, violent shudder. "I've only finished eating. Don't speak of it."

We were gonna be just fine, Toverre and me. Now that we weren't engaged anymore, we could focus on being friends, which'd always been the best part of the arrangement—at least, that's how it was for me, anyway. I figured it'd do him some good to come visit me and Gaeth at the estate, too; he'd already proven he could get down and dirty the same as the rest of us if he really needed to, and a little dirt hadn't killed him. Knowing that'd made me real happy—I could believe there was hope for us yet if even Toverre was capable of getting over himself.

Judging by the way he acted around Gaeth, he'd gotten over more than just his quirk about keeping everything ship-shape. All them dragons and missing students seemed almost to have knocked the notion of falling in love with someone new right out of his head. Even if that'd been all we got out of coming to the city, it would've lived up to Toverre's high expectations.

And even if neither of us had expected things to shake down the way they did, I figured we'd handled ourselves okay for two hayseeds from the country who nearly got robbed our very first day in Thremedon.

"If that's all, I suppose I'd better go and help Gaeth pack," Toverre said, folding his napkin and stacking the plates up neatly, cutlery sorted by order and balanced on the very top plate. "Otherwise he really *will* be a mess when the two of you get up there. I should think you'd be more concerned about your corps looking dignified."

"It's not *my* anything," I pointed out quickly. "And don't call us that. We don't have a name."

"Speaking of names," Toverre began shrewdly, "have you named your dragon yet?"

I sighed, casting a glance toward Toverre's gleaming window, the only one in the first-year dorms that you could *actually* see through when it was closed. Maybe I'd been overthinking the whole name thing, but once I named this dragon, she was gonna be the one to live with it. I didn't want to pick something like Troius had, just because it sounded strong, and it didn't seem like proper tribute to name her after my ma, even if she would've liked it.

There was a third option that'd been swirling around in my head for a while now—since I'd first clapped eyes on her, in fact—and Toverre wasn't gonna accept an "I don't know" for an answer. All the dragons I'd ever been mad for had been given real specific names, and even if the Margraves who'd named them had been one broken runner short of a rocker, you couldn't deny the names sounded real powerful when spoken aloud. I guess those Brothers of Regina knew what they were doing when they wrote down those prayers, because some of 'em had a real impact. It was make up my mind now or never, and I guessed I was gonna go with my gut instinct, since that usually saw me through all right. Toverre was probably gonna laugh at me, but he could go and suck a knob, since I was the one with the dragon.

"Inglory," I told him.

"Ah," Toverre said, like the first drop of rain before a whole downpour came flowing out of his mouth. I braced myself, just in case.

"Got something to say?" I asked. I didn't take his reaction personally since I knew it was just because of Toverre's high standards. If *he'd* been put in charge of naming anything, even something small like a mouse, he'd've devoted two whole weeks to searching in books until he found the most ridiculous name imaginable. He'd call it appropriate; everyone else'd call it bat shit.

And that was another reason we couldn't get married. I'd never doom a child to walking around with a name worse than my friend Ermengilde had been stuck with.

"Not at all," Toverre said, surprising us both, I think. "Given the circumstances, I feel it's rather appropriate; it's as if you're paying tribute to the legacy that came before you. You and Gaeth have both done quite well for yourselves."

"Gaeth named his after a cow," I pointed out.

"Yes, well," Toverre said, suddenly busying himself with straightening the napkins. "I didn't say there was anything *wrong* with it; I was just surprised."

I could tell he was dying to get all the dirty flatware out of his room so he could go torture the life out of poor Gaeth by teaching him how to fold socks, and it was probably time for me to go and get some of my own packing done as well, for once free of Toverre's "help." Neither of us was much for proper good-byes, and it definitely didn't make sense to make a big deal out of my leaving the 'Versity—not when I knew Toverre would be visiting as often as he could, or else.

I probably should've been nervous about starting my new life, or maybe even a little scared, but I wasn't either of those things. So far, I was the only one of the four without the proper means of controlling my dragon, but we were getting to know each other—and getting to like each other, too.

Besides, the others hadn't been dealing with a man like Toverre their whole lives, like I had.

Compared to him, reasoning with a dragon was bound to feel downright simple.

BALFOUR

It wasn't the first time I'd packed my life up to go and live with Volstov's dragons, but there were a few key differences between this time and the first.

The most important was the secrecy surrounding my new position. When I left for the Airman, my family was proud of me, and my childhood companions envious. This time, I could tell no one what I was doing nor why I'd resigned my diplomatic post dealing with the Arlemagne embassy. In some ways, my very public breakdown with the fever had done me a service since I could simply allow everyone to assume that I'd cracked under the pressure and was retiring to lead a quiet life in the countryside somewhere to focus on my health. My family would worry for a time, but I would devote myself to writing as many reassuring letters as it took. Eventually, even my mother would come around. The rest of the city might amend a few of the stanzas to "Balfour Steelballs," but I found that I didn't altogether mind the idea as much as I'd thought I might. I was even looking forward to what the new lyrics might be.

In the face of recent events, having all of Thremedon questioning my sanity seemed like a very small price to pay for actually managing to maintain it.

The second difference—this one perhaps even stranger than the first—was that I had an entire host of company, *real* friends, who had volunteered to help me pack up my belongings.

I'd had my doubts about whether or not we'd manage to fit into the tiny apartment, especially with Ghislain among us, but Luvander had soundly ignored all my protests in his usual way, and once Luvander had announced he was coming to help me, it seemed the others couldn't resist joining in. Adamo had committed himself last, stating that with Ghislain along, I probably wouldn't need any further help with the boxes, but that I might need *him* to corral all that extra help the other airmen were giving me so, as he put it, shit actually got packed.

Fortunately, I hadn't been living in the apartment long enough to accumulate anything very valuable *or* breakable, so I wasn't too worried about losing any heirlooms. My apartment did look as though an earthquake had hit it, but since I was leaving it behind, I figured it didn't matter that much—save maybe for the poor fellow doomed to move in behind me.

Even the dulcet tones of my neighbors making their morning rounds, feet clad in concrete blocks, was like music to my ears.

Since it was the *last* time, I no longer flinched every time bits of plaster came crumbling down from the ceiling above me; Luvander used it as a sort of metronome, setting the beat while he hummed and tossed things into crates.

Mostly, I was glad for the company, since it didn't leave me much time to brood on all the things I was worried about, such as whether or not I was really ready to deal with another dragon and what I was going to name her, besides.

Dear Thom, I began in my head, which was the only place such a letter could ever be written. *It seems that once again I have you to thank for changing the course of my life, though I wonder whether or not you ever intended to in the first place. I only hope you are able to make such strides in your own. I wish you all the best, and by the by, do you have any suggestions on what to name my new dragon? She is blue, if that helps you any.*

It was strange to think that without Thom's letter, none of us might have ever been forewarned of what the Esar was planning. The magicians would have suffered most, though I also couldn't bear to think of the poor children who'd died because of that fever. And yet I couldn't ever tell Thom what he'd done for us just by his insistence on writing. I knew that he wasn't the sort of man to revel in being praised, but it seemed a shame he might never know.

And for Rook, the only one of the remaining airmen who wasn't in on the little secret . . .

If he ever came back to Thremedon, he'd thrash us all with one arm tied behind his back.

"None of these cups match," Raphael commented from

where he was standing on a chair and emptying out my cupboards. "How can this be, Balfour? I always considered you a kindred spirit, dedicated to the finer things in life, and now I discover you're just as slovenly as the rest of them."

"There *were* sets," I protested, faintly. "It's just that certain parts got broken when I was first learning to use my hands."

"Oh," Raphael said, pausing in his work to look guilty. It passed quickly; he never harbored the same emotion for very long. "I suppose you're right, how terribly awkward of me. Now I've put my foot in it."

"That's right," Luvander said, coming up on my left with another full box to hand off to Ghislain, who lifted it in one hand like it was no heavier than a pillow. "I bet you feel terrible now, and it's no more than you deserve. Forgot you were dealing with the *new* Balfour, didn't you? This one's feisty. And watch out. When he hits back, I can only imagine how much it *hurts*."

"I was only stating a fact," I said, somewhat embarrassed. In truth, it was almost nice to be around someone who'd forgotten about my hands entirely—though I didn't envy Raphael being in the position of catching up on everything he'd missed since being lost in the war.

Evidently he was quite resilient, just like the rest of us. He'd manage well enough, and he wouldn't be doing it completely alone, either.

"Carriage's getting pretty full," Ghislain reported, coming back up the stairs and into my apartment. He was taking them three at a time, and the whole building shook with his massive strides. "Hope there aren't many more boxes."

"How kind of Lady Antoinette to lend us her driver to take Balfour out to the house," Luvander commented, hefting another heavy box to pass it to Ghislain, groaning under its weight. "I wonder why she agreed to do that? Perhaps a personal interest in our well-being . . . ? We *are* eligible bachelors, after all."

"If she was interested, it wouldn't be in you," Ghislain said, taking the first box, then waiting around for a second. "I've got a free arm if anyone else's got their shit packed."

"Be very careful with these," Raphael said, hopping down

off his chair and holding out the crate that held my mis-matched tea service. "These teacups made it past Balfour Steelhands. They deserve to be treated with some respect."

I glanced around the apartment—which looked less like a storm had hit and more like no one had ever lived in it at all. It reminded me of when we vacated the Airman, but since I had fewer fond memories of this place, I wasn't nearly as sad to be leaving it behind, without a trace of myself left.

"Ah-ah," Luvander chided, pulling a fountain pen out of some hidden pocket. "Before we go, we must make our mark."

"The landlady was very specific about not scuffing the floors or walls," I warned, knowing Luvander wouldn't listen to me. He was already crouching by the kitchen window, scratching something under the ledge of the sill. "It's a little habit I have," he explained, after he'd finished. "I left one in the Airman, as well. It said, 'Niall lost, Luvander won.'"

"*No,*" Raphael said. "My money was on Niall."

"That's what you get for being a traitor," Luvander replied.

I had no memory of the game Luvander and Raphael were referring to, but of course, knowing them as I did, it might just as easily have been made up. With Adamo down by the carriage, and Ghislain rocking the very foundations of the building, it was only the three of us. They were lingering, so I could tell there was something on their minds, but Lu-vander was right—they weren't dealing with the old Balfour, and I wasn't going to be the one to cave first.

"Well," I said, "I suppose that's everything. Thank you so much for the help."

"It was our pleasure," Luvander said.

"Yes," Raphael agreed. "I love doing menial tasks for other people without any promise of reward."

"Of course, there is *one* reward we *might* be granted," Lu-vander added slyly.

"No, we couldn't ask," Raphael replied. "He's bound to think we're rude."

"He thinks that already," Luvander said. "We won't have to worry about his opinion changing for the worse."

"But still," Raphael concluded, "it won't *improve* our image any."

"You might as well come right out with it," I said, though I had to admit, the routine was very well scripted. They might well have a future in the Amazement, if Luvander ever got tired of the haberdashery.

"You haven't named her yet," Luvander explained. "And the anticipation might kill Raphael a second time."

"Luvander's the one it's really been bothering," Raphael confided in me. "He won't shut up about it. Though I suppose that doesn't make it much different from any other topic that interests Luvander."

"It's only that I have a few suggestions," Luvander said. "I'm afraid you'll do something uncomfortable for everyone—like name her 'Steelballs.'"

"You can't very well do that," Raphael added. "She lacks the proper anatomy, and it will only make her feel inadequate among the other dragons."

"Shh," I said, in case my landlady was eavesdropping on us. Then, because I was going to have to tell them sooner or later—and because, even though it was technically none of their business, I'd never hear the end of it if I didn't choose a name everyone approved of—I relented. They *had* come to help me, and I could only imagine how deeply they resented me, the only one of the older order to be given a second chance at what had made us who we were.

That they weren't letting on just proved their character, and I was grateful to them—more grateful than I would ever be able to show.

"I was thinking 'Steelhands,' actually," I replied. "Call it a sudden inspiration."

For once, I could tell I'd gotten the better of them, since both Raphael and Luvander looked equally shocked. I supposed that sealed it.

"I hope you know this is entirely *your* fault," Raphael informed Luvander, after a long pause.

"She does have hands, at least, after a fashion," Luvander reasoned. "We'll just have to make sure she understands her namesake. Since no one *else* will be singing it to her."

The familiar sound of Ghislain coming back up the stairs heralded his return; he was followed closely by Adamo, and I realized there were no further boxes left. We were finished, with relatively little incident, and I had never been more happy to bid final farewell to a place as I was then.

"Just one more thing we need to do before we're done," Ghislain said, which brought me up short.

"There is?" I asked, wondering if I'd forgotten a room.

"Adamo tells me you've been having some trouble with those upstairs neighbors," Ghislain explained, jerking his thumb upward. "Figured I could give 'em a few good-byes of my own."

I stared at him for a moment, speechless. Then I couldn't help but toss my head back and laugh, the others joining in, despite us all knowing Ghislain was dead serious.

"Go right ahead," I told him. "Whoever moves in next will never know what a true hero you really are."

"I'm fine with that," Ghislain said, and started for the door.

With all of us together, it felt as much like old times as I'd needed. Just like the first time we'd been brought together by the dragons—though now I was armed with the knowledge that there were other, more resilient ties between us. I wasn't going to forget it, and I didn't plan on allowing the others to, either. It was a far cry from the timidity I'd exhibited in their presence once, but I liked to think I'd grown—perhaps into the kind of man worthy of a song or two in his honor.

I was a new man, and though certain parts of me were steel in name only, I would have no qualms about displaying my newfound resilience among my comrades. Somehow I felt as though I was the one who'd been rebuilt alongside these new dragons, and I wasn't about to let the opportunity at a second chance pass me by.